Blood is red.
You pigs are blue.
Start counting victims.
There'll be quite a few.

The poem was addressed to Jim Dempsey, Fairport's Chief of Police. Dempsey was a brilliant man, a determined man, a man who never came in second. Jim Dempsey was a winner.

Until today.

Diamonds are red.
Clubs are black.
Carry your buddy
Home in a sack.

THE ULTIMATE GAME

RALPH GLENDINNING

A JOVE BOOK

This Jove book contains the complete
text of the original hardcover edition.
It has been completely reset in a typeface
designed for easy reading, and was printed
from new film.

THE ULTIMATE GAME

A Jove Book/published by arrangement with
Wyndham Books

PRINTING HISTORY
Wyndham Books edition/September 1981
Jove edition/July 1982

ISBN: 0-515-06524-2

Jove books are published by Jove Publications, Inc.,
200 Madison Avenue, New York, N.Y. 10016. The words
"A JOVE BOOK" and the "J" with sunburst are trademarks
belonging to Jove Publications, Inc.

PRINTED IN THE UNITED STATES OF AMERICA

An Autumn
Afternoon

THE BOY stood in front of the kitchen stove. He hesitated for a moment, then jerked open the oven door. Checking the knobs under the burners, he turned the one marked "oven." The smell of gas was overpowering. The boy coughed, wiped his eyes and backed away. He stumbled into the living room, catching himself on the edge of the end table. The sight of the fat man snoring on the sofa and the stench of stale gin turned his stomach. He regained his balance and turned toward the front door.

The boy closed the door tightly and ran down the steps toward the woods, gulping in the clean, fresh air. His mother wouldn't return from her job at the library until after dark. His stepfather would never fondle her again.

They'd never suspect him. He'd go back into hiding, back where no one could find him. When he was ready, he'd come out. It might take years. The boy laughed aloud. He could wait. Then he'd show the world, and especially that prick Jimmy.

The boy headed deeper into the woods. The leaves made crunchy sounds under his feet. The fresh smell of pine filled his head. He inhaled deeply. The boy felt keenly alive and, for the first time in his life, happy.

1

Sunday, June 1.
The Plan

THE PLAN was perfect! The Man knew it was perfect. Nothing had been left to chance. Methodically, he drummed his fingers on the antique leather-topped desk, smiling to himself. It still wouldn't hurt to check it one last time.

He pushed back his chair, leaned forward and reached under the desk in his paneled den. His right thumb released a small hidden catch. The secret drawer opened silently. He removed a manila envelope and slid out the well-thumbed notebook. Sipping his beer, he read slowly, reviewing with total absorption the information it contained. He was right. There was no need for any last-minute changes. His actions were programmed in infinite detail and with split-second timing. Everything had been thought through. The plan was perfect in every detail.

The Man's leathery face broke into a triumphant grin, revealing his even white teeth. After a lifetime of frustration, now he'd move to the center of the stage and be important. The attention of the entire nation would be focused on his actions. He set his glass down gently on his desk.

It wouldn't take long. In just a few weeks millions would know of his existence, and of an intellect that no one could outwit. He took a deep breath. A tiny shadow of doubt came into his mind. He pushed it aside. He would pit himself against all of the recent scientific and technological developments in crime detection, and he would win. Lazily, he drew circular designs on the condensation that had formed on the outside of his glass.

The Man removed a thin black metal box from the drawer. From his pocket he took a small key. He unlocked the box and took out a series of black-and-white photographs, riffling through them slowly. Then he arranged them carefully in four rows on his desk, studying each one carefully. He switched the position of two of them, muttering half-aloud, "Age before beauty. No, dammit. They want equal rights. They'll get them." Satisfied, he scooped up the last three rows, snapped a wide rubber band around them and placed the pile back into the box, locking it securely in the drawer. Now he concentrated intently on the photographs remaining on his desk. One by one he numbered them in the bottom right-hand corner with a black marking pencil. Then he scotch-taped each one securely to a preselected page in his notebook. Finished, he snapped the notebook closed, slid it back into the manila envelope and replaced the envelope in its secret cache.

As the Man rose, uncoiling his tall, lean body and stretching the kinks from his muscular legs, he picked up his glass and wiped the puddle of water away with the palm of his hand. Then he glided noiselessly down the stairs, through the kitchen, leaving his glass in the sink, and then down into the basement. There was no one else in the house, but he moved as if he were stalking a victim.

He went directly to his wine rack and removed a bottle from each of three specific niches—a Château Lafite Rothschild 1964, a Dom Pérignon 1969 and a Puligny Montrachet 1970. The wine rack swung open on concealed hinges, revealing an impressive arsenal of weapons and a unique collection of disguises. He smiled confidently. No one would ever figure out that combination lock.

From a container he selected a familiar tape, inserting it into his portable recorder. Totally absorbed, he listened carefully to a series of different voices he had recorded secretly during the past six months. Then, on a blank tape, he practiced the inflections of each voice again. Satisfied, he snapped off the recorder, removed the tape, put it back into the container and locked it.

One by one, he had carefully selected and gathered the

disguises and weapons needed to execute his plan. They ranged from the simple to the exotic. From his extensive arsenal, he selected a pair of brass knuckles, a surgical knife and a hacksaw. Wrapping them in a piece of toweling, he tied the bundle tightly with a string and placed the package in a large, new Styrofoam container. After removing a pair of dark pants, a black pullover and black rubber-soled shoes, purchased months before from Goodwill, he swung the wine rack back into position, locking it in place with the three critical wine bottles.

Back in his den, the Man picked up the local paper and slumped into his favorite chair, losing interest almost immediately. There was never any hard news in the Fairport *Press*. Nothing exciting, just boring gossip and local chitchat. He knew that would change. In just a few days, the sleepy residential town of Fairport, Connecticut, would become front-page. There'd be banner headlines every day. Television specials. His palms itched. He rubbed them together, glancing at his calendar watch. It was the first of June. Today was D day, minus one. It was time for action. He was ready. No one would suspect him. Not his friends. Not his neighbors. Not his family. And certainly not Dempsey. That Boy Scout shithead. He would destroy Dempsey. He would outwit and embarrass Dempsey, and then kill him. Laughter echoed in the room. . . .

On Long Island Sound, sixteen sleek, graceful sailboats were cutting foamy wakes through the sparkling blue waters. Like seagulls, floating across the sky, they wheeled one by one in line formation around the last mark and set a course for home. In the lead Atlantic, from his position at the tiller, Jim Dempsey was shouting instructions.

"Get that kite up! You wasted three seconds. Watch the Genny. Don't let it dip in the water. Great work, Brenda."

Dempsey glanced behind him. A broad smile split his face. "We've got them now."

Brenda looked at him and nodded. His face was copper-colored in the late afternoon sun. It had been handsome once, but it was beginning to show the accumulated effects of an

outdoor life and years of sailing in small boats with wind, sun
and salt spray as constant companions. His jet-black hair had
lost its sheen, and wisps of gray were starting to show. She
loved to see him smile. When he did, his whole face lit up
and years melted away.

Shifting her weight slightly for better balance, the Atlantic
reacted almost instantly with an imperceptible lift. Jim gave
her a thumbs-up sign. She felt warm and contented. Even
after fifteen years of marriage, looking at Jim gave her a
special feeling. It was an inner glow of happiness. She looked
again, and smiled.

As they approached the finish, the sailboats were almost
surfing at maximum hull speed. Brenda turned and looked
behind them. The billowing spinnakers of the other Atlantics,
with their colorful designs, provided an almost unbelievably
beautiful sight. She heard the gun on the committee boat,
signifying that they had won the race, and with it the club
championship.

Jim was grinning from ear to ear. "Three years in a row,
thanks to my crew." He leaned over and gave Brenda a pat
on her knee. Brenda laughed. She appreciated the compliment, even though she knew it wasn't true.

Dempsey craned his head to see who had finished second,
as the two closest Atlantics swept across the finish line together. He couldn't tell; it was too close.

As they pulled into their slip, Spike Briggs, who had nosed
out Ned Nichols for second, pulled alongside. "Congratulations, you two. Jim, why don't you let Brenda crew for me?
It would give someone else a chance."

"No, thanks. You'd win and then everyone would know
my secret." He nodded appreciatively at Brenda.

Brenda laughed and jumped lightly onto the dock. She
shook some of the salt spray from her hair.

"Honey, while you wash down the boat, I'm going to run
up and powder my nose."

As she hurried up the walkway to the clubhouse, in navy-
blue shorts and white halter, Brenda was aware that her
well-proportioned figure still caused male heads to turn. She

thought to herself that the twenty minutes of exercise each day was probably worthwhile after all.

From his Atlantic, Ned Nichols watched her retreating figure. Out of the corner of her eye, Suzy Nichols watched her husband's gaze. She thought, I'll never change him. He'll always have an eye for a pretty ass. For a pretty anything. Ned likes pretty young things both coming and going. Especially coming. She shook her head sadly.

Jim and Spike watched Brenda's progress also. Spike broke the silence. "That girl is fantastic. She's always cheerful, fun to be around."

Jim nodded almost absentmindedly. Brenda was really special. Not only was she attractive on the surface, but she had depth. She rarely complained, even after Cindy's accident and the resulting brain damage. Brenda coped remarkably well. She hid her sadness behind her warm personality and constant energy. Only rarely did it surface.

He snapped out of his momentary depression. Cindy would make it. She was his little Buttercup. His everything. She would bloom, like her mother. It would just take a little time.

Jim finished hosing down his Atlantic, buttoned it up for the week and walked up to meet Brenda. They accepted lighthearted congratulations from the other crews they passed. Spike Briggs watched the two of them leave together. His pulse raced as he watched her tight-fitting blue shorts disappear up the walkway. He closed his eyes. His mind took over. The blue shorts were still there. Walking slowly. He knew every motion she had. For the next several moments, he replayed them all. Then he opened his eyes and took a deep breath of the salt air.

That goddam Dempsey. He was good, no doubt about it. Thorough and meticulous, yet innovative and daring. He was getting tired of sucking hind tit to him. Briggs finished stuffing the Orlon sails into their bags and drew the drawstrings tight. He ran his hand back and forth over his close-cropped crew cut. He smiled. Not bad for forty-two. And his lean body was still rock-hard.

He opened a new package of Tiparillos, took one out and lit it. At least he'd beaten Nichols. That jock. Maybe, at last, he had Ned's number. Blowing out a mouthful of smoke, he watched it dissipate in the breeze.

Across town, in the basement of an attractive yellow Colonial frame house on Sunrise Lane, a strange ritual was about to take place. Carrying a small wire cage containing four field mice, Dr. David Orton snapped on the fluorescent ceiling light to his small laboratory. Closing the door, he walked directly to the glass display case containing four pit vipers and checked the thermostats controlling temperature and humidity. He adjusted one slightly to duplicate more exactly conditions in the Arizona desert—dry, hot days and cool nights.

Orton placed the wire cage on the floor and for a few minutes watched the snakes. The smaller diamondback rattlesnake was stretched out to his full length of three and a half feet. The larger one was coiled loosely, resembling a ship's hawser arranged neatly in a large, circular heap. Both were sleeping. One of the sidewinders was lazily moving from one pile of rocks to another, leaving an irregular pattern in the sand on the floor of their den. Orton was enthralled by the primitive beauty of the rattlesnakes.

The doctor slid open a small glass opening at the top of the case. Through it he manipulated a long snake hook and one by one prodded and maneuvered the vipers into their separate feeding compartments. All four were now awake, aroused and hungry.

Closing the aperture at the top of the case, Orton pushed open a very small trapdoor into the first chamber and released a mouse through it. The trapdoor snapped shut. The mouse peered about and slowly started to explore his new environment. Suddenly he froze, instinctively sensing danger. The diamondback hit the mouse with enough force to drive his fangs through the sole of a man's shoe. Deadly poison was injected instantaneously. The rattlesnake released his hold and recoiled to a striking position. The mouse reeled drunkenly, staggered and fell over dead. The snake now uncoiled slowly and prepared to swallow the mouse.

Orton moved on to feed the other snakes, enjoying his

secret and fascinating hobby. He decided he would wait until tomorrow to milk the pit vipers of their venom.

On the way out of the laboratory, he passed three ventilated jars, each containing a scorpion. Orton had completed his research on their poison and had concluded that it was not virulent enough to kill an adult man in one day. Its hemolytic action, while often fatal, was not instantaneous. He had no further use for the scorpions. With a sadistic smirk, he unscrewed the tops of the jars and dumped the three scorpions into the same jar, screwing the top back on, knowing that in the confined space of one jar the scorpions would fight to the death. From this battle only one would emerge alive. If still strong enough, the survivor would eat the victims.

Orton snapped off the light and went up the stairs, whistling. He lit a Tiparillo, poured himself a cold beer and turned on the stereo in his den.

It was evening, and the Man was ready to move. After showering, he put on a pair of white silk pajamas and his navy-blue dressing gown, walked to the den and turned on the 7:00 P.M. news on the television. His wife watched briefly with him, but left at 7:20 P.M for a special meeting of her volunteer group, saying she'd be home no later than 10:30.

As soon as her station wagon pulled out of the drive, he picked up the phone and dialed a number. When the phone was answered, he said, "Good evening. This is Sam Shute." The Man spoke in a soft, aristocratic drawl. "If you have a few minutes this evening, I'd like to stop by. I've got a beauty for you."

"That would be fine, Sam." There was a twinge of anticipation in the voice on the other end of the line.

"You're sure it's convenient? I normally wouldn't bother you at home." The voice of Sam Shute hesitated. "But this one is so unusual. I knew you'd want to see it."

"What is it?"

Shute's voice lowered in a confidential tone. "A Jefferson reverse, with an inverted date . . . in mint condition."

"A Jefferson reverse!" Astonishment came over the phone. "I've never even heard . . ."

"It's one of a kind," Sam drawled softly.

"I'll be home alone all evening. Any time is fine, Sam."

The Man put down the telephone, in elation. The imitation of Shute was the one in which he'd had the least confidence. That was one reason he'd decided to use it first.

The Man knew that the person he'd called was an avid collector of rare coins. Sam Shute was a reputable coin dealer and a recognized authority in the field. The Man had been sure that a Jefferson reverse in mint condition would attract attention. It had. The Man laughed. It was such a rare coin, he had no intention of ever parting with it.

Less than fifteen minutes later, clothed in a black pullover, dark pants and black rubber-soled shoes, the Man pulled his car into a blind cul-de-sac less than a hundred yards from his unsuspecting host's driveway. He swept silently across the well-manicured lawn, circling the house once to make sure his host was indeed alone. Then he retraced his steps to his car, started it and drove into the driveway, parking in the shelter of two large rhododendron bushes. He mounted the front steps and rang the doorbell.

The door opened. A smiling face appeared with an outstretched hand of greeting. An iron fist smashed into the bridge of its nose. The smile vanished in a mass of shattered teeth and bones. The face reeled back, stunned and temporarily blinded. The Man moved forward fluidly, allowing no respite. His victim retched and folded almost in two as a piledriving left slammed into his solar plexus. A karate chop, delivered expertly to the back of his neck, snapped his vertebra with a sharp crack. The victim dropped lifeless to the floor.

The Man knelt and assured himself that his victim was dead, then carried the corpse into the bathroom and placed it in the bathtub.

He quickly undressed the body, putting the clothes and shoes neatly away in the victim's closet and dropping the shorts and socks into the clothes hamper. Then, wielding a surgical knife and hacksaw with professional skill, he dismembered the body into six sections, turning on the water to help the blood flow down the drain.

For a fleeting moment, the Man thought he was going to be nauseated. He turned away for a few minutes and studied the wallpaper pattern. Seventy-nine daisies across. One hundred sixteen down. The nausea disappeared. He looked again. Only water was running down the drain. He waited a few minutes longer, then turned it off.

He slid each section into a separate trash bag and then wrapped each bag carefully in that day's edition of the Sunday New York *Times*. He packed the bags neatly in the large container he had brought with him. Finished, he washed the knife and hacksaw clean and repacked them in the toweling, then thoroughly scrubbed the bathtub and floor. The room looked pristine.

The Man carried his parcels to his car and placed them carefully in the trunk. He made three trips from his car back to the house with heavy packages, carefully hiding their contents in preselected locations. He turned off all the lights, carefully wiped away all fingerprints, locked the front door and drove away.

At home, he immediately replaced the items he had used in his concealed arsenal. He dropped a playing card, the ace of spades, into the Styrofoam container and placed the container at the bottom of the deep-freeze that was reserved for storage of fish he had caught on his numerous fishing trips, then covered it with three other containers of exactly the same shape and dimension, all packed with frozen fish wrapped in the New York *Times*. At the proper time, he would move the container to a different location.

He removed his clothes, wrapped them in newspaper and put them in the trunk of his car, planning to dispose of them first thing in the morning. He showered again and put on his silk pajamas, removed his notebook from the secret drawer and with a black marking pencil crossed off the first name on his list. It had gone exactly as planned. He slid the notebook back in the drawer and locked it carefully.

When his wife returned home at 10:25 P.M., the man was just drifting off to sleep. She didn't wake him, he looked so peaceful.

2

Monday, June 2.
A Dynamite Start

THE MAN opened one eye and checked the Westclox on the nightstand. It was 6:30 A.M. As if by reflex, he reached out his hand for his wife's thigh. Like two performers who had played the same role over and over, their ritual was almost mechanical.

On good days, it took exactly seven minutes for both. As he bounced out of bed and headed for the shower, he noticed it was 6:37. Digital time. He smiled. Today was going to be a perfect day.

After breakfast, the Man removed three pounds of hamburger from a small refrigerator in his basement. On the workbench next to the sink, he sprinkled the meat with a measured quantity of white powder, kneading the mixture thoroughly, dividing it into six large patties. Rechecking his measurements carefully, he was confident it was strong enough to make them very ill, but it wouldn't kill them. He had decided that they were too beautiful to kill.

From his arsenal, the Man selected a small red plastic box and a brown paper sack. He checked again. The switch on the box was off. The receiver was deactivated. It couldn't pick up any extraneous signals. Now he checked the contents of the sack, rolled it cylindrically and taped it firmly bottom and top with bands of strong fiber tape. Next he taped the plastic box securely to the side of the cylinder, cautiously attaching the wire leads emerging from the mouth of the sack to the clips on the box. He checked it again.

Finished, he locked his arsenal and bounded up the stairs, a plastic bag of hamburger patties in his left hand and a strange device tenderly cradled under his right arm like a football.

On the way to his office, the Man took a scenic drive along the Gold Coast of Fairport, past a series of magnificent estates overlooking Long Island Sound. Through breaks in the hedges, there were glimpses of rolling lawns, formal gardens, spouting fountains and bronze statuary with the green patina of age. In the distance, the early-morning sun glinted off the gentle waves. Adjusting his sunglasses, he took a deep breath of the salt air. It was an invigorating smell. He stopped his car outside the high, wrought-iron fence surrounding one of the most beautiful of the waterfront estates.

Quickly he tossed the patties of meat over the fence. Then from his pocket he removed a high-pitched whistle and blew on it twice. It was inaudible to human ears. Slipping back into the driver's seat, he heard the snarls of the onrushing Dobermans on the other side of the fence.

At 8:30 A.M., Jim Dempsey arrived at police headquarters, a modern glass-and-brick two-story building in the center of Fairport. He glanced around. Both he and Brenda loved Fairport. It was the quintessence of New England: the quiet streets, lined with ancient trees spreading leafy shade; a white Colonial church on the main square; white clapboard houses; historical markers studding the lush green landscape; and the picturesque Housatuck River winding through the center of town, down to the Sound. He was thankful that the zoning board had a restrictive building code. All the storefronts were Colonial brick, and all were set back, separated from the main street by green plantings.

As usual in warm weather, Dempsey wore lightweight dark-blue slacks. an open-necked blue sport shirt, and a conservative sport coat. A blue shoulder holster held his .357 Magnum. Dempsey wore no insignia of rank. Everyone in town knew that he was the Chief of Police. It was a rare occasion when he wore his official police uniform, but he kept two crushed captain's caps, with braid on the visor, close at hand for use when needed. One was in the lower right-hand drawer of his office desk, the other was in the glove compartment of his car.

Dempsey took a last breath of the tangy salt air from the Housatuck, listened to the cry of the seagulls circling overhead, entered the police station and walked across the tiled lobby toward the duty desk. Sergeant O'Rourke knew the footsteps. He shuffled some papers and pretended to look at them. Then he looked up, simulated surprise on his weathered, crumpled Irish face.

"Top of the morning, to you, Chief," he boomed in his loud voice.

"Morning, Harry. Anything important?"

The Sergeant shook his head negatively. "Nothing out of the ordinary. Just the usual."

"How's Eileen?" Dempsey asked.

"The wife's much better." O'Rourke smiled his thanks. "It was just something she ate."

Dempsey could see a corner of the morning's sports section peeking from underneath the police blotter. He walked over to the stairs and went up to his corner office. O'Rourke watched him. The Chief had all the moves of a professional athlete. He carried his 194 pounds on a muscular six-foot frame. His body rippled as he moved. O'Rourke was convinced that, if necessary, the Chief could leap tall buildings in a single bound.

As he walked into his office, Dempsey's administrative assistant was standing, her back to the doorway, in front of a white wrought-iron baker's rack filled to overflowing with greenery and plants of all descriptions. Dempsey shook his head. Mary's garden was becoming the largest greenbelt north of the Amazon rain forest.

She held an empty watering can in her right hand and was leaning over, talking softly to the Rex Begonias.

Dempsey smiled before he spoke. "Mary, Mary . . . quite . . . I'm afraid only the weeds are listening."

Mary stopped her whisper in midsentence and turned around, an embarrassed look on her face.

Dempsey was still smiling. "Morning, Mary. I don't know what you say to those monsters, but it sure works."

"Morning, Chief," she said, returning his smile. "I'll get your coffee. The meeting is at nine." She retreated from the office with her watering can.

Dempsey walked to the window and looked out at the Housatuck. A flight of Canada geese was circling over the river. He opened a drawer and took out his binoculars. He adjusted them quickly, marveling at the grace and grandeur of the soaring birds and their ability to ride the wind currents faultlessly, as they chattered back and forth. He watched them use the wind to their advantage as they landed in the water and nodded approval. Soaring and sailing. The principles were the same.

He put down the binoculars and sat at his desk. His eyes surveyed the room. The office was spacious and attractively furnished. Brenda had done a nice job. She had a flair for decorating. She'd suggested the extra furnishings, and it had been a right decision to buy them, even though he'd had to pay for them himself. They certainly made a difference. It had been Brenda's idea to put the marble top on his desk. He'd taken a good-natured ribbing, but it worked well as a conference table. Now he could seat six in comfortable leather chairs.

Brenda had also suggested the conversational grouping of a leather couch, two matching chairs and a marble coffee table. He'd picked out the picture that hung on the wall. It was a large color photograph of the yacht *Intrepid* defeating *Gretel* in the fourth race of the America's Cup. It brought back pleasant memories. He'd crewed on the *Intrepid* in that series.

Mary came in with a tray and set up the coffee pot. He glanced appreciatively at her as she walked out. She was an attractive, personable widow, with beautiful auburn hair. She'd been the first female recruit in the Fairport police force and had advanced rapidly to the rank of sergeant. Just two months after her promotion, her husband, a computer programmer, had been killed in a tragic automobile accident. To try to overcome her deep grief, Mary had thrown herself totally into police work. It was now her whole life. She was both his assistant and his secretary.

Dempsey rose and poured himself a cup of black coffee,

still thinking about Mary. He'd like to promote her. She was efficient and highly competent with a good instinct for detective work. What a dilemma! Good police officers could come and go, but a good secretary was damn near indispensable. He sighed. At the first opportunity, he'd make the sacrifice and promote her.

Promptly at 9:00 A.M., Lieutenants Tom Farrow and Gus Belli entered Dempsey's office, as they did every Monday morning to review their activities and discuss the week's routine. They exchanged pleasantries and at Dempsey's suggestion poured themselves coffee. At five feet nine, Belli was the shorter of the two. He had a powerful, broad-shouldered, muscular build and moved like a bull. Farrow was at least three inches taller, loose and well-coordinated. He walked on his toes and moved in slow, fluid motions.

They sat down at the Chief's table, Belli on one side, Farrow on the other. Dempsey sat in his leather desk chair in the center. As they talked, Dempsey was struck by the contrast in the two men. Both were excellent police officers, both were intelligent, and both had unusual credentials for a town as small as Fairport. But there the similarities ended.

Belli had a dark, rugged look. The edges of his square face were blurred by deep-set eyes under heavy black eyebrows. His luxuriant black hair was parted straight. Belli would have been handsome except for a ridge of scar tissue above his left brow, which stood out as a pink line on his swarthy face. Belli wore the scar proudly. He'd won it along with a Silver Star in a firefight in Korea. In action, almost hand-to-hand in intensity. Belli's platoon had delayed the Chinese advance for half a day.

Farrow's boyish, freckled face was topped by a shock of unruly reddish-brown hair. A pair of cold blue eyes were wildly at variance with his generally mild, pleasant disposition. Farrow's skin was always pink. Since he didn't tan and he burned easily, Farrow avoided the sun.

Belli was tough-minded, organized and dedicated. He worked hard, perhaps too intensely, close to his capacity. Farrow was artistic, imaginative and creative. He was relaxed about his work and rarely used all of his abilities. He had almost unlimited potential, if he could be persuaded to use it.

Dempsey laughed aloud. He was lucky. He had both the wet and the dry look. Both were winners.

He suddenly realized that his assistants were staring at him. His face flushed slightly. He hadn't been listening. A long moment passed before he spoke.

"Sorry, my mind was elsewhere. It must be a sign of age." All three laughed good-naturedly. He rose and poured himself and Belli another cup of coffee. Farrow declined more coffee with a wave of his hand.

Dempsey sat down again, now all business. He leaned forward attentively as Farrow outlined the highlights of Senator Benson's planned visit to Fairport the following weekend.

Farrow spoke slowly. "He'll arrive on Saturday morning. I think his wife arrives this Thursday. I'm not sure of that yet. They'll stay at the Winchesters' house." Farrow pointed out the location on a map.

"Apparently they're old friends. There's a dinner dance in their honor at Longwood on Saturday night. Sunday afternoon is the big celebration at the high school He unveils a statue to commemorate Fairport's Bicentennial, with appropriate patriotic remarks. They leave after the ceremony for a political dinner in New York City. The Democrats plan to make a big thing of his visit."

"You can't blame them," Dempsey remarked. "He's a damn good speaker. Probably run for President next time."

"He'd be a hell of a lot better than the guy we got now," Belli said matter-of-factly. "He's awful."

Dempsey ignored Belli's comment and cut off Farrow's reply by asking, "What's the security setup?"

"The state police will cover his motorcades and the Governor's, too." Farrow stood up to trace the routes on his map. "Anytime he moves, it's their responsibility. We're committed for a security protection when he's stationary. At the Winchesters', at Longwood and at the high school." He pointed to the red X's on his map.

Belli leaned forward. "I can't understand why we're erecting a statue. The British landed here before the town was formed. Nothing important has happened since.''

Dempsey grinned. He had to agree with Belli.

No one spoke the obvious. All three knew that no matter what precautions they took, if someone was determined to kill Benson, or any other public figure, it could be done.

The phone rang. ''It's for you, Chief,'' said Mary on the intercom, as Belli and Farrow rose to leave. ''Bill Donnelly.''

Dempsey pushed the flashing button on the phone and picked up the receiver. He had a real fondness for Donnelly, Fairport's First Selectman. Built like an inverted triangle, Donnelly was a gregarious, lovable bear of a man.

''Bill, I planned to call you as soon as we finished here. I want to brief you on the security plans for Senator Benson's visit.''

''Good, Jim. The Senator's a close friend of mine, you know.''

Dempsey held the phone at arm's length as Donnelly talked on. Talking to Donnelly was like talking to a radio. One way, nonstop. He was a name-dropper, and a born politician—all things to all people.

After waiting a reasonable time, Dempsey interrupted the monologue. ''Great, Bill. When would you like to get together for a briefing?''

''We've got our monthly Rotary meeting today. Why don't you stop by at twelve? That will give us half an hour before lunch.''

''O.K., Bill. Damn good thing you called. I'd forgotten about Rotary. Thanks. I'll see you in an hour.''

Dempsey hung up the phone, put his feet on the desk and leaned back in his reclining chair. How could he have forgotten their luncheon? He was getting absentminded. It was going to be an important meeting, too. Ned Nichols had agreed to update the group on the purchase of some property near Candlewood for a summer day camp. It had started as a Rotary project. He opened his desk drawer and pulled out his file on the property. He quickly skimmed through it, then put the folder back in the drawer. Dempsey let his thoughts wander to the property. It was a beautiful spot, with a fishing lodge in the center of the heavily wooded 150 acres. The lodge sat high on a knoll, overlooking Candlewood Lake. Each spring, a hummingbird built its nest on a vine framing the rustic front porch. The nest always hung by a slender thread. It was a symbol of life, thought Dempsey. Fragile and tenuous, yet incredibly resilient and durable. The filmy thread was strong enough to support the nest against all of nature's pressures. Yet a man, if he wanted, could destroy it all with a mere flick of his finger.

Mary interrupted Dempsey's thoughts by bringing in the day's mail—two letters and *Sports Illustrated*. She took out the tray with the coffee pot and cups. The first letter was a request that Dempsey head up a special building-fund drive for the YMCA. He set that letter aside. He'd have to think about it. It would eat up a lot of time, but he knew that he'd ultimately agree. Most of the suburban crime and vandalism was due to bored and restless teenagers. A better Y would help.

The second letter brought him bolt upright in his chair. It was typed on plain 8½-by-11-inch white bond paper and the envelope was addressed to him, with a local postmark. It read in its entirety:

> Blood is red,
> You pigs are blue,
> Start counting victims,
> There'll be quite a few.
>
> Spades are black,
> Hearts are red,
> Before very long,
> You, too, will be dead.
>
> Diamonds are red,
> Clubs are black,
> Carry your buddy
> Home in a sack.

Dempsey drew a deep breath to steady himself, then leaped to his feet and shouted for Belli and Farrow. As they appeared in the doorway, he pointed to the letter on his desk. "Don't touch it," he cautioned. Then he buzzed for Paul Rice, their lab expert, as the two young lieutenants read over his shoulder. Both swore softly, then offered similar opinions.

"Some crank. He probably specializes in obscene phone calls, too," suggested Belli, his dark eyes flashing.

"It has to be a practical joke," Farrow added hopefully. "If not . . ." He hesitated, then finished his thought. "We've got trouble. It's a crazy."

Both looked questioningly at Dempsey, who was staring out of the window. The geese were gone. After a full minute of silence, he turned just as Paul Rice slouched through the doorway.

A former high school basketball star, Rice was tall, wiry and athletic. But he gave the impression of being of average height, because he walked hunched over. Except for his carriage, the thirty-year-old specialist was meticulous. His thinning blond hair was set in one-inch waves. His matching blond mustache was trimmed precisely.

Dempsey considered Rice to be a superb lab technician. He had a penetrating, incisive, rapid and facile mind. Yet he was a maverick. He liked to do his own thing. His nonconformity was almost a passion. His scented aftershave lotion was his trademark.

Dempsey gestured at the open letter on his desk.

"Paul, check this out thoroughly. My prints are all over it. Shit, I opened it and read it, like any other letter." Dempsey swallowed hard. "Maybe we'll be lucky and you'll find something."

Rice leaned over the table and read the letter. His blond eyebrows raised appreciably, but he said nothing.

"If it's a real nut . . ." Belli's deep voice trailed off. "You can't be too careful. You can't defend against insanity. Insane people do crazy things. They're totally unpredictable."

Dempsey nodded. "I hope Tom's right and this is a joke, but I've got a gut feeling it's not. I learned a long time ago not to be surprised . . . by anything. When you least expect trouble, that's the time to expect it. Let's keep our fingers crossed. I'm going to lunch with Donnelly."

• • •

The Man hit the steering wheel with the side of his fist. He was annoyed. Annoyed with himself. Earlier in the day he had thought that he would have enough time to swing by Barbara's for lunch. Now there wasn't time. It was D day.

He glanced into the back seat. His package was there, a CARE package. He laughed and said aloud, "It's eleven-fifty five A.M. Do you know where your package is?" He hit the steering wheel again. He sure did! A strange excitement was building inside him.

That Barbara. She was a different kind of package. Just the thought of her made his pulse quicken. He could feel the swelling begin. She usually wore knee-length skirts, without panties, and was always receptive. He liked that. The first touch on her inner leg would make her light-headed. Her heart would skip, and within seconds she would be moist with desire. Her sexual interest equaled his. Together they could go on for hours.

He was breathing heavily. Barbara's hand reached over and unzipped his fly. She fondled him with one hand; with the other she raised her skirt and reached for herself. Barbara's musky odor made him totally erect. He closed his eyes. He opened them instantly. Damn, what was he doing with his eyes closed! He was driving. He hit the steering wheel again. He'd find time to see Barbara later.

Dempsey pulled his unmarked police car into the parking lot behind the Selectman's office, just as the clock in the tower of the town hall was striking noon. Dempsey loved fast cars, and his police cruiser contained a specially constructed turbocharged Ford engine. He affectionately called it his "Bullet." It tested full out on the turnpike with flashing red lights at 143 miles per hour. He parked alongside Donnelly's Ford station wagon.

The First Selectman was pleased to learn that he was going to ride in the same car with Senator Benson. His round, ruddy Irish face was beaming, as always.

"That's great, Jim. It'll give us a chance to talk over old times."

"Wilbur can probably use your advice on his campaign, perhaps on some of the major national problems." Dempsey was pulling Donnelly's leg, but the Selectman took it seriously, as a compliment.

"There are a few things I plan to suggest." Donnelly's face turned serious. "I'm going to introduce Ella, and she'll introduce Senator Benson. I don't plan to talk for more than five or ten minutes."

Dempsey grimaced. He knew how Donnelly could ramble on. "Make it brief, Bill. Most people will be there to see the unveiling of the statue."

The two men concluded their meeting and walked together to Manny's, the local steak restaurant, just a block away. Dempsey noted that Briggs' Jaguar was parked two rows behind his car. On the way, Donnelly commented, "I think your security precautions are fine, Jim, but a trifle overdone. We ought to ride in an open car if the weather's nice." He put his hand on Dempsey's shoulder. "Of all people, you should know that nothing ever happens around here."

They entered the restaurant, dazed momentarily by the darkness of the interior in contrast to the bright sunshine outside. A heavyset man with a beard brushed closely past them, almost colliding with Donnelly. They crossed the foyer and took the stairs down to a private dining room in the basement.

Dempsey's eyes scanned the room. Five men were already there: Spike Briggs, the State Police Colonel; Bob Baker, owner and manager of Fairport's Sport Shop; Don Dillon, owner and president of Dillon Insurance Company; Sam Tilden, president and majority stockholder in the Fairport Savings Bank; and Andrew McAlpin, owner and manager of the Fairport Drug Center. Dempsey and the Selectman barely had time to say their hellos and order drinks when Ned Nichols and Harry Hoyle arrived.

Nichols came into the room triumphantly, as if he'd just won a major court case. He was smiling, cool and composed. He set his briefcase down on a chair and turned to help Hoyle through the doorway. Hoyle was wrestling with a large map mounted on heavy cardboard. His forehead was glistening with perspiration, his face flushed, and his suitcoat damp.

"It's a steambath out there. This is going to be a bitch of a summer," he complained.

Nichols gestured to him. "Harry, put the map behind the easel. I'll set it up after lunch."

Nichols, a rugged six-footer with steel-gray hair, thick and neatly combed, was immediately surrounded by most of the other men, asking questions. Without answering, he greeted each one in turn with his iron handshake. Then he held up both of his hands. Grinning broadly, he said, "Gentlemen, this is a great day for the kids of Fairport. We've got the property locked up at a very fair price. I'll give you the details after lunch."

Dempsey stood aside, sipping his drink, watching Nichols. It was Ned's day, and he was putting on quite a show. Easy to see why he was such a successful lawyer. It was a powerful combination of intelligence and personal magnetism. Yes, no question about it. Nichols was smart and persuasive. But underneath everything, he was ruthless, driven by a consuming ambition to accumulate wealth. To Nichols, money represented power. It was that simple. He considered himself a winner, and once Ned had selected a goal, he would let nothing stand in the way of his achieving it.

Dempsey drained his Perrier and lime and ordered another one. It was like drinking soda pop, he didn't really like the stuff, but never drank liquor on duty. He glanced at Hoyle, and wondered. Harry had inherited a very successful real estate agency, but lately he acted as if he were Nichols' personal lackey. Something funny was going on.

At exactly 1:00 P.M., they sat down to a Manny's Special—thick slabs of roast beef, baked potatoes and salad with Gorgonzola cheese dressing. It was during coffee that Ned Nichols stood up, placed a large map of the property on the easel and explained, with the help of an acetate overlay, the preliminary plans for the day camp.

Dempsey listened carefully. He liked the plans. It was the price that bothered him. Where the hell would they get that kind of money?

Nichols seemed to read his mind. "One and a half million

may seem like a lot of money. Actually it's only ten thousand an acre. That's cheap. With corporations moving into Fairfield County, the price of large parcels of land is skyrocketing. Hell, next year you won't be able to touch this property for fifteen thousand an acre. Isn't that right, Harry?''

The heavyset real estate man wiped his forehead and nodded in agreement.

Nichols glared at Hoyle, who then stood up and added, ''No question about it. This is a fair deal. It's the best we're going to find, if we want a summer camp.'' He sat down and wiped has forehead again.

''We all voted for a summer camp,'' Nichols reminded them. ''We've already raised two hundred and fifty thousand dollars. I've arranged with Sam for a half-million-dollar mortgage. Don't forget, we'll get matching funds from Washington. This is a great day for Fairport.''

Dempsey glanced down the table at Tilden. The old banker was nodding his approval. Somehow he didn't feel right about what Nichols was saying. The lawyer was selling too hard. He had a gut feeling there was something wrong. But both Hoyle and Tildon agreed with Nichols. Hell, they were the experts. He didn't know anything about real estate. But he did know people, and Nichols was cold and calculating. His heart was nothing but a pump.

Reluctantly, Dempsey raised his hand with the others. The vote to buy the property carried unanimously.

Nichols smiled, took a Tiparillo out of his inside coat pocket, peeled off the cellophane and lit the small cigar.

Dempsey saw Nichols wink at Hoyle. He finished off his coffee. It was cold. Suddenly the room seemed stuffy and hot. The meeting broke up. As the others crowded around Nichols, Dempsey left the restaurant and walked back to his car, glancing at the clock in the tower. It was 2:20 P.M. His mind was racing. Ned Nichols was a mean piece of work. That hardnosed shit wouldn't do anything for anyone, unless there was something in it for him. Dempsey drove out of the parking lot.

•   •   •

Dempsey would have been considerably more upset if he had heard the whispered exchange between Ned Nichols and Harry Hoyle after he'd left.

"Ned, we bought that property for six hundred thousand dollars. What happens if they find out who really owns it?" Hoyle's eyes showed his worry.

Nichols put his hand lightly on Hoyle's arm. "Harry, only the two of us know. It's buried deep. No one else need ever know. If they do find out . . . well . . ."

Hoyle stared at the lawyer. Nichols' eyes were the coldest he'd ever seen.

"I told you, we can really clean up if you get the options on the adjoining property. But you've got to relax and keep your mouth shut. I'll take care of our buddies."

Hoyle could feel the increased pressure on his arm. If felt as if it were being squeezed by an iron band.

From his vantage point across the street, the Man waited patiently. He had watched Donnelly return to his office at 2:40 P.M. Based on the Selectman's behavior pattern, the Man knew he would spend no more than ten minutes puttering around his office, then leave to play golf. Normally, Donnelly would tee off before 3:30, so that he could finish nine holes before cocktail hour.

"Not today, buddy. It's going to be a maxi-bummer." A grin split the Man's face.

Minutes before, the Man had walked unhurriedly by Donnelly's car. Checking to make sure he was unobserved, he had slipped a cylindrical object under the front seat, and holding his breath, had flipped a small switch. Nothing had happened. He had inhaled deeply, then had lingered for a moment at the rear bumper.

The remote-control device the Man now fingered had been adjusted to be effective at almost a hundred yards. He dropped his head and took a last drag on his Tiparillo. Exhaling smoke, he snuffed out the small cigar in the ashtray. He had spotted Donnelly leaving the Municipal Building. It was 2:47 P.M. The Selectman was wearing a straw hat and a rumpled seersucker suit. In his right hand he held a can of lemon soda.

The Man was pleased to see that Donnelly was alone. "I just want Donnelly. That pompous oaf." He laughed inwardly.

The Selectman opened the door of his station wagon and slid into the driver's seat. He started his car, backed out of his parking space and prepared to turn into Main Street. The Man aimed his device. As soon as Donnelly had cleared the other cars, he pushed the button. The bottom half of the Selectman disappeared in the ensuing explosion. The rest of him was splattered about the smoking remains of his car.

Donnelly would never ride with Benson or introduce the Governor. The Man had claimed his first public victim. He had started his program off with a bang!

Traffic on Main Street was quickly blocked off by three patrol cars. Two fire trucks arrived and began hosing down the smoldering wreckage. In the few minutes it took for Dempsey and his assistants to arrive on the scene, the curious had already gathered. At first, most of the townspeople thought it was a stunt. Someone was filming another movie. Probably Newman. But the bits of flesh and large smears of crimson were just too real. They stood around quietly, watching with eyes intent as a circle of vultures. They gave ground grudgingly to the police.

"Get back! You there, get back!" commanded Dempsey, gesturing with his hands. "There could be a delayed explosion!" The crowd moved back rapidly.

"Do you think?" Belli began, nervously glancing at the wreckage.

"Of course not, but we need breathing room," Dempsey said, studying the wreckage intently.

Belli noticed that Dempsey was wearing his captain's cap. The gold braid on the cap made him look official as hell.

As soon as the fire department had finished, the police ambulance crew removed Donnelly's remains in a large canvas sack. The ambulance attendant wiped his red-smeared hands on his smock and closed the rear doors. It was not a sight for squeamish stomachs. The crowd thinned out. A small boy left the scene, kicking a crumpled lemon-soda can down the sidewalk. A Good Humor man, a toasted-almond bar melting in his hand, stood open-mouthed on the curb, his face the color of his uniform.

"This was no accident. It was murder. Dynamite. Two or three sticks, fulminate of mercury fuse, probably activated by a remote-control device." Dempsey spoke grimly to his assistants as he probed carefully in the wreckage.

Neither showed any surprise. They'd concluded it was murder, also.

"Why not a pressure trigger?" asked Belli, picking up a piece of the steering wheel, then putting it down again.

Dempsey glanced up at him. "It would have gone off the minute Donnelly slid into his seat, not out here in the street."

Belli nodded sheepishly, then added, "But with a delay mechanism."

"Not likely," Dempsey answered without looking up. "It would work, but there's no reason—"

"It could have been a timing device, Chief." Farrow leaned over and picked up a small piece of red plastic. He held it loosely in his palm.

"Possible, but not probable. Donnelly wasn't in his car for more than a minute or two. The murderer would have had to be incredibly lucky to hit the time that exactly." Dempsey straightened up and looked around carefully. "I suspect a remote-control device. If so, the killer had to be close by at the time of the explosion. Probably sitting in a car."

As the others watched, Dempsey extended his arm in front of him. Then sighting down the arm, he turned his body slowly in a 360-degree circle. Finished, he said simply. "There are four or five spots where he could have been parked. Most probably in that alley across the street." Dempsey pointed. "That's at least eighty yards, probably closer to ninety. That's pretty far for a remote-control mechanism."

Dempsey turned to Belli. "Have the distance from those five spots to the wreckage measured." Belli nodded and made a note on his memo pad.

"Why would he use a remote-control device? Why would he risk it?" Belli asked.

"Control. He could be selective, make sure his victim was

alone. Many reasons. Maybe . . ." Dempsey hesitated. "Maybe he just wanted to watch."

"That's a sickening thought. I'll get the measurements and start checking for witnesses," Belli volunteered, moving away from the wreckage. He felt queasy.

Dempsey turned to Farrow. "Tom, have your men check this wreckage, piece by piece. We're looking for small bits of plastic."

"Plastic?" Farrow swallowed his surprise.

"Plastic and little chunks of wire. A miniature receiving device."

"Plastic? Like this, Chief?" Farrow opened his palm.

Dempsey looked carefully at the small bit of plastic. "Exactly." His eyes brightened.

In the next ninety minutes, Farrow's squad sifted meticulously through the wreckage. They found four additional bits of red plastic, three small twisted copper wires and several pieces of dynamite wrapping. From these scraps, they were now certain it had been dynamite placed under the seat and detonated by a remote-control unit, just as Dempsey had predicted minutes after arriving on the scene.

"The Chief is a goddam genius," muttered Sergeant O'Rourke, his weathered, crumpled face showing his admiration.

"A small talent," joked Farrow. But seeing O'Rourke's frown, he added quickly, "The Chief's really remarkable. At his best in a crisis." Farrow meant the compliment sincerely. Dempsey never ceased to amaze him.

Belli had made the rounds of the neighborhood. Dempsey had checked with Donnelly's office staff. They walked back to the wreckage together.

"Unbelievable," he reported to Dempsey. "Nobody saw nothing. A big fucking zip."

Dempsey muttered an oath. "That's too bad. I didn't do any better. We'll have to check again. There's got to be someone."

"It's America today. No one wants to get involved," Belli explained hesitantly. "It's see no evil, hear no evil . . ."

"Evil has wavelengths, like sound and light. Sometimes

you've got to feel them. Get your antennae out." Dempsey paused, then added, "Motive. We've got to concentrate on motive. Why would anyone kill Donnelly?"

Belli shook his head slowly. "He didn't have any enemies. He was a big lovable bear. It's unbelievable."

"You'd better start interviewing his friends," Dempsey said evenly. "Bill didn't blow himself up. One of his friends did. It would be nice to know why."

"Chief . . .the note, the threats . . . Shit. It was no joke. They carried him off in a sack." Belli's hands were sweating. He didn't like death close up. He wiped his hands on his trousers.

Dempsey nodded grimly. "The letter was for real. No question about it. The bastard told us to start counting the victims."

"Including you, Chief." Belli's eyes met Dempsey's.

Dempsey shivered involuntarily.

Farrow reported another find. It was a badly burned playing card taped to the inside of the rear bumper, the king of spades. It made no sense at all, except that the letter to the Chief had mentioned spades, hearts, diamonds and clubs—suits of playing cards.

On his way back to police headquarters, Dempsey stopped to visit briefly with Spike Briggs at the State Police barracks. It was a spur-of-the-moment decision. Briggs was on a long-distance call, so Dempsey waited briefly outside his office, admiring the brass sign, "Steven Briggs, Colonel, Connecticut State Police." So Steven was his real name. He hadn't known.

Briggs finished his phone call quickly. He welcomed Dempsey warmly. "About time you came to visit your traffic department. Awful news about Bill. Unbelievable!"

Dempsey had now heard the word at least four times, but he had to agree. It was unbelievable. Briggs had been monitoring the local police frequency, so he knew most of the details about the bombing.

"It makes no sense," Briggs said.

"None," Dempsey agreed.

"Donnelly would be the last person. Who the hell would murder him?" Briggs scratched his head.

"And why?" Dempsey shrugged his shoulders. "He never hurt anyone. He was a kid at heart."

"Mind, too." Briggs' bluntness hurt. Dempsey winced. Briggs continued, "He never grew up. Fairport grew up around him. He was Selectman . . . well, it's an easy job."

"Apparently thankless, too," Dempsey added grimly.

"Any clues?"

"None to speak of."

"Witnesses?"

"None."

"Motive?"

Dempsey didn't answer. He thought he detected a slight flicker of a smile on Briggs' face. If so, it was as fleeting as the blink of an eye. Briggs was beginning to annoy him.

"Cut the shit, Steve. I stopped by because I thought you might be able to help."

"It flashed through my mind. But so soon?" Briggs grinned, his teeth clamped on the plastic end of his small cigar. He ignored the reference to his real name.

"Something's up. Something big. I don't know what. I just feel it." Dempsey then related the chilling contents of the letter he'd received earlier in the day.

"That's a whole new bucket of worms," Briggs said slowly. "Sorry. I didn't mean to be a smart-ass. I get carried away sometimes. My shrink says I'm too damned competitive. You know, once a leatherneck . . ." Briggs looked down at his hands. "How can we help?" He looked up, straight at Dempsey.

Dempsey looked him in the eye. "A remote-control device is not difficult to set up. You can use a garage-door opener, but you've got to know what you're doing. Handling dynamite . . ." He smiled fleetingly. "It's not your basic amateur sport."

Briggs nodded his understanding. "You'd like a list of people who know how to use explosives."

"Right. It had to be someone with nitro in his blood. You've got one of the best computer hookups—"

"Both regional and national. It's the very latest. It's so sophisticated none of us amateurs dares to touch it. I'll get my computer expert started immediately. What else can we do?"

Spike was now all business. Organized, concise, tough-minded. It was a dramatic about-face.

"If you could track the source of the dynamite."

"We'll give it a try. You'll have our full cooperation. By the way, did you find the plastic box?" Briggs' eyes were laughing as they met Dempsey's.

The question jolted Dempsey. He locked eyes with Briggs. His mind raced. His jaw muscles tensed. He hadn't said anything about a plastic box. He knew nothing had been said about one over the police frequency.

"How the hell?"

Briggs' face exploded into a broad grin. "You should know. You wrote the book for the FBI, *Detection and Defusion of Explosive Devices*."

Dempsey had almost forgotten. "It was only a pamphlet," he said lamely.

"Modesty doesn't become you, Jim. It's still the bible on the subject. I've almost memorized it. It didn't take a great deal of imagination. I thought you'd be looking for a small plastic receiver."

Dempsey had to smile. Briggs wasn't a bad detective. "We found it," he said simply. He paused, rose from his chair and took several steps toward the door. Suddenly he turned and said, "You must have just missed the bombing?"

The grin left Briggs' face. "No more than ten minutes," he answered. "I walked back to the lot with Ned. Donnelly must have been right behind us. I said goodbye to Ned and drove off. Ned was just getting into his Ferrari when I left. Too close."

Briggs' Tiparillo had gone out. He struck a match and relit it. Dempsey watched as Briggs, out of habit, folded the match between thumb and two forefingers and put it in his pocket.

Once a Marine, thought Dempsey. Aloud, he said, "Good thing you didn't leave with Bill."

"Amen," said Briggs.

Briggs walked Dempsey to his car. As they reached it, Briggs spoke in a subdued tone. "Jim, I'm sorry . . . the way I acted before. It was . . ."

"It was nothing." Dempsey knew the apology had been difficult for Briggs.

"Yes, it was. I'm competitive. I grew up that way. First to survive. Then to get ahead. It's a technique, not a strength. Well, I'm getting better." A flicker of a smile touched Briggs' lips. "I'm not as uptight as I used to be. I'm much more relaxed, if you can believe it."

"You, relaxed? You're a coiled spring." It was Dempsey's turn to smile.

"I'm not as compulsive. There was a time . . . I was so competitive I didn't think anyone could beat me, at anything. I was the world's greatest. Now, hell, I even let you win occasionally . . . even at sailing." Briggs snuffed out his small cigar. field-stripping the remains and placing the plastic tip in his pocket.

Dempsey snorted. "I can't let you win. A sore loser's one thing. But a sore winner. There's nothing worse."

They shook hands and Dempsey drove off. He appreciated the apology. Spike was proud. He'd been a highly decorated Marine colonel, and still exhibited the aggressiveness and decisiveness of combat command. He was direct. Much too direct. The type who could start a fight in an empty room. Dempsey shook his head. The guy was different. A free spirit—his own man.

Briggs watched Dempsey turn the corner. His handsome, weathered face was taut, lips in a thin, crooked line. He snapped to attention, clicked his heels and gave Dempsey the Boy Scout salute.

Dempsey was back at headquarters by 4:30 P.M. There had been four telephone calls from the news services and reporters who had learned of the bombing. Belli had handled these.

"Take this yellow one, it's magnificent." Hetty Starr inhaled deeply and said to the world, "Don't you just love the smell? It must be what heaven smells like."

Hetty's housekeeper, Mrs. Foxx, said, "Yes'm," and

retreated toward the house with the bouquet of freshly cut roses. Mrs. Foxx had learned not to listen too closely to her mistress. Hetty's thoughts were beyond her. She had only one reply—"Yes'm."

Hetty sat on her marble bench. It was her favorite spot in all the world. Mrs. Foxx had set out her afternoon tea. Hetty's eyes continued around the rose garden, inspecting each flowering bloom. There were roses of all colors and shades; blushing reds, lavenders, pinks, whites and yellows. Golden yellows were her favorites. She inhaled again. It was the smell of the roses intermingled with the fresh smell of the sea. An intoxicating aroma. Today, the sea was calm.

She poured herself a cup of tea and closed her eyes. This was her tranquil hour. It was the time of day for meditation and memories, the only time that Hetty allowed herself to look backward. What memories! Hetty Starr had been the Queen of Cinema for two decades spanning the '30s and '40s, during the heyday of Hollywood. On two separate occasions, she had been awarded cinema's prized Oscar as Best Actress for her dramatic screen portrayals. She was acknowledged by almost every critic to have been one of the greatest dramatic actresses that Hollywood had ever produced.

Now, at the age of sixty-nine, she was considering a new career. Her old friend Josh Morgan had offered her a role on Broadway. She opened her eyes; picked up her cup and held it in her hand; live, onstage, bright lights, after all these years. The thought quickened her pulses. Her adrenaline bubbled. She hadn't felt this way since George died.

After her marriage to George Webster, a successful stockbroker, he and Shore Haven, their waterfront estate, had become her life. Retiring from acting, she had devoted herself to benefit performances and charity appearances, and had become Fairport's *grand dame*. For the past four years, after George's death, she'd been in limbo, her brain dormant, living on the surface, not allowing herself to get into depths, frozen in time, emotionally unemployed. She took several sips of tea, then set her cup back on its saucer.

Hetty turned her head and inhaled the salt air. She'd always wanted to try Broadway. There was nothing that had ever frightened her, except death. She had a mortal fear of death. It was so final. There was no curtain call. She couldn't face that. No, it's not too late to try the stage, Hetty thought. I'll do it.

Why not? If Bette, Katharine, Helen and Ginger could succeed, so can I. I was always the best.

A smile lit her face, a confident, self-satisfied smile. It was almost like announcing her engagement to a man she hadn't yet met, not knowing what role or what play Morgan had in mind.

Rising, she touched her statue. Before his death, George had commissioned three life-size marble statues for the garden. Two of them depicted Hetty in her Oscar-winning roles. The third was the bride on their wedding day. It was the real Hetty, her favorite. Touching it always brought good luck.

She looked forward to watching herself on television tonight. One of her greatest secrets was that she achieved a certain exhilaration in reliving, virtually reenacting, each of her celluloid roles. Even now, after all these years, she would become completely absorbed in the film, enjoying each nuance of her acting through a perfectionist's eyes. She often wondered if other actors and actresses experienced the same deep emotion in watching themselves on the screen.

This week, Channel 5 was featuring a series of Hetty Starr movies on its late show. Tonight was one of her favorites, *Bermuda Honeymoon*. This was the first movie she had ever made. Her sympathetic portrayal of the young and innocent bride had catapulted her overnight to stardom. What few people knew was that George, her leading man in that movie, had been her first real love. Her first lover. For six months theirs had been a sizzling Hollywood real-life romance. Her heart fluttered at the memories and the prospect of watching the movie again.

Hetty walked toward the fish pond. Where were her babies, Tony and Oscar? She hadn't seen them all day. She called. Silence. Then she heard the low whimpering noises coming from behind the hedge that rimmed the fish pond. She walked over to investigate.

Hetty ran hard toward the house, shouting, "Mr. Foxx,

Mr. Foxx, come quickly! It's Tony and Oscar. Call Dr. Sprott. Something is wrong with my babies!''

Gus Belli swallowed hard and pushed the doorbell. Minutes passed until the door was opened by Donnelly's sobbing twelve-year-old daughter. "My daddy's dead," she choked out and buried her face in her hands. Belli nodded and swallowed again. Momentarily he put his arm around her, then moved past the young girl to talk to Madelaine, the Selectman's widow, seated on the couch in the living room. She was weeping softly, but openly. Sobs were rising from deep in her chest. The tears came, then stopped, then flowed again. Her face had fallen apart, eyes swollen, cheeks puffy. Belli offered to return another time, but Madelaine wanted to talk.

"It's better if I let it all out." She sobbed. "I miss him so terribly, already. There's such an ache, such a lonely feeling. I've never felt such a hatred as I feel toward the man who killed him. I'd kill him myself." Her heart was in her throat, throbbing. The words coagulated. She swallowed them back and continued. "I have a knot in my stomach. I don't think it will ever go away. Why did this happen to us?"

Belli had no answer. This was the part of police work that he hated. But it was essential to cut through the grief and agony for the needed information. Sometimes a detective had to be as sympathetic as a priest, sometimes as brutal as a hit man to get what was needed. He left when the doctor arrived to give Madelaine a sedative.

Down the street, touching the back of his hand to his eyes, he took a Kleenex out of his pocket, blew his nose and swallowed the lump in his throat. Belli talked to Donnelly's neighbors and friends as well, looking for a motive, finding none. It wasn't glamorous. It was drudgery, hours of questions, questions, and at times it was heartbreaking.

The traffic on the Post Road was unusually light for early evening. The Man checked his rearview mirror and floored the accelerator. Two blocks later he made a high-speed right turn, a sharp left at the next intersection, then another right. He checked again. There was no one following. He slowed to normal driving speed, feeling alive, really alive. The Man inhaled deeply. Barbara would be waiting.

It was time to be cautious. Discovery would screw up his action. His game of multiple choice. He believed in enduring relationships. Right now, in addition to his wife, he was involved with three of them. Each of the girls knew about his wife, but not about the others. That would blow it. Each seemed to accept the fact that there could be no permanent arrangement. There had been no pressure. No one had ever . . . In fact, the girls each seemed to live for the moment. They were that type. Yet each was different. A brunette, a redhead, and a blonde. He laughed aloud. His girls were like his plan—perfect.

Barbara was waiting for him. She heard his car in the driveway and met him in the backyard. She was dressed in a short red skirt and white blouse that accentuated her attractive figure. She had a pleasant face, a nice smile and big brown eyes, with dark-brown hair cut medium short for the summer, pulled back and tied with a red ribbon. Her skin was a deep golden tan. Underneath was a wild, sensual spirit. She lived for the Man's visits. "Hi, darling. Missed you this noon. Pat and a friend are watching television. We'd better use the pool house."

The Man nodded. Pat was Barbara's nine-year-old daughter, who thought the Man was super. Both he and Barbara were very careful not to show any affection in front of Pat. She thought they were friends, nothing more.

The Man followed Barbara down the narrow path. Her ranch-style house was at the end of a dead-end lane, and the yard was well sheltered from any outside view by dense shrubbery and woods. In the rear of the property ran a brook about six feet in width that had been dammed to make a small swimming pool. Next to it was a changing room, which Barbara called the pool house.

As soon as they reached the changing room, he closed the door. They kissed affectionately, then longingly. Barbara reached behind her back and snapped the lock. He could tell that she was hungry for him, and the murder had aroused him, even more than normal. He reached under her short skirt. She was already moist, his fingers slippery in her pleasure. She unzipped his pants and they fell to the floor. She slid his shorts over his thighs and down his legs. He kicked them into the corner.

Automatically, they moved to the wide wooden bench with its comfortable foam cushion. Their lovemaking was intense. Three times Barbara put the back of her hand to her mouth, so she wouldn't cry out in pleasure. She could feel him finish and held him tightly to her. Together, they rose slowly and kissed intensely. Then, laughing happily, Barbara skipped away and plunged into the pool. He quickly showered, toweled off, dressed, waved good-bye and drove out of the driveway. The Man had spent less than twenty minutes with Barbara.

Dempsey spent the evening at home. Brenda had heard about Donnelly's death on the 6:00 news. It had shocked her, as it had shocked all of Fairport. "I don't understand it," she said over and over. "It's unbelievable. Everyone loved Bill." The bombing had been reported in a brief, factual way on all three national networks. Brenda had kept his dinner warm and talked to him about the Selectman and his wife while he ate.

Later, while Jim pondered Donnelly's death, Brenda read a simple book with Cindy. Her stomach tightened at her daughter's slowness. Trying not to let her concern show, she encouraged Cindy every time she read a word correctly. Brenda repeated each word slowly. She wanted to help her child more, to read aloud for her. But the doctors had said no. Cindy had to learn to do simple things for herself. Brenda's eyes blinked back a tear. It was so horribly frustrating. She hugged Cindy to her. Their daughter looked so fragile.

The Man clicked off the television set. The 10:00 P.M. news had briefly mentioned the bombing. But there had been no pictures. "Just wait." He leaned back in his leather chair and mentally replayed the day, well satisfied. D day had gone well. Donnelly was gone. Just as planned, he'd been able to place the dynamite package under the front seat and tape the playing card on the rear bumper in less than thirty seconds, undetected, without a disguise, knowing it wouldn't be necessary.

Exhilaration . . . at long last, his plan was underway. Murder was the ultimate crime. In all history there was no great murderer. He couldn't think of one who stood out above all others. Jack the Ripper, Bluebeard, Lizzie Borden, Manson. Not a great mind in the group. Psychopaths all! Mental freaks! Each was notorious because each had murdered more than once. A crooked smile split his face. If murder was the ultimate crime, then mass murder had to be out beyond the ultimate, ultimate.

Rising from his chair, he crossed to the desk. The plan was perfect. He would explore new dimensions. He knew he was the greatest. He would prove it. To everyone. Taking out his notebook and a black marking pencil, he crossed off the Selectman, the king of spades, number two on his list. Donnelly had been selected deliberately as his first public victim. Donnelly had been a close friend of Dempsey's, that Boy Scout Chief of Police.

3

Tuesday, June 3.
A Falling Star

IT WAS after midnight and the Man was on the move again. Like a shadow, he glided down the stairs, through the kitchen and out to his car in the garage. He started the engine and drove out of the driveway, encountering no traffic as he threaded his way across town. As he came in view of the Sound, he marveled at the diamondlike beauty of the moonlight dancing on the black velvet water. A cool nighttime breeze blew along the coast.

He stopped in front of a massive but elegant iron gate guarding the entrance to a large estate. The bronze plaque on the fieldstone gate pillar read "Shore Haven." The red light glowed on the electronic Securi-T monitoring system, which covered the entire perimeter of the estate. The system was on. Any intrusion of that electronic beam would flash a signal and sound an alarm at the police station. The police would be there in force within four minutes. The Man had timed it at three minutes, fifty-two seconds.

He took a key from his pocket. It was an exact duplicate that had been fashioned weeks before from the master key. Inserting the key in the outside control at the gate, he turned off the system. He was sure his victim wouldn't notice. The Man knew that she was otherwise involved; the light in her television anteroom was on, as he expected. The wing over the kitchen was totally dark. The couple who were her servants were both old and hard of hearing and undoubtedly asleep.

The Man chuckled. Those damn Dobermans wouldn't bother

him. From his hip pocket came a small leather case containing a set of lock picks. In less than thirty seconds the padlock holding the gates in place fell loose. The gates swung open, and with no headlights he drove noiselessly into the estate.

After removing her makeup, Hetty Starr had leisurely taken a hot bubble bath, toweled herself dry and powdered herself with a lavender scent, and now she was finishing applying the last layer of face creams. She checked her face in the mirror above the dressing table, taking elaborate care. She had learned early that time always moves fastest for your face.

Hetty was proud of her skin. People marveled at its silkiness and her youthful appearance. If only they knew how she worked at it. She brushed her short hair into her classic little-girl style. It was her trademark. Two more days and she'd have Basil touch up the color. He was a marvel at frosting it with just the right balance of natural and ash blond.

She slipped on her silk nightgown and satin negligee and lay down on the quilted gold lamé divan in the anteroom just off her bedroom. With her remote-control unit, she adjusted the television. The movie had just started. She splashed some Scotch over three cubes of ice in a short crystal Waterford glass, sipped it slowly, and waited expectantly.

Now, she was totally immersed in the role of Jane Alden, child bride. Once again, in George's powerful arms, being smothered by his kisses, stifled by his affection. She sighed deeply, at peace with the world.

The Man climbed agilely up the trellis to the balcony outside Hetty's bedroom, swung nimbly over the railing and, moving quietly on his rubber-soled shoes, moved to the French doors and looked in. As he had expected, Hetty was lying on her divan with the back of her head toward him. The door was already open. He unlatched the screen door noiselessly and slipped into the room, waiting motionless to see if Hetty had noticed his presence. She hadn't. She was totally engrossed.

Unclipping one of two canvas bags from his belt and loosening the drawstring at the neck, he crept silently toward the table at the back of the divan. He set the bag gently on the table and stepped back into the shadow of the flowered drapes.

Seconds later, the triangular head of a rattlesnake emerged from the bag and peered about. Rapidly, the body slithered out full-length onto the table. Its heat-detecting organ, located in the pit between its eyes and nostrils, sensed the warmth of Hetty Starr's body. Curious, it moved silently to within striking distance and coiled its body. Its head poised menacingly. Its beady eyes watched with fascination the white nape of Hetty's neck.

It was during the second commercial that Hetty reached for her drink. The motion excited the viper. Its tail rattled violently. As Hetty's head rose, the snake struck with lightning speed, burying its fangs deep into the side of Hetty's neck. Hetty gurgled a terrified scream. Her hands tore at the snake at her neck. The virulent neurotoxin poured into her system. Already her throat was paralyzed and she was having difficulty breathing. She slumped unconscious on the divan.

The Man moved quickly. With his loop, he recaptured the rattlesnake and placed it back into the canvas bag, which he clipped onto his belt. Then, from his other bag, he removed a mask of the queen of spades, which he had fashioned weeks before from a modeling set. On the shelf above, her prized two Oscars watched mutely as the Man's gloved hands gently placed the death mask over Hetty's face.

He snapped off the television set, turned out the lights and went back through the French doors. Once past the electronic fence, the Man stopped at the main entrance, closed the gates, reinserted the padlock into the hasps on the gate and snapped it shut. With his duplicate master key, he reactivated the security system. The glow of the red light showed that everything was in proper order.

About fifteen minutes later, the Man dropped the side-winder back into its glass display case through the opening at the top. The other three vipers crawled over to greet him, as if to welcome him home. The Man closed the opening to the case, replaced the snake loop on its hook and went up the basement steps.

Later, he sat quietly in his den, reviewing Hetty Starr's death. It was mildly surprising that he had been upset by the look of abject terror registered in her eyes. She must have died as much from fright as from the poison. A black marking pencil crossed off Hetty Starr, the queen of spades, number three on his list.

He put an Oscar Peterson tape on the stereo and sat back contentedly in his comfortable leather chair to listen. He felt lightheaded, fuzzy, now suddenly a continent away on the stage of the Opera House in Vienna. As the world's most celebrated flutist, he signaled to Oscar to begin playing. Then he picked up his solid-silver flute and tested it. The trilling sounds danced above the music from the stereo. The packed audience sat in hushed silence as he produced an incredible shower of notes, birdlike in the upper register, sweetly liquid in the lower ranges. The shower of notes increased in intensity to a storm of melody and finally to a musical hurricane.

He ranged the scales over three and a half octaves, from a low B-flat to a high F. On long, sustained notes, his purity of tone was breathtakingly sweet and even. With a full, smooth sound that was almost trumpetlike, he finished his performance with a flourish. The audience rose as one and exploded in a torrential cascade of sustained applause. The Man shook himself out of his reverie, turned off the stereo and waited expectantly.

His fantasies were increasing in frequency, and after every one it was always the same. The voice pushing aside all other thoughts. An old man's voice, clear and resonant, a one-word message. "Kill."

Tuesday morning started out as a hot, sticky, humid day. It was going to be a steambath. Streaks of condensation formed on the inside of the windows in the Chief's air-conditioned office. Dempsey, Belli and Farrow were trying to compile a list of possible bombing suspects. They had gotten nowhere.

It was almost a relief when the phone rang. Farrow reached for it. Out of force of habit, Dempsey glanced at the clock on his desk. It was 9:50 A.M.

"What!" Farrow sounded incredulous. "Hetty Starr? We'll

be right there." He jabbed a button on the phone and shouted directions. "Lou, call Securi-T. Get them over to Hetty Starr's estate immediately to turn off the alarm. She's been murdered."

"Murdered!" echoed Dempsey. "What the hell's going on?"

As they raced for the patrol car, Farrow filled them in on what little he'd been told over the phone. "Housekeeper called. She just found Hetty Starr dead."

"Are you sure she was murdered?" asked Dempsey.

"There was a death mask on her face, the queen of spades."

"Jesus Christ!" exclaimed Belli, crossing himself. "The crazy!"

When Dempsey drove through the open gate of Shore Haven, a police cruiser was already in the driveway. The alarm system was ringing incessantly. The man from Securi-T had not yet arrived.

"Get that damned thing turned off," shouted Dempsey. "I can't hear myself think."

Belli raced off, and in less than a minute the alarm went silent.

"Thanks," said Dempsey, as Belli returned, his blue shirt wet with perspiration, his hair glistening like patent leather.

"I didn't do anything. The guy from Securi-T just got here. The alarm went off when they opened the gate for the police cruiser," explained Belli.

"It wasn't on before?" questioned Dempsey.

"No," replied Belli. "Must have been an inside job."

"Don't touch anything," Dempsey reminded the policemen from the cruiser, who were milling about the body on the divan. His men knew that he was a fanatic on examining a crime scene himself, before it had been trampled by others. He had learned that the fresh clues were usually the important ones. Through the years, he had drummed into his men not to touch anything at the scene of a crime. His lecture always ended, "Keep your hands in your pockets. Over half the time it's the detectives who leave the fingerprints."

Doc Brody, the Medical Examiner, arrived with Paul Rice, the lab technician. Dempsey was pleased to see them. He had a high regard for Brody's ability. His profession had swallowed up his life, but even at age sixty he was energetic and excited about his craft. Brody had a wrinkled, round face, with tired, watery eyes magnified by thick bifocals. The top of his head was shiny bald with a thick fringe of curly white hair. The body was squat and rumpled, distended in front by a noticeable paunch.

Brody bent over Hetty's body, checking her pulse briefly, jowls flapping as he sadly shook his head. Then he removed the death mask. Underneath, Hetty Starr's face was contorted in a grimace of pain and fear. Her neck was swollen grotesquely. Brody bent low over the victim, his practiced eyes staring at her neck.

"I'll be son of a bitch!" Doc Brody exploded. "It looks like a poisonous snakebite on her neck."

"A snakebite? You've got to be kidding!" Dempsey crouched alongside Brody to get a better look.

"No. See the fang marks on her neck? Here." He pointed out the marks. "When I practiced in Arizona, I treated any number of them." Brody pushed his bifocals back on his nose.

"What kind of snake are we looking for?" Dempsey asked in a low whisper.

"Probably a viper of some type. Most likely a rattlesnake."

"A rattlesnake!" Rice turned around, his mouth open.

"Yeah, and judging by the dimensions of the marks," Doc said, "a big bastard."

Rice gulped audibly, swallowed uncomfortably, then asked, "Where the hell would anyone get a rattlesnake around here?"

No one answered. Dempsey called Farrow aside and instructed him to have his men search the house carefully for a large snake. Farrow blanched, his freckles showing clearly. He would have preferred to search for an armed intruder.

Dempsey and Rice watched closely while Brody continued his inspection of the wounds, giving the others a running medical report. "This swelling on the neck. It's caused by the hemolysins. But she was killed by the neurotoxins in the venom. That attacks the nerve centers. It causes paralysis and has a special affinity for the nerves supplying the respiratory system."

"But . . . but I didn't think a rattlesnake bite was fatal," Rice interrupted with a puzzled look on his face.

The doctor looked up quizzically at Rice. "You haven't spent much time out West, have you?"

"No. St. Louis is about as far—"

"Well, let me tell you. A big snake . . . in the face, neck or chest it's almost always fatal. Combined with the victim's fright, the poison works incredibly fast." Brody stood up. "A frail woman . . . a big snake . . . shock . . . surprise . . . on the neck . . . she had no chance at all. Jim, I'd like to remove the body for an autopsy as soon as you get all the photos you need."

Dempsey nodded. He and Rice now went over the room inch by inch as Rice's men dusted for finger and palm prints. They decided that the killer had probably entered the room through the French doors from the balcony.

Tom Farrow felt more than uneasy. Snakes gave him the creeps. Now, here he was playing hide-and-seek with a large rattlesnake. What a job for a grown man. He moved slowly, his eyes searching everywhere, totally alert, every sense on edge.

The rooms upstairs had been dedicated to Hetty's movie career. Farrow couldn't help but notice. The walls were covered with hundreds of photographs of Hetty, at gala Hollywood parties, at charity benefits, at elegant dances. They showed her receiving her Oscars and with celebrities of every type. Many of the pictures were scenes from her movies. Under different circumstances, he would have thoroughly enjoyed touring Hetty's home. Sally would—

Farrow's heart leapt at the sudden thud behind him. He spun around, his hand automatically reaching for his holster. A large cream-and-chocolate colored Siamese cat crouched in the corner. The cat's blue eyes stared disdainfully. Farrow's hand relaxed. He took a deep breath and did a double take. The damned cat was cross-eyed. Farrow whistled softly. He thanked God it wasn't black.

Dempsey and the others joined Farrow as they continued

their search, room by room. Miss Starr and her former husband had furnished the house with exquisite taste. They had been avid collectors of Chinese cloisonné, Ming Dynasty pottery and translucent white jade; the house abounded with beautiful vases, lamps and statues of museum quality. The floor was carpeted with palace-size Kirmans, the walls were adorned with paintings by El Greco, Manet, Picasso and Cézanne. Virtually all of the rooms were bright and airy and afforded magnificent views of the sparkling blue waters of the Sound. Dempsey had a momentary thought that the sunshine cascading into the downstairs rooms provided an ironic twist to the lifeless body upstairs.

After finding neither the rattlesnake nor any additional clues, they centered their investigation on the grounds, paying particular attention to the electronic alarm system, the fence around the perimeter, the main gate and the base of the trellis leading to the balcony outside. Hetty's room. Rice's team checked the soil carefully for impressions of footprints and took photographs from all angles. They found nothing.

On the way back to the house, Dempsey asked Farrow to check with Securi-T. "I'd like to know how their system could be compromised. Find out if it's possible for a person to get hold of a duplicate key. Whoever killed Hetty planned this carefully. He brought a deadly snake with him, along with a specially designed death mask. Somehow he neutralized her Dobermans."

"Dobermans!" Farrow stopped abruptly, his pallor showing his freckles again. "I haven't seen or heard—"

"That's the point," said Dempsey. "Hetty had two Dobermans, Tony and Oscar. They were her constant companions. Her security blanket. They had the run of the grounds. No one has—"

"Are they friendly?" Farrow looked hopefully at the Chief.

"Without Hetty, I'm afraid not. They'd be vicious. They'd chew any intruder apart."

Farrow looked around anxiously, readjusting and patting his holster. It was a beautiful estate, but he couldn't wait to get back to headquarters. He was going to practice his quick draw. He disliked Dobermans almost as much as snakes. The combination was almost too much.

They joined Gus Belli in the kitchen, where he'd been interviewing the Foxxes. The three were seated at the pine-planked kitchen table. A bouquet of yellow roses had been pushed aside to one end. Belli introduced them. Dempsey extended his condolences to the Foxxes. He had previously met them, and Brenda had commented that they were the perfect live-in couple.

Will Foxx was extremely handy about the property. He loved gardening and could fix almost anything. Jovial-looking, but quiet by nature, he was dressed in rough work clothes. His enormous, gnarled hands seemed several sizes too large and older than the rest of him.

Hannah Foxx was a hawkish-looking woman with a sharp tongue. A crow, and a born housekeeper. She considered the cleanliness of Miss Starr's home to be the most important thing in her life. The house was always spotless. Both of the Foxxes were devoted to Hetty.

Belli took Dempsey and Farrow to one end of the kitchen and in a low voice told them what he had learned. "The French doors were open. Hetty never used her air conditioning. She liked fresh air."

"She must have felt secure behind her electronic screen," mused Farrow.

"Mrs. Foxx also said the lights and the television were off when she found Hetty. It doesn't make sense." Belli glanced over at the Foxxes. "The killer turns everything off before he leaves. A neat bastard!" He shook his head.

Dempsey nodded. Almost impatiently he asked Belli, "The dogs?"

"They're at the vet's. They were taken ill yesterday."

Dempsey nodded again. "Anything else?"

"The Foxxes went to bed about nine-thirty P.M. She said that Miss Starr had been looking forward to watching her movie on the late show."

Walking back across the room, they rejoined the Foxxes at the table. Dempsey had more questions. He was gentle, but incisive. Hannah was still visibly agitated by the death of her mistress. Her husband had himself under reasonable control.

"Mrs. Foxx, was the alarm system turned on when you went to bed?"

"Oh, yes, sir. Miss Starr always had the system on. Only she turned it off . . ." Hannah put her handkerchief to her face. It was almost a minute before she could continue. Dempsey waited patiently. "She turned it off when someone was going through the gate. Then she turned it right back on."

"So it was on last night?"

"Yes, sir. I saw Miss Starr turn it on after my husband locked the gate, after . . . after Dr. Sprott took Tony and Oscar away." Tears were swimming in her eyes. Mr. Foxx reached over and gently took one of her hands in his.

"Do either of you have keys for the system?"

"Oh, no. Miss Starr had two. One is on her key ring. She always had that with her. The other is in her wall safe."

"Do you know the combination?"

"No, sir, only Mr. Nichols does."

"Do you mean Ned Nichols, the lawyer?" Dempsey glanced at Farrow and Belli.

"Yes, he was Miss Starr's lawyer. They were close friends. He stopped by often." Hannah's voice was wavering. Dempsey knew she was close to breaking again. One or two more questions at the most.

"Does anyone else have a key to the alarm system?"

"I believe Securi-T has one."

"Yes, I'm sure they do. They keep a master key for their customers. Who had keys to the gate?" He asked the question slowly.

"Only my husband and Miss Starr. That one's on her key ring also, with her car keys, front door, liquor closet and wine cellar." Tears were running down her cheeks. She dabbed at them with her handkerchief.

"Was anything taken from the house? Is there anything missing?"

"I haven't looked. I've been too . . . Hetty was my friend. We've worked for her ever since . . ." Mrs. Foxx's voice choked again and she began to weep uncontrollably. Mr.

Foxx put his arm around his wife, looked at Dempsey pleadingly and spoke for the first time. "That's enough . . . Maybe later."

Dempsey agreed. He and his two assistants rose to leave. Farrow told the Foxxes he'd return later to inventory whether anything of value had been stolen. In the meantime, he planned to obtain a complete list of Miss Starr's valuables from her insurance company for the Foxxes to check in detail.

Before leaving, Dempsey took Rice aside and said in a low voice, "Paul, I want you to get Ned Nichols over here right away. He had access to the wall safe, and it supposedly contains a key to the Securi-T system. I want you to have him open the wall safe. Don't let him touch anything. Just open it. I want you, personally . . ." Dempsey paused and pointed his index finger at Rice. "I want you to check to see if the extra key to the system is in the safe. If it is, close it and lock it again. If it's not there, then Nichols has to be suspect."

Rice's eyes flickered, but otherwise his face showed no surprise.

When Belli and Dempsey arrived back at headquarters, there was a small swarm of reporters waiting for them. The news of Hetty Starr's murder had traveled quickly. Dempsey gritted his teeth and started toward the entrance.

"Chief, give us a statement."

"What's going on in Fairport?"

"Who killed Donnelly? Who killed Hetty Starr?"

"Why were they killed?"

"How were they murdered?"

"What's the significance of the king and queen? Why spades?"

The reporters crowded them closely. The questions rained down unanswered. Then one young reporter made the mistake of baiting Dempsey.

"I understand she was raped," he smirked.

Dempsey turned the color of a ripe plum. He spun around, took a step toward the reporter, stopped himself, glared hard at him, started to answer, then caught himself. He turned on his heel and entered headquarters, muttering under his breath. "That shithead!"

Belli saw the strain lines on Dempsey's face. He knew that Hetty Starr's murder had been difficult for him. Belli held up his hand and said in his soft, deep voice. "I'll answer your questions, but one at a time, please."

"No, we do not believe she was sexually assaulted in any way. No, we don't yet know positively how she was murdered. We think she was bitten by a rattlesnake."

Belli nodded his head for the disbelieving newsmen.

"Yes, I said a rattlesnake. We'll know for sure later. Yes, we know she was murdered. We will pass on whatever other information we can as soon as we have the Medical Examiner's report. I can't tell you much more now. Yes, we are pretty sure that the same person killed both the Selectman and Miss Starr."

When Belli came into the Chief's office fifteen minutes later, he was breathing heavily.

"The pressure's growing. Those guys like to stir up trouble," he said, matter-of-factly. Then, with his eyebrows knitted, said, "Say, I thought for a moment you were going to belt that young s.o.b."

"I must admit," Dempsey replied calmly, "the thought did cross my mind." He winked at Belli.

The private phone in the Man's office rang. He asked his secretary to step outside for a minute and then he picked up the phone. It was Jeanne Hoover. The Man was surprised, but pleased. Jeanne was a beautiful girl. At twenty-six, she had the face of a goddess, a model's figure and grace, long, flowing strawberry-blond tinted hair, and the vitality of youth. Jeanne was also a smart young businesswoman and a leading advocate of women's liberation. An accomplished photographer, Jeanne specialized in fashion and design. She was unmarried and unattached. Best of all, thought the Man, Jeanne was uninhibited.

"Hi, sweetheart. Are you too busy for a late lunch? How about my place? . . . Great! Give me ten minutes. I'll have to race home and change." Jeanne's enthusiasm bubbled.

The Man was looking for relief. He was there inside of fifteen minutes. He pulled into the drive and parked alongside her car.

Jeanne lived in a charming three-room beach cottage which she had painted and decorated herself. The front door was open. As he closed it behind him, Jeanne called from the living room, "Hi, darling." Seated on the sofa, she was indeed beautiful in her pure-white jump suit, unzipped to the waist, displaying her tanned, small, firm breasts. She beckoned, then kissed the Man teasingly.

She kissed him again, this time hungrily. Then she whispered softly, "I've missed you. I've been thinking about you all morning, your rock-hard body . . . your firm muscles . . . especially this one." Jeanne laughed and touched him. "I decided I wanted to have you for lunch."

Jeanne meant what she said. He sat on the sofa. She knelt on a cushion on the floor. She was the most accomplished oral sex artist he had ever met, with a devil's tongue. He had coached her originally, and she had learned well. She obviously enjoyed it, and so did the Man. The soft, teasing sensations built slowly into a most intense sexual feeling, until each lick felt like a flame. Watching the gulls out the picture window, he was soon soaring with them, higher and higher.

"Honey, you are just delicious. I just love to make love to you. Thanks for letting me." Jeanne was purring like a cat who had finished a bowl of cream. She licked carefully to make sure she got the last drop.

"It's my turn now," the Man murmured. "I'm on a diet, and I understand that strawberry blondes have fewer calories."

"Thirty-four and a half," Jeanne suggested, as the jump suit came off and they reversed positions.

Later, they soaked in her hot tub. She served him a bowl of New England clam chowder, a grilled cheese sandwich and a glass of chilled Chablis. Considering everything, the Man thought it was a perfect lunch.

The Man thought about his relations with Jeanne while driving back to his office. Strange as it might seem, they had never made love in the usual way. At her request, he had never entered Jeanne. To the best of his knowledge, she was technically still a virgin. But what a talented virgin!

He was back in his office by two. Jeanne called from her office five minutes later to say that she'd had a wonderful time. She hoped she'd see him again later in the week.

Across town an unusual scene was taking place in the locked office of Andrew McAlpin, owner and manager of the Fairport Drug Center. On McAlpin's desk were twenty glassine bags, each filled with a white powder. A powerfully built blond man close to thirty, dressed in a light powder-blue business suit, sat opposite McAlpin, stroking his full golden beard.

"It's pure Mexican heroin, Mr. McAlpin." The young man had a cocky, arrogant manner that annoyed the druggist.

"You promised me fifty. I need enough to cover my whole area, including Stamford and Bridgeport." McAlpin's ruddy face showed his distress. His glasses magnified his tired eyes. Standing up, his shoulders sagged.

"Sales are hot, eh, Pop?" The younger man laughed, slapping his hand forcefully on the desk. "Don't worry, you'll get the rest. I haven't let you down yet, have I?"

"No, but business has been growing. My contacts are getting . . . anxious." McAlpin was pacing nervously as he spoke.

"You'll have thirty more bags next week. More if I can get them. I'll mash a few toes." The blond was at ease, secure in the knowledge that he had control of the situation.

"But we're selling at the rate of fifty a week. We need more." McAlpin's voice rose, pleading. He slumped back into his chair.

"You'll just have to cut the H a little more." The youth leaned forward and spoke, now with a hard edge in his voice. "Oh, yes . . . next week's shipment is going up in price."

"What?" exploded McAlpin.

"Mr. McAlpin, for a member of the Boy Scout Executive Committee and an elder in your church, you have a terrible temper. It's only a twenty-five percent increase." The blond grinned again, the wisps of hair from his beard making his even white teeth appear jagged, almost fanglike.

McAlpin sputtered, and almost threatened the young man. But he choked back the impulse, knowing that a threat would be useless and probably dangerous. He'd have to pay the increased cost. Golden beard knew it, too. The extra cost would be passed along the chain to the ultimate user. As it was, the addict was now paying $150 for a single dose of cut and recut junk. The original pure heroin was produced in Mexico at a cost of less than two and a half cents per dose. With profits of this enormous magnitude, McAlpin knew that if he opted out of the drug scene, others would step in immediately to exploit the need and reap the gains.

The blond hulk rose from his chair and picked up his empty briefcase. He felt for the bulge of the fat envelope of bills in the inner pocket of his jacket. He grinned. Suddenly he turned and faced McAlpin, his lips a tight, thin line, his voice little more than a whisper.

"I heard the news. One of your club members was blown up yesterday. Bits and pieces. Let it be a warning." He made a gun out of his hand and pointed it at McAlpin's chest. "It could happen to you, too, Pop. Don't do anything foolish."

He turned, unlocked the door and left, driving away in his white company car labeled with the name of a prominent U.S. drug firm.

McAlpin's hands shook. For a full minute he couldn't control them. That blond guy had seemed huge. He was a mountain. His words echoed in McAlpin's head. "One of your club members was blown up . . . it could happen to you, too." Could this blond have killed Donnelly? Had the Selectman been involved in drugs too? He should tell Dempsey. His hand reached out and touched the phone. My God, what was he thinking? That would be foolish. Foolish? Christ, it would be stupid.

McAlpin rose slowly, relocked his outside office door and put the twenty bags into his safe. That evening they would be distributed to his contacts in the neighboring cities. He made sure that none were distributed in Fairport. He didn't want his grandchildren hooked on drugs.

He sat back at his desk. For a long while, Andrew McAlpin just sat thinking, head of shaggy white hair slumped forward, face flushed more than usual. McAlpin was worried, and felt old and tired, inadequate and ineffective. Perhaps he shouldn't have gotten involved, but he was. In less than six months, he had cleared almost a million dollars from his heroin sales. Now there was no way out. None. It was too risky to even think about. Realistically, he had no choice. No one got out . . . except as a stiff in the morgue.

Living was better. If he didn't do it, someone else would, and they might let drugs into Fairport. Besides, he mused, what is a crime anyhow? It's what society decides it is. Tomorrow, society may decide drugs are legal. For twenty-five years, all during prohibition, it was a crime to import, sell or buy alcoholic beverages. Then, with a stroke of a pen, it was all over. One day a crime, the next day no crime! Crime is what culture decides. Respected families had built their fortunes during prohibition. Someday his grandchildren would be proud of the fortune and the life of ease and power he had built for them. There was no need for them to know the source of his wealth.

McAlpin remembered how he'd persuaded himself to start. Heroin wasn't really dangerous. In Britain, physicians prescribed heroin in cough medicines to people of all ages, babies to adults. It couldn't be that dangerous. Now, McAlpin thought, I'm in too deep to back out. As a druggist, I'm supposed to dispense drugs.

He rose wearily, unlocked his inside door and went back to his store, muttering, "Got to finish by three, got to get to my church meeting on time."

Jim Dempsey had finished his lunch and sat at his desk staring out of the window. He leaned forward and picked up a pencil. It was hard to understand. He was having difficulty reasoning what had happened. In two days, two prominent residents had been murdered, the First Selectman and a famous actress. One by a bomb, the other probably by a rattlesnake bite. Both were close friends of his. There didn't seem to be any other connection, no similarity in the crimes, except for the playing cards, the king of spades for the Selectman, the queen of spades for the Queen of Cinema. What was the motive? Why Fairport? What did the cards signify? The dev-il's picture books! What did the letter mean? "Start counting the victims. There'll be quite a few." Did the killer really mean that? How many? The whole suit of spades. Thirteen? The whole deck? My God!

Suddenly he felt a queasy emptiness in the pit of his stomach. He'd seen death before, but it had never affected him this way. He put the pencil down. He hadn't written anything.

Farrow returned and joined Dempsey in the Chief's office. Belli was rechecking for witnesses, and Rice was still at Shore Haven. Dempsey closed the door and asked Mary to send in Belli and Rice as soon as they returned. Otherwise they were not to be disturbed. Unless. He just mentioned the word. He didn't elaborate.

Together, on a pad of paper, they listed the facts that they knew about the murders and the questions whose answers might reveal a clue to the identity of the killer. It was two pages long when they finished.

Dempsey looked over the list, checked it again, asked Mary to type it and Xerox ten copies. Belli returned at 3:20 P.M. The three of them agreed that he should take prime responsibility for solving Donnelly's bombing and that Tom Farrow would be responsible for investigating Hetty Starr's death. Both would be assigned a team of four men. Dempsey would work on both cases on an overall basis.

As he put it, "I'll try to find the common thread. There has to be one." He continued, "The two killings were good, the work of a professional. We know he knows how to use dynamite. The way he detonated the bomb indicates a good basic knowledge of explosives." He looked at Belli. "Have you come up with a list of bomb suspects yet?"

"Hot off the press," replied Belli, producing a typewritten sheet of paper and handing it to Dempsey. "Briggs sent over a list of forty-two names. I could only add three to it. We haven't had a chance to start checking yet."

Dempsey scanned the list impassively and passed it on to Farrow. "O.K., Gus, don't eliminate anyone." He looked straight at Belli. "Check out all forty-five. We can't be too careful. The best surprise in this business is no surprise."

Belli met his gaze, then looked down at his own copy of the list. "You probably noticed, Chief, in addition to you, me, Farrow, Briggs and two other policemen, five of your Rotarian buddies are on the list, too—Ned Nichols, Bob Baker, Don Dillon, David Orton, and Harry Hoyle." He looked up. I never realized how many prominent citizens have had experience with explosives."

"Neither did I." Dempsey inhaled audibly, then asked, "Any luck on the source of the dynamite?"

"No. Every sale in the county we've been able to account for. Of course, it could have been bought anywhere." Belli gestured with his hands. "Briggs has agreed to check sales in the rest of Connecticut, New York and Massachusetts. That's as far as—"

Their meeting was interrupted by a knock on the door. Sergeant Lou Piccollo thrust his massive bald head into the room. Physically, Piccollo resembled a bulldog. His large, ugly, square head was set solidly on a short, powerful body. Dark eyebrows jutted out over eyes that were about five inches apart. Piccollo had no neck at all. His wife Rosie's favorite joke was: "When Lou was born, God screwed hs head on too tight."

As always, Piccollo came directly to the point. "Chief, I thought you'd like to know, Doc Brody called in and said Miss Starr was definitely killed by a rattlesnake bite. There was no sexual abuse."

"Thanks, Lou." Dempsey had a high regard for Piccollo's ability. He was tenacious, tough and fearless. He'd come up in the police force the hard way, starting as a patrolman. His thirty years of practical, day-to-day experience more than made up for his lack of education. Piccollo had a lot of good common sense. He was street-smart.

"Was Doc Brody able to pin down the time of death?" Dempsey asked.

Piccollo moved into the office and stood by the desk. "He said it was probably about one A.M., give or take a half hour either way. I pushed him hard, but he said he didn't think he could be more definite. Death occurred between twelve-thirty and one-thirty A.M."

"Her movie was still on at one. It didn't finish until two-fifteen," reported Farrow. "I called the station."

Dempsey excused Belli to get his team started on checking out the bomb suspects. At the door, Belli turned and said, "I almost forgot, Chief, we've got some pretty good pictures from that alley across from the town hall. That looks like the place he parked. Clear line of sight. Eighty-seven yards to the spot where Donnelly's car blew up." Dempsey nodded thoughtfully. Belli left the office.

Dempsey handed Piccollo a list of the names of the policemen assigned to Belli and Farrow and asked him to rework the duty roster.

"Where the hell is Rice?" Dempsey asked.

"I think he came in about ten minutes ago, Chief. He was planning to grab a sandwich and a cup of coffee from the machine. Said he hadn't eaten. I'll send him right in." Piccollo left the room.

"Mary, some coffee, please," Dempsey shouted through the open door.

Rice entered the room, carrying the remains of a liverwurst sandwich and a cup of coffee. Dempsey greeted him with one word. "Nichols?"

"No luck, Chief." The disappointment in Rice's eyes emphasized his words. "I had Nichols open the safe. He knew the combination, all right. The extra key to the Securi-T system was in there. So I locked the safe again. Nichols didn't blink an eye. He was Mr. Cool. But I've been thinking, he could have borrowed the key earlier, made a duplicate—"

"And put it back unnoticed," Dempsey completed Rice's thought for him. "It's possible. The blanks are hard to come by, but it could have been done. Anything else?"

Rice had just pushed the last of his sandwich into his mouth, and Dempsey's question caught him by surprise. He washed it down with a swallow of coffee, wiping his mouth with the back of his hand. "Sorry, Chief. I went over the house once more, and my men dusted everything for fingerprints. We're checking them out. Miss Starr's prints and those of the Foxxes were everyplace. But we did pick up a man's print in the TV room, and in her bedroom.''

"Great! That could be the break we need," exclaimed Dempsey, his eyes brightening.

Rice didn't look too hopeful, and he explained why. "I'm not sure, since we picked up the same prints in about four other rooms upstairs and downstairs as well, mostly on the window frames. Mrs. Foxx said they had a window washer clean all of the windows last Friday. I checked the company. It's Ajax Cleaning. They're reputable. I sent over a cruiser to get the fingerprints of the fellow who washed the windows. We'll know later today whether they're his or not." Rice kept flexing his shoulders as if his back hurt.

Farrow answered the buzzing phone. He talked for a minute in a low tone, then he reported on his conversation. "The dogs were poisoned. The vet said they're still pretty sick, but they'll recover. He thinks it was a small amount of arsenic, mixed with hamburger meat."

"Could have been tossed over the fence onto the grounds," Rice suggested, putting his hand in the small of his back and trying to straighten up, his face showing a flicker of pain.

"It certainly got the dogs out of the way," said Dempsey.

At that moment, Mary came in with the coffee and some home-made brownies.

"Thanks, Mary, you are one helluva short-order cook," said Dempsey, reaching for a brownie.

Mary laughed good-naturedly. The half-dozen brownies had completely disappeared while she was pouring the coffee. As she walked out of the office, she was trying to puzzle how three men could eat six brownies in less than two minutes. She was pleased. Duncan Hines, whoever he was, would be pleased, too. It was his mix.

Rice licked the chocolate frosting from his fingers before he continued. "I sent the death mask to the crime lab to be analyzed, and Doc took the body away for an autopsy."

"Piccollo gave us his preliminary report. Death by rattle-snake bite," Farrow informed Rice.

"We rechecked the grounds carefully," Rice continued, "especially the fence. I don't see how anyone could get over that. It's in good shape, high and barbed. No breaks and no place to squeeze through or crawl under, either. The electronic beam would have picked up any intruder, even if he used a ladder and went over the top. I tried it this morning. Damn near broke my neck." He rubbed his back again. "The main gate is solid. It was locked by a padlock."

"How secure?" asked Dempsey, sipping his coffee, his eyes on Rice.

"A cupcake for a pro. Old-model S&W. A good pick man could open it with a hairpin in ten seconds. Maybe a little longer in the dark."

"But the electronic beam would have nailed him," added Farrow, with a quizzical glance at Rice.

"The second he opened the gate," Rice answered emphatically. "That's what happened this morning when Foxx opened it for the cruiser. The system had to be compromised."

"How about an approach by boat?" asked Dempsey, pouring more coffee for Rice and himself.

"Impossible. I checked this carefully. There's a series of electric eyes. A criss-crossing pattern, almost fifty yards deep from the shoreline. You couldn't crawl it even if you knew where the beams are. A month's salary he came through the front gate." Rice drained his coffee.

"That's my thought, too." Dempsey spoke with emphasis. "Tom, I'd like you to start with Securi-T. Get your team organized and get going." As Farrow and Rice were leaving his office, Dempsey said, "Paul, you'd better have Doc take a look at your back." Rice nodded and flexed his shoulders again.

Dempsey sat back in his chair, his feet on his desk. The one thing sure about this type of killer was that nothing was sure. Back to the details, he thought. It's always the little things that give them away.

Less than twenty minutes later, Belli burst into Dempsey's office, his dark face florid with excitement.

"Chief, we traced the dynamite that killed Donnelly. It was the same lot stolen almost five months ago from the National Guard Armory in Poughkeepsie."

Dempsey leaned forward. "How much was stolen?"

"A case. But that's not all. Hang onto your seat." Belli's manner was so unlike him that Dempsey was apprehensive.

"Whoever stole the dynamite also got away with four antipersonnel hand grenades, an M-16 automatic rifle, an M-15 sniper rifle and night scope, a flamethrower, two land mines, a canister of napalm, a shoulder-held rocket launcher and six antitank rockets."

Dempsey sat stunned. Slowly his air escaped in an escalating whistle. The concern showed on his ashen face. "Good Christ! Our murderer has an arsenal of weapons. Get the word out to all of our men, as well as to the state police. This man is extremely dangerous. The demented prick really does plan to kill thirteen people . . . or more."

The Man clicked in a tape and flipped on his stereo. It was one of his favorites, "Frank Sinatra's Greatest Hits." He splashed a tumbler full of Scotch and settled into his favorite leather chair. "When somebody loves you, it's no good unless he loves you, all the way . . ." He drummed his fingers in time with the music. That Sinatra . . . in a class by himself.

The Man felt light-headed, fuzzy. He joined in with Sinatra. His baritone voice was in perfect harmony. Suddenly, he was singing solo. Sinatra had stepped aside for him. He was center stage. The spotlight on him.

The song over, the audience rose in thunderous applause, the women were screaming and reaching for him. Through the screams, he heard the penetrating voice, the one-word message, "Kill." His eyes scanned the audience quickly, row by row. He couldn't find the old man with the voice. "Kill." The voice was louder now. He couldn't recognize . . . but then he'd never seen . . . what did the old man look like? He couldn't think. His mind wouldn't function. He nodded his head up and down. Instantly the audience faded away. The noise ceased. Silence. He shook himself. Damn. His mind had wandered again. The tape had finished. He'd play the other side. No, there was work to do. He swallowed the rest of his drink and rose from the chair.

He passed through the kitchen, nuzzled his wife's neck and patted her bottom affectionately, then bounded down the basement steps. In his lab, he put on a pair of rubber gloves and ground up a small quantity of powder. He finally succeeded on his third attempt to insert the powder into the tube, with a hypodermic needle, and now knew what they meant about putting the toothpaste back into the tube. Completing his work, he put a few selected items into a small kit bag, took off his rubber gloves and scrubbed his hands and arms meticulously. The Man smiled. The old man with the voice would be proud of him.

For dinner Brenda had cooked a meat loaf, with her special Parmesan-cheese filling. Brenda enjoyed cooking. Often she found time spent in the kitchen to be restful, almost therapeutic. There was a certain pleasure, a satisfaction, in creating enjoyable meals and serving them in an attractive manner. Tonight she fed Cindy early, then she and Jim had a quiet candlelit dinner together with a simple red Beaujolais. They talked briefly about the death of Hetty, but there were unusual long periods of silence during dinner. Brenda had been shaken badly by the two murders, and she knew it had been rough on Jim. Knowing he didn't want to discuss the subject, she asked no further questions.

After coffee, Dempsey went upstairs to kiss Cindy goodnight. At 8:30 P.M. he left to drop in on the special meeting being held by the town council to choose a new First Selectman. He got home at 10:00, just as Brenda was finishing her bath, her second of the day. Jim thought to himself, If clean is sexy, Brenda would be dynamite.

"Dry you off," he offered. "Special service."

"No, thanks, honey," she said and laughed appreciatively. He sat on the edge of their king-size bed and watched in the mirror as she climbed out the tub and patted herself dry, applied cologne and powder and slipped on her shorty nightgown. "You've still got a great body, sweetheart. You're very pretty. Do you know you can see through that? Peek-a-boo!"

"Thanks, sweetheart. Aren't you exhausted?" Brenda was

experienced enough with Jim to quench his obvious and growing interest in her by changing the subject. "What happened at the meeting?" She turned back the light covering on the bed.

As Jim undressed, he answered, "Oh, it was interesting. They tried to get the other Selectmen, Ed Witchum and Tom Klein, to accept the position. Both of them turned it down. They were obviously scared to death. They hadn't gotten anyone to take the job when I left."

"I don't blame them. Do you think they'd be any good?" She slid into bed.

"Witchum would be great. He could do a lot for this town in the way of better financial planning. I tried to persuade him to take the job, but I didn't have any luck." Jim swung his body into bed and reached up and clicked off the light.

Brenda kissed Jim goodnight and curled up next to him to sleep. With the air conditioner on, he was warm and toasty.

The Man was also just going to bed. He should be tired, but he wasn't. He was exhilarated. He reviewed the day carefully in his mind, step by step. After killing Hetty Starr, he had driven home and slept for only five hours. Hetty, with her little-girl smile. She reminded him so much of his mother. Warm, tender, loving. His girl. Until that salesman had come by. Then she had given away her affection. He hated that fat slob. So he'd killed him. But that was long ago. Today he had spent a full and busy day at his job, knowing that no one could possibly suspect him of the two murders. So far, the Plan was perfect.

Tonight, disguised as a television repairman, with bushy black hair and a flowing black mustache, the Man had easily gained access to the condominium home of his next victim, and in less than five minutes had set the stage for his next murder.

It had been just as easy as planned. He had simply bluffed his way in. The doorman had met him at the locked front door of the luxury condominium. They faced one another through the glass.

"I'm from Acme Television. A-C-M-E. It's on the back of

my coveralls." He mouthed his words through the glass and turned around once, so the doorman could read the A-C-M-E.

The doorman unlocked the door and opened it a crack. "Who do you want to see?"

"The penthouse."

"They just went out to dinner. You'll have to come back in the daytime, tomorrow." The doorman put his foot against the bottom of the door.

"It's a surprise for him. She called Acme. He just got a big promotion."

"That's what they're celebrating. They told me about it when they went out," confirmed the doorman.

"She wants this remote control installed on their bedroom TV." He held up the unit. "It has to be tonight, she said. It's a surprise for him. It won't take ten minutes."

The doorman shook his head. "I can't let you go up there."

A look of disappointment spread over the repairman's face. Then his face brightened. "Call her at the restaurant and get her permission. Don't talk to him, though—it's a surprise."

"I can't do that." The doorman didn't budge.

The repairman threw up his hands. "Look, I came all the way out here. You won't call her to get permission. O.K. You're going to have to explain it to her, buddy. It's your ass." The repairman pointed at him through the door, then turned to go.

The doorman hesitated. He thought quickly. It might be his ass. The penthouse was important. He opened the door. "Come on in, but I've got to go up with you."

They walked across the polished lobby to the elevators. Less than a minute and a half later, they got off the elevator together at the penthouse floor. The doorman opened the apartment door with his master key. A minute later, they were in the bedroom. The TV repairman turned on the set and began to install the remote-control unit.

Minutes later, the repairman walked into the bathroom. "What are you doing in there?" exclaimed the doorman as he rushed across the room.

"I'm taking a leak, what did you think?" shouted the

repairman from behind the partially closed door. The doorman could hear plainly. The guy was, indeed, urinating.

With his left hand, the Man removed two items from the
shelf immediately above the sink and put them in his coverall
pocket. He replaced them with two others of identical make,
then flipped a playing card into the wastebasket under the
sink. Finished, he zipped up his fly, flushed the toilet and
returned to the bedroom.

"Thanks, I couldn't wait. It's a combination of weak
kidneys and too much coffee." He turned off the TV, puttered
about for perhaps another minute at the back of the set and
said, "That does it. I told you it wouldn't take long. Let's
go."

The doorman looked surprised. "Aren't you going to try
it?"

The repairman laughed. "Hell, no. When Acme installs
something, we guarantee it!"

At the front door of the condominium, the Man thanked the
doorman again and said, "Oh, my card, in case anyone else
needs TV service—twenty-four hours a day," handing the
doorman an Acme card he had found on the street months
before.

The doorman never even noticed the transparent, thin pair
of fitted plastic gloves the Man was wearing. As the repairman left the condominium and walked down the street to his
car, the doorman muttered, "I'm in the wrong business. That
hairy bastard probably will charge thirty-five dollars for less
than ten minutes' work."

The Man laughed softly at the memory, kissed his wife and
went quickly off to sleep. He snored contentedly.

4

Wednesday, June 4.
The Brush-Off

THE MAN awoke with a throbbing sensation. He had spent a restless night. His dreams had been one erotic fantasy after another. Clearly, his murders were stimulating him. They were turning him on. He hadn't planned on that. He choked back a laugh. Hell, sex was an unexpected bonus that he could handle.

His wife awoke to find him gently kissing her in the most sensitive places. It was very pleasant, and as she feigned sleep, her ardor grew until interest was replaced by desire. She began to breathe unevenly. Suddenly she was on fire.

The Man took his time and continued in the most unbelievable, magical ways. It was exquisite. Her toes curled. Her back arched. Her pleasure built, higher and higher, to a lofty peak. It was sheer ecstasy. This was like nothing she'd ever felt before. She could feel the warm waves running through her, flooding her whole body; one, two, three and four of them. Her entire body was tingling excitedly. She pulled her man to her.

Later, after showering, she slipped on her housecoat and went down to the kitchen, determined to outdo Julia Child at fixing her lover a breakfast worthy of him. Maybe, she thought, as she whipped the eggs for his omelette, he really does love only me.

The Man was shaving and chuckling to himself. I'll have to wake her up that way every morning. I should have tried that years ago. Damn.

His wife tingled all through breakfast. As she kissed him

65

good-bye at the kitchen door, she almost thought of asking him to stay home for a while. She wanted more.

Less than half a mile away in the penthouse of the fashionable Okonokee condominiums, overlooking both Long Island Sound and the exclusive Longwood Country Club, Judge and Isabel Waller were just getting up. At least, the Judge was out of bed. The Judge was a punctual man. He always arose at seven sharp. Today he was forty minutes late. But then, he thought, last night had been a special occasion. They had dined with friends at the country club to celebrate his promotion from Federal District Judge to Judge of the Second Circuit Court of Appeals. It was the highest appointment a judge could obtain except for the Supreme Court. Isabel had been so pleased at the news. In her enthusiasm over his promotion, she had consumed far too much Dom Pérignon.

The Judge leaned over and kissed Isabel lightly on the cheek. She opened one eye, then closed it again. He whispered softly, "Good morning, beautiful." He loved her brown eyes. They always glowed with warmth and humor. Her dry lips wrinkled into a partial smile. She knew she wasn't, with her short, plump body and horsy face. But she liked to hear the Judge say it. Trying to raise her head off the pillow, the smile disappeared. Ooh, her head . . . it was plop-plop, fizz-fizz time. Her head fell back on the pillow, eyes closing again.

The Judge stopped daydreaming and kissed Isabel again. She stirred slightly and murmured, "I'll get right up, just five minutes . . ." She was sound asleep again.

He smiled and padded off to the bathroom. After relieving himself, the Judge washed his hands and face, stared into the mirror at his full head of wavy white hair, and looked at his craggy face and teeth. Not bad, he thought. They're still all real. He reached for his regular toothbrush, and in its place was a brand-new one.

That Isabel. I'll never change her. She keeps buying me things, thought the Judge. There was nothing wrong with my old toothbrush.

He opened the tube of Crest and squeezed some on his

toothbrush and began brushing his handsome white teeth, twice scratching his gums. They bled ever so slightly. The sight of the blood disturbed the Judge, since his gums had never bled before. He attributed his slight dizziness to the champagne and put more Crest on the brush. Within forty seconds, he grew faint. His breathing slowed and became difficult. Gasping for breath, nauseous, staggering, the Judge reached for the support of the sink, missed it and crumpled to the tile floor.

Isabel heard the crash when the Judge fell. She rose quickly and tottered across to the bathroom in her bare feet and nightgown. She saw the Judge on the floor, screamed and collapsed in a faint alongside of him.

Paul Rice and Tom Farrow were seated across from Dempsey at his desk. Paul was talking. "We checked Hetty Starr's death mask in the lab. It's homemade—papier-mâché."

"Homemade?" Farrow questioned. "It looked professional."

"A damn good job," replied Rice. "Torn newspaper and paste. Someone spent a lot of time. Someone who knew what he was doing." He touched his hand lightly to his wavy hair. "An artist . . . a sculptor . . ."

"Why not someone connected with the playhouse?" asked Dempsey, without much conviction.

"It's possible," Rice explained. "But we found some recent dates on the newspaper scraps. Late May. It doesn't look like a discarded stage prop. It was made special."

Farrow sat forward, a questioning look on his face. "I can't visualize . . ." He hesitated, searching for words. "Someone creative . . . creative people are warm . . . they create things. I have an image of a cold-blooded monster. A destroyer. Anyone who would kill innocent people has got to be inhuman."

Dempsey shook his head slowly. "Don't kid yourself, Tom. There's no set profile for a mass killer. There's something wrong with this man, but it's inside. Up here." Dempsey tapped his head with his finger. "On the outside he's probably perfectly normal. This man is clever, very clever. He's careful. He'll go out of his way to cover his tracks. Because his acts are repulsive, we think of him as a degenerate, a ghoul, with blood dripping from his teeth—"

"Exactly," interrupted Farrow, "a Frankenstein . . . a Jekyll . . . a bearded Manson, with laser eyes."

"I don't think so," continued Dempsey. "Most of the time, our man is going to look and act perfectly normal. This man will do his best not to arouse suspicion. He's going to be difficult to find. But the man will make a mistake. We'll nail him." Dempsey rose from his chair and walked to the window.

"Chief, that's a great name for him," said Rice, uncoiling himself and turning to look at Dempsey.

"What's that?"

"The Man. You called him 'the Man' four or five times."

"The Man. That's not bad. It's nondescript. It fits. But . . ." Dempsey's face was grave. "Whatever we call him, let's not forget he's a dangerous, diabolical killer . . ."

Suddenly Farrow laughed out loud. "The Man. With our luck we'll call this bastard 'the Man' and . . . he'll turn out to be a woman."

The ringing phone interrupted them. Dempsey gestured and Rice picked it up. He talked briefly and hung up with a crestfallen look on his face. "Chief, we struck out on the fingerprints at Hetty Starr's. They were the window washer's."

Dempsey wheeled and stared out of the window. "It's June, the Canada geese are still here. Even the birds are screwed up. The world's gone mad. Maybe . . . maybe it's a woman." His smile was less than reassuring.

It was 9:35 A.M. when Mary rushed into the room, her face flustered and pale. "Chief, something has happened to Judge Waller. He's dead. You're wanted at the Okonokee."

Dempsey closed his eyes momentarily, took a deep breath, then issued commands. "Let's go, Paul. Tom, you'd better stay here and work on the Starr case. Mary, tell Doc Brody to join us."

There were two police cruisers on the scene when Dempsey and Rice arrived at the Okonokee condominiums. It was 9:40 A.M.

The maid had discovered the two bodies when she had arrived at 9:20. The Judge's wife, in shock and under heavy sedation, was just being removed on a stretcher to the hospital. Dempsey glanced at her as she passed by. Her face was a whitish-gray mask.

Quickly, the policemen on the scene briefed Dempsey. "We found them both on the floor. He was dead. She was hysterical, told us the Judge collapsed this morning in the bathroom. Looks like a heart attack. Poor bastard, gets a promotion one day, dies the next."

It took Dempsey and Rice less than two minutes to discover that it was not a heart attack, and that they had a third murder on their hands, by the same killer. It was as simple as finding the jack of spades in the otherwise empty wastebasket under the bathroom sink.

His men reassured Dempsey that nothing had been touched. Carefully, he and Rice reviewed the murder scene. The Judge was still lying three-quarters face down on the floor, clutching his toothbrush in his right hand. It was Rice who first noticed the pink stains on the toothbrush.

Both examined the body carefully. Rice pointed out the wide dilation of the Judge's eyes, the bluish tint of his face, and the stiffened condition of his throat. "I'd guess poison," he offered tentatively, waiting for the Chief's opinion.

Finally, Dempsey straightened up and said thoughtfully, "The autopsy will prove what killed him. If it's poison, his blood will test black. He could have been poisoned last night . . . no . . . no . . . then the killer wouldn't have known where . . . The Man put the jack of spades right here." Dempsey pointed with emphasis. "Under the sink, almost like a big X."

"He marked the spot!" Rice exclaimed, glancing up from his kneeling position next to the body.

"Exactly. If the Judge was poisoned . . . it had to be a deadly nerve poison, like curare."

"But, Chief, how would the killer know the exact . . ."

"Don't touch that toothbrush!" The force of Dempsey's shout startled Rice. "Sorry, Paul, but it might . . ."

Rice stood up carefully and waited for Dempsey to explain.

"The poison . . . it could have been introduced through small cuts in the Judge's gums . . . cut glass or a sharp wire imbedded in the bristles of his toothbrush.'' Dempsey demonstrated by pretending to brush his teeth with his index finger.

''The red stains!''

''Right. That's what tipped me off. Curare . . . it would only take a pinch.''

''It kills that fast?'' Rice looked at Dempsey.

Dempsey nodded emphatically. ''It's lethal in tiny, minute doses. Once it gets into the bloodstream, it attacks the neuromuscular system. Then, goodnight!''

Leaving the body for Doc Brody to examine, they went over the apartment carefully. They found no obvious clues, but noticed that both the Judge's and Isabel's clothes were strewn about the floor from the night before.

Rice said, ''Looks like they had a few too many. They drink the champagne, we get the headaches. I'll bet they barely made it home.''

''Too bad for him they did,'' remarked Dempsey, shaking his head sadly.

It was Rice who discovered that the television set in the bedroom didn't work. He commented. ''It's strange. With their money, you'd think they'd get something like this fixed.''

The living room was beautifully furnished with Early American antiques. Dempsey recognized a set of Queen Anne armchairs. He'd seen a picture of similar ones that had recently been sold at Sotheby's for $55,000. He knew that the Chippendale highboy, the kettle-base desk, the pair of William and Mary settees and the Federal breakfront were almost priceless. The furniture in the dining room was equally magnificent, featuring a very rare Queen Anne dining set, polished to a bright sheen and in perfect condition. It belonged in a museum.

Dempsey turned to Rice. ''If any of this is missing, you know where to look. Brenda and I have a thing about American antiques. Inexpensive ones,'' he added, when he saw Rice's expression.

Dempsey's face showed his admiration. ''This is probably the finest private collection I've ever seen, and in a condominium at that. Look at the paintings. Two original portraits of the Adams family by Stuart. Fabulous!''

Rice gave instructions to his men. He wanted photographs of the body before it was moved. The toothbrush, toothpaste tube, drinking glass and playing card were all to be analyzed by the lab. Everything was to be dusted for fingerprints. All doors and windows were to be checked for signs of forced entry.

The doorman didn't remember anything unusual about the previous day. He went off duty at 6:00 P.M., replaced by the night man. He knew that the Wallers were going out to dinner at the club to celebrate the Judge's promotion, and commented that they were a close, gentle couple. "Those two. They were always acting like love-struck kids. Even held hands walking across the lobby." He shook his head.

Paul Rice got the phone number and address of the night doorman, Fred Stanhope. "I'll check him out as soon as we get back to headquarters, Chief. He's a top-priority witness, maybe even a suspect. The penthouse is on the sixth floor. The murderer had to use the elevator. I don't see how he could have gotten past the doorman."

"Our man could, and did," emphasized Dempsey. "Incredible, isn't it?"

The news of the murder of Judge Waller spread like wildfire. Coming on top of the murders of Donnelly and Hetty Starr, it caused a sensation. The Judge was an important national figure. By the time Dempsey and Rice returned to headquarters, it was under full frontal attack by reporters and newscasters.

"No questions, boys, not now. We think the Judge was murdered. We'll let you know how, as soon as we've done the lab tests. We're pretty sure it's the same killer." Dempsey gritted his teeth and pushed past the reporters into the building. The telephones were ringing incessantly.

Dempsey set up Mary with two of her staff to handle public relations. In five minutes he dictated set answers to the questions expected to be asked. Then he went into his office and closed the door to be by himself to think.

Gus Belli's team had eliminated twenty-two of the forty-five names on their list of possible bomb suspects. It was grueling, pick-and-shovel investigatory work. When you're a detective and you're assigned a murder case, it becomes your whole life.

They had not yet indentified any real suspect. But Belli had not lost his confidence that they would. Belli excelled at digging for details. Methodical and thorough, he believed that a good detective had to be distilled out of his own sweat. "A plodder after facts and intelligent enough to know how to interpret and use the information he uncovers" was the way Dempsey had described him in his dossier.

Belli believed in hard work, remembering the past. He'd been raised as one of eight children of an Italian immigrant on the Lower East Side. His father had started with a pushcart and ten years later had opened a small grocery store. He'd been killed in 1964 during a holdup of his store. Killed defending the seventeen dollars and twenty cents in the cash register. Gus's older brother had taken over the store.

Gus was the only one of the family who had made it through college, and the whole family had expected him to amount to something. His father's murder had propelled him into police work, and Belli was determined to become a top detective. Marie, his high school sweetheart, and he now lived in a small Cape Cod house in the East Creek area of Fairport, with their three young children. He had accepted the job in Fairport in order to be able to work with Dempsey and had not been disappointed.

Looking at the list of remaining bomb suspects, Belli suddenly had an inspiration. Nichols, Baker, Dillon, Orton, Hoyle. All members of the Rotary. Donnelly and Judge Waller had been Rotarians, too. There might be a motive there. He'd check them personally. Nichols was too smooth, oily smooth, with a silk tongue. Hard as nails underneath.

Briggs and the Chief were also Rotarians. Briggs was an enigma. Combat-tough, but with a real softness for the ladies. A swordsman. He'd heard the rumors. Some young fashion photographer. But, hell, infidelity had nothing to do with murder. If it did, half of Fairport would be in prison. Throw a tent over the town, it would be one giant whorehouse. Besides, Briggs was a cop. And a top cop at that.

• • •

Lieutenant Rice rang the bell to Fred Stanhope's apartment. Sergeant Piccollo stood to one side, his hand on his service revolver. Rice had noticed that Piccollo had unbuttoned the flap on his holster. Stanhope answered the door with a towel draped around his waist. His face was still asleep, his eyes heavy-lidded.

"Murder! Judge Waller!" Stanhope's jaw dropped, his lips parted. "Oh, shit, the only decent tipper in the building. I loved the guy." Stanhope was now fully awake. He adjusted his towel to serve as a loincloth. "But how?'

"That's what we want to ask you," replied Rice coolly, as he and Piccollo pushed forward into the apartment.

Piccollo quickly checked the three rooms. Stanhope lived alone. His pad was filthy. The distinctive stale odor of marijuana permeated the air. Three or four days' dishes were piled in the sink. The couch and both easy chairs in the main room were sweat-stained and threadbare. There were no curtains at the windows, and the shades were drawn.

The mattress was on the floor in the center of the sparsely furnished bedroom. A pile of dirty clothes occupied one corner, a cheap dresser the other. The faded and sun-streaked wallpaper was peeling from one wall. Two goosenecked floor lamps were set on either side of the mattress. Oddly, there was no shade on the bedroom window. A glance out of the window confirmed Piccollo's suspicions. There were ten or twelve other apartments overlooking Stanhope's bedroom. Piccollo grimaced.

As Piccollo emerged from the bedroom, he heard Stanhope tell Rice, "I don't know nothing. I've got nothing to say."

Piccollo motioned Rice aside. Wordlessly, he pushed a straightbacked wooden chair under Stanhope, who sat down hard. Piccollo swung another chair around, facing the doorman, and straddled it in one fluid motion. His bulldog face was just inches from Stanhope's. His thick forefinger pointed at the doorman's throat.

For almost two minutes, Rice watched, fascinated, as they sat motionless. The only sound in the room was Stanhope's irregular nasal breathing. The doorman's widened eyes swiveled from Piccollo's face to his forefinger and back again.

Rice held his breath, afraid that with one jab of his stubby finger, Piccollo would puncture the doorman's larynx.

Finally, Stanhope came unraveled. At first it was a flicker of uncertainty, a stiffening of his body, betraying his inner emotions. Then, looking away from Piccollo, slumping lower in his chair, closing his eyes, hesitantly at first, then in a babble, he told them about the television repairman, concluding, "That hairy bastard! He must have done something when he took that piss. I was with him every other minute. Oh shit!"

"Could you recognize him again?" asked Rice.

"No question about it. He had bushy black hair, a flowing black mustache and strange eyes."

"Strange eyes?"

"Yeah. There was something unusual. I'll never forget them. I thought they were looking right through me." The doorman shuddered.

"What was so unusual about them?"

"They were slate-gray. The color of stone." Stanhope raised himself off the chair to adjust his towel. "Hey, he gave me his card." He jumped up and his towel fell to the floor.

"Get some clothes on and get the card," commanded Rice. "You're coming with us. We want to tape your story and have our artist make a sketch of the man you saw. This could be our first real break."

With Stanhope out of hearing, Rice clapped Piccollo on the back and said, "Nice going, Lou. What did you do, hypnotize him?"

"Naw." Piccollo grinned. "I puckered up. He thought I was going to kiss him."

Tom Farrow was puzzled. There were no herpetologists in Fairfield County. He'd inquired as far away as Hartford and New York. No one had any record of anyone in the Fairport area raising rattlesnakes.

"Who's crazy enough to do that?" was the unsettling question from the Curator of the Bronx Zoo.

Farrow had also talked to Securi-T at length, and they were

at a loss as to how anyone could have penetrated their security system. They were confident that it could not be compromised. They were also positive that no one could make a duplicate key, since the blanks were specially made for them by Medeco.

Bullshit, Farrow thought. I'm tempted to steal one from their office to prove that it can be done. The Man found a way to compromise the system. He most likely used a key. Nichols wouldn't even have to steal a key from Securi-T. Having access to Hetty's safe, he could have borrowed her key at any time and had a duplicate made. Ned Nichols . . . he grew up in New Mexico. They've got lots of rattlesnakes out there.

This was really becoming a first-class puzzle. Farrow could feel the creases in his forehead deepen. No, not one puzzle. Three of them. Three interrelated puzzles. A master jigsaw.

It was his love of puzzles that had steered him into criminology in the first place. During his second year at Boston University, he'd realized that his football scholarship was only a four-year escape from the family farm in Maine. Having no interest in farming, he was searching for an interesting career. He found it the day he learned that detective work involved solving puzzles.

He married Sally in his senior year. She had just graduated from Katharine Gibbs and was working as a secretary for Prudential. She'd been a great help, calming him down and making him see the serious side of life. Now she was always after him to work harder.

He'd come to Fairport because of Dempsey. The Chief had a reputation as a master detective, a supercop. His inductive and deductive reasoning and ability to solve crimes were acknowledged among criminologists throughout the country. Farrow knew that his reputation was well deserved.

Dempsey had been impressed by Farrow's open-minded, creative approach to problems. But several times Dempsey had hinted that he wasn't using his full potential. Now they had a giant interlocking puzzle. Three murders in three days. It was time to show everyone what Tom Farrow could do. If he solved the puzzles first, it would guarantee his future—his own reputation. He'd show both Dempsey and Sally—by working his ass off. ·

Farrow thought the multiple killings might be a screen thrown up by the murderer to conceal the real motive behind one of the deaths. The man might be after just one victim or a specific item of value from one victim. By killing a series of individuals, he might draw attention away from the specific motive of one of the crimes. The motive for each murder would have to be looked at carefully and separately.

Hetty Starr was loaded. She'd probably leave a multimillion-dollar estate. Nichols had ingratiated himself with Hetty in the last few years. As her lawyer, he would know the contents of her will. Was Nichols mentioned in it? Could it contain a motive for murder?

The private phone in the Man's office rang excitedly at exactly 11:30 A.M. He closed the door before answering. His secretary had instructions that neither she nor anyone else was to answer or use his private phone. He was sure no one ever did. The scuttlebutt around the office hinted that it was his private "hot line." No one realized what an accurate description that was. Only three people knew the unlisted phone number—Jeanne, Barbara, and Gayla.

It was Gayla on the line. "Honey, I'm back. I missed you. When can I see you, Tiger?" She emphasized the "Ti—ger," like a sexy college cheer.

"Hi, precious. I'm terribly busy this morning. How about later in the day?" The Man cradled the phone on his shoulder as he lit a Tiparillo.

"Darling, anytime. I'm really bushed anyhow. We had a rough flight on the last leg from Copenhagen, and I can use a few hours shuteye. I'll leave the door unlocked. Four days is a long time away from you, Tiger. I'm really ready for one of your special treatments."

"I missed you, too, Flygirl. I'll be over as soon as I can make it." He gave her a throaty growl and hung up the phone.

For a few minutes, the Man let his mind dwell on Gayla. She was some sweet girl. She still epitomized the All-American cheerleader, perfected at the University of Alabama. Now, almost ten years later, she was a dedicated stewardess for Pan American and an A-1 ambassador for the pulchritude of young American women. Blond, blue-eyed, peaches-and-cream complexion, intelligent, warm, outgoing, cheerful personality and measurements of 36-26-36, Gayla was damn near perfect. He inhaled deeply and blew out a cloud of smoke.

Before she had met the Man, Gayla had been promiscuously searching for love, for true affection, for an indefinable something that had always eluded her. Usually the men to whom she had been irresistibly attracted would have been more attracted to her brother, if she'd had one. As a result, Gayla was unhappy, depressed, almost to an extreme.

Roommates and friends would talk of orgasmic ecstasy and extreme pleasure from their sexual activities. Gayla listened quietly, feeling nothing. There was no automatic response for her. She had reached a point where she alternately contemplated group sex or lesbianism or both together.

Fortunately, neither of these extremes proved necessary. Gayla met the Man, accidentally. He laughed, thinking about it again. It was still a vivid memory, even though it had happened almost three years ago.

After an all-night flight from Frankfurt, Gayla was driving back in her Volkswagen from JFK to her country cottage on the Brookings estate that she shared with two other girls, when she ran into the Man. Literally ran into him. Just after pulling off the turnpike, a cocker spaniel darted out from underneath a parked car into her path. She swerved violently and sideswiped the Man's brand-new Jaguar XKE. Fortunately, he had just crossed the street and was about to enter Jerry's Diner for an early-morning cup of coffee.

Apprehensively, she pulled to the curb. He approached angrily, swearing softly to himself about women drivers. Aloud, he said, "Well done. You missed the dog."

"Gee, I'm sorry. I didn't mean to hit your car. Did I do much damage?" Gayla's big blue eyes were brimming with tears and innocence.

The Man took in her warm gaze, laughed gently and replied, "Just the left front fender. Nothing that can't be fixed. Better the car than the dog. Let's take a look at yours."

As she got out of the car, the Man gave her a most appreciative once-over before he remarked, "Your lucky day. A slight dent on the end of your bumper. That's all. It's barely noticeable."

Gayla laughed nervously, and in an apologetic tone replied, "I really appreciate . . . you're being awfully nice. Do you want to see my license, or do I need to fill out any forms, or anything? I'm insured. This is my first accident."

"Your form is already filled out perfectly. But I wouldn't mind looking at your license to learn your address, since we've got to stop meeting like this. How about a morning cup of coffee?" The Man laughingly offered the bait.

"I'd love to, Tiger. I like your vibes. I'm Gayla." She gave him her beautiful toothpaste smile. She had accepted the bait willingly.

He held out his hand. "Since you called me Tiger, I'll learn to like it." He took her arm as they walked toward the diner.

Twenty minutes later, they both knew they had found something special. They really enjoyed each other's company, and were on the same wavelength. He suggested that maybe they'd lived together in a previous existence. She laughed uproariously when, in answer to the question that all single girls ask a new, interesting male friend, he replied, "Yes, I am, but it is a well-known fact that the Tasmanians, who never committed adultery, are long extinct."

As they left the diner, Gayla noticed that her mood-stone ring had turned from jet black to royal blue. She had been impressed by his sense of humor, his milk-white teeth, and his sun-wrinkled eyes. She liked his directness. He seemed to be all man.

Two days later, Gayla achieved her first orgasm. It was far better than she had been led to believe or dared hope for. It exceeded even her wildest fantasies. The Man had stimulated her in a way no one had before. It had been exquisitely sensitive, an incredible wave of vibrations. It was, she acknowledged, the happiest day of her life. She was normal.

Gayla had represented the type of challenge that brought Tiger to the peak of his manhood. The proper balance of affection, tenderness, love, compassion, understanding, patience, and the experienced manipulation of two high-powered electric vibrators—one fast, one teasingly gentle—had been the key to the achievement of Gayla's miracle. Since that memorable occasion, Gayla had been completely loyal to her Tiger, and she had been rewarded by miracle after miracle. Sexually, Gayla was now happy, satisfied and content.

The Man laughed. He'd figure out some way to spend part of the afternoon with Gayla.

Dempsey was sitting at his desk, deep in thought, the rugged face showing lines of strain about the eyes. His dark mood deepened.

Three murders on three consecutive days. What was the pattern? One a day. Just like vitamins. Did the murderer plan to keep up his one-a-day pace? Oh, shit! What was the motive? There was no apparent robbery. What had the criminal gained? Were the killings motivated by revenge? It so, revenge against what, against whom? Where was the common thread? There had to be one. The motive was usually love or money, unless . . . the killer was a psycho, a crazy. They killed without motive. Sometimes they killed just for fun. But most crazies were totally wild. They killed on impulse, at a whim, hit or miss, without a plan. Who was this Man, this murderer? Did he live in Fairport? Did he know him? Somehow, he was sure he did. He felt it very strongly. There didn't seem to be a modus operandi. He opened the drawer and took out a pencil and noted on his pad:

Selectman	—bombing	—king of spades
Actress	—snakebite	—queen of spades
Judge	—probably poison	—jack of spades

The one consistent element in each murder was the playing card at each murder scene. The killer clearly wanted people to know that the same person was responsible. Why? One killing of an important person each day. It had to be a psychopath, another Manson. But different. Very different. These murders were planned. They weren't done on the spur of the moment. It looked like a controlled type of "Helter Skelter," and oh so clever.

Each murder different—unusual for a psycho. Mass murderers always kill the same way, over and over, like Son of Sam. Was the murderer trying to prove something to himself, to others, perhaps the whole community? Would he kill again? Would he try to run through all thirteen of the spades, and then the whole deck of cards—fifty-two murders? It would be the horror show of the century. He swallowed and felt the sour taste of bile in his throat. A sudden summer storm blackened the sky, interrupting his thoughts. He turned on the lights in his office, blinking his eyes at the sudden glare.

He leaned back in his chair and watched the progress of the rivulets of water running down the windowpanes, beginning as individual drops, then a trickle, a steady flow, and in minutes growing into a cascade. It was now raining torrents, beating against the slate roof with an eering drumming sound. The few pedestrians in the streets had scrambled for cover. A defiant youngster, soaked to the skin, was splashing his bicycle through the sudden rush of water flushing the streets of days of thoughtless litter.

Just as suddenly as it had started, the rain was over. The skies brightened, and the sun blazed through from behind a wall of swirling, dark cumulus clouds. He rose and went to the window, hoping to see a rainbow. The prism of colors might provide the clue he needed.

Since childhood, rainbows had fascinated him. When he was just seven, his grandfather had talked about the two of them finding the pot of gold at the end of the rainbow. "All we have to do is follow the arch and we'll find it," he'd say. The scene was still vivid. The old man with snow-white hair, bent with crippling arthritis, but still enjoying one of nature's miracles, the sun shining on the droplets of water creating a display of vivid colors of indescribable beauty.

There was no rainbow, no colored arch to lead the way. Perhaps his problems would disappear as fast as the summer storm, and the sun would shine again. That was it. He sat down at the desk again and picked up his pencil. He'd have to dig deeper. Think harder. He was oblivious to the rat-a-tat sound the eraser end of his pencil made hitting the pad. He still had no answers. He didn't even have a theory.

A nationally known, well-respected federal judge had been killed with a fiendishly clever but simple plan. Dempsey was confident it was poison and probably curare. Doc Brody was checking now. It had to be. Suddenly, it hit him. The king, queen, jack of spades. Where was the ace? The ace of spades was missing!

By 1:00 P.M., the Yankee Clipper was already crowded, and the cigarette smoke was thick enough to make the bar seem even smaller than it was. The proprietor grunted a greeting to Farrow and pointed to the corner booth. Through the haze, Farrow could distinguish the outline of a husky man seated with Gus Belli. He shouldered his way toward them.

"Tom Farrow, meet Joe O'Cello," Belli said. O'Cello took off his silver-rimmed sunglasses.

Farrow almost laughed out loud. The name fit. The guy looked like a sponge. His bald head was pumpkin-round, with a cauliflower nose. The skin on his face was soft, almost mushy, with large pockmarks. He had small, quick eyes that were hidden in deep dark-brown sockets. O'Cello. One glance told him that lunch wasn't going to be much fun. He never drank on duty . . . but . . . he took another look at O'Cello. "Beck's," he said to the waitress.

"Make it two," Belli added. Farrow grinned inwardly. Belli never drank at all. He was a two-beer goner. But then, Belli had to watch O'Cello eat.

"Extra-dry martini, up," ordered O'Cello, his voice a hoarse whisper.

The waitress turned and shouted to the bartender, "Two Germans and a white loudmouth." Turning back, she wiped the crumbs from the table with a damp cloth. As she leaned over, Farrow noticed that the clipper ship stenciled on her T-shirt was under full sail.

"How's the pool business?" asked Farrow.

"Billiards," corrected O'Cello. "Good, thanks to jai alai. It's saving Bridgeport. Good crowds mean good business."

For the next half hour, over corned-beef sandwiches, they

talked about nothing in particular. O'Cello's Billiard Parlor was a known manhole cover. It was a major opening to Fairfield County's underworld. From it, O'Cello's connections ran out in all directions. It had been almost two years since Belli had saved the life of O'Cello's son after a motorcycle accident. He'd slowed the bleeding from an artery until the ambulance arrived. O'Cello had given Belli a verbal chit. Up to now he'd never cashed it.

Over coffee Belli came to the point. "We've got three murders. What do you hear?"

O'Cello sat in silence, puffing a thick Cuban cigar. He showed no surprise at the mention of a third murder. Finally, he shook his head sadly, stirring the heavy smoke.

Farrow and Belli exchanged glances. Farrow spoke, "Nothing?"

"Nothing," O'Cello said simply, his pudgy hands open on the table. "And . . . believe me . . . I've asked around."

"That's it?" Belli asked, his swarthy face showing disappointment.

O'Cello glanced slowly around the room. Satisfied, he showed his yellow teeth and whispered hoarsely, "Nothing about murder. But . . ." His head swiveled about again, blowing a cloud of thick cigar smoke into Farrow's face. "We hear other things about your town."

"Like what?" Farrow choked out.

"Funny money and hard drugs." O'Cello ticked them off on his stubby fingers. "Independent, but big. Real heavy bread. . . . That's all I know."

For the second time, Farrow and Belli glanced at one another, disbelief on their faces.

"That's all I know," O'Cello repeated. "But . . . I'll keep asking. Murder . . . it's not good."

It was a few minutes later, after O'Cello had left the bar, that Belli said disgustedly, "We've got three murders and the Sponge gives us riddles."

"Can you imagine? Funny money and hard drugs. We've never had any problems like that in Fairport. We need a new source." Farrow inhaled deeply on his Tiparillo, and blew a perfect smoke ring.

*   *   *

Immediately after lunch, Rice reported to Dempsey on the details of his conversation with Stanhope, the night doorman at the Okonokee condominiums.

"The stupid ass actually took the murderer up to the Judge's apartment in the elevator and let him in with his own passkey. The man was supposed to be a TV repairman from Acme. I checked. Acme has no one employed matching the description provided by Stanhope—white male, six feet tall, about thirty-five to forty years old, one-ninety to two hundred pounds, bushy black hair, flowing black mustache, piercing slate-gray eyes.

"The murderer actually gave Stanhope an Acme business card with the name Alvin Ross. Acme claims that Ross left its employ three months ago. He moved to Chicago. I checked." Rice sighed. "He's there. Besides, Ross is about five feet four inches tall and weighs a hundred and forty pounds."

Dempsey listened carefully, then commented, "Business cards are easy to come by. They're given away every day. Forget it. But the description of the murderer interests me. It's our first tangible clue." A faint smile creased his lips.

Surprise showed in Rice's face. "Hell, Chief, bushy black hair, flowing mustache, slate-gray eyes. Sounds like a Halloween disguise. I've got our artist making a sketch, but I thought it was a long shot."

"Probably is, Paul. But a man who wears a bushy hairpiece and a fake mustache must feel pretty well disguised. It isn't necessary to alter the rest of his appearance."

Dempsey rose from his chair and sat on the edge of his desk, his eyes now level with Rice's.

"We can be reasonably sure that he's a white male, about six feet tall, weighing approximately one-ninety to two hundred pounds. Stanhope's estimate of age would be more questionable, especially if the hair and mustache were fake. But at least we've got something."

Rice nodded his understanding. "Don't forget the slate-gray eyes. Stanhope kept mentioning them. They must have made some impression. He said they were the color of a . . ." Rice swallowed. "of a tombstone."

"They sound as fake as the hairpiece and the mustache," Dempsey replied. "Cat's eyes. Pop them in. Pop them out."

A knock on the doorframe and Belli and Farrow entered the Chief's office.

"I hear the killer just talked his way into a guarded condo. Our man has got balls of brass," said Belli.

"When we catch him, it'll be a real pleasure to find out," replied Dempsey. "The guy who nails him first gets first kick." Belli could tell from the Chief's expression that he wasn't kidding.

After a brief discussion, Dempsey assigned the responsibility for investigating the murder of Judge Waller to Rice and asked him to select a team of three men. Rice left quickly. He had some ideas of his own he wanted to try.

Belli reported that the interviews with Donnelly's acquaintances had yielded nothing of substance. Dempsey requested that the scope of the interviews be expanded to include Hetty's and the judge's friends and associates as well.

"We've got to find a pattern," Dempsey said.

"Like what?" Belli and Farrow asked simultaneously.

"The same name on each list," replied Dempsey thoughtfully. "That would be a common thread. Particularly if he's white, about six feet tall and weighs between one hundred ninety and two hundred pounds."

"Chief, it may not be a single individual. Maybe it's an organization," suggested Belli. "The three victims were all prominent citizens. Maybe it's an extremist group out to kill off rich people." He looked up hopefully.

"The Selectman wasn't rich. He was wallowing in debt up to his armpits," commented Farrow. "But the idea of a group . . . that's got merit. Maybe they're out to ruin our political system. Donnelly and the Judge were both active in politics, and Hetty Starr was a power behind the scene in state Republican circles. She virtually dictated the candidates."

"That's possible," mused Dempsey. "Hell, at this point, anything's possible. But if someone's out to ruin our political system, why a little town like Fairport? Why not start in Washington?"

"In Washington, this type of thing might do some good," said Belli, with a wry smile.

"An underground organization, a radical group, maybe even a cult. We can't overlook it," said Farrow. "The spades might be the key to identifying them."

"Possibly, but I've got a gut feeling that it's one person," said Dempsey, pouring himself some black coffee. "One man with a dislocated mind. One man out to prove something."

"What's he proving—that he can kill people?" asked Belli. "What the hell kind of a fruitcake is that?"

"Exactly! That he can kill people and succeed. That he can commit murder over and over and get away with it. He's thumbing his nose at us, giving us the old finger—the Royal Rockefeller sign." Dempsey gestured. "He's out to prove he's a great killer."

As the others left his office, Dempsey rose and walked to the window. The billowing clouds from the morning storm covered the western horizon like huge mounds of vanilla ice cream. The sun was now shining brightly, and on the horizon was a faint hint of a rainbow.

The Man had not been able to free up time to leave his office for Gayla's until slightly after 3:00 P.M. He told his secretary that he had an important meeting, and he'd be back by 4:00 or 4:30 P.M. Just before he left his office, Barbara phoned. She had arrived at her daughter's camp safely, thought of him constantly, missed him enormously, and would be back probably late Friday or Saturday. He had forgotten she was going to Vermont.

On his way to Gayla's he snapped on the radio. It was tuned to WINS, 1010, "All-news twenty-four hours a day."

"Another terrible murder occurred today in Fairport, Connecticut. Horatio Waller, newly appointed Federal Judge to the Second Circuit Court of Appeals, was killed this morning in his penthouse atop the luxurious Okonokee condominiums overlooking Long Island Sound. The police suspect that the Judge was poisoned. They expect to release a more definitive report on cause of death later this afternoon. This is the third murder in Fairport—"

The Man clicked off the radio and lit a Tiparillo. He puffed contentedly, knowing that the murders would be featured over and over, on every newscast, every television station, every radio station, in every newspaper and in every news magazine throughout the length and breadth of the country. The media were spreading fear across the country. They were doing the job for him. What was happening in Fairport could happen anywhere.

He blew a badly shaped smoke ring. The plan was perfect. In the next several days, television crews would begin crawling all over Fairport, televising specials on the murders to every home in America. It was all part of the plan. He was going to give the public an unexpected thrill. It would be a first. A prime-time murder they'd never forget. He smiled again at his own ingenuity.

As quickly as the murders had taken over the Man's thoughts, Gayla replaced them. Tiger again, he turned into the lane leading to her cottage. She now lived alone. Her roommates had moved into New York shortly after their relationship had begun. He parked the car, snuffed out his small cigar in the gravel, and walked up to the vine-covered fieldstone cottage.

Clad only in a wrap-around beach towel, Gayla was genuinely delighted to see him. As she rushed into his arms, the towel fluttered to the floor. They kissed hungrily at the front door, again in the living room, again on the edge of the bed. She'd really missed him. He undressed while she opened her carry-all and took out a present.

"For me? What is it?" he asked, smiling.

"It's really for us. I got it in Copenhagen." There was a show of color in her cheeks.

"Is it what I think it is?" He grinned broadly.

"Ti—ger, how can I surprise you? You're too smart. I saw it in the window of . . ." Gayla hesitated, smiled shyly and continued. "A specialty shop! Our old one is almost worn out. This one has variable speeds and attachments. I'm anxious to see how it works. The brochure said it was guaranteed to enable the user to reach new heights of enjoyment."

Growling playfully, Tiger unwrapped the package and removed the new vibrator from its box, checking to make sure it was designed for 110-volt current before he plugged it in.

It really did have six speeds, and it more than lived up to all of its advertising claims. Even on speed three, it worked very well, for both of them.

At 4:05 P.M. Rice burst into Dempsey's office with reports from Doc Brody's lab.

There was a look of admiration on Rice's face. "Chief, you were right. There was a small jeweler's wire, almost a needle, imbedded in the bristles of the Judge's toothbrush. He couldn't possibly have used the toothbrush without cutting his gums. The lab picked up traces of poison on the brush, and the toothpaste is loaded with it. Doc reported death by a nerve poison. He's pretty sure it's Pavulon—"

"That's a synthetic type of curare, isn't it?"

The look of admiration on Rice's face deepened. "You expected that, Chief, didn't you?"

"Frankly, yes," Dempsey replied. "It's used in hospitals—given to surgical patients to relax their muscles. It's available. It's probably where the Man—"

"I've already started checking," Rice replied with a tone of pride.

Calmly, Mary came into the room, her face ashen gray. She handed Dempsey an envelope similar to the one he had received on Monday. On the envelope was typed, "Number 2 in a Series." It was addressed simply, "The Boy Scout Chief, Fairport Police." It had been mailed locally the preceding day.

Before opening the letter, Dempsey buzzed for Farrow and Belli and motioned for Rice to come around to his side of the desk. He asked Mary to stay also.

Then he put on a pair of thin plastic gloves. As soon as the others arrived in his office, he slipped the letter out of the envelope and unfolded it. Then he read aloud:

"Hearts are red
Spades are black
You've found three—
King, queen, and jack.

"Clubs are black
Diamonds are red
The ten of spades
I've saved for Fred.

"Fred who? you ask.
Tomorrow, by noon
The devil will have him
And none too soon.

"You have some time
And a solid clue.
Can you find Fred
Before I do?"

"Paul, have this checked for fingerprints!" Dempsey was livid. "Mary, where did you get this?"

"It came in the regular mail delivery."

"That cocky bastard! Now he's gone too far. He's given us a victim's name. Mary, get me a list of every man in Fairport whose name is Fred." Dempsey hit his desk with the side of his fist.

"How do I do that?" asked an incredulous Mary.

"Get a telephone book and set up a group of girls to check every name. List down everyone with the name Fred," suggested Dempsey.

"But, Chief, won't some just have the initial F in place of a first name?" asked Farrow, a hint of challenge in his voice.

"Probably they will." Dempsey glanced quickly at Farrow, then turned his head to Mary. "List those with initials separately, then check with the phone company, or call the people directly, to see if their first name is Fred. When you get your total list compiled, we'll go over it together to see if we can pick out a possible victim."

"How about unlisted numbers?" asked Rice. "This bastard is smart enough to—"

"Good thought, Paul. I'll get those directly from the phone company," answered Mary.

"Chief, do you really think we can narrow it down to the right Fred?" asked Belli.

"We'll need a little luck. But this could be the Man's first mistake. Let's hope so," Dempsey answered, then turned away.

In the police lab, under Rice's direction, his team of technicians examined the two letters from the Man. The letters were being handled carefully, with plastic gloves, checked for fingerprints, stains, fibers, hairs, watermarks, anything that might provide a lead. Both postmarks had been traced to the main post office on Housatuck Avenue.

The paper, typewriter ink and even the glue on the seal of the envelopes had been chemically analyzed. The letters had been examined under ultraviolet and infrared light in search of any possible leads.

In an experimental procedure to detect prints on paper, the letters had been sprayed with ninhydrin. This chemical would enhance traces of any prints that had been left. It would pick up ridges, whorls, loops, minute partials, little curly lines smaller than a dime and invisible to normal procedures.

The lab technicians methodically went through each investigative ritual that could lead them to the Man. So far they had discovered nothing of importance. On the first letter, they had found Dempsey's fingerprints. On the second letter, they had found nothing.

At her desk, Mary was radiant. The Chief had given her a very important assignment. She flipped out another Merit 100 and lit it. "I'll show the men what I can do. I've got a natural instinct. I know it. Woman sense. Female intuition."

She'd already recruited her team and cleared it with Dempsey. Two secretaries and two girls from Traffic. They'd divided up the phone book and now were hard at work. She'd emphasized the importance of going over each section, name by name, and the need for accuracy.

She relaxed and drew deeply on her cigarette. Rice had been assigned the Judge's murder. If there was another murder, perhaps the Chief would assign it to her. A field promotion. Lieutenant Mary Potter and her all-girl team of detectives. Terrific!

She could feel the smoke deep in her lungs. She coughed violently. Another murder? What the hell was she thinking? She shivered.

At the Fairport Savings Bank, Samuel Tilden, banker, was irate. Eyes flashing fire, he ranted at three of his vice presidents and two bank examiners. "What do you mean, there's a shortage of almost two hundred thousand dollars?"

"Well, sir, there just is," moaned the first vice president.

"There can't be," shouted Tilden firmly. His hand shot out and gripped the vice president's trembling arm.

"But, sir, the counterfeits were almost perfect," explained the second vice president.

"Counterfeits? Two hundred thousand dollars' worth? What kind of idiots do we have in this bank?" Tilden was shouting even louder. Suddenly he noticed through his open office door that the clerks had looked up, their faces frozen. He slammed the door, muttering under his breath, "Idiots. Goddam idiots."

"No, sir, not money. One counterfeit was a savings withdrawal slip for a hundred thousand. It was an exact copy. The second counterfeit was a hundred-thousand dollar cashier's check. Another exact copy," exclaimed the third vice president. He showed far more backbone than his two associates by standing up to Tilden.

"Call the police," Tilden thundered.

"Sir," said one of the bank examiners, "I don't think the police will be that helpful. You'll want to notify them, of course, and you'll want to get Justice involved, as well as Treasury. But . . . whoever did this . . ." He hesitated, trying to pick the right words.

"Why? Why do you say that?" Tilden interrupted, turning his wrath toward the examiner.

"It's the Xerox 6500 color copier your bank installed last month. It brings counterfeiting capacity to the rank amateur. This is the fifth bank in the last three months where I've discovered fraud on a major scale. The machine accepts all types of paper, and its reproductions are excellent. You can't tell a reproduction from the real article just by looking at it. You have to test them. Let me show you.''

The examiner then produced two $100,000 cashier's checks. They looked exactly the same. He carefully rubbed a corner of each with a piece of white tissue paper. When he rubbed the first, a smudge appeared on the tissue paper that was the same color as the document.

"That's genuine," the examiner said. When he rubbed the second check, the color on the tissue paper was different. "That's the fake . . . machine ink, you see." He passed it to Tilden.

"You mean," exclaimed an astonished Tilden, "someone just put these fake documents into the day's receipts, took out the same amount of cash and adjusted the records? Is that what you're saying?"

"Right, Mr. Tilden. Right the first time. That's why I don't think the police will be able to trace who did it. It was done at least a week ago, and the money's probably long gone by now. The best I can suggest is that we install a foolproof system on your 6500 color copier so that it can't be repeated.''

"When it comes to getting ripped off," snapped Tilden, "I see red." Tilden's face flushed.

"We'll install a two-key system on the machine, and I suggest, Mr. Tilden, that you keep one of the keys yourself.''

"That's not good enough," stormed Tilden, his head bobbing up and down. "I want this shortage investigated. Everyone in the bank has to be suspect. Everyone. Everyone has access to the Xerox, and . . .'' He looked around accusingly. "They're all looking for a sure thing.''

Suddenly he turned and grabbed the examiner's wrist. "What's the best firm for this type of investigation?"

"Sir, we're not supposed to—"

"I don't care what you're supposed to do. I want to know," Tilden snapped.

"It's Bond & Bond. Out of Boston. They're very good— old, reliable firm—but they're expensive," the examiner said quietly.

"Hang the expense. I want to get rid of the rotten apple." For the first time, Tilden's face relaxed.

Later, after everyone had left Tilden's office, the insurance company had been notified, arrangements had been made for the two-key system, Justice and Treasury had been advised of the shortage and Tilden had called and retained Bond & Bond, only then did Samuel Tilden permit himself the pleasure of a satisifed grin.

"You're damn right. A man who tells lies only hides the truth. No one will ever find the money! It's well hidden, and it's all tax-free. It's a good thing I learned about the capabilities of the 6500 color copier before my employees did. One of those idiots could have robbed my bank!"

Six thousand miles away, on a remote beach on the island of Kauai, a slim, pretty, dark-haired young lady lay motionless on her rattan beach mat. She raised her head to let her eyes take in the glorious view. The huge rolling surf . . . the bright-blue sky . . . the green-covered craggy cliffs thrusting out into the sea . . . the smooth, white sandy beach totally secluded from the rest of the world. She smiled, loosened the strap on her yellow bikini and settled back. The warm Hawaiian sun massaged her body.

It was the fourth day of her vacation. She was beginning to feel like herself again. The knots in her body had left. Kauai was beautiful. The condominium she had rented at Princeville was perfect. It was paradise. The right place to reassemble all the pieces, to get her whole act together again.

Judy Rogers was torn between two loves, her career or Rick Taylor. He'd put it just that bluntly when he'd asked her to marry him.

It had been too sudden for Judy. She'd turned him down. Probably too quickly. The life of a gentleman farmer's wife in Greenville, South Carolina, wasn't for her. She loved Rick deeply. That was the trouble. They'd both been hurt. One remark had led to another. They'd said things they hadn't really meant. Now, she missed him. The last six weeks her world had been misty blue. She needed to get away, sort it out again, think it through. She wanted to be sure. Capping the suntan oil, she settled back on the mat.

Her career. She'd determined to put all of her energy into her future. She liked Boston. At Bond & Bond they'd picked her as a flier. She had a knack for investigation, a magic that could sort through details and come up with answers. Was it magic, brains or luck?

During the last two years, she'd solved three different insurance cases. No one else had even come close. Her obsession was that she wouldn't accept defeat. Hard work, attention to details—was that her magic? She wondered.

She sat up, retied her bikini straps and raced for the surf, knowing she was right. Rick could go pick cotton. She had her own pride. Everything was in front of her. She'd make it on her own.

At 4:45 P.M. Rice advised Dempsey of the first real break in the three murders. In addition to Judge Waller's prints, the lab had picked up a very good partial set of unidentified fingerprints from the almost-new tube of toothpaste. They had a clear thumb print and reasonably clear reproductions of the central whorls of the index, second and third fingers of the left hand.

They both stood at Dempsey's table examining the photos of the prints. Rice, grinning from ear to ear, was so excited he almost forgot the back pain.

"We'll get him now. I've sent copies of the prints by telephoto to the FBI Identification Division in Washington. Silvester, the guy in charge, said it may take a few weeks." Rice glanced sheepishly at Dempsey.

"A few weeks!" Dempsey exploded. "Why? Everything's on computer."

"That's what I thought. But Silvester told me that without a known suspect, it still has to be done by hand."

"Oh, shit!" Dempsey hit his open palm forcefully with his fist.

"I told him, Chief, the murder of a federal judge . . . it's a federal matter. He told me he knew that and they'd start immediately, print by print."

"This place will be crawling with FBI agents now. I just talked to Sam Grady on the phone. He's going to have dinner with me, so I can bring him up to date."

"Who's Grady?" Rice asked.

"An old friend of mine. You'll like him. Right now he's running the FBI regional office in Hartford." Dempsey paused. "With Grady involved, this investigation will get top priority."

By 5:20, Mary's team had compiled a list of all the names in the phone book with the first name of Fred. Dempsey was surprised to learn that, even including two Freddies and four phone numbers listed for Mrs. Fred so-and-so's, there were only eighty-four Freds in Fairport.

Dempsey and his staff went over the list, name by name, and winnowed the list down to five who could be considered prominent enough to be possible victims. Fred Stanhope, the doorman, wasn't prominent, but he was the obvious choice, having seen and talked to the murderer, and with the best chance to identify him. For his own safety, they decided to lock Stanhope in a cell and keep him under guard. If necessary, they would arrest him "on suspicion," and free him after the danger had passed.

They again discussed whether to release the contents of the two threatening letters to the media. Dempsey took a strong position against it. "We'd better play this close to the vest, or we'll have mass panic. Overnight, this place could become an armed camp."

"Or a ghost town," added Farrow emphatically. "I think we should keep the contents of the Man's notes private. Keeping the bastard's personal thoughts out of the press might make him frustrated enough to give us more detailed clues."

"Agreed," exclaimed Rice. "The press would have a field day with those letters. I can see the headlines. 'The Man Challenges Police. Can You Find Fred Before I Do?' We can't let him use the press for his own kicks."

In his soft voice, Belli's comments seemed almost confidential. "Let's keep them to ourselves. There's stuff in them that will help us identify the Man when we catch him."

Dempsey looked at Mary. Her nod made it unanimous.

Although no one wanted to release the Man's letters to the media, they all agreed that they had to find a way to warn Fred.

"Chief, will this do?" Mary handed Dempsey a typewritten press release.

He scanned it quickly, changed one word, looked at Mary appreciatively and said, "Perfect." It read:

During our investigation, we learned today that the Fairport murderer has identified a possible victim as a man named "Fred." We don't know the identity of Fred. so anyone with that name should be particularly careful.

> Signed: Chief Dempsey
> Fairport Police

"Mary, make sure this gets immediate general release. I want mentions on local radio every hour." Mary took the release and hurried out of the office, returning almost immediately.

Dempsey stood up and started pacing around the table, talking to the others. "We've got two groups of Freds. The first contains the five who are the most likely victims."

Dempsey paused, then continued, "Paul, take Stanhope into custody. He's in the most danger. Tom, I want you to cover the other four . . . do it personally . . . warn them of the danger. Suggest a short out-of-town vacation. If they insist on staying, offer them protection."

"The second group . . . the other seventy-nine Freds . . . Mary, have your team phone them, one by one. Identify yourself and read the press release. Don't miss anyone. I don't care how many calls it takes. Let's go."

Alone in his office, Dempsey sat on his couch, deep in thought. If they only knew the Man's motives. They were guessing. Which Fred would this psycho go after? He hoped they'd get lucky.

As Dempsey pulled into his driveway, he was surprised to see Briggs' Jaguar. Brenda and Spike were sitting on the patio, having a cocktail. She jumped up, genuinely pleased. Spike looked perturbed. A flush of red momentarily crept up his neck.

"Darling, what are you doing home? I didn't think you'd be home until late. Now the Judge! What the hell's going on? Three murders. We were just talking about them." As Spike rose, Brenda kissed Jim with feeling.

After shaking Briggs' hand, Dempsey said, "Boy, am I glad to see you here. I tried to reach you at your office to invite you over for dinner. You must have read my mind. Sam Grady, an FBI director, is coming down from Hartford. He'll be here at about seven-thirty. They're involved because Waller was a federal appointee. I thought you'd like to sit in."

"I'd like to very much. I'll give Alice a call and tell her I won't be home for dinner." Briggs went to use the phone in the kitchen, feeling relieved that Jim didn't mind that he was having a drink with Brenda. He had stopped by on an impulse just to look at her . . . those blue shorts . . . couldn't get them out of his mind.

Returning to the patio, Briggs reported, "Alice said fine. The Colonel's chicken will keep." He smiled at his own joke, then turned to Jim and spoke in a low voice. "I hope you can bring me up to date. That's great news about lifting a partial set of prints. If they're the murderer's, we should be able to nail him."

"It looks like a lucky break, one I didn't expect. The Man's too clever to leave that prominent a clue. Spike, do me a favor—start the barbecue while I say hello to Cindy. Everything's there." Dempsey gestured to the corner of the patio. "I thought we'd grill some steaks. It will give me a chance to brief you. We're going to need help from your troopers."

"Sweetheart," Jim gave Brenda a loving pat on the seat of her Kimberley slacks. "Fix me a vodka and tonic, too. I'll get the steaks out as soon as I come down. And mix one of those special salads of yours, will you?"

"O.K., hon." Brenda tossed her dark-brown hair back and pulled up her white halter. "I'll fix Cindy's dinner first, and get her to bed."

Upstairs, Dempsey poked his head into Cindy's room. She

was glued to television. Miss Piggy and Kermit the Frog were dancing with some furry animals.

"Hi, Buttercup. How's my little girl?" Dempsey leaned over to kiss her forehead. Keeping her eyes on the screen, Cindy wrinkled her face into a smile and gave her father a big Muppet hug.

Sam Grady arrived promptly at 7:30 P.M., having driven down from Hartford in slightly over an hour. When Sam got out of his car, Dempsey was astonished. Grady limped noticeably and managed the three steps to the patio terrace only with the help of an ivory-tipped cane. Later, Sam told them the reason. Three years before, he had been thrown from a horse, while trail-riding in the Superstition Mountains, and his left leg had been crushed. After three operations, he still walked with a decided limp and had to limit all physical activity.

They had a round of drinks and sat down to a simple but elegant dinner by candlelight. Jim noticed that Brenda looked particularly lovely in a light-blue Lilly. It was her best party dress. He mouthed silently, "I like your dress," across the table. She smiled appreciatively. The conversation at dinner was mostly small talk. They skirted around the edges of the murders, reserving their serious talk for after coffee.

Dempsey spent part of the dinner renewing his friendship with Grady. At the age of forty-three, Sam was still a forceful, dynamic personality, a promising executive in the FBI, marked for a top office in Washington. For a while, their lives had been closely parallel. Both had graduated with honors in criminology from Columbia, and they'd worked together for three years in the FBI. They they'd chosen separate career paths. Dempsey had gone to the Police Academy for graduate training, Grady had stayed with the FBI.

Dempsey remembered Grady as both extremely intelligent and physically strong, recalling their close karate matches during training. At one point, he started to remind Sam. He caught himself just in time.

Brenda was surprised at how much Grady reminded her of Jim. He had the same broad shoulders and the same type of handsome, rugged outdoor face. His eyes were shrewd, but twinkling. However, when Grady tried to move about, the resemblance ended.

After Brenda had left to do the dishes, Dempsey brought the other two up to date. It was Grady who suggested, "Why don't we check the fingerprints you found at the Judge's against the fingerprints of your bomb suspects? If your list is a good one . . . hell, we might identify the Man in a matter of hours."

Dempsey and Briggs nodded their agreement quickly. Briggs spoke first. "The good ideas are always simple."

"We'll get on it first thing. You should have an answer tomorrow morning," Grady said confidently.

Dempsey then leaned forward and spoke in a low voice. "If he's killing important people or those connected with politics, I'm really concerned about Senator Benson and the Governor, who are visiting this Sunday in connection with the town's Bicentennial celebration."

"Good Lord, I'd forgotten about that." Briggs hit his forehead. "The s.o.b. could have a field day."

"There'll probably be a number of celebrities attending Hetty's and the Judge's funerals, also," added Dempsey. "We're going to need your help, Spike. With three murder investigations, I can't possibly provide security."

Briggs agreed instantly. "You're dead right, Jim. Hey, sorry, that's a dumb choice of words." He smiled his apology. "We'll take over security. You concentrate on solving the murders. Our men can work out the protection details in the morning."

"Thanks, Spike. I appreciate that." Dempsey's facial expression showed his relief. "We've got to discourage dignitaries from coming to the Judge's funeral. Sam, do you think your people in Washington can help?"

"I'm sure they'll try, but you know politicians. They don't listen to reason. They're always too anxious to mingle with the crowds and shake loose the votes. The media boys may accomplish more than we can. I was listening to the radio on my way down, and your town's reputation is taking quite a beating.''

"What can you expect? With a murder every day! We've got to stop this guy," said Dempsey, as he refilled their brandy glasses.

"Hetty's funeral will be the real problem," commented Briggs.

"She'll draw the international jet-setters and the Hollywood crowd."

"I'm trying to persuade her relatives to hold the services in New York and bring her body back here later for a quiet family service," Dempsey said. "She wanted to be buried here. This was her home."

Brenda interrupted their discussion briefly to say goodnight. During the interruption, Brenda again offered Sam the use of their guest room, but, declining with warm thanks, Sam said that he had reserved a room at the old Fairport Inn and had a breakfast meeting there with his regional agents.

The three lawmen talked until almost midnight, agreeing that to avoid duplication of effort, the investigation needed a single head and that Dempsey was the logical man. They also agreed to meet as often as needed.

Dempsey was pleased. He now had the firm, agreed cooperation of both the state police and the FBI.

They said goodnight, and Dempsey watched his two friends walk toward their cars. Grady hobbling slowly, his cane making a hollow sound on the walkway, and Briggs moving with fluid grace, almost like a tiger on the prowl.

When he'd arrived home, the Man had flushed the remainder of the Pavulon down the toilet. Disguised as a visiting intern, he'd appropriated a supply sufficient for his purpose from the anesthesiologist at the hospital six weeks previously. He knew the theft had not been reported, and had not even been noticed.

The Judge's murder had received major coverage on all

three television networks. It was their lead story. The pressure was building. People were beginning to appear nervous, too look behind them, to lock and bolt their doors and windows. He could sense the fear. It hung in the air. One could smell it.

The fear would grow day by day until it stifled all life in Fairport. People would start to hear footsteps, they would buy new locks for their doors, deadbolts, guns to defend themselves. Starting as a trickle, it would grow to a torrent inundating everyone. Tomorrow, some would start to leave town. A few would leave at first, then more each day, until only a few would remain.

Before going to bed, he took a black marking pencil and crossed out the Judge, the jack of spades, number four on his list. He smiled as he put his notebook back into its secret cache and locked it carefully. Leaning back, he sighed and slapped his knee. The plan was perfect.

As he thought about the killing he'd planned for the next day, he had a sudden apprehension, a moment's hesitation. Should he stop now? The next murder would horrify the nation.

No, the world would remember him as the greatest. A man whom no one could identify, totally confusing all of the law-enforcement agencies. He was not a mad dog, not a psychopathic killer, not a wild crazy. No, he was perfectly sane. He was the greatest, and he had to kill, and keep on killing.

The Man was exploring new dimensions. He would go beyond the ultimate. Way beyond. That was his plan. It was that simple. That made it right. He was not a psycho, not a weirdo, not a kook. For it was he who had the greatest criminal mind of all time. He would go on and prove it. The moment of doubt, the flash of conscience, the instant of guilt, had all passed. He chuckled to himself. Look out, Fred, you're as good as dead.

5

Thursday, June 5.
A Royal Flush

IT WAS past midnight at Gunn's Gunshop on Main Street. After the police warning, Fred Gunn had decided to barricade himself against the worst. With his father, affectionately called Pop, and two gun enthusiasts, Zeke Snider and Luke Baldwin, Fred was ready for the Man. In fact, Fred was ready for anything.

The store resembled a fort in an old western. Tables had been turned on their sides, blocking doors and windows and providing secure firing positions. Each of the defenders had two M-16 rapid-firing automatic rifles and a bandolier of high-powered ammunition. Each also wore a loaded .38.

Fred had set up a two-on, two-off guard and schedule with four-hour shifts. Fred and Pop were awake and alert. Fred was smoking nonstop. Zeke and Luke were preparing to bed down on canvas cots set up in the corner, near their emergency food and water supplies. Both were big men, tough former Green Berets. Hammers.

Suddenly there was a distinct scratching noise at the front door. All four heard it at the same time. Two rifles swung in unison to cover it. Zeke and Luke picked up their M-16s and took positions near the windows. With his left hand, Zeke opened a tiny slit and peered through the pulled blinds. "It's only a drunk," he whispered.

"Don't be fooled. It could be that crazy nut in disguise."

There was anguish in Fred's voice. "He could have a gun. Don't forget, when you return his fire, aim just to the right of the muzzle flash."

"Yeah, sonny, that'll work just fine, unless he's a lefty," cracked Pop.

"He's taking something out of a paper bag," reported Zeke in a low voice.

"It could be nitro," warned Fred.

Outside, a local derelict, searching for a resting place for the night, oblivious to all wordly cares, lurched against the door. He slid down to a sitting position.

Inside, behind the barricades, it sounded as if the door was being forced. Two automatic rifles fired at once, the noise shattering the silence of the still night. The bullets splintered the door inches above the derelict's head. Undaunted by the sudden commotion, the drunk shrugged, took one last swig out of his bottle and passed out.

Two police cars were on the scene almost immediately. They carried the drunk off to jail for safekeeping, and they spent the next fifteen minutes lecturing the Gunns on gun safety. One policeman concluded, "Mr. Gunn, guns don't kill people. People kill people. They misuse guns. Of all people, Mr. Gunn, you should know that!"

Judy Rogers was enjoying a glow—a rich Hawaiian glow. She touched the heart-shaped ebony-colored sea bean she'd found on the beach. It was a sign of good luck. Each day of her vacation had been better than the last. She'd met a very interesting man and had no time to think about Rick. In fact, right now Rick was the farthest thing from her mind.

She and her new friend, Jack Winchell, spent the afternoon sightseeing and finally stopped for a quiet moonlit dinner on the patio of a native restaurant overlooking the long Pacific rollers. The view was breathtaking, the evening breeze comfortable, the maui-maui with the wiki-wiki sauce delicious, and the conversation stimulating. Judy was impressed. Jack was not only a very interesting architect, but also an exciting man. He believed that women should pursue their own careers, and said something she'd long remember: "A man of quality should not feel threatened by a woman of equality."

Judy wasn't sure whether it was the soft breeze, the moon-

light, the wine, the guitar music, the charming conversation
or the long, lingering kiss at the doorway that almost persuaded her to invite Jack in for a nightcap. At the last
moment, she'd cut short the temptation. Tomorrow was another
day. They had planned a morning tour of several remote
beaches by helicopter. Then Jack was going to teach her the
fundamentals of surfing. By tomorrow night, she'd know
him better and maybe then take the next step. She kissed him
goodnight, quickly.

Walking into her condominium, Judy noticed the blinking
red light on her phone. Two messages were propped against
it. She picked them up. The first read, "1:20 P.M. Mr. Bond
called. Urgent you call your office in Boston. You are needed
for an important assignment."

The second message read, "4:50 P.M. Mr. Bond called
again. He has arranged transportation for you to Honolulu on
Hawaiian Air at 10:00 A.M. tomorrow morning. Connecting
flight United 96, leaves Honolulu at 12:45 P.M. for Boston via
San Francisco. He will brief you on your assignment and will
arrange travel to Fairport, Conn. He suggests you sleep on
the plane."

Judy slumped onto her bed, muttering an oath. Drat the
black luck. She and Jack were just getting acquainted, and
had the basis for a growing relationship. Now she would have
to leave before her heart found out. Her career was killing her
personal life.

There was a six-hour time difference. It was now 5:00 A.M.
in Boston. Impossible to call Bond at that hour. Besides, she
didn't know his home phone number. What could be so damn
important? Fairport? That was the sleepy little town on the
Sound where her sister, Brenda, lived. What a coincidence!

She slid out of her blouse and slacks and walked into the
bathroom.

Clearly it was an important assignment or they wouldn't
have interrupted her vacation. They wouldn't have asked her
to fly back. It was a tough break, but it could be a steppingstone
for her career. She turned on the water in the tub, tested the
temperature, took off the rest of her clothes and slid into the
tub.

She'd call Jack and ask him to drive her to the airport. He'd understand—opportunity was like the perfect wave, when it came along, you had to ride it. Besides, it would be a good test of their newfound friendship.

The Man's wife woke early, and for several minutes just looked at her husband sleeping alongside her. Her other half. She smiled and thought, What a fantastic lover, what a wonderful, talented total man. Love had been good to her. She felt so lucky to have him. Lately there had been a nagging concern that there might be another woman, but yesterday morning had convinced her that there couldn't be.

She moved closer and cuddled next to him until the alarm went off, some twenty minutes later.

At breakfast, Dempsey read about the Judge's murder on the front page of the New York *Times*. They had most of the facts right and said some nice words about the progress of his investigation.

The Today Show featured all three murders, and Jane Pauley announced that Sam Grady would be interviewed on Friday morning's program. Dempsey remembered now that Mary had told him about a call from NBC-TV, but he'd ignored it in the press of events. He and Brenda would have to make it a point to watch the program. Sam would handle the interview perfectly. *The Today Show* was still one of Brenda's favorites, but she missed Barbara.

Dempsey checked his watch and rose to leave. He kissed Cindy's forehead, tousled her hair, smiled and said, "Buttercup, be a good girl for Mommy."

Cindy's eyes stayed glued to the television. Through a mouthful of cereal, she giggled her goodbye.

Brenda walked to the kitchen door with Jim and kissed him with feeling. "Be careful, darling. You mean everything to me. There's a madman out there someplace, and I'm terrified he may try to kill you next."

"Don't worry, sweetheart," he said, putting an arm around

her shoulders. "My mother didn't raise a fool. Besides, he's after Fred today." Dempsey picked up his briefcase from the chair and added, "Don't forget to meet me for Bill's funeral services at two. I'm one of the pallbearers."

He kissed her again, closed the kitchen door and headed toward his "Bullet" parked in the driveway. Suddenly Cindy jumped from her chair, opened the door and raced out to get her doll from the wagon in the driveway.

Seconds later, a violent explosion shook the kitchen and shattered the windows. Brenda screamed and ran through the kitchen door.

Cindy was huddled silently by the doorway. She was shaken, but unharmed. The "Bullet" was a flaming wreck. A livid Dempsey was emerging from the swimming pool, soaking wet, but otherwise unhurt. With an instinct learned only in combat, he had hurled himself over the hedge into the swimming pool a split second before the explosion.

"That son of a bitch tried to kill me with a grenade," Dempsey was shouting. "Look at my car! That no-good murdering prick, he wrecked it!"

Brenda was sobbing with relief at seeing both Cindy and Jim unhurt. She clutched Cindy to her and called out, "Jim, are you all right?"

"I'm fine, don't worry about me. Call the fire department! That bastard has to be close by." Dempsey had unholstered his .357 Magnum and was looking around the yard.

"Darling, be careful . . . be careful." Brenda, clearly frightened, looked at Cindy.

Her daughter's face registered horror. Tears welled in her eyes and flowed silently down her cheeks. She stared and pointed mutely. There in the driveway, her doll was burning. The lifelike features were melting into one amorphous lump of burning, molten plastic. Wisps of black smoke curled up from the flames.

Cindy shuddered and blurted out, "Daddy, Daddy, he killed my dolly."

Brenda hugged Cindy to her protectively. She whispered reassuringly, "Sweetheart, everything's all right. Your daddy's not hurt. That bad man tried to kill him. We'll get you a new dolly." She carried Cindy into the house, half running toward the phone.

Dempsey realized that before he could search for the Man, he'd have to put out the fire. Flames were now dangerously close to the house. Dashing into the garage, he seized a portable fire extinguisher. Three minutes later the fire was out.

The wreckage was smoldering when two fire engines and three police cars, sirens screaming, arrived.

Dempsey directed the police in a search of the immediate neighborhood. They found no trace of the Man. No one had seen him. Farrow arrived with the second wave of police cars, his red hair more tousled than usual. Dempsey told him that he hadn't seen the Man either, it was just a sudden premonition, a sixth sense, that made him dive for cover.

"Tom, assign a detail to clean up this mess. I know it was a grenade." Dempsey's face was a grim mask. "See if your men can find fragments. I'll bet anyone a new car it was one of the stolen grenades."

The Chief had no takers.

Dempsey was suddenly aware Spike Briggs was there, too. He hadn't seen him pull his Jaguar next to the curb. Briggs was walking across the lawn.

"Where the hell did you come from?" Dempsey asked, with a quizzical look.

"I was on my way to work when I heard the report. I was close by, so I stopped to help. Glad to see you're O.K."

Dempsey thought he saw that flicker of a smile on Brigg's face again. Or was it his imagination? "Thanks," he replied, simmering. "I think we've got everything under control. I haven't had time yet to tell Farrow about last night, but I'm assuming your troopers will handle security. I need my men to solve these murders. This guy is annoying the shit out of me."

"Maybe we should assign a couple of men to guard you," Spike said and laughed. "You're not young enough to be jumping over hedges into pools. Haven't you heard? The wet look is out!"

"Go fuck yourself!" growled Dempsey, heading back into the house to change into dry clothes. He ignored the twinges he'd felt in his chest. They must be a sign of age.

Brenda was crying. The explosion had horrified her. Jim and Cindy had both come close to death. Thank God they hadn't been hurt. The chills swept through her. What kind of a man would try to kill a child? And . . . she shuddered violently . . . the Man . . . he'd surely try to kill Jim again. She closed her eyes and talked silently with God.

Jim did his best to console her. He hadn't known that Cindy had been outside. He hugged Cindy, but she kept wriggling away. Somehow she held him responsible for the loss of her doll. But, as Brenda explained, biting her lip, it was difficult to expect a child, especially Cindy, after what she'd been through, to understand violence and death. Even the death of a doll.

Cindy kept asking over and over whether her dolly felt any pain while she was burning. Brenda winced at each question and kept repeating, "No, your dolly had no feelings. She felt no pain."

Cindy wasn't convinced, knowing how much it had hurt when she'd burned her finger. And it hadn't even been on fire.

As soon as he could, Jim left, reassuring Brenda, "Sweetheart, it's my job and I'm damn good at it. Don't forget, if he's the Man, I'm Superman. I'm indestructible." Brenda relaxed. She knew he was right; he knew what he was doing and was good at it. No one was better. Just last night, Grady had said so. Now, almost back to normal, she'd take Cindy down to the Carousel and pick out a new doll.

Dempsey borrowed Farrow's unmarked blue-and-white cruiser, skirted around the group cleaning the wreckage in the driveway and headed to work. He felt lousy. He wasn't worried about himself, but the Man had gone too far. He'd almost hurt Cindy. That was more than his considerable pride could take. He had to catch him fast.

The Man drove slowly, weaving his way through morning traffic. Then it happened. A red Ferrari passed him. He felt lightheaded, fuzzy. Instantly, he was the world's greatest Formula I race driver.

That had to be Niki Lauda who had passed him. Yes, Mario Andretti in his John Player Special was in the other lane, and John Watson in his Brabham was behind them. He hadn't yet spotted Jody Scheckter or James Hunt's McClaren, but was sure they were close to the pace. They always were.

It was the Grand Prix at Monaco, Princess Grace would be watching, her eyes on him. He needed this race for the championship. Flooring the accelerator, within seconds he overtook Lauda. Engine screaming at 6,800 rpm, he swung in front of the Ferrari, keeping Lauda in a pocket.

Damn, they must have lapped the field. Cars were bunched in front of him. He'd have to pull around. Downshifting, he swung to the inside, slid perilously close to the curve, then barreled into the straightaway. Behind him, he heard the squeal of brakes and the crash of metal against metal. He'd pass them on the grass. What the hell were pedestrians doing on the course? "Look out, you damn fool!" he shouted. "Kill," whispered the voice in his inner ear. "Kill."

The distant wail of the police siren snapped the Man back to reality. Quickly, he braked and pulled back into the traffic flow. Christ, he was losing his grip on reality. His mind was stuck in neutral. If he wasn't careful, he'd wreck his whole plan.

The Man was not disappointed that Dempsey was still alive. He hadn't planned to kill him with the grenade. It had been thrown deliberately and accurately under his car. At the worst, if Dempsey hadn't taken evasive action, it would only have wounded him. The explosion was intended to frighten Fairport and to embarrass and torment the Chief even further.

As for that brat, Cindy, it didn't make any difference. She was getting to be a pain in the ass. She'd almost ruined his plan.

Dempsey was way down on the Man's list, the very last name. The Man had assigned him the two of clubs, the lowest card in the deck. A special death was planned for him. "I'll rip his mind out." The Man laughed, a strange, demented laugh. He had to keep Dempsey going until then. The Chief was a fireball. A comet. The danger was he'd burn out too soon.

"No." The Man laughed again. "The ten of spades belongs to someone else. It belongs to Fred."

On his way to headquarters, Dempsey stopped twice. First, he pulled into the parking lot at St. Vincent's, the parish church where the funeral services for Donnelly would be held. Dempsey knew that the First Selectman had been a regular at St. Vincent's since he'd entered politics. It was good politics to be seen in church every Sunday, every holiday, every special service, and Donnelly had been a superb politician.

St. Vincent's was a modern granite-and-glass church with spacious grass lawns attractively framed with flower beds and roses. The rectory, of matching construction, was located behind the church and connected to it by a stained-glass walkway. Dempsey had always thought the church to be attractive, but completely out of character on a street of white frame Colonial homes, many of them built before the Revolutionary War.

Father O'Leary greeted Jim warmly. Although of different religious belief, he had great respect for Dempsey. He knew the feeling was mutual. Each summer for the past four years, Dempsey had arranged sailing classes for a group of boys from St. Vincent's. Jim had taught the class on racing techniques himself. It had been his idea, and it had been a huge success.

Dempsey smiled his greeting. Father O'Leary was a caricature of a young Irish priest, with a broad, beaming face. Just ten years before, he had been an All-American tackle for Notre Dame, with a bright financial future as a professional football player. But Father O'Leary had never given it a second thought. He had only one calling. His older two brothers were also priests, and his only sister a nun. He had a great way with people and was well respected in the community. Dempsey usually kidded the priest about his weight problems, but not this morning.

"Terrible thing, these senseless murders, Jim." O'Leary sighed, putting his huge hand on the other man's shoulder. "The people are upset. At our parish meeting last night everyone was talking about them. The fear . . . it's like a grass fire, spreading out in all directions. People are arming themselves. They're frightened, angry, and there's talk of vigilante groups. There's a violent, dangerous mood developing. Violence always begets violence. What can we do to help?"

"Nothing, Father." Dempsey wished he had a better answer. "I'm sure we'll solve this quickly, but . . ." He hesitated, then looked straight at O'Leary. "A few prayers wouldn't hurt."

After a moment of silence, he continued, "We have a good lead on the killer. He left a pretty clear set of prints at the Judge's place. We hope to be able to identify him today."

The priest nodded and bowed his head, his hands clasped together. Neither of them spoke for almost a minute, then Dempsey said, "I stopped to check on the funeral arrangements for Bill."

After getting the information he wanted, Dempsey left. He saw Donnelly's widow and daughter drive into the church parking lot just as he was leaving. He waved, but didn't stop to talk.

Less than a quarter of a mile away, he pulled into a parking space in the town square and went into Tony's barbershop for his monthly haircut. There was an undercurrent of talk about the murders, but Dempsey didn't enter into the conversation. He felt glum and uncommunicative. Other than to say, "We'll get him soon," he ignored the discussion about the killings. He seemed deep in thought, and the others in the shop, knowing the pressure on him, respected his silence. But Dempsey could sense the circle of eyes staring at him.

With his hair neatly trimmed, Dempsey crossed the street and entered the side door of the Congregational Church. It was one of the oldest churches in New England. Dempsey had always thought it was one of the prettiest, too. The interior was neat and plain, with twenty rows of white pews facing a large white cross raised on the altar at the end of the center aisle. The Reverend Paul Fredericks was bent over in front of the cross. He turned at the sound of footsteps. Dempsey was surprised to see how frail and feeble the minister seemed. His shock of pure-white hair added to the impression of age, as did the thin, almost cadaverous face.

"Morning, Reverend." Dempsey spoke loudly for the other's benefit.

The elderly clergyman peered closely at Dempsey, as if he were a stranger. A flash of recognition came into his eyes, and he smiled warmly. "Morning, Chief. How's Brenda?"

"Just fine, and Cindy, too," Dempsey added, to forestall the minister's next question. He didn't have time to get into a long social conversation. "I stopped by to ask about Hetty Starr's funeral arrangements."

"Four P.M. on Friday. Private burial service. Family only. Funeral service is one P.M. at Riverside Presbyterian Church in New York." The minister ticked off the facts with the speed and precision of a telephone recording. Considering Fredericks' physical condition, Dempsey was astonished at the clarity of the man's mind.

"And Judge Waller's funeral?" Dempsey asked.

"Not sure yet. Probably two P.M. on Saturday." The minister answered, his eyes searching Dempsey's face. "Will there be any more killings, Jim?"

The question caught Dempsey off guard. "I hope not, Reverend," he answered quickly. "We should catch him today. But we're drawing up security plans now for the funerals . . . just in case."

The minister blanched at the thought of possibly more violence. His wizened hands shook. He clasped them together and turned away, toward the cross.

Dempsey said goodbye, stopped for a few minutes to use the church lavatory, walked across the square to his car and drove directly to headquarters.

From his vantage point, the Man had been watching Dempsey's every move. That meddling Boy Scout Chief would never catch him. He almost laughed out loud as he listened to Dempsey reassuring the minister. The police would catch him today. Pure cow manure. Meadow muffin malarky! It was time for the Man to take over and act. It was time to fulfill a promise. A promise to the voice. The unknown old man. It was time to kill Fred.

As soon as Dempsey said goodbye to the minister, the Man stepped out of the shadows. The Reverend Fredericks had turned toward the altar and had knelt to pray.

"Forgive this evil devil, Father, for he knows not what he does. Provide the police with the vision and wisdom to catch him before his dark hand comes out of the black night and kills other innocent men and women."

The minister never heard the Man whisper, "Go with God and he'll go with you." He never even sensed his presence until it was too late, much too late. Powerful fingers encircled his neck, choked off his prayer, choked off his scream, choked off his breath, choked out his life. The gloved hands relaxed their grip and the minister slumped lifelessly in front of the altar. Fred was dead.

The Man moved quickly, sliding Fredericks feetfirst to the foot of the large wooden cross. He went directly to the maintenance closet and brought back an aluminim ten-foot stepladder. The Man lifted the frail corpse as if it were a rag doll and rapidly climbed the ladder. He set the minister on the top of the ladder with his back toward the cross. Then, one by one, he lashed the man's wrists to the cross with short pieces of rawhide thong. From a sheath on his belt, he removed an ice pick and plunged it through a playing card into the minister's chest, then removed the ladder, tied the ankles to the cross and returned the ladder to the closet.

Finished, he glanced once at the Reverend Fredericks hanging on the cross, lit a Tiparillo and walked out the side door of the church.

Belli met Dempsey in the hall and walked with him toward the Chief's corner office.

"Sorry to hear about your car. Are you O.K.?"

Dempsey's curt nod and facial expression told Belli that he didn't want to talk about his narrow escape, so Belli switched subjects. "We've almost completed interviewing the list of possible bomb suspects. Funny thing, one of the suspects on our list has not been seen since last Sunday afternoon, the day before the bombing.''

"Who is it?'' asked Dempsey.

"Dr. David Orton, the psychiatrist.''

"Dave? Where the hell is he? Hey, that's right. He missed Rotary.'' Dempsey waited for an explanation.

Belli stepped back and let Dempsey enter the doorway first, then followed him into his office. "Orton's nurse, Miss Shepherd, reported that he called her Monday morning, said he and his wife, Catherine, were going sailing in their Rhodes Reliant. Orton said he'd be back next weekend and asked his nurse to cancel his appointments this week.'' Belli gestured. "Gave her the week off, too.''

"That sounds like Dave.'' Dempsey smiled faintly. "He's always been impetuous, does what he wants, when he wants. Works when he feels like it. Wouldn't it be nice to take a week off and go sailing? I'd head straight for Nantucket.'' Dampsey sounded envious, a faraway look in his eyes.

"Chief, I know that Orton's a friend of yours. Did you know that in the Army he had extensive training in the use of explosives?'' Belli looked at him steadily.

"No, but I'm not surprised. Dave's a talented guy. Keeps himself in great shape, a real jock. Don't play him anything for money.'' Dempsey held up his index finger, as if in warning. "He doesn't like to lose. We used to play poker. Dave's a wild gambler, with balls. I remember one time we were playing table stakes, he bet his entire stake—two hundred bucks—on a pair of threes. Fortunately, I shaded him with a pair of fours.''

Dempsey smiled at the memory, then impatiently said, "I wish we'd get that fingerprint report from the FBI. Let's hope we find a match.''

"Don't forget, both of us are on that list,'' said Belli, sucking in his stomach. As he left Dempsey's office, he thought, Better cut down on Marie's pasta. He was getting a gut.

Police headquarters were buzzing with the news of the

grenade attack on Dempsey's car. Friends flowed in and out, congratulating the Chief on his narrow escape.

On the twenty-fifth floor of the RCA building in New York, a one-way discussion was just concluding in the teak-paneled executive office of Filbert Flagg, director of network news for the NBC television network.

"It's the biggest news story of the year. We've got to cover it live," summoned up Flagg. "First the Selectman, then Hetty Starr, then Judge Waller, now a grenade attack on the Chief of Police. I want a live interview in Fairport with him. What's his name? He's hot news."

He turned for an answer to Tuesday Fields, his girl Friday.

"We already called. The Police Chief was too busy to talk," said Miss Fields. "His name is Jim Dempsey."

"He'll talk to us. Just let Dempsey know in a subtle way that we can handle this story several ways, giving sympathetic treatment to Fairport's mass murders, or tearing his town apart."

Flagg put his hands flat on the desk and looked at his freshly manicured nails. "Ask Dempsey which it will be! Don't forget to remind him that we reach over fifteen million homes across America every night. The American people have a right to know what's going on in Fairport."

Miss Fields shook her head. "It's not as if he were sitting on his rear doing nothing, chief. The poor guy is trying to solve three murders, plus protect his own life."

Flagg ignored her. "Better yet, set up a group discussion for tomorrow night. Dempsey might not be able to talk in front of cameras. We don't want a dull show. Line up that fellow Grady of the FBI and the head of the Connecticut State Police, too. John Churchman will interview the three of them. I like the way this is shaping up."

"But, chief, Grady has already agreed to be on *The Today Show* tomorrow morning," Miss Fields explained. "Jane Pauley is interviewing him."

"More exposure won't hurt. It will help his career in the FBI. I understand he's a bright rising star." As usual, Flagg's logic smothered any opposition to his ideas.

"But, chief," Miss Fields interjected, "John Churchman is in China with the president."

"That Churchman's never around when we need him." Flagg shook his head in annoyance. "Never mind, use Warren Petty for the interview. He's a man's man . . . be even better."

"Great plan, chief. You're a genius." Flagg's assistant director, known around the network as Mr. Yes-Yes, complimented him.

Tuesday Fields bit her lip. As she walked past, Flagg commented, "Sorry if I offended you, G.F. Don't forget, NBC didn't become number one in news by considering people's feelings. Our job is to inform America by getting the news out in the most exciting and interesting way possible. Now get your pretty ass in gear!"

In the executive office of the Man, his private phone rang. Before answering, he asked his two associates if they would mind postponing their discussion until a later time. They left his office. He closed the door and answered his hot line. A kittenish voice was purring softly on the other end of the line. It was Jeanne.

"Darling, I'm starving to death. You're not feeding me often enough. Meow! Meow!"

"Hey, pussycat, I've been busy. Don't you fashion photographers ever have a busy season?" He leaned back and put his feet up on the desk.

"This is it, but I took a day off. It's too beautiful to work. I'm sitting on my lounge in my bikini, taking mental snapshots of you." There was a moment of silence. "They're for the centerfold of *Cosmopolitan*."

He laughed. "Do you think you can fit all of me on two pages?"

"You braggart! Say, I've had a sexy fantasy all morning. It's the two of us having a picnic today in my little boat." She whispered softly. "It's simply gorgeous out on the Sound, and I'll promise you the best box lunch you've ever eaten, if you bring a pint of your special cream for me."

"That sounds too good to miss, kittycat. I'll try to make it.

But I've got a busy day, so if I can't make lunch, I'll stop by later. Your parlor tricks are plenty good enough for me. We can save the boat idea for another day. It sounds exciting.''

"I'll be waiting for you. Try to make it for lunch. Take some vitamin E. You're not as young as you used to be! Meow, meow, meow,'' purred Jeanne.

"You silly nut. Goodbye, see you later,'' said the Man, laughing. Hanging up, he could hear that she'd turned up the volume on her stereo, which was playing "I'd Like to Make It with You.''

At 11:30 Mary buzzed the Chief to tell him that Sam Grady was on the line.

"We've almost struck out, Jim.'' Sam's voice sounded flat, disappointed.

"What do you mean?''

"Well, I've been waiting to call you with a full report, but we don't have it yet. We've been able to check the fingerprints on forty-four of your suspects. Sorry to tell you . . .'' Grady hesitated. "They're all negative—no match.''

"Oh shit!'' Dempsey muttered. "How about the other one?''

"We don't know. His card is missing from the files. He doesn't appear on the microfilm records, either. It's most unusual. The Washington Bureau can't explain it.''

"Who is he?''

"David Orton. A psychiatrist.''

"Orton!'' exploded Dempsey. "I know him well. His name came up this morning. Been out of touch since the murders started.'' Dempsey cradled the phone on his shoulder and buzzed for Mary. As soon as she appeared, he told her, "Tell Gus to contact the Coast Guard. Have them locate Orton's boat.''

On the other end of the phone, Sam listened patiently. Then he continued, "That may not be necessary, Jim. We'll have his prints this afternoon. We've tracked down a duplicate in the Army Bureau of Records. They're sending it over to our lab.'' He laughed softly. "There's some good in the federal bureaucracy. We've got duplicates of everything.''

Dempsey never got a chance to reply or to thank Sam for his help, for at that moment Sergeant Piccollo burst into the office, white-faced and breathless.

"Jesus, Chief, they just found Reverend Fredericks crucified at his church!"

"Good Lord," uttered Dempsey, as he dropped the phone on its cradle and raced for his borrowed car, with Piccollo alongside.

Over the phone, Sam had heard everything and sat stunned. He called Briggs to give him the incredible news. Briggs had left for an early lunch.

They screeched to a halt in front of the Congregational Church. Dempsey and Piccollo leaped out on a dead run toward the church. The ambulance was arriving from the opposite direction. It braked at the last minute, but not enough, and too late. The ambulance smashed into the side of Dempsey's borrowed cruiser. Dempsey never even looked back.

Inside the church, a small, horror-struck crowd had gathered, milling about silently. Even the faces of the hardened police were frozen with anger and disbelief. There, behind the altar, on the wooden cross, hung the lifeless body of the Reverend Paul Fredericks, clad in his white cassock. His long, flowing white mane obscured his gaunt but gentle face. His arms and legs had been tied to the cross with strips of rawhide. An icepick protruded from a small red stain on his chest. There was no need to check for a pulse. The ambulance was not needed. It was much too late.

Once again, Dempsey cautioned his men not to disturb anything until everything had been checked carefully for clues. They hustled the onlookers out of the church. Later, gently lowering the minister's body down from the cross, they saw that the icepick firmly held the ten of spades over his heart.

Dempsey was visibly upset, his face bunched up, angry with himself. "The Man told us the ten of spades was for Fred. It wasn't a first name, it was a last name. Fredericks. Damn, I talked to him myself, this morning. We should have thought of last names. Damn!"

While Dempsey searched for clues, Piccollo had been looking for witnesses. The church sexton, Charles Thomby, had discovered Fredericks on the cross and had called the police. Piccollo was questioning him. Suddenly, he waved excitedly for Dempsey, who hurried over to where they were seated in the front pew.

"Tell the Chief what you just told me," commanded Piccollo with an eager intensity.

The old sexton was clearly frightened. He looked around, slumped lower in the pew and stammered, "Well, as I came in the front door . . . I saw a man . . . hurrying through the chapel . . . he went out the side door."

"Did you recognize him?" asked Dempsey, leaning closer and watching the sexton's face closely.

"I thought it was Mr. Nichols, the lawyer," quavered Thomby. "But now I'm not so sure. I don't want any part of this." He buried his head in his hands.

Dempsey put his hand reassuringly on the sexton's shoulder. "Take it easy, Mr. Thomby. No one will hurt you." Then he turned to Piccollo. "Lou, have one of your men take down Mr. Thomby's statement. You pick up Ned Nichols and bring him to headquarters. I want to talk to him."

"A minister has been crucified." The word spread like wildfire through all of Fairport in minutes, across the nation in less than an hour. All three television networks and the major radio networks carried special news bulletins featuring the "crucifixion."

Dempsey was angry. He told Mary, "It wasn't a crucifixion. Fredericks was choked and stabbed with an icepick. Then he was tied to the cross. Damn sensationalists. This kind of reporting doesn't help us."

The damage had been done. The world had been told that the Man had crucified a religious leader. The people were incensed.

In Congress, Senator Barker, from California, interrupted the debate on the Farm Bill in the Senate to report on the crucifixion and to say that he was sponsoring a bill to double the budget of the FBI. "Our people deserve protection from maniacs, and they're going to get it," he thundered. "If local policemen can't protect our citizens, we'll build a national police force." A surprising number of Senators rose and applauded.

The Man was gleefully aware of what was happening. Newspaper and television reporters, photographers and camera crews were descending on Fairport in swarms. The Motor Inn had more requests for bookings than ever in its history. Most motel and hotel rooms were filled within a forty-five mile radius. Some of the journalists who had driven out from New York had to drive almost back to the city to find a vacant room. The media men expected more killings, and they were determined to be on the scene of the next one.

The Man had planned it that way.

Dempsey sat in his office, thinking. He rubbed his head, trying to stimulate his thought process. He was hoping for an inspiration. None came.

He was waiting for Piccollo to bring in Ned Nichols. Ned was fast becoming an enigma. He'd been seen hurrying out of the church. Why? Christ, he'd known Ned for years. He was no mass killer. Or was he? How does a mass killer act, when he's not killing? Probably as normal as possible.

Ned had a disciplined, rational and brilliant mind, with a quality of icy self-assurance that turned many people off. Lately he'd become argumentative and arrogant. There was a difference between assurance and arrogance. Assurance listens to other people, arrogance doesn't. Dempsey's neck muscles tightened. Recent discussions with Ned had been hostile confrontations. There was a deep-seated hostility about him. But Ned had used this hostility in a creative way, made it work for him, turned it into money.

Dempsey rubbed the back of his neck with his strong fingers. Was Ned's need for money so great that he had thrown away all compassion? It couldn't be. Nichols was a wealthy man. Whatever was driving him, whatever the evil influence, it wasn't a need for money. It had to be greed. A lust for money, the drive to accumulate material possessions that becomes so persuasive, so all-consuming that, for some, it occupies every waking moment. Dempsey had seen it before. It drove men to do unbelievable things, clouding their minds and ultimately so possessing them that they couldn't reason right from wrong. Was Nichols approaching that condition?

Why the hell was money so important to some people? He shook his head. He and Brenda got along just fine without much money. Of course, they had each other, and Cindy. He glanced at Cindy's picture on his desk and reached out to touch it.

What had been the relationship between Nichols and Hetty? He hadn't heard any rumors. Fairport had its gossip network, and Dempsey kept his ears open. Their relationship must have been strictly business. Hetty had been very wealthy, millions. How greedy had Nichols become? He'd better take a look at Hetty's will. Nichols was the administrator of Hetty's estate. Hell, he'd also drawn the will and had custody of it. A greedy, crooked lawyer could accumulate substantial wealth quickly. What the hell was he thinking? Ned Nichols wasn't crooked.

It was 1:15 P.M. when Piccollo arrived at headquarters with an iron grip on Ned Nichols' arm. The lawyer's steel-gray hair was disheveled. His face flushed in indignation, lips bared over his teeth, eyes blazing. Nichols was seething.

"Jim, what the hell is going on?" he asked, in a hostile voice. "Tell your bulldog to get his teeth out of me. He just dragged me out of my car. I was on my way to have lunch with a lady friend of mine. My arm feels broken. I'll sue the fucking town."

"Shut up, Ned, and sit down." Dempsey's voice was firm and icy. "It's been a rough week. We don't need any bullshit from anyone, including you."

Piccollo released Nichols' arm, and the lawyer moved toward the couch, rubbing his arm vigorously.

"Chief, he was driving down toward the beach," Piccollo started to explain. Dempsey interrupted.

"Thanks, Lou. Why don't you leave us alone for a while?" He held the door for Piccollo and closed it behind him.

Dempsey sat on the soft leather chair opposite Nichols on the couch. He gave the lawyer a long quizzical look, then asked, "O.K., Ned. What were you doing at the Congregational Church?"

Nichols started to deny being at the church, but the cold look on Dempsey's face changed his mind. Fighting his emotions, he spoke calmly. "I stopped to see Fredericks. I was making final arrangements for Hetty's service. I'm administrator of her estate and executor of her will. But you know that."

"Did you see him?" Dempsey was still staring at Nichols intently.

Nichols shook his head. "Not alive. He was hanging on the cross. It was a horrible sight. I got out of there as fast as I could."

"Why didn't you call us?"

"I saw the sexton coming in the front door. I knew he'd report the murder. I didn't want to get involved."

Dempsey noticed that the blazing light had left Nichols' eyes, but they were still hostile.

"That's not very smart, Ned. You know better," Dempsey said quietly.

"It was a spur-of-the-moment decision. It was wrong. I should have called you."

"Did you kill him?" Dempsey asked bluntly.

"Good God, no. I can't stand the sight of blood. It makes me ill." Nichols swallowed.

Dempsey abruptly changed his line of questioning. "Ned, are you mentioned in Hetty's will?"

Nichols hesitated, inhaled deeply, then answered, "Yes, I am. Our firm updated her will several years ago. You'll find out soon enough. I'll inherit almost half of her estate."

Dempsey gave a low whistle. "Sounds like a real motive."

Nichols blanched, nodded affirmatively and added quickly, "You should also know that I handle some of Judge Waller's financial investments. I'm executor of his will, also. If you're looking for a financial motive, I'm clearly your man."

Their eyes locked in a long, cold stare before Dempsey

spoke. "Ned, it all boils down to one simple fact. Your bare ass is exposed."

Nichols's glare seeped slowly into a smile, ever so faint. "I don't think so," he said. "I've got a firm alibi if I ever needed it. In fact, I've got three of them. Three young—"

The insistent knocking on the door interrupted Nichols. Belli burst into the room. "Chief, sorry to interrupt you, but Orton's yacht is still tied up at his dock. He's not on it."

Before Dempsey could comment, Mary buzzed. "Chief, it's Sam Grady on the phone. He says it's urgent."

Grady's phone call changed the whole complexion of the murder investigation.

"You've got him nailed, Jim. Your man is David Orton," said Grady.

"Orton? It can't be!" Dempsey sat stunned. "Are you sure?"

"Positive! The prints on the Judge's toothpaste tube match Orton's exactly. There's no question about it," exulted Grady. "They've sent up radiophoto copies of Orton's prints from Washington. He's your man. I'm sending them over to you."

"Thanks, Sam. We needed a break. We're putting out an APB immediately." Dempsey leaped from his chair, his hand extended towards Nichols, a wide grin on his face. "Ned, I'll give you a call. Thanks for dropping by. Nice of you. I appreciate your cooperation.

"Mary, give my apologies to Madelaine. She'll understand." He checked his watch. The funeral service was only twenty-five minutes away.

"Gus, it's Orton. He's the Man. Positive identification. Put out an APB. Get Tom, Paul, Lou and your team. Put on your vests and let's fly. We don't need a warrant. I'll take full responsibility." Dempsey ran out of his office, toward the parking area. He had appropriated a new police cruiser on his return from the church. Farrow's had been towed away by the police wrecker.

At 1:40 P.M., Ned Nichols sauntered out of police headquarters, his steel-gray hair neatly combed, a broad grin on his face.

• • •

Seven minutes later, two police cruisers blocked off the entrance to Sunrise Lane. Four others screeched to a halt in the circular driveway of a charming yellow-frame Colonial set in the center of a well-manicured lawn in a tranquil, upper-middle-class residential neighborhood. Flower beds, blooming with petunias, marigolds and snapdragons, framed the front entrance.

With Dempsey in the lead, a picked team of twelve policemen and officers, all wearing bulletproof vests, with drawn service revolvers and Winchester 12-gauge riot shotguns, surrounded the house. There were three entrances, the front, the kitchen and the office. Despite strict zoning ordinances, Fairport allowed doctors and dentists to operate their businesses in a portion of their own homes.

Dempsey glanced at three days' collection of newspapers on the front steps. He rang the front doorbell directly below the nameplate, David S. Orton, M.D. There was no answer. He knocked loudly. There was still no answer.

He signaled to Piccollo, who had the talent of a master locksmith. If it operated with clicks, springs or slides, he could open it. Piccollo inserted a pick and jiggled the pins in the tumbler. In one minute, the front door swung silently open. Dempsey eased fluidly inside. The front hall was empty.

He waved Piccollo forward, and together they searched the house and office, room by room, from top to bottom. There was no one home; both the house and office were empty. The Monday New York *Times* was on the nurse's desk.

Dempsey now signaled for a team of seven policemen to search the house in minute detail. Five policemen maintained a guard outside.

The two cruisers that had been blocking Sunrise Lane were released back to headquarters. Dempsey directed the search team. "I want everything checked carefully. We're looking for an arsenal of weapons. We also want pictures of Orton and anything that will give us background on him."

Within minutes, there was a triumphant shout from Paul Rice in the back bedroom. There, in the corner of a closet, covered by a blanket, was an M-16 automatic rifle and two land mines, matching the description of those stolen from the armory.

Minutes later, in the pine-paneled game room in the basement, under the pool table, they found a case of dynamite with seven sticks missing and a canister of VX nerve gas, marked WD-1-No.4. A Mauser .243 rifle with a Bushnell telescopic sight was leaning against the doctor's wine rack.

In a small, locked laboratory, adjacent to the game room, they found a glass display case with four live rattlesnakes. "Jesus, Mary and Joseph!" Belli crossed himself and backed out of the room. "The place is crawling with snakes. Let me out of here!"

Dempsey called a war conference of his officers in the psychiatrist's office.

"David Orton is undoubtedly the Man. His fingerprints were at the Judge's, and now, in his basement, we've found the same type of snake that killed Hetty Starr, as well as some of the items stolen from the armory, including the type of dynamite that killed Donnelly. Orton still has a sizable arsenal, probably with him. He's extremely dangerous. The most disturbing thing to me is that the VX nerve gas wasn't reported stolen. VX is the most potent nerve gas ever developed. One canister could kill thousands of people. If the Man has more of this toxic gas . . ." Dempsey left his gruesome thought unfinished. "We must find out how he got it and how much he took."

"Tom." Dempsey pointed menacingly. "I want you to find out how much VX the Man has. I don't want you to do anything else. This is top, top priority. Believe me, this VX is extremely dangerous. I've seen it tested. It killed everything in sight. Get in touch with both Grady and Briggs immediately. We need their help. Stress the urgency." Dempsey's face reflected his deep concern. "I want a report in an hour. And for God's sake, don't let the media know anything about this gas. There'd be mass panic. We'll inform them in due time and with the right caution. Get going!"

Farrow nodded silently, his young face grave as he left the room.

Dempsey stood up, looking directly at Belli. "Gus, I want a full description of Orton released to the wire services just as soon as you can get back to headquarters. Do we have any good, up-to-date pictures of Orton?"

"We've found two that I think are Orton, one with his wife and one of him alone," replied Belli, handing the pictures to Dempsey.

"This is a good one," said Dempsey, returning the picture of Orton alone. "Get this on the wire. I want his picture and description on every news show tonight and on every front page in the country. Have enlargements made for our men, as well as the state police and the FBI."

He set the other picture on the table.

"I also want your men to check on Orton's wife, Catherine. If she's with him, it should make it easier to find him. If she's not, we may have another murder on our hands. Gus, let's move. I want a dossier on Orton by three-thirty."

Belli nodded, rose and left the room.

"Paul, you and Lou stay here with four men and take this place apart. I want you to find a pin, if he's hidden one. Anything of major importance, call me," Dempsey commanded. "Now, let's get going."

Alone in the psychiatrist's office, Dempsey had a nagging sensation of worry. He couldn't shake it. It kept throbbing in his head. There was something wrong. There was something missing. What was it?

A lone bagpiper played mournfully by the doorway of St. Vincent's as Donnelly's family filed into the church behind his coffin. Some four hundred people, friends, neighbors, politicians and curiosity seekers, lined the walkway and crowded into the church. State policemen in crisp, neat uniforms were spotted strategically around the perimeter of the church.

Donnelly's wife, Madelaine, and their two daughters sat in the front pew. They were surrounded by family and friends. Brenda sat on the aisle in the center of the church.

Father O'Leary looked directly at Madelaine as he began his brief eulogy.

"We all die a little death when we lose the people we love. We ache, we hurt, we agonize, we want to shake a fist at someone. Even you, God. We pray that you will guide us and make us better, not bitter.

"Bill Donnelly spent his lifetime in the service of our community. He shared his abilities, his dreams and his love with us, and he made the supreme sacrifice. He gave his life in our service. He died of an illness; yes, an illness. Not his own illness, but an illness in our society and an illness of one particular individual."

The audience stirred slightly, and Father O'Leary held out his giant arms. Once again, there was total silence.

"Someone has said that a death at any age is dying young. Death is like a door. We move through the corridor of not darkness, but light; not pain, but peace; not extinction, but to God. We now commit our beloved Selectman into the hand of God, whose love does not fail and will never cease.

"We are told that to mourn is blessed. Does this mean that out of darkness will come dawn? That out of the rain may come a rainbow? That out of death will come eternal life? True faith is the only means of understanding death."

O'Leary bent low over the casket, blessed it, turned and said, "Let us pray."

After the service, Brenda waited outside. Madelaine was helped out of the church and into a long black limousine by her two brothers. Other relatives shifted their bodies around her to keep strangers away.

Brenda felt a light touch on her elbow, and a low voice. "Grim, isn't it?" It was Spike Briggs.

She nodded, silently.

"It's hard to get used to funerals," Briggs said matter-of-factly. "They're all painful."

"I don't look forward to the rest of this week." Brenda shuddered.

Briggs shook his head slowly. "It has all the dimensions of a Greek tragedy."

To the muffled beat of drums, Donnelly's casket was carried past two rows of Fairport firemen and police. Their hats came off and went over their hearts as the body passed by.

Briggs walked Brenda to her car. She was surprised to notice he still had his hand lightly on her elbow.

"I don't like death," she said as she slid into her car. "It gives me the shivers."

"It's a fact," Briggs replied lightly. "Everyone wants to go to heaven, yet no one wants to die. But . . . you can't have one without the other."

Back at headquarters, Dempsey learned that the lab had isolated a right-hand thumbprint on the blunt end of the icepick used to stab the minister. It had been compared to the telephoto copy of Orton's right thumb. They were identical.

"We've got him now," exclaimed Belli. "What incredible luck."

"Not yet," cautioned Dempsey. "We just know who the Man is. Now we've got to catch him. Anyway, I feel a hell of a lot better than I did earlier today." He inhaled deeply and blew out a lungful of air.

Dempsey called both Briggs and Grady and brought them up to date. The FBI had put David Orton at the top of their most-wanted list. Both lawmen were shocked to learn that Orton might have a quantity of VX nerve gas. Both agreed to assign a team of men to help Farrow find out how much had been stolen. Grady said that he would call the Director of the FBI directly and ask him to contact the War Department on the old boy network.

They all knew the seriousness of the situation. Dempsey asked them if they could meet at 4:00 P.M. to review the situation. Grady asked if he could bring two of his assistants, and Dempsey readily agreed. Briggs had attended Donnelly's funeral. There had been tight security and no incidents.

At about 2:30 P.M., Farrow reported some good news to Dempsey. He reported his find calmly, but there was a gleam of pride in his blue eyes.

"Orton doesn't have any more VX."

Dempsey rose from his chair, exultation on his face. "Are you sure?"

"Positive." A smile wreathed Farrow's freckled, boyish face.

The Chief came around the desk and extended his hand to Farrow. His other hand clasped Farrow's shoulder. "Thank God."

Farrow nodded, then explained, "One of Grady's assistants, Bob DeLuca, and I made about twenty phone calls. At first, no one knew anything about any missing VX. Then someone in the War Department remembered that one canister had been tested by another agency. They wouldn't say which one, but DeLuca suspects the CIA. Finally, they admitted the canister was marked WD-1-No.4. They claimed that only one ever left their system. They've accounted for the rest. They have no idea how Orton could have gotten the canister. They asked that we keep this quiet, no publicity."

Dempsey grinned broadly.

"I thought it was strange he'd left the VX behind," said Farrow. "But it didn't seem to surprise you."

"No, it didn't," Dempsey said. "I don't think he's interested in mass destruction. Just individual, selective killings. It's crazy, but that seems to be his pattern."

"The Man's a psychopathic killer."

"Yes, and a trained psychiatrist. It's a strange combination."

Dempsey walked slowly with Farrow to the office doorway. "We don't have to worry about Fairport being wiped out by nerve gas. Let's return that canister."

"I've already taken care of that," Farrow answered casually, concealing his pride. "I turned it over to Briggs. A couple of his troopers are returning it to the War Department. Their bureaucratic faces must be beet-red."

At 3:30 P.M. Gus was ready with his dossier on Orton. He went over it carefully with Dempsey, made a few additions, then had twenty copies Xeroxed. The photo lab had run off twenty enlargements of Orton's picture on their automatic film processor. The enlargements had been given to the wire services. Within the next few hours, Orton's picture would be coast-to-coast on all of the television news programs.

Rice had reported by phone that they'd found nothing else

of major importance at Orton's, other than an old U.S. Army issue .45 pistol in a dresser drawer and a quantity of brown hair dye. Dempsey's ears perked up at the mention of the hair dye, until Rice said that they'd found it on his wife's dressing table. They had also found Orton's typewriter and were bringing it back to headquarters to check the typeface against that on the threatening notes from the Man. Dempsey asked Rice to have his team go over Orton's house once again from top to bottom.

"What the hell do we do with the snakes?" Rice's nervousness was obvious, even over the phone.

"Leave them alone," advised Dempsey. "Get an expert in to feed them, until we can find them a home."

Sam Grady and two of his regional FBI agents, Bob DeLuca and Warren Shuster, arrived within minutes of Spike Briggs and his chief detective, Slade Custer. Dempsey had worked once before with Custer on a narcotics case, and had been impressed. A shrewd, incisive mind, he'd thought. Belli and Farrow joined the group, and there were introductions all around. DeLuca and Shuster reminded Dempsey of Mutt and Jeff. DeLuca was a giant of a man, towering over everyone at six feet seven. Shuster was at most five-one with a slight build.

The eight of them crowded around the table in the Chief's office. Dempsey chaired the meeting. "When I suggested this get-together, we didn't know how much VX Orton had with him. We're now pretty sure he doesn't have any."

"Amen," whispered Grady, almost inaudibly. It was a sentiment they all shared.

Dempsey nodded. "The Man has now been identified as David Orton. We've got a positive make on his fingerprints left on the Judge's toothpaste tube and again this morning on the icepick used to stab Fredericks. At his home we found a cage of rattlesnakes, a case of dynamite with seven sticks missing, and a number of weapons stolen from the Poughkeepsie Armory. Orton still has a formidable arsenal and is extremely dangerous. We've got to catch him fast." Dempsey paused. "I know him well. He's an extremely intelligent man. A wild gambler, who'll take chances. But, I've got to say, he's one of the last people I'd ever suspect of being a mass killer!''

"It should be easy now that we know who he is," Briggs said with confidence.

Dempsey, let Briggs' remark go unanswered and continued, "Gus has put together a dossier on Orton. He'll give you each a copy, and I'd like you to follow along as I read it. Stop me at any time for comments or questions."

Belli passed out copies of the dossier, and Dempsey began to read.

"David Samuel Orton was born February 12, 1939, at Claremont, California. He is now forty-two years old, six feet one inch tall, weighs one hundred ninety-four pounds and has thinning, light-brown hair, which he wears fashionably long. He has a small mustache, or at least he had one last week. He has unusual slate-gray eyes. Orton walks with an imperceptible limp. He is missing the three smallest toes on his left foot. He is married, with no children.

"His parents were John and Patricia Orton. His father was an electrician. Orton's mother is still alive. She now lives with her married daughter, Joan Simmons, in Alameda, California. He has no brothers and one sister.

"Orton was an outstanding student, graduating as valedictorian from Claremont High School in 1956. He was active in school activities, especially sports, where he was a three-letter man; captain of the swimming team, member of the wrestling team, undefeated in his senior year; and a state champion at track in the javelin event.

"In the summers of 1956 and 1957 he worked as an electrician for an air-conditioning company.

"He attended two years at the University of California at Santa Barbara, where he majored in electronics. He enlisted in the Army in July 1958, one month after he married his high school sweetheart, Catherine Pollard.

"While in the Army, he received demolition training

at Fort Ord, California. Orton was awarded a sharp-shooter medal for his marksmanship with a rifle. He also holds a brown belt at karate."

"Orton sounds more dangerous all the time, almost lethal," interrupted Grady.

"He is, no question about it," answered Dempsey. "He clearly has the ability to use explosives. But listen to the rest of this.

"Orton returned to college, but transferred to the University of California at Berkeley, studying pre-med. He graduated with honors in June 1962. Studied medicine in graduate school and did postgraduate work in psychiatry. He interned at Columbia Presbyterian Hospital.

"He was drafted as a doctor and sent to Vietnam in 1967. As a result of his previous military experience, he obtained a commission as a major and served as a surgeon. After six months he was wounded in the left foot by a bamboo stake in an anti-personnel trap. His foot became infected and, as a result of gangrene, he had three toes amputated. He was awarded the Purple Heart and was discharged from the Army in March 1969.

"Orton set up his very successful practice in psychiatry in Fairport in February 1970. He's a member of the Fairport Yacht Club and Longwood Country Club and active in the Rotarians. Orton's neighbors claim that he and his wife seem to be an ideal couple, with no apparent marital problems."

"As a doctor, he would have access to curare and know how to administer it," commented Briggs.

"Unquestionably. Given a motive, he certainly has the physical capability and the experience necessary to commit all four of these murders. Gus' report doesn't include the fact that Orton's name appeared in the FBI Activist Files for Anti-War Activities in 1970."

"Considering what happened to him in Vietnam, Chief, you really can't blame him," commented Belli sympathetically.

Moments before, Grady had limped slowly to the window. Suddenly he spun around, leaning heavily on his cane. "That's got to be his motive. A grudge against the System. Anti-war activities, then a paranoid vendetta against society . . . murdering community leaders."

"It's hard to guess why anyone would kill four innocent people," replied Dempsey, looking at Grady. "So far, we haven't found any connection, or the motive. Today's murder was made to look like a crucifixion. Why?"

"For the shock effect," suggested Briggs.

Dempsey nodded agreement.

"He's sick," said Belli. "His mind is like a jigsaw puzzle, with a key piece missing."

"A crucifixion . . . one doesn't come along every day," commented Briggs, looking around the room slowly. "It's bound to get everyone's attention. That's what the Man wants."

The meeting continued until after 6:00 P.M. They all agreed that the three law-enforcement agencies would now concentrate on finding and catching Orton.

Briggs summed it up. "We now know who the Man is. Let's catch the son of a bitch. After we have him, we'll know why he committed the murders. We won't have to guess."

They were unanimous about using the power of the media to help catch Orton. "It will be tough as hell for Orton to hide," enthused Grady. "We'll turn such a large spotlight on him he'll have to crawl under a rock."

"Unless he's disguised," cautioned Dempsey. "Orton has shown a real ability at disguise. One thing I can't understand . . ." Dempsey frowned, thinking out loud. "Why would Dave leave such glaring clues—obvious fingerprints—on the toothpaste tube and again today on the icepick? It's almost . . . almost as if he wanted to be identified."

"Why would a murderer . . ." began DeLuca, his face showing puzzlement.

"To get credit for the murders," answered Grady. "If he's not gaining anything else—no money—maybe he wants credit. But it seems like such a lousy motive."

Dempsey gestured affirmatively. "Psychos often have a

compulsion, a need to be identified. The stolen weapons were not well hidden, either. We found them in a few minutes. If Catherine had found two land mines in the closet or a case of dynamite under the pool table . . . It's pretty obvious. They were left there for us to find.''

Briggs ran his hand over his crew cut. "It just doesn't make sense." He glanced at his watch and stood up. "Sorry, but I've got another appointment. I'm going to have to leave."

Before they broke up the meeting, it was agreed that for maximum publicity Grady would go ahead and appear on *The Today Show* and Grady, Briggs and Dempsey would be interviewed together, live, on the NBC network news at 7:00 P.M. on Friday.

Across town, in a secret subterranean suite under Rocco's Cadillac Agency, a heavyset man in a blue blazer was seated in a corner, counting stacks of twenty-dollar bills. Tony Rocco always sat in a corner with his back to the wall. He had learned early in his business that corners, especially dark ones, are safest. The reflecting one-way mirrors on the green velvet walls and the electronic alarm system in the secret passageway leading to his private fortress increased the Rock's feeling of security.

"We need ten thousand more, and each package will be full. Two hundred grand each." The Rock rolled his large green eyes toward the ceiling and wheezed. Then he snapped lid shut on two of the three suitcases and locked them.

Whitey, his personal bodyguard and companion, disappeared into an adjoining room and returned with ten additional packages of crisp, new twenty-dollar bills, banded into small thousand-dollar bundles.

"That does it," exulted the Rock, as he finished packing the money into the third suitcase. "Now we're ready for tomorrow's meeting.

Rocco's Cadillac Agency had long been a Fairport landmark. Established in 1946 by Enrico Rocco, it had done well until his death in 1964. But it had really flourished under the guidance of Tony Rocco, becoming one of the largest Cadillac agencies in New England. Only a few close confidants knew how well the Rock had prospered. He was now worth a cool twenty million. The Cadillac agency had produced almost a million of the Rock's personal fortune; the other nineteen he had made himself. Literally. Rocco's twenties were virtually indistinguishable from Uncle Sam's.

He had been one of the first to recognize and take advantage of the breakthrough represented by photo-offset printing. For ten percent of the face value of his production, his syndicate contacts in Vegas supplied him with an unlimited supply of official bond paper used for federal notes. Rocco's photoengraved plates produced exact images of the U.S. Treasury's twenty-dollar bills. It was impossible to tell them apart. To his knowledge, not one of his twenties had ever been questioned.

"I was glad to hear that prick Waller bought it yesterday," exulted Whitey, fishing in his mouth with a gold toothpick. "He gave Joey six long ones for simple possession. Shit, there are twenty kids at Fairport High who carry their grass around in knapsacks."

"Whitey, I don't like it. These murders . . . they're bad news. We've had a good thing going. Over two years. No one knows about it. No one even suspects. It's a perfect setup. This guy could fuck it up good."

The Rock stood up and moved about aimlessly. "I don't want state cops or the Feds snooping around, poking their noses into dark corners. If the police can't stop this man, we'd better do it for them. I'm getting nervous. Get me Little Louie in Vegas. Real private."

While Whitey dialed, the Rock opened the small refrigerator behind a wall panel and poured himself another glass of buttermilk. He gulped it down. When the light flashed, he picked up the white phone.

"Hello, Louis, this is Antonio. How's your Cadillac business? I'm glad to hear it. You gotta plan ahead. Yeah, it wasn't raining when Noah built the ark, either. Did you get the check? . . . The new model sales are going very well, very well indeed. That's why I called. We've got a heavy loose in this town. A real spook. Killing at random. No

pattern. It's no laugher. Right. It could hurt our new-car
sales. I think we may have to stop this looney. Exactly! No,
don't know who he is. We gotta find out. Well, I'd prefer
Lefty, but if he's another job, Spider will do. I'll assume
it's Lefty, unless I hear different. Put him on the plane tomorrow morning. I'll make arrangements on this end. Same as
before. You get what you pay for. It's good value. Say hello
to your family. God Bless.'' Tony Rocco put down the phone
and gave Whitey a thumbs-up signal.

Jeanne was waiting expectantly for the Man. She had spent
the afternoon catching the sun on her secluded wood deck that
overlooked a cliff of craggy rocks, with the crashing sea and
its constantly changing patterns of foamy wake and spray.
The potent combination of the hot sun on her well-tanned
body, three glasses of chilled Chablis and four hours of
dreamy, erotic fantasizing about her man had set Jeanne's
whole body tingling. Jeanne was ready, in fact anxious, for
relief.

Hearing the car in the driveway, she met him at the door,
kissed him teasingly, her bikini-clad body pressing hard against
his muscular build. The odor of Musk Oil perfume filled his
head. He felt light-headed and fuzzy.

"Darling, I've been thinking about you all day. Follow
me." She led him into her bedroom and with one fluid
motion pulled the flowered drapes closed and threw back the
matching bedspread on her queen-size bed. On one of the
white wicker bed tables, Jeanne had set a pitcher of chilled
Montrachet and two goblets. On the other was an assortment
of lotions and body oils.

The stereo was playing "Chase the Clouds Away." The
Man nudged the bass control slightly, listening with cocked
head to the baroque emphasis of the bottom line. "That bass
is superb," he commented. "That's Chip Jackson. He's even
better than Ron Carter." He was tempted to join in on the
flügel horn with Mangione, when Jeanne took his hand and
led him away.

She poured them each a glass of wine as he undressed.

Clad in her beautiful skin, she lay down on the cool flowered sheet. The Man began rubbing the tension from her neck and shoulders, kneading the oil into them with his powerful, gentle hands, then massaging her back, her hips, her legs, her inner thighs. She rolled over, and he completed rubbing the oil over her entire body, emphasizing the most sensitive places. It was touch and glow time, and Jeanne was smoldering.

Slowly, she pulled him down to her and kissed him longingly. They both knew today, for the first time, Jeanne wanted him, needed him, inside her.

Gently, tenderly, he loved her, all the secret spots that reacted to the lightest touch of his fingertips, then pleasuring the deepest parts, a feeling she'd never felt, never enjoyed before. It grew, slowly at first, then with a rush, until it filled her whole inner self with a warm glow. Jeanne could feel everything he had to offer, and he could feel her deep reactions. The Man paced himself, slowly and deliberately. Her moans increased in tempo and sound. His movements increased until every fiber of her body shook and trembled reaching for her man. It was timed perfectly. She was drenched in pure pleasure. He kissed her gently.

"That was wonderful," purred Jeanne. "You're the greatest."

The Man smiled, a self-satisfied smile, knowing that from that moment on, his kitten might never again be satisfied with just a dish of cream.

The Man's thoughts were interrupted by the incessant ringing of his private phone. Annoyed, he answered it. On the other end, it was Jeanne, all coos and purrs. "I'm lying here waiting," she said.

He couldn't believe his ears or his own voice. "I'll be right over, lover."

My God, the whole thing—all the way—had been a fantasy. A figment of his vivid imagination, fantasex, in 3-D living color. In the background, he could hear the old man's voice, laughing.

He tried to calm himself. He was hooked on dreams . . . with a black hole in his head . . . a mind collapsing in on itself . . . no longer master of his own fate. His mind was being taken over by fantasies and by an old man's voice. An old man whom he couldn't even identify. Walking backward through the looking glass to Wonderland, he couldn't even tell Tweedledee from Tweedledum.

He had to regain control! Had to hang in, remember everything, whether it happened or not. If his own mind couldn't be trusted, he was in deep trouble. What the hell was he worried about? All he had to do was trust the old man and fear nothing. He breathed a sigh of relief.

Oh, shit! He'd just screwed the ass off Jeanne. It had been superb, and now he was off to be the wizard . . . and do it all over again. What incredible luck! If this kept up, he'd either need a pacemaker or they'd put him in a canvas blazer with wraparound arms.

Sitting back in his chair, he put his feet up and thought. If this hadn't been the real thing, how about all the other times . . . with Jeanne, Gayla, Barbara and even . . . his wife? How many of those had been fantasies? Hell, what difference did it make? They sure felt real. He laughed loudly and readjusted his shorts. He was the greatest, Jeanne had just told him so.

Pulling his car into Jeanne's driveway, he could hear the gulls calling to one another, challenging one another to soar higher and higher. Jeanne met him at the doorway. She kissed him hungrily, pressing her bikini-clad body tightly against him. Anxiously, she led him into her bedroom and . . .

The goddam phone was ringing again.

Marie Benson, the attractive wife of Senator Wilbur Benson, arrived at La Guardia at 8:30 P.M., on American Airlines Flight 184 from Chicago. She'd arrived two days earlier than the Senator to visit with her college classmate and close friend Muriel Winchester. Muriel and her husband, Tom, had vacationed twice with the Bensons and had visited them in Minneapolis. The Winchesters were delighted that, at long last, the Bensons were going to be staying with them in Fairport.

"There she is. Hi, Marie."

"Don't you look great! You don't look a day older."

"Neither do you. I like your hair."

"Oh, thanks, do you really? It's a little lighter. The sun, you know."

"Tom will get your bags. We've got our car outside, and we'll be in Fairport in an hour. I can't wait till you play Longwood."

The murders weren't mentioned until they were out of the public eye, in the privacy of their car.

It was bright sunshine when Judy Rogers took off from Kauai, heavily overcast when she arrived in Honolulu, and raining torrentially when she took off for San Francisco. The flight had been delayed almost an hour to let the rain abate. This delay would make her connection in San Francisco a tight one. She hoped the rain wasn't an omen.

Jack had been so understanding and thoughtful. He'd driven her to the airport, even wanted to fly over to Honolulu with her. But as she'd told him, it was a long run for a short slide. He'd agreed to visit her in Boston in the late summer. They'd go sailing on the Cape. Even hinted . . . his firm had a branch office in Boston. Would he really change his whole life for her? Little butterflies fluttered deep inside. Were her feelings coming from her heart, or her head? She wasn't sure. Her hand reached out and touched the empty seat next to hers.

Finally, she'd reached Peter Bond by phone and learned what had been happening in her sister's sleepy little town. A killer loose. Three murders in three days. Hetty Starr murdered. What a waste . . . such incredible talent.

Bond was giving her two assignments. They sounded challenging. A $200,000 shortage at the Fairport Savings Bank and some background investigation into Hetty Starr's will and insurance policies. No explanation. Said he'd fill in the details after she arrived. It sounded like major fraud.

She couldn't wait to talk to Brenda. Jim would be in up to his armpits. He was always so proud of his town. There'd never been an unsolved crime in Fairport. Judy wondered if they'd be upset if Brenda's little sister solved two crimes in their town. They'd keep it in the family. Hell, maybe she'd find the killer, too. Little chills danced up and down her spine.

She took several deep breaths, settled back and dozed off. It was a light, uneasy, tense sleep.

Dempsey was glad that the police cleanup crew had removed the burned-out frame of his "Bullet" and all evidence of the grenade explosion that morning.

"Things are happening so fast it seems as if that happened a week ago," he told Brenda at dinner. "I hate to run out again, hon, but I told the boys that I'd be available tonight. We're pushing the search for Orton at full speed. I know he's someplace right here in town. He's got to be."

Later, Brenda was seated in the den. The television was on, but only for company. Brenda wasn't watching, but thinking. Poor, dear Cindy. The burning of Cindy's doll had been traumatic, forcing her deep into a protective shell. She hadn't spoken all afternoon, sitting in her room rocking back and forth, hugging her new doll. She'd insisted on eating in her room and then had only picked at her dinner. Jim had gone in to kiss her and Cindy had cried, finally falling asleep with her arms wrapped tightly around her new doll.

After all their work with Cindy, all the hours of frustration, the slow painful progress, in just a few seconds she had slipped way back. How far back Brenda didn't know. She'd make an appointment with Dr. Markum tomorrow. Tears came to Brenda's eyes. It was a world of hurt and sorrow. Poor Jim, he had so much pressure on him, and some lunatic was trying to kill him. She put her hands to her throbbing head. Another tension headache.

At 10:15 P.M. Brenda called Jim to tell him that Ed Witchum had stopped by and said that he'd act as First Selectman, until the next election. Jim was pleased. He told her he missed her, and they exchanged kisses on the phone. Exhausted, she was going to bed.

By midnight, every male guest of every hotel, motel and rooming house within thirty miles had been checked out carefully. Fourteen men who resembled Orton had been questioned and cleared. One had almost been shot when, protecting the identity of his female visitor, he'd slammed the door on three policemen. Seconds later, he was lying prone on the floor with two of them sitting on him, with drawn revolvers. In the background, a very frightened young receptionist was trying to hide her nakedness behind a skimpy motel towel.

"There's not a sign of him, Chief. No trace. His wife, either." It was a weary Lou Piccollo talking. "They've disappeared completely, probably squirreled away at a friend's house."

"They can't be. We've checked them all out. Maybe they're holed up in a vacancy, but by tomorrow we'll have covered all of them," exclaimed Farrow, who'd volunteered to work the night shift.

"Tom, Lou and I are going to call it a night. If anything develops, call me immediately. Orton's still out there, moving around in the night, flicking his Bic. Somehow, I feel he's watching all this, watching us, watching our frustrations and laughing his fucking head off."

It was a puzzled Dempsey who said goodnight and drove home.

The Man was seated at the desk in his den, in his pajamas and smoking jacket. He finished his Tiparillo and snubbed it out in the crystal ashtray, spirits buoyant, feeling wonderfully gratified. His plan was working exactly as he had anticipated. It was perfect! What a glorious day. Dempsey's "Bullet" had been blown to bits. Laughing, he recalled that scene . . . the Chief, soaking wet, with a drawn .357, running around in circles after him. He laughed again. There's nothing worse than a soft-hearted man with a gun. He'd never find him. Shit! Couldn't!

Then he'd brazenly choked the minister . . . that holy

spook . . . hung him on the cross in his own church. The Man hadn't known until tonight that Fredericks had only had three months more at the most to live. It was no worse than shooting a sick dog. The Man laughed so hard he doubled up. Hell, I really did him a favor . . . saved him a lot of pain . . . freed his soul to be born again!

It had been eerie when the minister had said, "Forgive him, Father." He didn't even know I was there. The Man beat a tattoo on his desk with his fists . . . should have been a drummer . . . even better than Krupa.

With his black marking pencil, he crossed out Fredericks, "Old Fred," the ten of spades, number five on his list. After locking his desk drawer carefully, he drank a glass of milk, took two vitamin E's and went up to bed.

Now the police are chasing shadows. Just about every home in the United States knows what I look like—rather, what I'm supposed to look like. They'll be searching for a man who looks like Orton's picture. They don't know what a mastermind they're up against. I don't have a mustache. I don't look anything like they think I do!

The Man sighed contentedly, rolled over and gently patted his wife goodnight. At least she was real. She was no fantasy. He reached out again to make sure. "Beddy byes," he whispered. The Man was still very much in Fairport.

6

Friday, June 6.
A Real Sizzler

AT BREAKFAST, Alice Briggs was nervous, almost irritable, buttering her toast for the second time. Awakening, she had rebuffed Spike's aggressive advances, and knew he was annoyed about that. Now, as he leaned over to kiss the back of her neck, she instinctively hunched her shoulders, shivering. Spike blurted out, "It must be that time again."

He could have bitten his tongue; it wasn't. Alice started to cry. Spike put his arm around her and whispered softly, "I'm sorry, hon." She buried her head on his shoulder and sobbed softly. Minutes passed. Finally, she lifted her head, reached for a paper napkin and dried her eyes.

"I'm so afraid. This madman . . . he's killing everyone in sight." Alice looked up, her eyes puffy red. "He's already tried to kill Jim. I'm afraid"—she sobbed again—"he'll try to kill you."

"Don't worry, honeypot." Spike picked up his cup and tasted his coffee. It was cold. "A lot of people have tried—two wars—but I survived. Got the instincts." He emptied his cup. "That's good coffee, sweetheart," wiping his lips with the back of his hand.

"I'm so worried. You're so preoccupied." Alice sniffled. "I don't see you anymore. Last night you were real late again. You know I can't sleep without you next to me. I worry about you." She took a deep breath.

Spike took her hands in his. "Hon, relax. I patted you goodnight, but you were asleep. We're working like hell,

142

trying to catch Orton. Until it's over, I just can't get home early.''

He took her face in his hands and kissed her lightly. "When it's over, we'll take a vacation. How about the Northwest? You've always wanted to go there. Get some brochures from the agency, and we'll make some plans.''

He kissed her again, this time with feeling. "I'll be late again tonight. Sam Grady, Jim Dempsey and I are going to be interviewed on the seven-o'clock NBC News. Be sure to watch.''

"Maybe I'll invite Brenda over,'' Alice said hesitantly. "It will give us a chance to see you two.'' She smiled. It was a weak, sad smile, but it was a smile. "Tomorrow I'm going to take the train into New York and visit mother. I'll be back Sunday.''

"Good idea. Your mother will cheer you up.'' Spike picked up his coffee cup, ran the water over it and put it in the dishwasher. "Don't forget the special tonight. It should be interesting.'' Spike spoke with emphasis. "Imagine me on TV. A star is born!'' He put his arm around her and whispered softly into her ear.

Alice shook her head forcefully. "I can't understand you. You're unbelievable. A killer on the loose, and all you think of is sex. That isn't the only way I show my love for you. There are other ways. That's why I got up early and made French toast for you.'' She bit her lip before continuing. "Lately . . . I've noticed . . . the more danger for you the more aggressive you are. I'm really not interested this morning.''

Alice looked up at Spike. His eyes were still hopeful. She shook her head again and lit a cigarette with trembling hands.

Spike muttered softly to himself, then grinned broadly. "How about tonight, sweetheart? I'll wake you up.''

Alice closed her eyes and sighed. Spike went out of the house, whistling.

Dempsey opened the front door and picked up the morning newspapers. He was gratified to see that Orton's picture covered the entire front page of the *Daily News* and four columns

on the front page of the *Times*. It was almost the same size as
the enlargement they'd sent the wire services. Standing at the
front door, he read the lead story about the four murders and
Orton's identification as the Man. Fredericks' killing hadn't
been treated as sensationally as he'd feared.

Back in the kitchen, he turned on Channel 4, then sat down
to breakfast with Brenda. Cindy was still asleep. *The Today
Show* came on at 7:00. The news featured the murders, and
then Grady was introduced. Sam looked relaxed and completely at ease. Dempsey ate sparingly, pushing his eggs
around the plate, watching the program.

Jane Pauley was charming, as usual, and showed great
sympathy for Fairport's plight. Sam fielded all of her questions
in a most forthright and open manner. His warm personality
came across even on television and softened the grisly subject
matter. Brenda sighed. "Sam exudes charm. He should be a
regular on television."

Grady was effusive in his praise of Dempsey. "Chief
Dempsey is doing a fantastic job in solving these crimes. He
has come up with the exact method used in each murder, and
in every case has done that within a few hours. Now we've got
a suspect, David Orton, and every effort is being made to find
him."

Sam explained the cooperative effort that Dempsey had set
up involving the FBI, the state police and Fairport's own
police force, concluding emphatically that he could think of
no one in any law enforcement agency that he'd rather see
heading the investigation than Dempsey.

Brenda looked proudly at Jim. She reached over and touched
his hand. He laughed quietly and said, "I'll be damned.
That's nice of Sam."

The Man pulled his car into Carroll's drive-in and ordered
a cup of coffee and a jelly doughnut. He sat in his car reading
and rereading the articles about his murders in the morning
newspapers. Orton's picture stared out from the front page.
He slumped down in his seat slightly and adjusted the visor to
block the sun from his face, finishing his coffee and lighting

a Tiparillo. Damn, it was his last one. He'd have to buy another pack.

He heard the distant drone of a small airplane. It brought back memories. He felt light-headed and fuzzy. It was the day after he'd won the National Aerobatic Championship in Peoria. He was putting on a special one-man performance. Ten thousand people were gathered below, watching his every move.

A wingover. Three slow rolls to the left, three to the right. He eased the nose down on his Pitts Special to gain speed, then he pulled back on the stick and the plane climbed steeply into a loop. On his back, he rolled out into a perfect Immelmann. Three snap rolls to the left. Three to the right. Then he rolled the plane over on its back and put it into an inverted spin.

He eased the stick back, kicked his right rudder and checked his inverted spin, pulling out just four feet above the ground in the center of the stadium. The crowd gasped in unison at the combination of daring, flair and precision. He climbed for altitude; gaining it, he dove for maximum speed. Then he threw the plane into an end-over-end cartwheel. The crowd stood as one and roared, seeing the impossible. No one else could do the cartwheel flip. No one else had ever dared try it. He was the greatest

The Man righted the plane and sneered. Jerks, all of them. Peasants. They didn't appreciate real talent. He was a legend in his own time. The next exhibition he'd have a real surprise fdr them. He'd drop a napalm bomb right in the middle of the crowd. He laughed out loud, oblivious to his surroundings. It was then he heard the old man's voice.

The Man nodded quickly, snapping out of his fantasy. His wild laugh had startled the disbelieving carhop. Smiling weakly at her, he started his car, and drove quickly out of the drive-in.

Dempsey was slumped back in his leather reclining chair, deep in thought, ignoring the empty coffee cup in his hand. It's this one-a-day murder bit that gets me. Monday, the First

Selectman; Tuesday, the actress; Wednesday, the Judge; Thursday, the minister. Who will it be today?

Was Orton trying to kill him with the grenade? Was Fredericks a replacement, a second-thought killing after he'd escaped? No, the killer's letter had said the next victim would be Fred. The minister was the planned victim.

He straightened up and set his cup on the desk. So Orton wasn't trying to kill him, just trying to scare him. The grenade wouldn't have killed him, even if he hadn't plunged into the pool. It probably would have wounded him. Odd, there'd been no fright at all. He'd known intuitively what to do; afterwards, he'd had a splitting headache all day. It had been difficult to think clearly.

He reached for a pad and pencil, leaned back in his chair again and wondered, Will Orton keep on killing? If so, who's next? I've got to think like Orton to catch the bastard.

Who would I kill next? Yes . . . a list of possible victims. He kept tapping the pad with his pencil point. The pad was still empty. Hell, I don't even know where to start . . . what's the motive?

Suddenly, Dempsey stiffened and sat bolt upright. Of course . . . Orton's a psychiatrist, treating people every day for emotional problems. Perhaps there's a clue, a motive, in his cases. There may be a link somehow among Donnelly, Hetty, the Judge and Fredericks.

"Mary," he bellowed. "Get Farrow in here." Mary reminded him that Tom had been on duty until 4:00 A.M. Dempsey gave the assignment to Gus Belli instead.

By late morning, Orton was still at large. He had been reported by alert, anxious citizens in thirty-two cities and communities across the country. Suspects had actually been arrested in Atlanta, Georgia; Portland, Maine; Tucson, Arizona; Cincinnati, Ohio; and New York City. All had been released except the one in Tucson, who was wanted for a felony.

On six separate occasions, Orton had been seen in the Fairport area. All reports were immediately checked out. All were negative. One teenager claimed to have been raped by Orton in a parked car at approximately 1:00 A.M. at Ridley

Beach. After questioning, she admitted it had been a close friend of her regular boyfriend, and it hadn't really been rape.

A small crowd was waiting in the lobby at Logan Airport. Judy Rogers walked down the ramp toward the baggage area. Suddenly she did a double take, as Peter Bond himself moved forward to meet her. Tall, distinguished-looking, almost handsome with his prematurely silver-gray hair, Bond stood out in the crowd. Judy smiled. Bond did his best to hide his personal magnetism under a cloak of conservative blue suits, Arrow button-down shirts and Harvard stiped ties. He was still conspicuous.

Peter was the administrative genius of Bond & Bond. The brains behind the scenes. His twin brother, James, handled most of the undercover work and took most of the headlines. But James was now in the Far East on a special government assignment.

Bond saw her almost at the same moment. His handclasp was warm, and a kiss on her cheek totally unexpected. He took her arm and steered her toward the baggage carousel, onto which bags from the San Francisco flight were already spilling.

"Awfully sorry, Judy, darling, messing up your holiday this way. I'll make it up to you. A promise." His hand squeezed her arm ever so slightly, or was it her imagination?

She pointed out her first bag on the carousel. He released her arm to reach for it. Judy noticed that Peter had a perfect smile and warm blue eyes. Her pulse quickened. He was Boston's number-one bachelor, the catch of the year, maybe of any year.

The question must have been in her eyes. As he opened the door to his Mercedes 340SL, he smiled. "After twenty hours of traveling, you really deserve a band, the whole treatment. A private chauffeur was the best I could do."

Sliding into the driver's seat, he turned and looked at her. "I didn't think you'd want to come into the office today."

She nodded and smiled appreciatively.

"You rest up. Take it easy. I'll pick you up for dinner

tonight at seven. We can talk over specifics of your assignment then. Tomorrow, you can drive down to Fairport. You're booked at the Inn.''

Judy was about to interrupt and explain that she could stay with her sister. Bond must have read her mind.

''It would be better if you stayed at the Inn. I don't want you involved with Dempsey . . . or these murders. I don't want you close to them.'' Bond glanced sideways at her, reached over and gently touched her hand.

''You're too important to . . .'' He hesitated long enough for her heart to notice. ''. . . to the firm. We have plans for you.''

On the drive to her apartment on Massachusetts Avenue, Bond filled her in a little more on the assignment. She was to do some background digging, preliminary investigation he called it, on fraud at the Fairport Savings Bank and possible fraud connected with Hetty Starr's and Judge Waller's insurance policies.

He reached his right arm over her shoulder and felt for a large manila envelope on the rear shelf, picked it up and handed it to her. ''Some background material.'' He held up his hand and smiled. ''After you get some rest.''

It was Bond's theory that there were several money-grubbing rats in Fairport. Judy was to try to find out who they might be.

She was shocked to learn of the murder of the minister, Paul Fredericks, but pleased to hear that they'd identified the killer, David Orton. She exhaled lightly and shook her head, suddenly aware of her fatigue.

Bond pulled his metallic-gray Mercedes to the curb, opened the trunk, grabbed the bags and helped her to the door. Then, as she reached for her door keys, his hand touched her chin. She looked up and was kissed lightly on her lips.

She watched as he slid into the car and drove away. She felt light-headed. Things were happening awfully fast. Her fatigue had disappeared.

It was half an hour later, closing her bedroom drapes and pulling down the sheets, that the thought hit her. What if there was only one money-grubbing rat in Fairport? And what if the money-grubbing rat was a killer rat, too? Maybe . . . just maybe . . . she knew how to catch a rat.

The Man was sexually aroused by the thought of his next murder. He had planned it to be a big event, and it was developing perfectly. He left his office earlier than necessary for his next appointment. From a corner toll phone he dialed Gayla's number.

"Ti—ger, I was hoping you'd call. I'm ready for another of your special massages. Ten minutes! Wonderful. I'll be waiting."

Gayla was just climbing out of her warm bubble bath when the Man arrived. Through the screen door he could hear her shout, "Come in, Ti—ger. I'll be with you in a minute." As he passed through the living room toward her bedroom, she bounced into view, still drying herself vigorously. The Man couldn't help but appreciate her beauty. Gayla was gorgeous. They kissed with feeling.

He pushed her away, laughing. "Darling, every time I meet you it's in a wraparound towel. Don't you wear anything else in the summer?" She let it drop to the floor as she led him into her bedroom. "C'mon, Ti—ger, into my den."

Within minutes, they had connected Gayla's infinite-pleasure machine, with attachments. The vibrator was not the only thing turned on. Gayla was, too.

Gradually, the Man increased the speed from three, to four, to five, then to six. Her orgasm started almost immediately and grew in tempo from level to level, from one peak to another higher peak. She was on top of the world. It was powerful. It was prolonged . . . intense . . . awesome to behold. The Man had never witnessed anything like it. Gayla had achieved the impossible, a never-ending climax. She was vibrating from head to toe in sheer, uncontrolled ecstasy.

Slowly, over minutes, he turned down the speeds to five, to four, to three, to two, to one and then off. Gayla was still quivering. Her entire inner self was pulsating with waves of tingling pleasure.

He unplugged her magic wand. She was completely spent,

drained of all energy, zonked. But on her beaufitul face was an indescribable, radiant glow of happiness, a look of total contentment. As the Man kissed her gently, she murmured, "That was unbelievable. Thanks, Ti—ger. You're a perfect lover. You're the greatest."

The Man paused at the doorway. Gayla was alseep, her golden hair shimmering on the pillow. She looked so young, like a little girl, with visions of sugarplums, an All-American little girl, curled up with her favorite teddy bear. With both arms, Gayla was hugging her newfound pleasure toy.

The Man shook his head. His teddy bare. That type of ecstasy could become addictive. When they'd first met, Gayla had said she'd liked his vibes. She'd never realized how accurate a prediction that would be. He walked back to the bed and kissed her softly again. "Gayla, you've come a long way, baby."

Dr. Markum wasn't being too reassuring. He'd given Cindy a thorough examination, talked with Brenda and Cindy together for about fifteen minutes and to Cindy alone for another half hour, getting nowhere. Cindy kept rocking back and forth in her chair, clutching her new doll tightly to her.

Now, Dr. Markum explained to Brenda, "It was a traumatic shock. She's retreated within herself."

Brenda nodded. She could have told the doctor that herself.

Dr. Markum stood up. Then he sat on the edge of his desk, next to Brenda's chair, talking now in a low, confidential tone. "Somehow, Cindy believes the doll was herself. She feels rejected, punished by the doll's death. It was almost . . ." Markum peered over his glasses. "Almost as if you, or Jim, had done it on purpose."

Brenda was perplexed and didn't understand what the doctor was saying. She wasn't too sure about him anyway. He hadn't really helped before. She and Jim had done most of the work with Cindy. They had pulled her out of her deep depression. It had been hours and hours of attention, love and affection. They'd just have to do it again.

Markum was still talking in his low voice. "It's going to take a lot of therapy. I'd like to see Cindy again on Monday." The doctor put his hand on Brenda's shoulder.

Brenda stood up, shrugging off the doctor's hand. She couldn't stand touchers. Jim had said several times that he thought Markum was a flake. Now, she agreed with him.

Smiling sweetly at Markum, they left his office. She took Cindy's hand in hers and walked out to her car, not bothering to make another appointment.

Sam Grady returned to Fairport on the New Haven at 12:12 P.M. Dempsey picked him up in his cruiser. They were to meet Briggs at Manny's Steak House for lunch. Jim complimented Sam warmly on his performance on the show. Sam admitted that except for the subject matter, it had been enjoyable.

As they drove, Dempsey brought him up to date on Orton. "Nothing new, just the weirdos seeking publicity." He slowed while the light changed. "The doctor's gone underground, and he's going to be hard to catch. I know Dave—he's goddam clever."

Sam absentmindedly rolled his side window up and down in rapid succession. He did it two or three times, until Dempsey turned his head and looked at him. "Sorry, Jim, I was lost in thought. Orton has been killing one person a day. It's the main pattern. If Orton is going to continue to kill, he's got to come out of hiding."

Dempsey pulled into Manny's parking lot, noticing that Briggs' Jaguar was already there. He pulled the cruiser up to the front door. They sat for a moment, and then Dempsey replied, "Orton will probably come out of his hole disguised. He's shown that he's good at it. To keep killing here in town, he's got to stay close. I'm convinced he's still right in our midst."

He waited for Grady to get out of the car, then eased into the parking spot closest to the front entrance.

Briggs waved to them from a quiet corner table. On duty, all three skipped drinks and ordered medium-rare Manny Specials. They discussed the murders, Orton, his possible motives and how they planned to handle questions on the live television special.

Briggs suggested that they put out an APB on Orton's wife. "She may lead us to him. Got to be in this with him. If he's disguised, she may be easier to find."

"Unless she's dead," Grady said, taking a bite out of a hard roll.

Briggs startled them as they were almost finished with lunch. He leaned forward and whispered, "Check our waiter. He's just about six feet one, hundred and ninety-five pounds. He's got thinning hair. It's gray, but that could be dye. Walks with a slight limp. There's a strong facial resemblance." Briggs' eyes continued to follow the waiter. "My God, it could be Orton."

Grady stared at Briggs, then at the waiter, and nodded silently, his coffee cup halfway to his mouth.

Dempsey continued signing the check, never looking up. "Spike, you've summed up our problem. Our waiter could be Orton about to poison all three of us. Fortunately, he's not. That's Joe Lombardi, been a waiter here for at least eight years. I know him well. You're thinking . . . still could be Orton, disguised as Lombardi. Crazy as it sounds, I thought of that, when we sat down."

Dempsey paused, then said, "There's a strong facial resemblance, but Lombardi lost his little finger on his right hand to a power lawnmower about three years ago. Our waiter really is Lombardi. I checked earlier. Even Orton wouldn't go that far to impersonate someone else."

Briggs raised his coffee cup and grimaced.

On the way back to headquarters, Dempsey's police radio crackled with a message.

"Chief, it looks like another one. The Grand Manor just called for an ambulance. One of their patients has been murdered."

"Oh, shit," muttered Grady, closing his eyes. Dempsey checked his rearview mirror, did an abrupt U-turn and put his foot to the floor. They were only a few blocks away. Swerving through the light traffic, sirens at full blast, they screeched to a halt in front of the luxurious health spa, the East Coast's rival to Scottsdale's Maine Chance.

"You go ahead," Grady said, touching his bad leg. "I'll follow along."

Dempsey raced into the front foyer, where he was met by Ralph Quinn, the Grand Manor's director, white-faced and quite upset.

"This way, Chief. It's Mrs. Arbuckle. She's dying."

Quinn and Dempsey walked quickly down the hallway to a deluxe corner suite. Nellie Arbuckle was one of the richest dowagers in the world. Her ancestors had arrived in America before the Revolutionary War and had established one of the most successful trading empires in New England. Through the years, the money had pyramided, generation after generation. Nellie was the last surviving member of the Arbuckle family. Dempsey suspected that Nellie represented a huge body of money completely surrounded by people waiting for the inevitable.

Dr. DeFoe, the resident physician, turned as they entered the room. He gestured excitedly. "She's barely breathing. Where's that ambulance?"

"It's on the way, should be here any minute," Quinn answered.

After the initial report on the police radio, Dempsey was surprised to hear that Nellie was still alive. "Let me take a look." He shouldered past DeFoe and leaned over the unconscious old lady on the bed. Her face was contorted in pain, her pulse faint.

Dempsey leaned closer, his nose twitching. "Has she had any garlic?" Dempsey asked, without turning his head.

"At the Grand Manor? Of course not," DeFoe replied haughtily. "It's not on her diet."

Dempsey stood up and spoke angrily to DeFoe. "Then it's phosphorus poisoning. That's not on her diet, either!

"Look"—he pointed—"there are small burn marks on her mouth. Probably yellow phosphorus, one of the deadliest poisons known. Have you treated her for poison?" He turned and glared at DeFoe.

The doctor looked stunned, stammering, "No, I didn't

know . . . this morning . . . she was fine. Then she complained . . . severe abdominal pain.''

DeFoe was interrupted by the arrival of the ambulance crew. Dempsey issued commands. ''Treat her for shock . . . watch for the toxic action of phosphorus on her heart. There's no antidote. The best you can do is flush her out fast.''

''No antidote?'' The young ambulance medic gulped, almost swallowing his tongue.

''None,'' replied Dempsey, ''Do the best you can, sonny, and pray.''

While they wheeled Mrs. Arbuckle into the ambulance, Dempsey turned his attention to her room. Grady arrived and stood just inside the doorway, visibly impressed by Dempsey's instantaneous deduction. If she lived, the old lady would have only Jim's quick and facile mind to thank.

Now, on his hands and knees, Dempsey checked all of the corners of the room, looked carefully on the floor of the closet, inspected her eyeglasses and a small tray of crackers and cheese on her bedside table. He turned to Grady. ''Sam, after the last five days, we've got to suspect attempted murder, but I don't think so. This was an accident.''

''An accident?'' Grady was perplexed and waited for an explanation.

Dempsey wheeled and snapped at Quinn, ''I'd like a straight answer. Have you had a problem with rats or mice?''

Quinn, shaken by Dempsey's directness, answered slowly.

''Yes . . . we've had a few mice, but what's that got to do . . .'' His voice trailed off.

Dempsey walked to the closet, opened the door and pointed. ''Mouse tracks. The most common source of phosphorus is in rat poison. Generally, the paste is spread on crackers as bait.''

Then he walked back to Nellie's nightstand. ''Now, on this tray are three Bremner wafers with cheese.'' He picked one up and smelled it. ''It's Brie, probably delicious.'' Taking a small bite, he nodded. ''But check the one that's been partially eaten. It's a Bremner wafer, but that's not cheese on it It's rat poison, probably containing at least five percent yellow phosphorus.''

A look of admiration flickered on Grady's face, then he asked, "Why eliminate murder? Someone could have put poison on one cracker and—"

"Yes, it would have worked beautifully," answered Dempsey. "Nellie obviously has serious cataracts. I noticed that when I checked her. Look at her glasses." Dempsey picked them up and handed them to Grady. "Thick as the bottom of milk bottles. Without them, she probably can't see six inches. She'd have eaten the poisoned cracker just as likely as not." He took the glasses back and put them on the nightstand.

"But she didn't finish it," said Quinn.

"It wasn't necessary. One tiny taste of phosphorus is enough to kill . . . even a strong human being. The odds are still against her, but I don't think this was done on purpose."

Dempsey walked over to one corner, turned and said, "The first thing I noticed was this broken cracker by the side of her chair. Nellie probably dropped it. Without her glasses, she couldn't see, so she felt for it, and, as luck would have it, picked up the wrong cracker, the poisoned one.

"Now, let's check the kitchen and see if I'm right."

Quinn led the way to the kitchen, walking slowly, so that Grady could keep up. Within minutes they found a large can of Rat Doom Zinc Phosphide, containing five percent yellow phosphorus. One of the kitchen helpers, José Gonzales, confirmed that he had spread the poison on Bremner wafers and put them in two rooms where the maid had reported mice. One of the rooms had been Nellie Arbuckle's. They quickly confirmed the helper's story by picking up the poisoned wafer in the other room.

"Quinn, this is terrible negligence," said Dempsey, "but it's not murder. I'll send a man over to make a report. Let's get going, Sam."

On the drive back to headquarters, Sam glowed in his praise. "Just delighted to see you in action, Jim. Fantastic. That was one of the finest pieces of on-the-spot detective work I've ever seen. You're a bloody Sherlock Holmes."

Dempsey turned his head toward Grady, tight-lipped. "There wasn't any playing card."

Grady blanched. He'd missed that, too.

"It's funny," Jim remarked, glancing at Grady. "Can you imagine the irony of being a guest at one of the most expensive private health spas in the world and dying because you ate a canapé of rat poison?"

"Almost unbelievable. But thank God that it wasn't another murder," commented Grady grimly.

"Amen," sighed Dempsey.

The NBC main news crew arrived in Fairport shortly after noon. They went directly to the Gold Room of the Inn, where they started to set up their television cameras, microphones and seating arrangements for the evening news special. They were a professional team that had worked together for over five years. Jules Fieldman, the producer, had direct responsibility for the entire news special. Fieldman was supported by three cameramen, two sound men, a staff announcer and a girl in charge of lighting. The electricians and equipment arrived in an NBC trailer, which parked directly behind the Inn.

As soon as Filbert Flagg had made a firm decision to have a live report on the murders, Tuesday Fields swung into action. An advance team consisting of Gary Barton, field producer, with responsibility for picture-taking; Bob Jackson and Megan Griffith, tape editors; and three field cameramen had been dispatched to Fairport. Over the past twenty-four hours they had been accumulating background information on the murders for a five-minute introduction in the live interviews.

Now, in the Blue Room of the Inn, Barton, Jackson and Griffith were reviewing the usable footage on the twelve reels of videotape cassettes taken by the cameramen. In this process, they ran each tape through their machine, projecting it on two nine-inch television screens connected to a tape-editing console. Using the console controls, they identified the sequences of film which seemed most suitable.

At 3:30 P.M. Barton met with Jules Fieldman and Warren Petty and gave them a rundown on the visual content of the introductory film. Both thought it was excellent. Together, they wrote an appropriate script for the film, and Barton, sitting at the editing machine, put the appropriate pictures and sounds together on a single master tape.

Today was a big day for Sal DeMarco, supervisor of maintenance at the Inn. Sal came from a large family of DeMarcos who had lived for generations in Fairport. All of the DeMarcos could use their hands, and all worked hard. Most had been star athletes for the local high school. They were carpenters, masons, contractors, electricians, landscapers and builders.

Along with the Giannonis and the Palmeros, the DeMarcos made the town function. Sal combined all of the DeMarco talents. He had been a three-letter man at Fairport High and could do virtually anything in the maintenance line.

This was the first live television program ever transmitted from Fairport. Sal had spent the last two hours working closely with the network electricians, making sure the wiring was adequate to handle the telecast. It wasn't as big a job as expected, since most of the main cables and lines were fed directly out of the NBC remote hookup trailer, but he'd been helpful on the stage connections. At 4:15 P.M. Sal excused himself and went back to his office in the basement to have a cup of coffee and use the facilities.

At just about 4:00 P.M., a lone Connecticut state trooper tooled his motorcycle into the parking lot of the Inn, braked to a halt and kicked his sidestand into place. He entered the lobby of the Inn, his face shielded by the wide brim of his hat, carrying a small leather bag.

Slate-gray eyes scanned the lobby efficiently in seconds through metallic, reflective sunglasses. All was serene and peaceful. The desk clerk was avidly reading about Orton's murders. Two couples were having early cocktails at a small table in the alcove. A lone businessman sat at the dimly lit bar, drowning the disappointment of a lost sale.

The trooper ignored the single elevator and crossed the lobby to the door marked "Stairs." The Man was exhilarated, watchful, and deadly.

Fifteen minutes later, Sal entered his small office, poured himself a cup of coffee from the Pyrex coffeemaker, took a few sips, set it down and walked down the small corridor to the men's room. The Man followed him noiselessly.

Less than ten minutes later, Sal DeMarco returned to his office, finished his cup of coffee, and, carrying a small leather bag, returned to the Gold Room. The makeup job done in the men's room was perfect. The slight difference in stature would go unnoticed.

With the wiring for the program completed, the NBC electricians drifted back to their trailer for a light snack and a break before the program. They would recheck all their circuits an hour before air time.

The Man worked deftly and with confidence. He unzipped his leather bag and removed a roll of thin electrical cable and a timing device. Less than seven minutes later, completing his work, he knew what he'd done could not be detected, even when the crew rechecked their circuits. The news special was wired for action, wired into the 220-volt laundry system. The program would be a special to be remembered. It would be a sizzler.

Sal DeMarco returned to the men's room in the basement. Ten minutes later, the state trooper emerged from the inn carrying his small brown leather bag. He kicked his motorcycle into action and roared off, the afternoon sun glinting off the metallic sunglasses.

Tony Rocco was seated in a white leather upholstered chair in a corner of a private suite leased on a permanent basis in the Fairport Inn. The suite was in a private wing separated from the rest of the Inn and had an entrance shielded by two immense flowering rhododendrons. The other two rooms were furnished in a simple manner and were occupied around the clock by two of the Rock's burly bodyguards.

Seated across from the Rock on a matching white leather couch, separated by a glass coffee table, were two beautiful young ladies. The one on the left had the face of a goddess, a model's figure and grace, long, flowing strawberry-blond tinted hair, and the vitality of youth. The other was blond, blue-eyed, with a peaches-and-cream complexion and All-American measurements of 36-26-36.

The Rock looked them over carefully. His large green eyes were almost luminous. There was no sexual connotation or lust in his glance or in his mind. His leer was strictly business. The Rock had no time for women. His only love was money.

Further, no one, absolutely no one, ever touched him. As Whitey so elegantly put it, "Mr. Rock don't trust nobody. He never has. When he was a baby, he diapered himself."

Finished with his anatomical survey, the Rock spoke quietly but firmly, his fat, piglike hands folded in his lap. "Same as last time. You get five percent when all the money's passed. Ten grand each. You pay your own expenses. Use the same method to invest the money and the same names. Jeanne, you have the East Coast, New York to Miami. Gayla, your territory again is Europe. I'll cover Chicago, Vegas and the West Coast, personally."

Jeanne asked the only question. "What's the timetable?"

The Rock shifted his heavy body and leaned forward. "Same as the last three packages. I'd like it all invested by the end of the month. We'll be ready with our new models then. I expect to have my second press already spewing out Grants as well as Jacksons. By the end of the year, you girls should be able to retire in style. Good luck, and remember, no matter what, you're on your own. Don't contact me under any circumstances, and don't talk to each other."

The Rock rose to his feet slowly, wheezing at the effort.

It was Gayla who made the mistake of reaching out to shake the Rock's hand. With the deceptive speed of a cobra, Whitey interceded and shook her hand for the Rock, the end of a gold toothpick just showing out of the corner of his mouth.

The Rock twisted his face into a half-smile. "Whitey, help the girls to their cars with their suitcases. They're heavy."

Reports on Orton's whereabouts continued to flood into police headquarters across the country. A plane to Rio was delayed forty-two minutes at Kennedy when a woman reported that a man answering Orton's description had boarded. "It's him all right. Same slate-gray eyes," she swore positively. Minutes later, an irate and sputtering Brazilian was allowed to reboard the plane, with the profuse apologies of the security police.

In Boston, police raided a massage parlor on a tip that Orton was busy inside. The Western Association of Psychiatrists, at their annual regional convention in Denver, voted unanimously that David Orton be barred from further psychiatric practice. In San Francisco, at a press conference, a noted psychic, Othello, stated flatly that Orton had fled to Cuba and was being hidden by Castro.

The Fairport police had checked seven additional Orton sightings. Dempsey insisted that each one be treated seriously and checked thoroughly. All were negative.

Jim Dempsey, Spike Briggs and Sam Grady all arrived at the Inn at 6:30 P.M., thirty minutes early. At Brenda's urging, Jim had consented to wear his police dress blues.

"Darling, you look smashing," she said proudly.

Briggs had on his state police uniform, complete with epaulets. Even with a new pin-striped suit, Grady gave the impression of an unmade bed, his crumpled, rugged face matching his clothes. Limping into the Inn, he whispered an aside to Dempsey: "Between you two dudes, I'm going to stand out. I'll look like the typical American hero."

There had been no murder that day, and it was almost seven o'clock. A feeling of apprehension, of tenseness, hung heavy in the air.

"Maybe he won't come out from under his rock today," Sam commented.

The three exchanged glances. None of them really believed it.

"When you least expect it, look out," spat out Dempsey.

As they entered the Gold Room, Jules Fieldman came forward, introduced himself and led them over to Warren Petty, seated in an easy chair. They'd all watched Petty on television. His was a household face, as familiar as that of any Congressman, sports personality, and possibly even that of the President himself.

Dempsey was surprised. In person, Petty was a much smaller man than he seemed on television. The newscaster was scanning some papers, smoking a briar pipe and wearing a tweedy coat. His dark-brown toupée was slightly askew, his tie open. Somehow it seemed all wrong. Dempsey smiled and glanced at Briggs and Grady. They were smiling, too.

Petty looked up. Seeing them, he rose and acknowledged the introductions. Dempsey's smile broadened. Standing, Petty came to his shoulders. Petty sensed the disappointment and shrugged good-naturedly. "It's not yet air time. I'll grow on you." Then he smiled, too.

Dempsey liked Petty almost immediately. He was obviously a solid professional newscaster, with real human qualities. He couldn't have planned it better; his relaxed manner and appearance put all three lawmen at ease.

Petty dismissed Fieldman and gestured to the three chairs around his. When they were all seated, he leaned forward and spoke quietly.

"This is a tough subject. It's got to be handled with delicacy and fairness to Fairport. These murders could have happened any place. Unfortunately, Orton chose your town."

Petty then reviewed with them the format of the program and the questions to be discussed. They decided who would answer each question, with major emphasis being given to Dempsey.

"Five minutes to air time. Please take your seats, gentlemen." Jules Fieldman guided them into position. "One minute."

Petty reappeared. He winked at Dempsey and sat on his chair, set up on a small platform, a level above the other chairs. Petty was wearing an NBC blazer, tie two-blocked, hair set properly, face tanned with makeup. Petty now looked the way Dempsey remembered him. The Chief winked back.

Each took a sip of water from a glass that had been placed next to each chair.

As the producer, off camera, pointed his finger at the newscaster, Dempsey noticed a red light flick on over the main television camera, which was focused on Petty and his three guests.

"Good evening, America. This is Warren Petty, speaking from Fairport, Connecticut. This is a special newscast of interest to all Americans. You are undoubtedly aware of the four horrible murders that have taken place in this picturesque Connecticut town located on Long Island Sound, less than sixty miles from New York City. Tonight we have three guests who are leading the search for the vicious mass killer, identified as David Orton, a local psychiatrist."

Petty introduced each of them in turn and then introduced the background five-minute introductory film. The red light flicked off, and the film appeared on the television monitor placed before the three guests, out of sight of the television audience.

Dempsey watched the film intently. It was a very fair report, a skillful blending of background information about Fairport, giving details of the four murders. It concluded with a plea for all viewers to be on the lookout for David Orton. The film gave his description in detail, with an enlargement of his picture that filled the screen for at least fifteen seconds. Then the red light flicked back on and the interview began. Petty asked Dempsey the first question. "Chief Dempsey, you have the reputation for being one of the finest investigative detectives in the United States. Do you think Orton—"

Warren Petty never got a chance to finish asking the first question. The full shock of 220 volts of electrical power surged through Petty's throat microphone, and in an instant he was beyond help, seized in a horrible electrical dance of death.

Sam Grady sprang to help Petty and was within inches of the newscaster when Dempsey, with a fluidity of motion that belied his age, hurled himself across the stage and in one motion knocked Grady away from the live power flowing through Petty's body, then vaulted to the control panel, where the operator was frozen motionless with horror. Dempsey hit the main switch, and Petty's body settled to rest. The NBC network went off the air from coast to coast.

Nielsen later reported that over nineteen million homes

were watching the telecast when Petty was electrocuted. The nation also saw Dempsey, with instant reflex action, save the life of Sam Grady and make a valiant attempt to try to save Petty. Then their screens went black. Less than two minutes later, NBC was back on the air from their New York studio with a rerun of *Columbo*. Periodically they interrupted the film for bulletins about the murder of Warren Petty.

In the Gold Room, the acrid smell of burning flesh permeated the air. The ambulance arrived and took Petty to the morgue. Sam was profuse in his thanks to Dempsey. "You saved my life, Jim. I just didn't think. I was trying to help Petty. In one more second, I'd have been fried to a crisp." He shuddered and limped away.

Briggs was checking the equipment. A playing card, the nine of spades, had been taped under Petty's chair. "It was Orton. It had to be. Of course . . . his background as an electrician. We should have guessed that he'd try to electrocute someone." Spike was fuming. "How could he get in here?"

Dempsey hadn't said a word. He was thinking. That clever bastard. Orton had cut in the 220-volt power from either the kitchen or the laundry and activated it with a timer.

Across the nation, nineteen million families had been horrified by the grisly murder. About a third were eating their dinners, watching the evening news.

"He just danced like a puppet. I saw a live murder. Wow! Maybe they'll have another special tomorrow night."

"Stop it, Bobby, you're making your sister sick. Eat your hamburger and watch *Columbo*."

"Why don't they use Columbo to find Orton?" asked Bobby.

"That's not a bad idea," answered his mother.

In Buffalo, Senator Benson, on the campaign trail, had been watching television in a motel room with his close personal aide, Florence Harper. Now, an hour later, nauseated with fear, he commented, "That was awful. I don't feel well, Flo. I think I'm getting the flue flu. Fix me another Scotch on the rocks, will you, please?''

''But you've had four already, hon.''

''You're beginning to sound more like Marie every day. Dammit, I'll get my own.'' The Senator poured a tumbler full of Scotch, adding two lumps of ice, reached for the phone and dialed area code 203 and the number of the Winchesters.

''Tom, this is Wilbur. They're not home yet from the club? I'm in Buffalo. Yes, wasn't it gruesome? I've never seen anything like it. Say, I'm coming down with the summer flu. I feel awful. I think I'd better stay here in bed for a couple of days. No, tell Marie to stay there and enjoy herself. Some of my staff can look after me. Ask Marie if she'd mind standing in for me on Sunday. It will be simple enough. Just read my speech and pull the string to unveil the statue. Tell her I'll call tomorrow night. Give her my love. Thanks, old buddy.''

The Senator hung up the phone and took a long swallow of Scotch.

Later, when Tom told Marie about the call, she said she'd be glad to do it. Inwardly, she fumed. That yellow chicken, I'll bet he's bedded down with that laying hen, Flo!

The Man wouldn't have been surprised by the phone conversation. Actually, he hadn't expected Senator Benson to come anywhere near Fairport, having researched his victims carefully. Senator Benson wasn't even on his death list. Marie Benson was.

Tony Rocco was eating dinner, watching the news special. When Warren Petty was electrocuted, the Rock was so startled he spilled his whole plate of Colonel Sanders' fried chicken onto his lap, mashed potatoes, gravy, mixed bean salad, and all.

The death of Petty, live, on television, had shattered the Rock. Now, an hour later, he'd decided to move up his trip to Vegas by a week. He explained to Whitey, ''We can both use a week's vacation. I think it's better if Lefty works alone here in Fairport. That way there won't be any connection between us when Lefty kills this Orton creep.''

•   •   •

Lefty Diangelo arrived at Kennedy on TWA Flight 148 from Las Vegas at 9:30 P.M. His thin, ominous face was shielded by the wide brim of his black hat; his eyes were watchful slits behind dark-green shades. His long, thin hands had an almost imperceptible yet constant twitch.

He was met by Whitey and whisked to the Fairport Motel, where a room had been reserved under the name of Larry Fleming. There he received an envelope with his assignment: $100,000 cash if he found and killed Orton in one week. Plane fare back to Vegas if he didn't.

Lefty liked the assignment. Of course, he had no way of knowing that the hundred grand was counterfeit. It wouldn't have made much difference. Lefty liked to kill, had twelve notches on his favorite gun, three on another. $100,000 was real bread. Lefty's problem was that he didn't know where to find Orton. Neither did anyone else.

It was 9:30 P.M. when they found Sal DeMarco in the closet marked "Supplies," bound, gagged and drugged. Coming out of his stupor, Sal blurted out, "I was standing at the urinal, peeing. This trooper comes in. I turn to look at him. Those slate-gray eyes—it was David Orton, so help me God! I tried to zip up, but before I could, he must have hit me with a sledgehammer."

Judy Rogers sat quietly on the edge of her bed in her apartment. The murder of Warren Petty on television had been horrifying. It had sickened her. Now, almost three hours later, she was still feeling uneasy.

She'd been pleased to see Jim save Grady's life. Jim had always been a natural hero. Admiring her older sister's choice, as a teenager, she'd been jealous of Brenda. Maybe that's why she'd been so choosy herself. Right to turn down Rick . . . right to be cautious with Jack . . . an interesting man . . . but after all, she'd only spent two days with him. Now Peter Bond . . . maybe . . . just maybe . . . They had so much in common, and he obviously cared. Let it develop slowly.

Her mind was still muddled. It had to be jet lag. How did those stewardesses cope? She didn't envy them. Getting up, she walked into the bathroom and splashed cold water on her face.

Peter had called at 4:30 P.M. and had canceled their dinner date. Called back to Washington unexpectedly. It was that damned Presidential investigation. The best he could do now was meet her in Fairport next Wednesday. At least he'd call her every night and review her progress. Promises, promises. She'd wait and see.

One thing was especially nice—the use of his Mercedes. She'd started to turn him down, but he'd insisted. "I'd like you to get used to it. When you solve this case, I plan to give it to you as a bonus."

Her own Mercedes . . . a 340SL! It was her dream car. But that wasn't the important thing. He'd said, "When she solved this case . . ." He hadn't said, "if," but, "when." He obviously thought she had talent. Real talent. She'd prove it. Wasn't it Nero who said, "Hidden talent counts for nothing?"

Judy had slept most of the day, but was still deliciously tired. She brushed her teeth, showered, put on pajamas, straightened the sheets and fluffed the pillows, then climbed into bed with the folders that Bond had given her.

The files made fascinating reading. Three insurance companies had retained their firm. They held major insurance policies on Hetty Starr and Judge Waller. They totaled, with double indemnity, over four million dollars. Oddly enough, Ned Nichols, an attorney, was mentioned on all three policies. Could Nichols be a money-grubbing rat?

Bond & Bond had also been retained to investigate a fraudulent shortage of $200,000 at the bank. This was the third major shortage in the last four years at the same bank. Samuel Tilden, the bank president, had demanded an investigation after each one. Nothing had been turned up. She wondered. It was too obvious, too pat. Could Tilden be a money-grubbing rat?

Murders were generally committed for money. If Nichols and Tilden were money-grubbing rats, how come Orton was the killer rat? Was this a syndicate operation? Were all three involved?

Her head was spinning. If she didn't stop thinking, she was going to dream of rats. Ugh.

It would be almost five in the afternoon in Kauai. She wondered what Jack would be doing now.

It would be almost eleven in Washington. She wondered what Peter would be doing now.

Reaching up and turning off the light, she wondered if they would be thinking of her.

It was late, but the Man was not tired. He had enjoyed the day immensely, felt wonderfully gratified. The only annoying thing was that the Boy Scout Dempsey had acted so heroically on television. Damn, he could have prevented that. But it wasn't important. A hero today, a bum tomorrow. He had Dempsey on the run, faked out. Dempsey's intuition. Ha! It was shitty. He saw things that Dempsey no longer noticed. If Dempsey was going to see anything, he'd have to open both eyes.

The black marking pencil crossed out the NBC newscaster, the nine of spades, number six on his list. He hadn't been sure originally which network would schedule the first live telecast from Fairport, or whom they'd assign to anchor it, and would have preferred Churchman. He was better known. But Warren Petty would do.

Before he locked his notebook securely in its secret niche, he briefly reviewed his plan for the next day.

I've got to lure him out in the open . . . just as they want to lure Orton out . . . then I can get him . . . no question . . . it will work.

As he slid into bed, he patted his wife affectionately. A sleepy voice reproached him. "Not tonight, honey. I'm too tired."

"Oh, rats," he muttered to himself.

7

Saturday, June 7.
Funny Money

DEMPSEY SLEPT fitfully. Visions of a silhouette man darting in and out of the shadows kept running through his subconscious. Over and over, he heard a taunting voice, "You can't find me. You'll never find me."

The smell of coffee hauled him out of his nightmare. Awake, he reached out in the fuzzy air, but his hand felt only emptiness. Brenda was already up.

Dempsey stirred and sat up. Damn. He still had that headache. He felt exhausted. He couldn't put Orton out of his head. He was there when he went to bed, with him all night and there when he woke up.

The combined aromas of his favorite breakfast, blueberry pancakes, Canadian bacon and coffee, drifted upstairs. He was still enjoying the pleasant odors when Brenda appeared, bright and cheerful, in a pink peignoir, with pink slippers, carrying a silver serving tray.

"Good morning, sweetheart," she said, setting down the tray. "After all you've been through, I thought you deserved breakfast in bed this morning."

Dempsey checked his bedside clock. It was ten minutes of eight. "I must have overslept."

"It will do you good. Lean forward while I fluff up your pillows."

Jim ate his breakfast and Brenda perched on her side of their king-sized bed, watching him. Finally she spoke. "Darling, I'm so proud of you and what you did last night. But I'm worried. I think Orton was trying to kill you."

Dempsey finished a mouthful of blueberry pancake and took a sip of coffee before answering.

"No, I don't think so. It's not his plan. Don't worry, precious. We'll get him. We just have to flush him out. Orton is now a known. It's the unknowns that bother me. If Orton had wanted to kill me, he would have made me his first victim, before I was on guard. It's much easier to kill someone who doesn't suspect you're trying to waste him. That's like shooting fish in a barrel."

Dempsey mopped the syrup on his plate with the last of his pancake. He swallowed it, then continued talking.

"I'm pretty sure . . . Orton wants me alive, as a competitor. He's playing a game, a deadly game of murder, but he's getting pleasure from it—a strange, almost erotic euphoria. We're competing. He must think he's got me on the run. Orton won't try to kill me unless he tires of the game, or I start to win. I intend to catch him long before that."

Brenda stood up. She was standing in front of the window. The sunlight poured through her peignoir. Jim stared at her, noticing nothing on underneath the robe.

He finished eating, and Brenda took the tray. "Thanks, sweetheart. That was a delicious breakfast and very thoughtful of you, but I . . ."

Brenda waved him into silence. She set the tray on the bench at her dressing table, undid the bow at the neck of her peignoir, and with hands on hips, turned slowly around. He was right, there was nothing underneath.

"Sweetheart, I thought we'd save that for dessert," she whispered, climbing in alongside him.

Dempsey grinned. The dessert turned out to be even better than blueberry pancakes.

The Man sat at his kitchen table drinking coffee and flipping the dial on the television set. All the major New York stations were running cartoons. Nothing but bubble gum for the kids' minds, damn, it's Saturday, no *Today Show* . . . parents still asleep . . . at least they're still in the sack. He grinned to himself, as he picked up the local news on the New Haven station. It was fuzzy, but they were showing the electrocution of Petty, with a panel of commentators discussing the murders. They also reran, in slow motion, Dempsey's heroic action in saving Grady's life.

The Man grimaced. Slow motion made it even more impressive. When one commentator suggested that Dempsey be awarded a special medal for his bravery, the Man rose and clicked off the television.

The headline on the *Daily News* caught his attention. "U.S. WATCHES NEWSMAN FRY." Unfolding the paper, he sat down in his chair again. The sub-headline asked, "How Did He Do It?"

That was more like it.

He turned to the back page and a one-word banner, eight inches high "SHOCKING." The article on page three was captioned, "Orton Kills Fifth on Network TV."

He grinned broadly and slapped his knee.

He glanced at the New York *Times* Its headline was more subdued, covering only four columns. "WARREN PETTY ELECTROCUTED ON NETWORK NEWS PROGRAM. ORTON SUSPECTED." Damn *Times*. No flair at all. Just the facts. Shit. It's a wonder they sold any papers at all.

On his way downtown, he stopped off several times. Petty's murder was the first topic of conversation. The people he talked to were frightened. Horrified would be more exact. He walked buoyantly, spirits high. The murder of Petty had been brilliant. It had gone right into people's homes and touched them personally. They couldn't get it out of their minds—an indelible mark. He could smell the fear building, hour by hour.

Despite the hot, sticky weather, residents were bolting their doors and keeping their windows locked. Guns were bought, loaded, kept at arm's reach. Visitors were being met with cold stares. The mass exodus he'd predicted had begun.

Today was going to be an even more exciting day.

As he passed the municipal tennis courts, a yellow tennis ball bounced over the fence and onto the edge of the macadam. He swerved the wheel, hit it and grinned, feeling the slight thump. The ball ricocheted down the road. Glancing at the courts, now, at this early hour, they were almost full. The running figures brought back memories.

He felt light-headed, fuzzy. He had that vague feeling again. It was center court at Wimbledon. The finals against Connors. He'd just beaten Borg 6–0, 6–0; Borg hadn't won a single game. Connors would be easier. He didn't think he'd allow him a single point. He tossed the ball up, then stopped himself in mid-serve. What was the use? Why should he play any more? He'd achieved perfection in every sport. He was the greatest!

In the last World Series, he'd pitched all four games and struck out every damn Yankee. Pitching the last three innings underhanded, just to rub it in. He'd offered to pitch blind-folded—but even a good man knows his limitations.

"Stop it," growled the voice in his inner ear. "You're making me ill."

The Man laughed at the old man's comment. He had become so good it was sickening.

That was the problem. Once he'd achieved perfection, sports had become a bore. Killing was more exciting. Far more exciting. Once again, he was the world's greatest killer on the prowl. A predator. A killer shark on dry land. He hit the steering wheel with his fist. Little shivers went up his spine. Killing! That was for real. He couldn't see, but he knew the old man was grinning, too.

The Man parked his car, wiped the evil smirk off his face and went into his office. Saturday morning, no rest for the wicked, he thought.

Sally Farrow's milkman expressed his fear in simple terms, as they stood outside her kitchen door.

"Lady, if Orton can kill a man like Warren Petty right on television with the Chief of Police, the head of the state police, and a top official of the FBI sitting right there on the stage and do it in front of nineteen million people, he can kill anybody. I saw him do it, and I'm getting out of here until he's caught. I got vacation time coming. I'm taking my family and heading for the Cape."

Sally bit her lip as she took the quart of milk and dozen

eggs from the milkman. "I'm scared most of the time," she confessed. "I've got this terrible fear deep inside that one night Tom . . ." Her voice quavered. ". . . won't come home." Her face wrinkled up. "I'd die, too."

The milkman saw the pain in her eyes. "Lady, unless your husband thinks growing old is boring, or has a death wish, he should get out of police work." He hesitated, then spoke softly. "It makes widows."

"Thanks. You really cheer me up," Sally said ruefully, biting her lip again and tasting blood. "Tom would never quit. It would be chicken."

"Lady, better to be a live chicken than a dead duck. I'll see you after Orton is caught."

The milkman tipped his cap, climbed into his delivery van and drove off. Sally watched him go, then turned and walked slowly back into her kitchen.

At house after house the questions the milkman heard were the same. Where was David Orton? How could he hide, when everyone was looking for him? How could he get by a screen of police and murder the newscaster on television? Why was he killing people in Fairport? Who would he kill next? How many would he kill?

These were the same questions that Dempsey, Grady, Briggs, Belli, Farrow, DeLuca, Shuster, Custer and Rice had been discussing for the past two hours. Orton had left another fingerprint on the playing card, at the scene of the electrocution. The lab had reported that Orton's typewriter had been used to type the threatening letters received by the Chief.

They had pieced together exactly how Orton had entered the Inn, subdued Sal DeMarco, impersonated him and wired the 220 volts into Petty's microphone. The electrocution was triggered by a simple timer set to go off at 7:07 P.M. The motorcycle had been stolen from state police headquarters and abandoned in the driveway of David Orton's house.

Dempsey was pacing in front of the others, his face a grim mask. "The nerve of that bastard! I thought his house was under twenty-four-hour surveillance." He glanced questioningly at Rice.

"It is, Chief, it is." Rice took a deep breath and looked

straight at Dempsey. "A man's in the house at all times. Yesterday afternoon, Paul Roberts, a state policeman, was on duty." Rice glanced hopefully at Briggs. Briggs nodded, almost imperceptibly.

"It was your suggestion, Chief. The state police are helping us out," Rice continued, somewhat lamely.

"Roberts saw a trooper pull his bike into the drive. It was about five-twenty P.M. He thought it was his replacement. The guy shouted to Roberts that he'd be right in. Roberts went to pick up his gear and when he got back to the front door, the other trooper was gone. Roberts waited, and in about ten minutes his real replacement arrived. They moved the extra cycle around the back into the garage, where they had theirs parked, thinking the other trooper would be back for it."

A look of disappointment came into Rice's eyes.

Briggs rose from his chair, snubbing out his Tiparillo in the process.

"Gentlemen, have my apologies. It was stupid. We should have caught him." He banged his fist against the palm of his hand in frustration.

Briggs began pacing with Dempsey. "Orton's got guts, no question. In one of our uniforms he can gain access . . . almost anywhere. It's an added problem." He put his hand lightly on Dempsey's shoulder.

Dempsey shrugged off Briggs' hand, sighed and sat back in his seat. "We can't warn the public that the killer is disguised as a state trooper. All hell would break loose. If they can't trust the police, they won't know who to trust." He looked down at his desk.

"We'd have anarchy," Farrow added.

Grady gestured with his cane toward Dempsey. "If Orton parked his motorcycle at his own house, there's a good chance he's holed up there. Jim, do you think there's a secret room, stocked with provisions and weapons, in his basement or garage with a hidden entrance?"

Dempsey stared at Grady for a moment. Then he nodded slowly. "It's possible. Piccollo's team is out there now with metal detectors and two bloodhounds. We went over the house yesterday, but then we weren't looking for Orton's hiding place. We are now.''

"It's about the last place you'd think a murderer would hide," said DeLuca. "Right in his own backyard."

Dempsey caught his breath. "It's the type of clever thing Orton might do. I'm beginning to respect his devious mind. If Piccollo doesn't find a hiding place on Orton's property, he'll search the entire neighborhood." Dempsey's grim face registered his determination.

"The alternative is obvious. He had a car nearby," suggested Grady.

"We're checking now," replied Dempsey. "People in every house within a quarter-mile radius of Orton's are being asked if they saw anything at all unusual yesterday afternoon."

Rice apologized for having to leave the meeting, but explained that his men were checking out an average of at least one Orton sighting every hour and needed help.

Belli reported that Orton's nurse had given him a list of the doctor's patients. None was related to any of the murder victims. There didn't seem to be any connection between Orton's patients and the killings. Belli hadn't seen any specific case records. He'd need a court order for that.

As they broke for lunch, the group agreed with Dempsey's suggestion that the Bicentennial celebration scheduled for Sunday should be postponed.

"We couldn't guarantee the safety of any of the visitors. It's senseless to expose them to unnecessary risks. After we capture Orton, the town will have something worth celebrating then."

Briggs agreed to call the Governor. "She'll be delighted to cancel Sunday's celebration. She's got a lot of common sense."

By 12:45 P.M., the Yankee Clipper was crowded and smoky. Belli, Farrow and Rice were seated in a corner booth, almost half-way through their corned-beef sandwiches. Their conversation had been totally about the murders.

"Why would the bastard do it?" asked Belli between bites. "It's not human."

Farrow put his sandwich down on his plate. "I'm not sure," he said quietly. "Killing is a very human impulse. It goes all the way back to Cain, the third person on earth, firstborn of woman. Times change, people don't. Hell. Cain killed his own brother."

Rice said, "And got away with it. That's what worries me—Orton may be another Cain."

The three exchanged worried glances, and finished eating in silence.

After the waitress had poured their coffee and put their check on the table, Rice leaned forward and spoke softly.

"We all worry about it. But dying's an ordinary thing."

"How the hell can you say that?" asked Belli, his dark eyes flashing.

Rice gestured. "Everyone does it. Sooner or later."

Belli hunched his broad shoulders forward, staring at Rice. "That doesn't make it ordinary. Not to me."

Rice pursued the point. "Life is transient. How do either of you know you'll be alive tomorrow?"

Farrow shrugged and spoke quietly, more to himself than the others. "Death has to be the ultimate experience."

Belli glanced at Farrow. He noticed his blue eyes seemed cold. Farrow's whole expression had changed. He was unwrapping a Tiparillo. Belli let the moment pass.

Rice broke the silence. "Death is part of our job, a constant hazard. Lurking . . . waiting . . . who knows when . . . or how. Every policeman had to deal with it. But we're not paid to die. I resent people thinking we're paid to die."

"What do you expect?" asked Belli.

Rice uncoiled himself, slid out of the booth and stood up. "I want people to remember what we do to preserve life."

As Farrow stood up and took out his wallet to pay his share of their lunch, he looked first at Rice, then at Belli, and said, "Dying really doesn't frighten me. It's almost seductive. But when it happens, I want to go quickly."

Farrow walked swiftly through the smoky haze, out of the bar, leaving Rice and Belli looking at one another. Belli shook his head and said sadly, "I wonder where this will all end."

• • •

Lefty Diangelo was stymied. He'd contacted every connection the Syndicate had in the northeast, turning up nothing. It was clear to Lefty that Orton had no connections with the underworld. The Doc was on his own.

Lefty knew all about the shadowy netherworld of the fugitive. He'd been practicing it all his life. Fugitives were his kind of people, and it took one to know one. They slept in closets, never argued, never tried to piss anyone off. He had firsthand knowledge of being holed up in a rundown room with an iron bed, a bare bulb hanging from the ceiling, dirty paint peeling off the walls, and roaches . . . even hiding out in hippie communes, and more than once he'd faded into the sleazy world of the drug cult.

On the run, there is only one objective—survival. Lefty knew how to go underground. If anyone could find Orton, Lefty could. He was determined. Eager. $100,000 . . . Bubbles would like that. Christ, could that hooker spend money. Maybe it was time to take a look at the Doc's files.

Lou Piccollo and his team had searched Orton's house and grounds meticulously, inch by inch, finding no trace of Orton and no secret room. Moving on, they were searching the neighborhood house by house.

Morning had proceeded into afternoon. Piccollo checked his watch. It was 3:20. It had started to rain. A light misty drizzle. Sergeant Booth of the state police was on duty, sipping a Coke, seated in Orton's favorite stuffed armchair in the den.

Booth stiffened, the skin on his neck crawling slightly. What was that scratching noise? He unholstered his .357 Magnum and quietly crept down the hall toward the doctor's office. He turned the knob silently and swung the door slowly open. Booth felt the searing pain in his shoulder before he heard the *plip*, the distinctive sound of a Mauser with a silencer.

Booth reached for his hip-pack radio and with lips trembling shouted, "Mayday. I've been shot by Orton."

He felt the pain tearing at his insides. His screams filled the room. Then he collapsed on the floor. Booth never saw Lefty vault over the doctor's desk, race out of the office door and drive away in his rented car, muttering to himself, "Fuckin' fuzz. I didn't find nothin', not a friggin' thing."

Piccollo was on the scene within three minutes, relieved to find Booth unconscious, but alive. The Sergeant had lost a quantity of blood, but Piccollo knew he would live. As he called the ambulance, Piccollo swore to himself, "We got burned again. Where the hell did Orton come from? Where the hell did he go?"

Piccollo could feel the tension growing.

Judy checked the rearview mirror and pushed down on the accelerator. The Mercedes handled like a dream. It simply flowed along. She crossed the state line and slowed to the speed limit.

It wouldn't do to start off with a speeding ticket. Connecticut was tough on speeding They took your license away. She knew the whole office would be watching, especially Peter.

It would be easier to do this job as a man. She'd be dealing primarily with men. Men had an easy rapport among themselves. Usually, men carried more authority. They found it easier to sidestep a woman. It was the old weaker-sex syndrome.

She smiled. She had no trouble being firm. Sometimes her toughness shocked her associates. Particularly the men. When she got tough, they jumped and said, "Yes, sir . . . uh, ma'am."

She checked her speedometer and slowed again. It had crept up to seventy. What a car! With a singing heart, she let the smile crease her face. An average performance just wouldn't do. As a woman, it had to be supergood. She was constantly being judged by men. She hoped she'd someday get to the point where she could be just as mediocre as a man.

She adjusted her sunglasses. That was a foolish thought. No, she liked being a woman. It was fun being superior.

In his office, Dempsey mentally ground through the evidence. David Orton fit every clue. He ticked them off again: demolition expert, dynamite in his basement, rattlesnakes, medical background, physically powerful, electrician, DeMarco's identification, typewriter, and, of course, the fingerprints found at the murder scene—not once but twice. Then there was the attempt on his own life. Orton had the stolen grenades.

Clearly, it had to be David Orton. He had an ironclad case against him. Then what was bothering him? Think it out. One, two, three. Christ, now he was patronizing himself. Write it down. He reached for a pencil.

Gus Belli burst into Dempsey's office to tell him that a state trooper had just been shot by Orton at his house.

"Let's go," said Dempsey. He folded his questions about the murders and stuffed them into his pocket.

Dempsey and Belli went over the shooting scene with Piccollo. They were there for about fifteen minutes. It was Piccollo's opinion that Booth had been shot by a Mauser. The lab people arrived as they were leaving.

On the way back to headquarters, Belli commented, "The Doc must have wanted something real bad to break in when he knew his office was being watched."

Dempsey looked intently at him. "Gus, what makes you think it was Orton? Booth never did see the man who shot him. He just assumed it was Orton. Let's not make the same mistake."

Belli didn't respond. His dark face clouded over. Totally confused, he drove the rest of the way in silence.

When the Man heard about the shooting of Booth, he wasn't amused. Some pissass is trying to help me. I don't need any help. This is my game, all the way. I'll find out who's butting in and sic my goldfish after him. He'll butt out in a hurry.

The Man pushed a small cigar into his mouth, and bit down hard on the plastic end.

Don Dillon was driven by ambition. A seven-day-a-week workaholic, he was totally committed to success. Normally, he concealed his restless drive behind a relaxed manner. Lately, he'd become tense, irritable.

Inheriting the Dillon Insurance Company from his father, at

age twenty-six, had been a mixed blessing. As his friends remarked, it had insured his future. His father believed that blood offered the best security for the business.

But the problem with taking over your father's business, as Don quickly learned, was that most people assume the son would have failed at any other venture. He was aware of the jealous "Thanks, Dad" remarks behind his back. As a result, Don spent his working life proving that he was even better at the insurance business than his father. He was. But Don's problem was that he hadn't yet proved it to himself.

Don and his wife, Deborah, lived in a glass-and-stone mansion built on a hillside overlooking the Housatuck. Their life-style was one of great wealth. Inside was a swimming pool, a movie projection room, a game room complete with a full-size Brunswick billiard table, a collection of fine art, a staff of servants, and closets and closets of expensive high-fashion clothes.

Deborah was a compulsive spender. Her hobby was shopping: clothes, antiques, art, minks, jewels, more clothes. It didn't matter what she shopped for, as long as it was expensive. She lived to shop and loved to buy. When the bills pyramided on the desk at the end of each month, Don would erupt. It was their monthly argument, and generally lasted two days. Finally, she'd wear him down with a combination of feminine wiles.

Deborah was good in bed, totally uninhibited, pretty to look at, almost sparkling. Introduced to Don as a Radcliffe girl, he'd never known that she'd never even seen the college. Deborah had been a B-girl and a semi-pro, hustling from the age of sixteen.

Deborah had grown in her role as Mrs. Dillon, until now she was one of the leading socialites in town and president of the LGA at Longwood.

Don had an endless fear that without his money he'd be helpless, a nobody, and lose Deborah. That was probably right. The glue that once held them together had dried and cracked. So, week after week, Dillon worked hard and made a great deal of money. While he worked, Deborah played hard, shopped and spent a great deal of money.

Since it's easier to spend than it is to earn, the Dillons were in deep financial difficulty. They were borrowed to the hilt, heading for bankruptcy. Deborah didn't know. Don didn't dare tell her. Their whole financial empire was about to collapse, like a house of credit cards.

He'd work this out himself. Clearly, he needed to get his hands on $400,000. He had an idea! Her estate would never miss it.

Jim and Brenda attended the funeral of Judge Waller. The misty rain had stopped. Dempsey noticed that there were troopers everywhere. The security for the dignitaries attending was airtight. Everyone entering the church, with appropriate apologies, was asked for identification and searched for concealed weapons.

In addition to the sorrow normally present at a funeral, there was an obvious sense of apprehension among the mourners. The visitors wanted this service over quickly so they could get out of Fairport.

Dempsey was relieved. There were no incidents.

Janice, the Judge's daughter, made a special point of coming over to Jim and thanking him for attending the funeral. "I know how busy you are. Mother and I both want to thank you. Every act of one's life casts a shadow forward. We appreciate what you're doing to catch this madman. Good luck, Chief."

Dempsey tried to look reassuring. Janice kissed him lightly on his cheek. He noticed the hurt in her eyes, but she'd handled it with class.

As they walked to the car, Dempsey asked Brenda to call the yacht club and explain that neither he nor Spike Briggs would be able to race the next day. She asked if they were going to call off the races, and he shook his head.

"Hell, out on the Sound may be the safest place around here. Can you imagine, it was just last Sunday we won the race. What an unbelievable, crazy week!"

Barbara arrived back home from her daughter's camp at about 4:00 P.M. She knew she should be bushed from a hard day's drive, but instead felt exhilarated. Most of the way home had been spent thinking about her man and plans for a long orgy. At one point, she'd become so excited thinking about him she'd pulled over to the side of the road and smoked a cigarette to calm down.

Now, comfortably home, she poured herself a straight vodka over ice and lay down on the couch. Within ten minutes, she was moist in her own pleasure. With no physical contact at all, she could feel him inside. What's wrong with me? I'm getting fuzzy, just thinking about him.

The Man arrived well before five. Hungry for one another, they needed no preliminaries. She was stimulated by five days of fantasizing about him. He was turned on to a fever pitch, driven by two primitive instincts—murder and sex. They went at it with a vigor that was almost uncontrollable. Probing every inch of her, he was stimulating waves of deep, powerful orgasms. It could not be sustained. Finally, she begged him to stop.

"Hon, ease up. I can't take any more. Please don't exhaust me."

They kissed tenderly, and she fell back into bed. He brushed back her hair. She was asleep before he left the room. The Man smiled. Barbara had been satisfied completely. All thoughts of a long orgy were now out of her mind. That was perfect, just the way he'd planned.

Right now, there wasn't time to stay in bed. Exhilarated, he couldn't explain it, but knew he was undergoing a strange phenomenon. He was obtaining an energy transfer from his sexual partners. Clearly, he was picking up strength, vitality and stamina from his sexual activities.

The Man left Barbara's house, no longer feeling vague or fuzzyheaded, once again a predator on the prowl. He took a deep breath.

Judy Rogers checked into the Fairport Inn at 5:20 P.M. The bellhop took her bags at the front entrance, and she parked the Mercedes herself, giving the car a gentle pat as she left. Aware of several admiring glances, she wasn't quite sure whether they were meant for her or the car.

The room was comfortable New England, with chintz curtains and bedspread, highlighted by a small balcony overlooking the crescent swimming pool. Attractive but impractical, was her first thought. She unpacked and put away her things. The empty suitcase went into her closet.

She sat on her large double bed and reached for the phone to call Brenda. The phone on the other end kept ringing. She lit a cigarette. No answer. Her sister was out. It was probably just as well. She'd made her manners, at least tried. After settling in, she'd call again and stop by tomorrow to see her. Sunday would be a good day to get filled in on a lot of background.

After a shower and change, it would be a leisurely dinner in the Colonial dining room. If she remembered correctly, their food was home-cooked and very good.

She opened her briefcase and sat down at the desk. Bond & Bond had provided some additional files that would require at least two hours of work. It would make her job so much easier if the police would catch Orton soon. The murders were confusing.

The murders had to be connected in some way. Big money was involved. But as far as fraud was concerned, there was nothing that implicated Orton in any way. She kept coming back to Nichols and Tilden.

Just a week ago, she'd left Boston for Hawaii, emotional and moody. Now, just one week later, she felt relaxed, totally confident, pleased with herself. Feeling kind of all together, at last. A week ago blue and alone; now she had two male interests and an exciting challenge. She improvised softly to herself, "What a difference a week makes."

Her reverie was interrupted by a knock at the door. The bellhop opened it and handed her a small florist box.

"These were left for you at the desk," he said.

Judy fished in her purse for fifty cents. He thanked her and left.

How sweet of Peter, she thought, glancing at the package.

She undid the ribbon and opened the box, Inside were several clumps of daisies with the dirt still attached. Her forehead creased as she opened the card inside.

Her smile froze. Her heart lurched. The typed message hit right in the pit of her stomach.

Welcome to Fairport, Little Miss Muppet.
> Love and Kisses,
> David Orton

Judy quickly locked and bolted the door to the room, then the door to the balcony. In a daze, she walked back to her bed and slumped down on the edge, still holding the box of daisies.

How the hell? Little Miss Muppet had been her nickname back in grade school!

Swallowing hard, she decided to have dinner in her room.

Across town, in his fortress, the Rock was nervously cracking the knuckles of his fat piggy hands, one after another, in rapid succession. His twelve-carat diamond ring glistened brightly in the fluorescent lighting.

Whitey was packing for his boss' trip to Vegas. They had obtained first-class reservations on United Airlines Flight 711, leaving Kennedy at 10:00 A.M. the following morning. The Rock wanted out of Fairport—wanted out bad. He hadn't slept all night and today had sat in the corner with his back to the wall for eight solid hours. The Rock had a premonition. He was going to die. The Rock didn't want to die. He had it made.

Whitey had never seen the Rock like this, and was shaken to see that that the Rock was a genuine, total coward. He had tried to reach Lefty, but he was out of his motel. Oh well, he thought, the Rock will be himself again once we reach Vegas.

The private phone rang, and Whitey answered. The voice asked for Mr. Rocco. Whitey was astonished. It was the Rock's voice on the phone, but the Rock was sitting in the room with him.

"For you, boss." Whitey pushed the phone nervously at the Rock.

Apprehensively, Tony Rocco picked up the phone. His own voice on the other end of the line asked, "Mr. Rocco?"

"Yes, this is Rocco," he managed to squeak out. "Who's this?"

"You don't know me personally, but I'm David Orton. They call me the Man."

"Orton—the Man!" Rocco's mouth opened wide. His face twisted, contorted and turned pasty green, bile rising into his throat. He swallowed it back.

"Yes, I want you to know you're next on my list. I'm coming to visit, to get my piece of the Rock."

The phone clicked dead in the Rock's ear. He clutched his stomach and wet himself, turning into a quivering mass of yellow Jell-O.

He spoke in a low whisper. "Whitey, bring the car around now, while I change my pants. For God's sake, get Lefty. We'll pick him up in front of his motel in fifteen minutes. He can ride shotgun to the airport. We're going to Vegas tonight!"

The Man's ploy had worked. With one phone call, he'd flushed the Rock out of his fortified subterranean suite, driving him into the open, out where the Rock was vulnerable.

When the car pulled up to the door, Rocco jumped in with two suitcases—one full of twenty-dollar bills, the other half-packed with clothes.

"Let's get to the motel and pick up Lefty. Step on it, Whitey."

"O.K., Mr. Rock." The driver smiled. His slate-gray eyes glanced into the rearview mirror.

The impersonation was so good, the disguise so perfect, that the Rock never knew that it wasn't Whitey who killed him. At the very end, the Rock pleaded, "Whitey, have you gone mad? How can you do this to me, after all I've done for you? Whit—"

At 7:45 P.M. a cruising police car found Whitey lying on the roof of a brand-new Eldorado in the parking lot of Rocco's Cadillac agency. The car's horn was blowing incessantly. It had been wired on. Whitey didn't know what had hit him, maybe a large truck. He had landed badly, shattering a forearm, his right leg and most of his face. He kept murmuring, through bloody lips, "Don't worry, Mr. Rock. You'll be all right when you get to Vegas. Whitey will take care of you."

At 8:12 P.M., a squad car was called to the Fairport Motel. They delivered Larry Fleming, a guest of the motel, to the hospital. Mr. Fleming had suffered an unfortunate accident in which both of his wrists had been broken and the trigger finger on his left hand had been completely severed. Mr. Fleming was in shock and was unable to give any details about his accident.

The driver of the patrol car reported that Fleming looked sinister, with a thin, ominous face. He looked like a real hood.

At 8:27 P.M. Lieutenant Rice, the duty officer, answered a call at police headquarters. The automatic recording system was on.

"Fairport Police, Lieutenant Rice speaking."

"Lieutenant, this is Mr. Rocco."

"Yes, sir. What can we do for you?" Rice recognized the voice of Tony Rocco, from whom he had recently bought a used 1972 Cadillac.

"Somebody just closed the door on me."

"What?"

"I'm dead, Lieutenant. The Grim Reaper. He got me. I bought it. This is my conscience speaking."

Rice swallowed in astonishment, not wanting to believe his ears, staring at the phone in his hand.

"At present, my future's not what it used to be. Some things change, some don't, some should. My soul's in command now."

Rice shook his head. He couldn't understand Rocco.

"Lieutenant, would you like to get lucky?" Rocco's question was flat, without expression. Rice nodded automatically. He needed some luck.

"There's a trapdoor under the rug in my office. It leads to Easy Street, Make Money, Monopoly, Dollar Daze, Bogus Bucks . . . keep going, you go straight to hell."

Rice looked up, his heart beating wildly, his eyes searching for someone to share the call. There was no one in sight.

Rocco continued, his voice unemotional and final.

"There's a plate of garbage outside your front door. A born-fat porker, stuffed with two hundred big ones, messing up a bright, shiny Caddy."

Rice rose from his chair, the phone still on his ear.

"Oh, Lieutenant, plant a clump of ivy for me, and send my body to the Smithsonian. They need a Pet Rock."

On the other end of the phone, Rice could hear a wild laugh, then a click. He was holding a dead phone.

His mind in a whirl, Rice yelled for Sergeant Bob Martin, and together, with drawn revolvers, they raced out the front entrance. Parked at the curb was a black Cadillac limousine, with Connecticut license ROCK-1. Lying in the back seat was Tony Rocco, dead, choked to death on wads of brand-new twenty-dollar bills. His cheeks and eyes were bulging. Protruding from every orifice of the Rock's body were twenty-dollar bills. A pile of twenty-dollar bills covered his fat, pudgy nakedness, his piggy hands clutching the money to him, even in death.

They learned later that the money in the car and in the Rock totaled $200,000. While removing the twenties from the Rock, the Medical Examiner found a playing card, the eight of spades, rolled up cylindrically and inserted deeply.

At 8:35 P.M. Rice called Dempsey at home and reported the murder of Tony Rocco. The Chief was back at headquarters by 8:45 P.M. Belli, Farrow, Piccollo and O'Rourke arrived shortly afterwards. Dempsey called Sam Grady at the Inn, but there was no answer in his room. He called the Briggs. They were out, also.

"Just a typical Saturday night," muttered Farrow.

Dempsey sent Farrow and Sergeant O'Rourke to interview Whitey and Larry Fleming at the hospital. Gus Belli and a backup patrol car went to check out Fleming's room at the Fairport Motel. Dempsey went with Piccollo to Rocco's Cadillac agency. Rice stayed on duty at headquarters, in charge of the continuing manhunt for Orton.

The next hour was most productive. Dempsey and Piccollo found an elaborate suite under the Cadillac agency. Behind the suite they found two rooms containing a printing press, a plate for printing the face side of twenty-dollar U.S. note, a plate for printing the reverse side of a twenty-dollar U.S. note, a sequential numbering head, and $450,000 in new twenty-dollar bills. They were stacked in one-thousand-dollar bundles. There was also a base set up for a second printing press, which had not yet been installed.

At the Fairport Motel, Gus Belli hit the jackpot. In Larry Fleming's room, under the mattress on the single bed, he found a Mauser with a silencer, two bullets missing from the magazine. One bullet was imbedded in the wall above the blaring television set. In Fleming's leather coat, draped over the desk chair, he found a letter. The envelope was addressed to "Lefty." The message was simple and straightforward. "$100,000 in twenty-dollar bills if you find and kill Orton in one week. Plane fare back to Vegas if you don't." The letter was typed and unsigned.

"Lefty, from Vegas. That would be Diangelo, one of the best in the business." Belli was back at headquarters, pleased with what he'd found.

"I think the lab will find that this is the Mauser that shot Booth this afternoon. It wasn't Orton after all. It was Diangelo. It's probable that Rocco hired Diangelo. A hundred thousand dollars is a lot of twenties, and Rocco sure had a bundle of them. He must have been concerned that the search for Orton was putting too much heat on his counterfeit operation. The lab is checking Rocco's typewriter to see if he wrote the letter offering the hundred grand to Lefty."

Dempsey slapped Gus on the back. "A counterfeiter hires a top hit man to kill a mass murderer for us. You never know who's trying to help." He shook his head, then grinned at Belli.

"Keep it up. You'll have your own detective show on TV. You can solve every crime in thirty minutes, with three minutes out for commercials. Good work. You forgot only one thing. Diangelo won't be called Lefty anymore!"

Belli grinned back at Dempsey. Things were looking up.

Farrow hadn't fared as well. Whitey was under sedation

and kept babbling that he'd protect the Rock. Larry Fleming was still in shock and was unable to talk.

It was almost 10:00 P.M. when Dempsey suggested they go home and get some sleep. "Tomorrow's just two hours away, and we've still got to catch Orton. We still haven't found him. While we've been looking, he's killed a well-known newscaster on network televison and the town's Cadillac dealer. He's also maimed a hood and a top-flight hit man. In addition, singlehandedly, the Man has just exposed a large counterfeit operation, which must have been running right under our noses in the heart of Fairport. Who the hell does Orton think he is—Robin Hood?"

A shadow came into Dempsey's eyes. He looked tired and suddenly old as he turned and left for home.

As soon as Dempsey had gone, Belli beckoned to Farrow and they went into Belli's office. Belli closed the door.

"Jesus," Belli exclaimed. "The Sponge told us. Funny money and hard drugs. He was sure right about the funny money."

Farrow hit his forehead with the palm of his hand and exhaled forcefully. "We didn't believe him. Did you tell the Chief, or anyone else?" His freckled face was pale. He looked ill.

Belli shook his head. "And I'm not going to . . . not now."

Farrow looked relieved. "We'll check out the hard-drug bit ourselves. Just the two of us. Remember Dempsey's rule of wallowing. When you're up to your nose in mud, keep your mouth shut." He extended his hand, and Belli grabbed it eagerly.

That evening Marie Benson learned that the bicentennial celebration had been postponed. It was a relief to her. Now she wouldn't have to sit through a dreary small-town parade, read her husband's ghostwritten speech full of patriotic platitudes and unveil a meaningless statue.

Most intriguing of all was the chance to catch an early-morning plane and be in Buffalo before noon. She'd walk into the Senator's motel room and catch him bare-ass naked, in bed with that floozie Flo. She'd confront him.

You can't have it both ways. You can't have Flo and me. Hell, no. She laughed to herself.

There was more than one way to get the Senator to buy her that new ermine wrap. Let him play games with Flo. She'd rather have the ermine. The fur would be hers alone. At last, her priorities were right.

Tonight, Marie was at a dinner dance at the club with the Winchesters, looking elegant in a stunning black silk gown with a deep, plunging neckline. Diamond sandpipers danced on her ears, and a matching diamond pin adorned her gown. She'd been the object of innumerable stares, jealous whispers and compliments. The evening had helped her bruised ego.

It had been a vintage evening. She'd mixed her usual Scotch with two reds, a white and a large quantity of the bubbly, and now was pleasantly high, in her own spirit world, gripped by the grape, in a fingerpoppin' mood.

They had finished dinner, and now, at her insistence, Muriel and Tom were dancing. With Tom, it was a close-contact sport. Muriel was still the same sweet, delightful girl she'd known many years before in college. How could she have ever married that oaf? He was nothing but a social moth and a bottom-grabber.

Marie brushed back her hair. If he puts his big paw on me once more, he'll get a knee right in the groin.

At that moment, her thoughts were interrupted by an attractive-looking man who touched her shoulder. He was tall, broad-shouldered and very masculine. Her smile was cordial, but not inviting. He introduced himself as the manager and told her that there was a telephone call for her in his office. She was to follow him. She rose unsteadily, and he took her arm.

A few dances later, Tom and Muriel returned to the table. Muriel commented, "Marie must have gone to the ladies' room. I think I'll join her."

Muriel was back shortly. She'd checked all of the stalls but couldn't find Marie. They waited about ten minutes longer before Tom looked around the dance floor and in the bar.

Both now made worried inquiries of their friends and club members at neighboring tables.

Had anyone seen Marie Benson?

"She went out with Harold, toward his office," shouted Irene Flynn, dancing past.

It was some time later, when Tom remembered that Harold Green was in the hospital recovering from a hernia operation, that they called the police.

It was then 11:47 P.M.

Rice called Dempsey at home at 11:50 P.M. to report that Marie Benson was missing. The Chief told Rice that as soon as he put on a pair of pants, he'd meet him at the country club. He asked Rice to try to reach Sam Grady at the Inn.

"If she's really missing, it's another federal case. She's a Senator's wife. Sam will want to be involved."

All three arrived at the club before 12:15 A.M.

The Winchesters were distraught. Muriel was weeping. Tom was visibly shaken, unsure of himself. Muriel knew that despite his gruff, confident exterior, Tom had a lack of self-confidence, especially in a crisis. To compensate, he tended to become bellicose and insult others. He was now shouting at Paul Rice.

"Stupid police, wasting taxpayers' money. Why can't you protect innocent citizens?"

It was Sam Grady who quietly but forcefully took Tom aside. Out of earshot of the others, Sam told him, "Buddy, we've all got enough problems. We don't need any of your cheap horseshit. Cool it." He touched the end of his cane to Winchester's shin. He got the message.

Under Dempsey's direction, the police searched for Marie. She had not returned to the Winchesters' house and had not checked into either the Inn or the Fairport Motel. There were six taxicabs on night duty. None had picked up Marie Benson.

The few bars, restaurants and clubs still open after midnight were checked thoroughly. Patrol cars crept along the country roads, shining their powerful searchlights into shrubbery and ditches by the side of the road. The pro shop and caddy house and then the entire golf course were searched.

The bright, almost full moon helped, but there was no sign of Marie Benson.

Sergeant O'Rourke and a patrolman were one of the teams searching the back nine, bordering the woods. The night was silent. Fireflies flickered just above the tall grass. O'Rourke looked into the wooded area and said, "Anything could happen in there. Anything at all." He wiped the perspiration from his face.

Spike Briggs arrived at the club at 12:45, having picked up a bulletin about the Senator's wife on his police radio while returning home from a movie. Briggs seemed annoyed that he'd missed the discovery of Tony Rocco's body and the excitement that followed.

Sam Grady called Senator Benson at his motel in Buffalo. There was no answer to his room phone. The Senator was out.

It was 1:15 A.M. when Sam Grady put his hand on Dempsey's shoulder and solemnly said, "I hate to say it, Jim, but I think Orton has kidnapped Marie Benson."

Marie Benson had followed the Man into the manager's office. He'd pointed to the phone off the hook on the desk. As she moved toward it, she heard him close the door behind them and snap the lock.

The last thing she remembered clearly was looking into a pair of expressionless slate-gray eyes. Trying to cry out, she felt the prick of a needle in her arm. Vaguely, her subconscious remembered the Man's lifting her onto the desk, tearing off her black lace panties and attacking her with an animal ferocity she'd never known before.

Or was she imagining things? Couldn't think clearly . . . bombed out . . . everything jumbled . . . that wine . . . couldn't focus her eyes . . . that champagne . . knew better than to mix the grape and the grain. If she got out of this, she'd give up the gargle.

Everything was totally black inside the trunk of a car. She couldn't move and was having trouble breathing. Now the car began to move.

•   •   •

It was much later when the Man completed his work. Let them find her in the place he'd originally planned. Marie Benson had been surprisingly youthful, with a superb body. Hadn't resisted him at all. Maybe it had been the drug, but when he'd put her on the desk, she'd opened her legs voluntarily and had moved with him all the way. She knew what she was doing. This was no amateur.

He sat down at his desk with a short snifter of brandy, took a sip, then slid out his notebook from its secret niche. With the black marking pencil he crossed out Antonio Rocco, the Rock, the eight of spades, number seven on his death list. As an afterthought, next to Rocco's name he drew a fat little pig, with curly tail and twenty-dollar bills for eyes. Then he crossed it out with a big X.

Rocco had been a shit. That fat slob reminded him of his own stepfather. His real father had died a month before he was born and had left him no memories. His mother had raised him, working in the library until nine every night. She made him study. "Work hard, it's the only way to success, and, sweetheart, I want you to be successful."

He took a mouthful of brandy and swished it around before swallowing. He could feel the warmth as it went down. Mother, sweet mother. Theirs had a been a close relationship, sharing a small, one-bedroom apartment. Then, when he was eight, that fat, oily salesman had come by and moved in. Shortly after, they moved to a two-bedroom flat.

The animal noises the salesman made at night with his mother disgusted and revolted him. His other self learned to turn the noises off and sleep, but he made himself listen. For four years he listened and hated. That's when he learned hate begins in the mind.

The Man stirred himself and finished off his brandy. It was easy to get lost in remembering. He couldn't look back, might turn to salt. His future was about to start.

That Rocco. Imagine running a major counterfeit operation in the center of Fairport, right under the nose of Jim Dempsey. That pompous Chief and his troop of Boy Scout police. They were so proud of the lack of crime in Fairport. He'd show them. They'd asked for it, they'd get it.

Rocco wasn't the only one. The whole fucking town was rotten. McAlpin was a major drug pusher, he was sure of that. Old Sam Tilden was a crook. That clever bastard might get the better of Ned Nichols.

The Man laughed quietly. No way! Maybe in the hereafter, but not in this world.

As he undressed for bed, he laughed again as he thought of the abject terror of the Rock, the weasel-like pleadings of Whitey, the trapped animal instincts of Lefty. He'd had a close call with Lefty. That snap shot from the Mauser had just missed his ear. He reached up and fingered his earlobe. It was still all there.

Tomorrow would be a big day, a red white and blue day, for Marie Benson. He yawned. He needed some sleep, or his brain would stop beating.

8

Sunday, June 8.
Red, White and Blue

"CHRIST, THE nights are getting shorter!" It was a weary Dempsey trying valiantly to open his eyes. Brenda stirred alongside him.

"Jim, don't use the Lord's name that way," Brenda said reproachfully. "When I came home from the movies, I took two sleeping pills and slept like a log. What happened last night?"

Brenda stretched and her hand touched Jim.

"You'd never believe it! Hon, do you mind waiting until tonight?" Reluctantly, he removed her hand. "Marie Benson's been kidnapped. We've got a full day ahead of us."

Dempsey sat on the side of the bed, feeling like a used tennis ball. There was no more bounce left. He struggled to his feet.

The Man was puttering around down in the basement. He was cleaning up after a good night's work, putting certain items back into his arsenal. Work finished, he swung the wine rack closed and locked it with the three critical wine bottles. He washed his hands thoroughly at the basement sink and checked his fingernails carefully uder the light. They were clean.

On reflection, he shouldn't have made love to Marie Benson. He'd taken a big chance, broken one of his cardinal rules, deviated from his plan. Marie could have been missed sooner. Someone might have come by; that no one had was incredible luck. That bitch had really asked for it, deliberately exposing those black lace panties. She hadn't complained.

He went upstairs to the kitchen, two steps at a time. It was a bright, sunny day. In the back of his mind, a new, even bolder strategy was developing. From now on things were going to happen mean and fast. It was getting close to crunch time.

The news section of the Sunday *Times* was on the table, along with a cup of coffee. The front page still featured the electrocution of Warren Petty. Sipping the coffee, he tapped his fingers on the table. The papers couldn't keep up with him.

The Sunday editions were printed early, and news of Tony Rocco's murder had come in too late to be included. The early editions were already on trucks moving to the suburbs when he'd kidnapped Marie Benson. The shooting of the state policeman, Booth, was featured in a separate column on the first page. They still thought that he'd done it.

He was sure that across the nation, the radio and television stations were filled with the news of Rocco's death, the uncovering of a major counterfeit ring in Fairport and the kidnapping of Marie Benson. As the day progressed, the emphasis on the kidnapping would continue to grow, pushing the six murders into the background.

He lit a Tiparillo, sat back and exhaled contentedly. Sunday morning . . . maybe he should go to church. The Man at divine services . . . no one would expect it. But then, he had a lot to be thankful for. He laughed uproariously.

"That poor woman, in the hands of a maniac. Orton will probably bury her alive. Can't the police find her? What's the matter with them? I never did have much faith in Jim Dempsey. He only acts when the cameras are around, like the other night on TV. It's time they call out the Army."

It was Mrs. Rizzo, the grocer's wife, talking to Father O'Leary on the steps of St. Andrew's after early mass.

"Mrs. Rizzo, faith is the evidence of things unseen. Look up to heaven and fear nothing. Dempsey is a good policeman.

He'll catch this Orton,'' the priest reassured her, wishing he felt that certain himself.

He looked up for guidance and strength. It was a beautiful summer day, with wispy white clouds flecking a deep-blue sky.

"Father, we need your help. It's time to stop these senseless crimes."

He shrugged his massive shoulders, turned and went back inside his church.

On the fifth tee at Burning Tree in the suburbs of Washington, four men were discussing the murders and kidnapping. One man, obviously senior to the others, spoke.

"Enough is enough. She's a Senator's wife. It's time to send a handpicked team up there. Grady needs help. I want four of your best detectives, Bob. And I want them there tonight."

He turned and put his hand on the shoulder of a tall, athletic-looking man. "I think it best if you go with them. We'll play on as a threesome. Good luck to you."

A second man interrupted. "Bob, you and your team can fly up in our plane. We've got three men leaving from Dulles at two P.M. I think you know Jim Thatcher. It's his team. We're going to dig into that counterfeit operation."

It was the Assistant Secretary of the Treasury speaking. He then addressed the ball and hit a screaming wormburner 150 yards down the middle of the fairway.

"Damn," he muttered, "another West Texas bug fucker. How can anyone play golf thinking about some crazy nut like this on the loose twenty-four hours a day, seven days a week?"

He strode briskly down the fairway. "Now, let's forget Fairport and play golf."

Gayla heard the news of Rocco's death on the 10:00 morning news as she was preparing to go to the beach. She sat on the edge of her bed, open-mouthed, the top of her bikini still in her hand, mind racing. If Orton had killed Rocco, she might be next. Maybe he had a thing against counterfeiters and their accomplices.

The story of the phony money operation under the Cadillac agency continued to pour from the radio. Numbly, she clicked it off. The Treasury agents would be checking everyone associated with Rocco, every meeting, every scrap of paper. Had anyone seen her enter the private entrance to Rocco's suite at the Inn on Friday? It was time to leave Fairport. This would all blow over and then she could return.

With her airline pass, some time off due, and $200,000, she could go anywhere. No need to invest it for the Rock now. No one would ever know. Should Jeanne be warned? No, the Rock had said they were on their own. Her first priority was to herself.

The first thing she packed in her carryall was her new pleasure toy, adding clothes almost as an afterthought. Finished, she dialed her man's private office number, needing protection. There was no answer. Damn, it was Sunday. Where was her airline schedule? She'd have to hurry, every minute counted.

Dressing quickly and locking up her cottage, Gayla was now perspiring nervously. Her doubts were fast becoming monsters. She'd write her man a note on the plane.

Driving onto the turnpike, she mentally composed the note. "Darling, I've come into some money. I've never told you about my rich aunt. She died last night, and I must fly down to settle her estate in Acapulco. It may take some time. Why don't you fly down and stay with me? What a beautiful place, we could have such a ball. I'll miss you, Tiger. Until I see you, be good!" She'd fill the page with kisses.

He'd come to Mexico, get a quickie divorce, then they could be married.

Gayla checked her rearview mirror. Was that Jaguar following her, or was it her imagination? She took a deep breath. At least it wasn't a police car.

The conference room at police headquarters had been turned into a command post. It was the center of both the manhunt for David Orton and the search for Marie Benson. Two desperate, frantic searches were now underway in Fairport.

Dempsey, Briggs, Grady, their assistants and dozens of other law-enforcement agents were involved. Lawmen from around the country had offered assistance. It had been a crushing week of defeats, of strained emotions, missed opportunities and frayed nerves. One disappointment piled on top of another. One shock yielded to yet another shock. The lawmen were tired and edgy. Tempers were short. Eyes were red and watery from lack of sleep. Faces were set, grim and determined. It was total-commitment time. It was sudden death, overtime.

In this desperate game of life or death, not one trace of David Orton, the will-o'-the-wisp, had been discovered. His constant action, his fluid motion, had the police totally off balance. On his own schedule, Orton appeared like an evil wind, committing murder after murder, kidnapping Marie Benson, and then, like the wind, was gone.

The lawmen knew that, sparked by the bright, penetrating laserlike focus of television and fanned by the tens of thousands of written and spoken words of newspapers, news magazines, and radio, public indignation was rising to the breaking point. The public wasn't angry at the murderer, David Orton, but was furious with the police for not protecting them adequately, for not catching Orton, for not rescuing a Senator's wife. Since he was leading the manhunt, the public's frustrations seemed to center on Dempsey. Orton was clearly outwitting and outmaneuvering him.

The interviews with the club members and guests at the dinner dance yielded little. Witnesses stated that Marie Benson had left the Winchesters' table with a man who closely resembled Harold Green, the club manager. Green's description was that of a tall, dark man with a handsome smile, practiced for too many years at too many country clubs. Marie had apparently gone with him willingly.

They had walked toward the manager's office, located in the rear of the building. There was some indication that they had used the office for sex; perhaps even rape had been involved. A pair of initialed black lace panties had been found in the office. They were Marie Benson's. Two other matching pairs were found in her luggage at the Winchesters'.

No one had seen them leave the manager's office or the building. That was not surprising. The office had a private door of its own exiting to the parking area behind the club-house. This lot was used by club employees only. Interviews with employees turned up nothing.

No one had seen Harold Green's car. He was still in the hospital unable to walk. A matchbook with David Orton's fingerprints had been found on the desk. There were no other fingerprints. Everything seemed to have been wiped clean. The trail of Benson and Orton outside of the manager's office was stone cold. It was nonexistent.

Dempsey was talking quietly to Sam Grady and Spike Briggs. "This guy's a puzzle. He's clearly brilliant—he's outwitted us at every turn. We don't know where he's hiding, can't locate his wife. We don't even have his scent. Not a whiff. Yet he leaves another set of clear fingerprints for us to find. It doesn't make sense."

Briggs stretched. He looked at Dempsey. "He's rubbing our noses in it, wanting more and more credit."

"The playing cards serve that purpose, identifying his victims. I can't understand leaving his fingerprints also."

"What are you getting at, Jim?" Sam had leaned forward in his chair, his hand on his cane, eyes intent on Dempsey.

Dempsey turned and faced Grady. "I really don't know yet. I've been thinking about the Man all week, day and night, and I've got a pretty good idea of how he thinks and operates. He's smart, efficient, and plans well. He executes with precision, with balls, and flawlessly . . . with one major exception." Dempsey held up his index finger.

"He keeps leaving clear fingerprints in obvious places for us to find. That doesn't fit his pattern. If he'd done it once, I'd consider it an oversight, a mistake. But he's done it four times."

Briggs nodded, took out a package of aspirin from his pocket, poured a glass of water and swallowed three of them.

"Why do people do such damned awful things to each other? It's unbelievable. My mind's unraveling. It's not wrapped tight anymore. The ends are frayed. I've got a splitting headache.'' Briggs rubbed his eyes.

"So do I,'' said Grady.

"Me, too,'' added Dempsey.

Briggs passed the aspirin around.

Out on the Sound, fourteen Atlantics were nearing the finish line. Less than a dozen yards separated the first eight boats. Without Dempsey and Briggs, it was going to be the closest finish to a race in several years.

Number 4, an all-green boat, crossed the finish line, the winner by less than a foot. There were loud cheers from the other boats.

John Frouge had never won a race before. He had sailed in the shadow of Dempsey, Briggs and Nichols ever since joining the club five years before. John was an avid sailor, but not of championship caliber. He was well liked and respected, because he tried hard, entering every race. He never complained and had contributed importantly to publicizing the Fairport Yacht Club. Hard work and agreeable personality had paid off, he was the current Commodore of the club.

The other finishers crowded around Frouge on the dock. Suddenly four of them seized him, swung him back and forth and catapulted him into the water. It was the traditional club baptism awarded a first win. The group shouted gleefully. "Frouge's a winner, three cheers for the Frog, the Frog, the Frog . . .'' The chant grew as others picked it up.

Mary Frouge blanched. The Frog. She bit her tongue and could taste the salty blood, trying to hide her feelings, but it was difficult. John had been a champion swimmer in college, and his friends had naturally called him the Frog. She hated that nickname, in fact despised it. She associated it with little green ugly things with warts.

It had taken her a long time to live down that nickname, and now it was starting all over again. Why did he have to win?

Jeanne Hoover was up at the crack of noon, and heard the news of the Rock's death as she was preparing to take her shower. She turned off the steaming water, put the soap back in the dish and went back to the comfort of her bedroom. Sitting naked on the edge of her bed, she lit a cigarette, trying to collect her thoughts.

Rocco dead. His counterfeit operation exposed! The radio had said the police had raided Rocco's printing plant under the Cadillac agency. She'd wondered where he had it hidden, but never even wanted to guess. Apparently they had raided it last night. Still hadn't arrested her. That meant they didn't know about her. She doubted if Rocco would have kept any files, any addresses. He'd told them over and over never to write anything down. If the police had found her address at Rocco's, they'd have been here by now.

With Rocco gone, who knew about her involvement? Whitey. He'd never talk. Besides, he didn't even know her name. Gayla. They were both in the same fix. If Gayla was caught, she'd talk. But Gayla would run . . . fly away fast . . . probably gone already. As a stewardess, she had wings and the perfect cover, but if Jeanne was to run, it would look suspicious. No, the worst was probably over. Why not sit it out?

She snubbed out her cigarette in the ashtray.

Two hundred thousand dollars. She had two hundred big ones. It was all hers! Rocco was his own boss. He had no connections. Except for Whitey, no one was close to him. Whitey was the only threat, but he'd be in prison for a long time, and would never talk. He was old-style loyal and would do what Rocco had told him. He wouldn't contact her. Even if he was released, there was no danger. It was counterfeit money. Whitey didn't think of it as real money.

Besides, Whitey liked her. She knew men. No, Whitey wouldn't bother her. The money was hers. She decided to leave the suitcase right where it was for the time being. No one could possibly find it there.

Jeanne got up from the bed with a new spring in her walk, picked up the soap, turned on the shower and stepped in. As the pulsating hot-water spray beat down, she thought to herself, If my world does fall apart, I've got friends in high places.

• • •

It was early morning in Vegas when Little Louie heard the news. It was a phone call from Eddie in Yonkers, who knew that Louie had some type of arrangement with Tony Rocco. Now Eddie could guess what it was, but he didn't try to figure it out in detail. It was better not to know.

Eddie put it this way. "Sorry to wake you, but I thought you'd like to know about Rocco."

"Thanks, Eddie. I'll do you one someday."

Little Louie carried his 265 pounds on a five-foot-eight frame and never worried about his weight. In his business, he'd be happy to live long enough to die of overweight. Besides, Louie felt he wasn't overweight, he was just a foot too short. Louie loved to eat. When happy, he ate to celebrate; when sad, he ate to commiserate. He'd get up from the dinner table just to get something to eat in the kitchen. But Louie was tough. The fat was layered with muscle. You could hit Louie in the stomach full force with a fist of iron knuckles and he wouldn't blink an eye, a result of pumping iron for over ten years.

Unfortunately, his head was almost as muscular as his stomach. But on one ever claimed Louie was smart. Before he had become respectable in Vegas, Louie had been an enforcer for Gambini. With a specialty of squashing testicles, he was known as the Nutcracker. Actually, he'd only done the trick twice, but that had been enough to establish a reputation. No one messed around with Little Louie. Even the thought of the consequences was too painful.

It was later when Louie heard the full details. He thought, Diangelo in the hospital . . . that wouldn't do . . . Lefty knew too much about Louie. Orton must be something. Lefty was one of the very best.

The police had picked up the Jackson plates. Nothing was said about the Grant plates. He had seen them. Perfect, brand-new, never been used. He knew where Rocco would hide them. The police had missed them. He'd get them and set up his own operation in Vegas. They were worth millions. He'd have to move fast. Today.

He'd take Spider with him. Spider would protect him and would blow away Lefty.

Marie Benson was still missing. There had been no demands for ransom, but the police knew Orton had her. Someplace in Fairport was a hideout. He was holed up there now with his wife and Marie Benson.

"Kidnapping doesn't fit Orton's pattern."

Dempsey was talking to Grady, Briggs, Belli and Farrow.

"He's clearly not interested in money. No ransom request, and last night, he left two hundred thousand dollars with Rocco. Counterfeit, but perfect. Very spendable. Other than weapons, he's stolen nothing of value. The pattern shows he's interested in only one thing—murder."

"You expect him to kill Marie Benson?" It was Farrow asking a question to which he already knew the answer.

Dempsey looked at him, nodded and sighed. "He probably has already. He'll want us to find her body today to keep up his fucking one-a-day routine. He's a walking, living, breathing time bomb."

"Sounds as if you're inside his mind writing his script," Briggs interjected, drumming his fingers on the table. "But I agree. If we don't find her soon, he'll probably call and tell us where to look."

"I hope you're both wrong, but I'm afraid you're not," said Grady. "I finally got through to Senator Benson. He took the news awfully calmly, I thought. Said it was just part of the risk a public servant had to take these days and that Marie would understand. I told him we'd find her. I didn't know what else to say."

Crestfallen, Belli shook his head. "He's got us on the run. We're stretched so thin we've got holes all over the place. There's no time to dig for facts. No time to think. I'd like to get my hands on that cock—"

"Let's go back to details," interrupted Farrow. "We've assumed Orton is acting according to a set plan. He's meticulous. A plan would fit the pattern."

"No question," Dempsey added.

"O.K. Therefore, he must have planned to kidnap Marie Benson all along," continued Farrow.

"Or Senator Benson. Remember, she was standing in for him," commented Briggs, as he exhaled his cigar smoke.

"That's what I'm getting at. She was going to make a speech and unveil a statue. Let's assume the celebration hadn't been called off. Where—"

Briggs interrupted Farrow with a shout. "The Statue. My God, the statue, of course."

Dempsey leaped to his feet. "It's worth a try. Sam and Spike, come with me. Gus and Tom, we'll meet you there."

When they pulled the cord that opened the huge olive-colored drape covering the statue of the Minuteman, they found Marie Benson. She was nude, reclining on the statue, glistening in the afternoon sunshine. Her entire body had been spray-painted in vertical stripes—red, white and blue.

A typewritten note proclaimed, "Fairport's Bicentennial Girl." A playing card, the seven of spades, had been stapled to the note.

Doc Brady later told them that Marie had died of an overdose of carbon monoxide, explaining that hemoglobin has an affinity for carbon monoxide more than thirteen hundred times greater than it has for oxygen. He claimed that the paint might have killed her by closing off the oxygen to her pores, but Marie had already been dead when she'd been painted. The report also mentioned an involvement in sexual intercourse within the last eighteen hours.

Orton was not only a killer, he was also a rapist!

Searching the area, they found one patch of weeds stained a bright crimson. From a distance, it looked like human blood. Close up, it was red paint. Marie's body had been painted while lying on the ground near the statue.

Gus Belli noticed two Tiparillo butts in the fringe of the woods, about forty feet from the paint stain. They looked fresh. They were probably meaningless discards. But then it was just possible they could have been flipped there by Orton. Hesitating for a moment, the young lieutenant had a funny premonition. He looked toward the others. They were all staring at the Senator's wife. He'd like to show them to the Chief alone. But Dempsey was talking to Briggs.

He picked up the butts carefully and put them in a Kleenex, rolled the tissue around them and put the wad in his pocket. He wondered if Orton smoked Tiparillos. Check it out . . . wouldn't say anything to anybody . . . lots of people he knew smoked Tiparillos . . . they were all around him.

After checking the butts, he'd flush them down the john. It was warm and sunny, but Belli had a sudden chill. If Dempsey found out that some possible evidence had been disturbed, he knew whose butt would get flushed.

Alice Briggs caught the 3:12 train from Grand Central, which was scheduled to arrive in Fairport at 4:50 P.M. She selected a seat in one of the less-dilapidated coaches and sat down gingerly. The seat back was stained from the perspiration of countless commuters. Although she had carefully selected the no-smoking car, there were numerous burn holes in the fabric from thoughtless smokers. The floor was littered with cigarette butts, used tissues and scraps of food.

As the train pulled out of the station, Alice settled slowly back and tried to relax. Even her mother had remarked at her tenseness. She felt like a bundle of frayed nerve endings.

She halfheartedly opened a paperback bought in the station. It was impossible to keep her mind on the pages. The murders in Fairport made this novel seem so trite, so contrived. She closed the paperback and put it in her Gucci bag.

The panorama flashed by the soot-stained window—Harlem, 125th Street, the sordid slums. People on fire escapes, seeking relief from the summer heat, one of their few pleasures, watching the trains clattering by. Kids in underpants, playing in the water squirting from open hydrants, the water rushing down the gutters, sweeping filth and dog excrement before it.

Alice closed her eyes. She and Spike were so lucky to be in Fairport, so very lucky. To live in a lovely clean house with lawns, flowers and giant old shade trees, enjoying a clover-shaped swimming pool with clear, sparkling water, sailing with friends, and playing golf. Yes, they were lucky. Visiting her mother lately so depressed her. She was anxious to get home.

In recent weeks, Spike had been acting so strange. He seemed preoccupied . . . even before the murders. Was there another woman, or were there women? She'd noticed that strong, lingering perfume clinging to his shirt. The girl behind the perfume bar at Altman's had identified the odor as Flower of Musk Oil.

Alice had retreated back into her own protective shell, away from Spike. In turn, he seemed to pull away further. They were losing the ability to talk, to communicate with each other. What was happening to their marriage? What was happening to her life and happiness?

She was a fool. A suspicious fool. Right now she'd resolve to forgive and forget. Spike was her man and she wanted him. Life without him would be nothing. It would be so lonely. She was a home person, and needed a nest. It was time to make up and recapture the magic before it was too late.

Excited now, Alice couldn't wait until the train reached Fairport. I'll smother him with kisses . . . all over . . . even try those kinky things he's always wanted me to do . . . let my real emotions surface . . . aim to please . . . come out with my tail wagging . . . do anything. Whatever it takes to keep him. I'll show that oversexed bastard. There was a hint of a smile on her lips.

It was 5:00 P.M. when the train reached Fairport. Not bad, only ten minutes late, Alice thought, eyes eagerly searching the platform.

Spike wasn't at the station to meet the train. Disappointed, Alice walked over to Tommy's Taxi Stand and took a cab home.

Judy spent most of the afternoon visiting with her sister. Brenda was surprised and delighted. Theirs had always been a close relationship, despite the six years difference in age. She was impressed at how well Brenda looked. She was still the same considerate sister, so gloriously feminine and as warm as sunshine.

Judy, now calmer, had told no one about the daisies or the note from David Orton, and didn't intend to. If Peter Bond found out, he might order her back to Boston. This secret might prove very useful. How did Orton know she was in Fairport?

"Remember my nickname, Little Miss Muppet?" she asked. Brenda laughed; she had forgotten all about it.

It had been a rambling conversation of bits and pieces, giving Judy a fairly complete background on each of the murders. Every time they'd talked about Jim, Brenda's eyes had brightened. Judy told Brenda sketchily about her assignment, keeping names and facts unspecific.

"Forgeries of negotiable bank drafts are being passed on a large scale in the metropolitan area," Judy generalized. "The banks don't want to talk about the problem, for fear of undermining consumer confidence. They'd rather lose the cash than risk an uproar. We go from town to town checking . . . ."

Brenda nodded, not really listening. This was her baby sister talking. Life was moving so fast. They hadn't been taking enough time lately to know, to enjoy, one another. Brenda smiled. Underneath her charming manners, enthusiasm, exterior softness and style, Brenda had caught a glimpse of Judy's flintlike hardness.

"My little sister, an investigator, a private detective. It's funny. You used to fly apart emotionally and dissolve in tears. When you were young, you were so shy, entering a room and walking along the nearest wall so no one would notice you."

Judy wrinkled up her nose. "Early impressions die hard. I'm still emotional. But I've learned to speak out, show happiness, even bitch occasionally. I'm hard on myself. I still feel my emotions inside, just don't show them as much."

Brenda leaned forward and put her hand on Judy's knee. "That's called maturity, sis."

"Yes, and experience. When I lose my temper, I don't hurt anybody but myself."

Over tea, Brenda related in some detail Cindy's traumatic experience and regression. "Judy, I'll never forget the look on Cindy's face that morning, or her words—'Daddy, Daddy, he killed my dolly.'" Brenda shuddered, and Judy's heart went out to her sister, seeing that talking about Cindy was like exposing a raw nerve.

"There's no magic formula," Brenda said. "We take it one day at a time." She brushed away the start of a tear. "It can only be solved by love and affection."

"It's that simple?" Judy asked.

"No, it's that difficult," Brenda said flatly.

"Judy, a mind . . . it's a terrible thing to waste . . . especially when it's your . . ." She didn't finish. Brenda looked down at the floor.

Judy thought Brenda was going to cry, but the emotion vanished quickly, covered by a sip of tea. When she looked up, her face was smiling. "I try to remember. You have to hit bottom before you can start up again."

The two sisters hugged on the couch and for a long time sat there without speaking.

Declining both the offer of dinner and the use of their guest room, Judy said that Bond & Bond wanted her to work out of the Inn and that also she was expecting a phone call from Peter Bond. She said that she was anxious to see Jim, but that there was plenty of time, and she didn't want to interfere with his work.

Judy was leaving when Cindy woke from her nap, came downstairs and entered the room. Her heart leaped, seeing Cindy's pale, fragile look. The child was staring, her eyes all white around the edges. There was a momentary uncertain silence.

Brenda jumped up and took Cindy's hand.

"Cindy, dear, you remember Aunt Judy."

Cindy stared blankly.

Judy knelt on the rug in front of the little girl, speaking softly as she looked into her eyes. "I brought you a present," she said, unwrapping a package and handing the open box to Cindy.

"It's from Hawaii. It's a King Kamehameha doll, for you."

She saw the child's eyes widen, with an expression she couldn't quite fathom. For one awful moment, she thought Cindy was going to turn and run out of the room. A tear ran down the girl's cheek, and, crying, she hugged the doll to her chest. The tears stopped as suddenly as they had come.

Trying to speak—her voice so low Judy strained to hear—Cindy said only, "Thank you, Aunt Judy."

Eyes more than misty, the two sisters walked out to the Mercedes together, their arms around one another. Brenda spoke softly. "Thanks, sis. It was a minor miracle."

Driving off, Judy saw in her rearview mirror the figure of the tiny girl, the doll clutched tightly in both arms, a smile on her face.

The planeload of federal agents arrived at the Bridgeport Airport at 5:35 P.M. Three Treasury agents under the command of James Thatcher were picked up by a local agent and driven rapidly down the Thruway to the Sheraton Motor Inn in Stamford. They immediately started to set up their investigation of Rocco's counterfeit operation.

The four FBI agents under the leadership of Bob Dillinger drove in two rental cars to the Holiday Inn in Bridgeport. Here they were met by Sam Grady, who briefed them thoroughly on the seven murders. Grady suggested that Dillinger's team conduct an independent investigation of the murders of Judge Waller and Senator Benson's wife. Both came under federal jurisdiction. Grady would serve as liaison with the Fairport police and the Connecticut State Police. His regional men would continue to work with him and Jim Dempsey.

Grady and Dillinger were old friends. Bob Dillinger, assured and authoritative, was well thought of in federal circles. In his early years with the FBI, the name Dillinger was a source of embarrassment to him. The greeting was always "Robbed any good banks lately?" But the name had its advantages. It attracted attention. His superiors, at first bemused by the name, remembered it. As a result, they gave him special assignments.

Dillinger had done well because he had unusual talent, and was now considered one of the best detectives in the FBI. He had all the normal abilities plus an intuitive second sense, almost psychic. He had a nose for murder.

Marie Benson's murder again stunned the nation. Fairport had now suffered through seven murders, one each day for a week. The mass murderer had been identified as David Orton, but he was a ghost, a ghost of death, who couldn't be found. Despite all of the efforts of the police of Fairport and neighboring communities, the state police and the FBI, he was still on the loose. Even worse, Orton was still murdering people, prominent people.

Today, June 8, was to have been an important gala day in Fairport's history, the town's Bicentennial celebration. Marie Benson's death and a week of murder, chaos and frustration had changed all that. Outsiders could sense the subtle shifts of feelings and emotions in the town's residents. An all-pervasive, ugly mass mood had developed and was spreading, enveloping virtually everyone.

Initially, it had been apprehension. By Wednesday, it had become fear, a numbing fear of death. By Thursday, fear had grown into hysteria, close to terror. The wave of hysteria had crested with the identification of Orton as the Man. Now, hysteria was giving way to resentment. The people were now becoming angry at their police and law-enforcement agencies. They couldn't understand why Orton, once he'd been identified, hadn't been captured.

Then there was the lunatic fringe across the country. To this group, Orton was becoming a national hero, a modern gunslinger, with seven notches on his gun. That made him special. On television, Orton was providing greater entertainment than the summer reruns of *Kojak* and *Charlie's Angels*. The Doc now had a following, and underground Orton clubs were being formed. Pools were being organized on how many murders he would commit. The odds were now down to 20–1 on thirteen successful murders, 1,000–1 on fifty-two murders.

To the average man in the street, it was apparent that Orton was killing only prominent people. Ordinary people didn't have to worry. They could sit on the sidelines as fans and watch. Orton was their star performer in a drama that unfolded day after day, with far more punch and impact than their daily soap operas.

As people realized that Orton was killing only important people, the mass exodus from Fairport slowed to a trickle, then stopped. Many who had fled their homes returned. Prominent people, thought leaders, decision makers, movers and shakers were still leaving. No one but Orton knew who he would kill next, but people had a week's track record to go on and were studying the form chart with grisly interest, guessing who would be next.

Dempsey, again at his desk, was worried. Not for himself. He'd go nose to nose with David Orton anytime and let Orton choose the weapons. It was Fairport. The people depended on the force, and he'd let them down. Seven murders. He should have his ass kicked. "Fred" was the Reverend Fredericks. Damn, they could have nailed Orton at the church. He'd told them—called it close—and got away with it. Then Rocco and Benson. Who the hell was next?

That nagging headache, it kept getting worse every day. He swallowed three more aspirins and washed them down with the last of his Fresca. Someone said that aspirin irritated the stomach lining and caused stomach bleeding, heartburn, nausea and allergic reactions. If these murders continued, he'd probably have them all.

He had to out think Orton. At every murder he'd been a step behind. He had to speed up . . . had to catch that murdering bastard. Where was the lady in red, his informer? Over sixty percent of all major crimes are solved through informers. People who, for one reason or another, are jealous, frightened or resentful enough to turn in information which leads to the arrest of the perpetrator.

Christ, he was beginning to think in stylized Police Academy language. In the last week they'd received not one valid lead. Not one single shred of evidence from ordinary citizens, although they'd been asked for help over and over. It didn't make sense. It didn't fit the normal pattern.

Orton was busy killing people at a one-a-day pace. But no one had seen him. There had been hundreds of reported sightings, but not one had checked out. That was unusual, so unusual it was suspicious.

Hold on. DeMarco saw . . . swore it was Orton who knocked him cold . . saw him for just a second or two . . .

slate-gray eyes . . . never forget them. But a master of disguise . . . could be done with practice in a matter of seconds . . . slip in a pair of slate-gray contact lenses and make them very noticeable. It would be the main identifying feature that people would remember, like a mustache or red hair . . . and easily removable . . . In a split second they'd be out of sight, back in your pocket. It was incredible.

Orton's known actions kept running through Dempsey's mind. He had to get organized. He had to find a clue, a pattern, a key. He picked up a pencil and made a list of Orton's actions on Friday. He estimated the times as best he could.

Dempsey checked his list and whistled appreciatively. It involved split-second timing. Christ, if Orton could do all that in less than an hour and a half, in an afternoon, Lord knows what he was doing the rest of the day. He could kill off half the town. All this, and no one had recognized him. On Saturday, Orton had been even more active. Dempsey jotted down the activities he knew about, from the time Orton called Rocco on the phone until he'd draped Marie Benson's body on the statue.

The Chief looked at his list closely, positive of the time the phone call had come in to Rice, estimating the other times from that one. Orton was really operating on a tight schedule. He'd listened to the tape himself. You'd swear it was Rocco talking.

Orton had left $200,000 in Rocco's car. Why? An honest murderer? It didn't make sense. Most people who murdered did it for money.

Maiming Diangelo was no small trick. Thinking about it made Dempsey's skin crawl. Lefty had a king-size reputation, a number-one hitter. You couldn't buy anyone more deadly. He'd never known Dave was that lethal.

He was clearly mobile, even after dropping Rocco's car off. How did he get around? His own car was still parked in his garage. The one thing that deviated from the plan was Orton's rape of Marie Benson. He'd actually fucked her on the manager's desk. That was risky, foolhardy. Why would he take such a chance?

Orton had spray-painted Marie out by the statue, probably about sunrise. The smear of red paint in the weeds meant he'd missed one shot of red. He'd obviously used a tarp. The grass was all tamped down in one spot.

Dempsey shook himself and stood up. He stretched and walked around his office, gritting his teeth. He was making progress, clearing some of the cobwebs, unplugging his mind.

The identification of Orton as the murderer had stopped all other investigation. No one else was a suspect. But . . . suppose he wasn't the murderer! What a ploy by the real killer.

Brilliant, absolutely brilliant. For four days, no one had thought of any other possibility. It had to be Orton. Everything pointed to him. Dempsey mentally ticked off the evidence. It was ironclad. But there was that nagging doubt. Just suppose it wasn't. Back to square one and chaos! Oh, shit!

What was he thinking? They'd found Orton's fingerprints at four different murders. Wait a minute! Four clear, readable prints, one a day for four consecutive days. The odds anytime on finding just one usable print were less than one in four. The odds of doing it four days in a row were astonomical . . . and all on small, portable items. Easy to plant.

No other fingerprints, not even smudges or partials on areas that Orton had to have touched. Everything wiped clean. It was too neat, too pat.

Supposing someone else was planting Orton's fingerprints? Fiendishly clever . . . courts accept fingerprints . . . juries convict with fingerprints . . . they're almost irrefutable. Lawyers blanch and plead insanity for their client when they learn his fingerprints were found at the scene of the crime.

Dempsey stirred, shook his head, rose from his chair and did a series of deep knee bends. Then he walked down the hall to get another Fresca and relieve himself. The afternoon was fast disappearing. Where did the time go? He couldn't begin to account for it. He felt disoriented. He wanted to finish his thoughts before evening.

Farrow walked into the men's room after him. They stood side by side at the urinals. Out of the side of his mouth,

Dempsey asked, "If you wanted someone's fingerprints on certain items—without his knowing—how would you do it?"

"Carefully, very carefully." Farrow laughed, but then he realized he was laughing alone. Out of the corner of his eye he saw the Chief's heavy-lidded, serious look and quickly added, "You might collect items handled by that person, do it over a period of time, until you're ready to use them."

"Easy for a matchbook cover, even a tube of toothpaste or playing card. It would be harder with an icepick."

Dempsey was reflecting on Farrow's thoughts out loud.

They both hit the flush buttons at the same time, flipping the last drop of urine into the foaming water, and zipped up. They continued their discussion side by side at the washbasins.

"Do you remember a case in California where an innocent man was convicted of bank robbery with fingerprint evidence? It got quite a bit of publicity."

"Yes, I do. *Reader's Digest*, sometime back." Farrow's encyclopedic memory and hobby of reading about unusual crimes was often helpful. "The DePalma case. His fingerprint was on the teller's cage that was robbed. Claimed he was seventeen miles away at the time. His story was supported by thirteen witnesses. Said he'd never been in the bank, yet he was still convicted and went to prison."

"Innocent?"

"Yes."

"Convicted by a fingerprint?"

"Yes, against everything else."

Dempsey and Tom dried their hands and continued talking as they walked slowly down the hall toward the Chief's office.

"Tom, I seem to remember that someone planted the fingerprint. Am I right?"

"Not exactly. The police lifted a fingerprint from the teller's cage. A fingerprint specialist testified in court that it was DePalma's. Exhibits compared the latent with DePalma's. They were identical."

"But, if I remember, DePalma was set up."

"He was. The expert had forged DePalma's fingerprint on the exhibit."

"How?"

"Quite simply. He made a Xerox copy of a fingerprint card of DePalma. Then he lifted the impression of DePalma's index finger off the paper with fingerprint tape and put it on the exhibit."

"So it's possible to transfer fingerprints. I thought so."

"But, if I remember," warned Tom, "that method leaves particles of toner powder . . . it's used in the Xerox machines. Very different from fingerprint dusting powder."

Dempsey nodded wearily. "I do remember. The lab's rechecking Orton's fingerprints now."

As they reached Dempsey's office, Mary gave them a subdued smile and said, "Lab's on the phone."

The Chief hit the flashing button, listened and repeated the conversation aloud for Tom's benefit.

"You say they're real fingerprints? Not copies? No traces of toner powder? Not transferred? They're Orton's. No question about it. Orton himself left those fingerprints on these items."

Dempsey looked crestfallen.

On Shoreside Drive, just three estates down the Gold Coast from Shore Haven, there'd been considerable activity all day long. Black limousines with drawn curtains had been shuttling back and forth from Fairport to an embassy in New York City and an estate in Glen Cove, Long Island. Ostensibly, this was Happy Acres, the estate leased and occupied by the Russian Cultural Exchange.

In reality, it was the nerve center of Russia's extensive spy network in the eastern United States. Some sixty subversive agents reported to the Soviet Union through this cultural-exchange front. It also served as the U.S. headquarters of the KGB, Russia's security police. Local residents referred to it as the Home of the Ugly Bears.

Inside the bear pit, Oleg Kamonov, first secretary of the Russian Cultural Exchange, was briefing an elite group of six KGB colonels.

"This place is total madness. Seven murders in seven days. In Russia we wouldn't have trouble like this. Psychiatrists are watched closely. Orton's sickness would have been detected early and he would now be receiving beneficial care from the state in an asylum.''

"The Third Secretary of the Politburo arrives this evening. He's here for four days, then addresses the United Nations on Friday. You are to protect his every movement. Nothing—do you understand, nothing—is to happen to him. Your very lives . . . You do understand me?''

Six heads nodded in unison, an abject expression of fear registering on every face at the mention of one word said softly: "Siberia.''

Kamonov ran his hand over his heavy beard. "The Third Secretary is an avid sailor. He'll want to sail on the Sound. I leave it to you to work out total security. I have asked the U.S. State Department for protection against this madman Orton. As usual, I have received no satisfaction. They say the police are doing everything possible. It's ridiculous. They've arrested no one. In Russia the jails would be full of dissidents. It is madness. It could only happen in the United States. Capitalist nonsense, perfect evidence of what happens in a country that grants too much freedom.''

One of the KGB colonels spoke for the group. "You're right, sir. There's no place like America.''

It was now twilight, and the red glow in the sky had almost gone. The light was shimmery. In a moment dusk would be all-enveloping.

The Man stood for a moment in the deepening shadows and watched the light fade. Then, wearing telephone lineman's cleats and carrying a small duffel bag, he walked directly to the tall mast set in a cement base that served as the flagpole at the Fairport Yacht Club. The few stragglers still at the club were either on their boats in the slips or on the upper deck on the other side of the clubhouse.

No one watched the flagpole. They missed quite a sight.

With the duffel bag clipped to his belt, the Man quickly scaled the mast. Originally, it had been the mainmast of a square-rigged brigantine from the post-Civil War era. The mast was fifty-two feet high and still had the original crosstree. The rigging was modern, light polyester cord. At the base of the crosstree, the Man rigged his nine-sixteenth-inch-diameter nylon rope to the heavy block and tackle already installed. Letting both ends fall to the ground, he checked to make sure that the cleat, high on the mast, would hold a heavy weight.

The nylon line had a break strength of six thousand pounds. After removing a can of grease from his duffel bag, he descended slowly, dabbing gobs of it on the mast. Once on the ground, the can of grease, greasy gloves and climbing spikes went into the bag.

Now, with a clean pair of gloves, he picked up a twelve-foot piece of nylon rope, set aside before. The rope had an oval metal ring on one end and a bowline noose on the other. He tied the long nylon rope onto the metal ring with a hitch, knowing the metal ring would pass through the pulley. By using a hitch, he would be able to release the long rope from the ring, at the proper moment, with a simple pull.

The Man took one last look at the flagpole, picked up his duffel bag and faded into the night.

Then the Man stopped at Barbara's. Her reading light was on. She was lying on the bed, dressed in a shortie nightgown.

"Hi, precious. Going to bed early, aren't you?" He kissed her softly.

She put down her novel. "I've been bushed all day, no energy at all. My legs feel rubbery. I'm resting up. Had to be the trip. It took a lot out of me."

"Sweetheart, let me pep you up."

Before she could answer, he lifted her nightgown and touched her, with hands that were gentle, sure and magical. In a moment she felt revived. She was moist . . . and ready. Knowing she shouldn't, being too spent from yesterday, but yet . . . saying nothing . . . she couldn't resist him.

It was heavenly. He used his lips and tongue in unbelievable ways. When he was inside, he filled her completely with a warm glow of happiness. She was ecstatic, but concerned.

She'd noticed it yesterday. Her man was gaining energy from her. He drained her strength, her ambition. She was fast becoming a prisoner of love, a prisoner without fetters in her own bed. This had to stop . . . she couldn't . . . it felt too wonderful.

Barbara was sound asleep long before the Man left. He set a glass of milk on the night table next to her bed, kissed her goodnight and tucked the sheet around her, then shook his head. Barbie Doll was winding down.

Belli was nervous. In his entire life he'd never told a lie, never had to. Last night he'd agreed with Farrow to say nothing about O'Cello's tip about funny money and hard drugs. Not a lie, but not the whole truth, either.

Now he was concealing evidence, with two used Tiparillo butts in his pocket. His face brightened. Maybe they weren't evidence after all, just two used cigar butts. He had to do something with them. They were burning a hole in his conscience.

It was late afternoon when he bumped into Rice in the men's room. He knew he could trust Rice, not a cigar smoker at all. He glanced around warily, then asked, "Does Orton smoke?"

"Yeah, why?" Rice glanced at him. Belli felt a tremor of guilt.

"I just wondered. What does he smoke?"

"Tiparillos. Why?"

At the word "Tiparillos," Belli felt his body tense. He felt Rice watching him closely, wondering what he was concealing. He glanced sideways at Rice. The blond was busy combing his hair, full attention riveted in the mirror.

Rice dried his hands, turned and said, "We found a couple of butts in an ashtray in Orton's bathroom. Want to see them?"

Belli nodded and followed.

As they walked, Rice explained, "Sometimes it's easier to compare dental impressions than fingerprints. It's not too hard to get accurate dental records. Dentists keep them."

Rice unlocked a file cabinet, took out a small manila envelope and shook out two Tiparillo butts onto a glass tray.

"These interested me because of the teeth marks in the soft plastic. Under a mircoscope they really show up."

With tweezers he placed one on a glass slide and put it under his microscope. "Take a close look. You'll see the plastic tips have been chewed viciously They're mangled, totally deformed. The corners have been bitten off."

Belli looked through the eyepiece. "Shows a lot of emotional strain."

"Yeah, we know."

Belli fished into his pocket and handed Rice the rolled-up tissue. "Why don't you compare those two with these?"

Rice's eyes widened. He started to ask, "Where . . ." then stopped himself.

Belli watched the blond studying the two butts under the microscope. He compared them with the ones found at Orton's. Rice whistled softly.

"The same madman chewed on these. They're identical." He looked at Belli. "The state police have a forensic laboratory in Bethany, and access to a forensic odontologist." Rice smiled. "A dentist. I'd like to have these run up there today to make sure I'm right."

Belli nodded and took a deep breath. Honesty was the only policy.

"I marked the exact spot by the statue, near the fringe of the woods, where I found them." Belli hesitated, then added, "So many of my friends smoke these things. It's Tiparillo country. I was playing a hunch."

"It's one of the few clues that isn't a fingerprint," Rice exclaimed. "It's important evidence."

With his tweezers, Rice put the two new butts in another envelope and scribbled an identification on the outside. He put his hand on Belli's shoulder and with a knowing wink said, "Gus, my lad, show me the exact spot where my lab men picked these up this morning. There's no need for anyone else to know."

Belli gave Rice a grateful look. "As soon as you're ready," he said, leaving the office.

Rice grinned. Damn, even Belli had a bit of free spirit in him. Old Gus wasn't as square as he'd thought.

• • •

Jim and Brenda had a quiet dinner at home. He was disappointed at missing Judy. He'd be fascinated to know more about her fraud investigation and what she might uncover. He wished there was time to help her.

It was almost eleven before they went to bed. Forgetting the promise of the morning, he fell quickly alseep. She knew he was exhausted.

Alice decided it was time for her new strategy of willing compliance. It would be Spike and Alice with the Round Heels. Boy, would she be sexy and available, a whore in the bedroom, giving everything he wanted, and more. Quizzically, she wondered, How does one hang from a chandelier? Spike was her man, no matter what.

After bathing in a hot soapy tub with just a touch of Flower of Musk Oil, she looked at her body in the full-length mirror. A slight paunch. She pulled it in. It pushed out again. Damn, exercise was the only answer. Turning sideways and inhaling . . . not a superstar, but pretty good equipment. Overall, she didn't look too bad.

Drying and powdering herself, she selected a most seductive pink peignoir with the free feeling of wearing nothing at all. Waiting, she thumbed through *The Joy of Sex,* looking for a new technique to please him. Her heart was speeding up, actually excited by the thought.

The hall clock struck 7:00 P.M., 8:00, 9:00, 10:00, then 11:00. She put the book away. The excitement had long since vanished.

The door slammed in the driveway at 11:30 P.M. She was angry enough to scream at him. Yesterday she would have. Not tonight, being Alice the Temptress.

Spike bounced into the room. "Hi, hon, sorry I'm late. It's been a tough week."

"Would you like dinner, sweetheart? I saved you a steak. It will only take a mimute." She came on softly, silky smooth.

"No, thanks, I had dinner with the boys. How's your mother? Don't you smell good? Mmmmmmmm!"

It had taken Spike only thirty seconds to get the message. Alice smelled sinfully delicious and looked so fresh, real, gentle, and so available. The tender trap had worked. He literally dragged her into the bedroom, tearing off his clothes. Maybe he'd been out with the boys after all.

He was all over her. She did her best to stay with him. But if she was flying, he was in orbit. It was total loving.

Tiring now, when he didn't stop when he should have, she began to question what was going on. She was exhausted. He seemed to be gaining momentum and strength.

"Midnight . . . he's come twice and he's fresh as a daisy . . . he's insatiable. Enough is enough." She dig her sharp fingernails into his back to cool his ardor. Nothing stopped his action.

"Sweetheart, let's save some for tomorrow," she cooed in his ear, and then she bit him, hard.

Spike finally got the message, grinned, kissed her fervently, bounded to his feet and went into the bathroom. The shower was running. He stuck his head around the door.

"That was great, hon. We'll finish in the morning. Would you like a beer?"

She gave him a strained smile and shook her head.

He turned off the water, dried himself and went down the stairs. As she fell asleep, she wondered, What's happened to him? He's impossible. Maybe I'd better share him with one or two others. He's too much for me.

Later, the Man was sitting in his den, his wife asleep upstairs. It had been a long, exciting day for him. He took out his notebook, and with the black marking pencil, he crossed out Marie Benson, the Senator's wife, the seven of spades, number eight on his list.

She had been in the trunk of his car with the motor running all last night. At 4:00 A.M. he had slipped out of bed and driven the car to the high school grounds. There, next to the Bicentennial statue, he'd spread-eagled Marie Benson on a large dropcloth and painted her with fast-drying paints from a portable spray gun.

She was appealing, almost sexy, even in death. He'd had a

hell of a time putting her up on the statue; he'd gotten paint all over an old pair of painter's coveralls and gloves. They and the dropcloth were still in a bag, hidden carefully behind his arsenal. They'd be disposed of in the city incinerator at his first chance.

On the way home, he was concerned about running into the newsman. He hadn't. Fortunately, on Sunday morning the newsman delivered papers an hour or two later than usual.

The Man had then slipped back into bed, nudging up close to his wife, and slept two additional hours.

Seven identified, but only forty-four to go. The plan was perfect. Yes, a few adjustments needed, but there had not been a single hitch. The police were still running in circles.

They reminded him of elephants in the circus. Around and around they went, each with his trunk holding the tail of the elephant in front of him. He was the ringmaster. The elephants were running faster and faster, running in place. They were getting dizzy. They were reeling. It was about time to stop their whirl and send them off on another blind trail, before the audience grew bored. Tomorrow he'd watch them try to climb a greased pole.

Earlier tonight, he had dialed the home of his next victim. Before calling, he had debated whether to use the voice of Spike Briggs or Jim Dempsey. He had decided on the Chief's voice. That ass! He wanted to be sure his intended victim took the bait. Just like the Godfather, he'd give him an offer he couldn't refuse.

"Oh, Mary, how are you? This is Jim Dempsey. Is John there?"

Over the phone he could hear Mary shouting, "Sweetheart, it's Jim Dempsey, for you."

The Man smiled.

"Hi, John, congratulations. I'm sorry I wasn't there to see you win today. I understand you nosed out Ned . . . Nonsense, you deserved it. Your sailing has improved. You've been getting closer all the time.

"That's really what I called about. Racing in the Nationals next month. I was going to ask you earlier, but I've been busy. Three of us, you, Briggs and me. Could we get together for a few minutes in the morning? How about seven-thirty? You can still catch the eight-ten. At the yacht club. It's on your way to the station. Keep it to yourself. We'll surprise everyone. Great! See you at seven-thirty. And bring your commodore's hat.''

Tomorrow was ring-around-the-collar day. He'd shock the world. He'd give them one murder and two bodies. It was time to play his top trump card. It was time to reveal his ace in the hole.

9

Monday, June 9.
Last Gasp

THE MAN awoke with a start. He felt light-headed and fuzzy. It was that vague feeling again, but pleasurable, very pleasurable.

His wife was kneeling on the bed next to him, her fingers making gentle circles on his chest, nails teasing him until he was fully aroused. She switched positions and kissed him gently, lovingly. He was all hers. It was something. It was quite a handful. She'd nicknamed it Thunderbolt. Suddenly, it struck her funny.

"What's so hilarious? It's five o'clock in the morning. I wake up with great expectations, and you're sitting there laughing. What's up?" He kissed her gently.

"You are." She gestured and laughed. "It's the Washington Monument."

The next fifteen minutes they romped all over the bed, playing, teasing, wrestling, loving, laughing, spontaneous love. Two people throwing their inhibitions aside for the enjoyment of each other, finally winding up at opposite ends of the bed. She was teasing herself to excite him. Faster and faster. He was reciprocating for her benefit. Faster and faster. By their actions on themselves, they were exciting each other, and it felt too good to stop, for both of them.

Afterward, he lay there wondering. Had he been dreaming? He pinched himself. No, he was wide awake. He looked at his wife. She was sound asleep.

• • •

The Man was up and on the move. He checked himself in the car's rearview mirror. He looked exactly like the Chief. The impersonation was perfect. Tiparillo lit, he inhaled deeply. It was early, so he drove slowly along the Housatuck River toward the Fairport Yacht Club. The fog hung heavy over the river, obscuring the other side.

John Frouge was excited. Dempsey had asked him to keep the news to himself, but he couldn't. At breakfast he bubbled over.

"Mary, Jim Dempsey asked me to sail in the Nationals with him and Briggs. It will be the three of us representing FYC against the best sailors in the country. He must think I'm good, since the combined time of the three Atlantics is the team's score."

Mary stared at him in disbelief. Then she turned toward the stove, hiding her astonishment.

"But sweetheart, you've only won one race in your life, and that was by a foot. If Nichols hadn't torn his sail . . ."

She didn't complete the thought, or add that neither Dempsey nor Briggs had been racing.

The uncertainty was in his eyes, too. After a moment of silence, he said quietly, "I'll do my best. You know me. I've got to try. It's like breathing."

"How's that?" she asked.

He smiled up at her. "You go it alone. No one can do it for you."

She leaned over and kissed him warmly. "That's the guy I love. You're my Peter Pan. I'm your Tinkerbell." She kissed him again, rubbing the back of his neck. "Don't forget, Peter, tonight's the night."

John's cheeks colored. He dropped his eyes toward the floor and nodded. It embarrassed him. Mary always reminded him when it was time for sex. Oh, well. He'd do his best, but she had such vitality. Swallowing the rest of his coffee, he checked his watch.

Mary gave him a long, lingering kiss at the doorway and ran her hand slowly down the front of his pants. "Come home early, Peter," she whispered.

Damn, he thought. She's in the mood already, But then, she's always . . .

He pulled away and ran toward the car, commodore's hat clutched under his arm.

At 7:25 A.M. John drove his powder-blue Thunderbird into the yacht club's parking area. The morning fog hung heavy over the coastline. The pavement was damp and glistening from the mist.

Probably burn off by noon . . . good sailing afternoon . . . red sky at night, sailor's delight. There had been a real red glow last night, he remembered.

He spotted Dempsey through the fog, out by the flagpole. What's he doing out there? he wondered, walking to meet him.

The Man waited patiently.

"Morning, Jim." John reached out to shake hands respectfully. Dempsey was some man. "Sorry about these murders. Anything new?"

"We'll get Orton today," the Man said with confidence. "You can bet your life on it."

The Chief's confidence both amazed and pleased John Frouge. He started to reply, but the Man cut him short.

"John, I want to mail our entries today. I need a photograph of you. I brought my Polaroid. Stand next to the flagpole. Good, right there."

The Man pointed to the spot where he wanted Frouge.

"In this fog? Why didn't you tell me? I'd have brought a picture," Frouge asked in a puzzled tone.

"No, I need one taken here. Did you bring your commodore's hat? Good, put it on," the Man directed.

It sounded foolish, but Frouge did as he was told. After all, Dempsey was club champion.

"That looks pretty good, but let me adjust it for you. Hold still." The Man stepped behind Frouge.

John never realized before that Jim Dempsey had slate-gray eyes, bulging, slate-gray eyes. The noose was already tight about his neck. He was gasping for breath, feet off the ground, struggling. His hands tore at the constricting band around his throat. He was being strangled, hanged. Trying to scream in pain, he couldn't. His last memory was of an evil-looking man grinning and pulling on a nylon rope. Can't kill me, he raved inwardly, I'll hold my breath!

The Man pulled Frouge's kicking body up to crosstree, then maneuvered the metal ring so that it caught on the cleat on the mast and made sure it was hooked solidly. Now, a sudden tug on the other end of the rope, the hitch parted, and the long nylon rope fell free to the ground.

John Frouge's body was suddenly very still. The Commodore was hanging by his neck, forty-five feet above the ground.

The Man looked up and said softly, "Run that one up the flagpole, Froggy boy, and see who salutes."

The Man coiled his long nylon rope and put it in the trunk of the car. Looking at himself in the rearview mirror, he adjusted his cap. What a damn good-looking Chief of Police.

Driving slowly away from the yacht club, he muttered to himself, "Damn fog . . . ought to lift by noon. I want to watch those elephants try to climb a greased pole."

Dempsey's face was grim as he looked at the morning newspapers. They screamed the news of Marie Benson's murder. The *Times* showed long-range pictures of her body, lying nude on the bicentennial statue. The *Daily News* featured a close-up. He could imagine the picture in the *National Enquirer*.

Dempsey skimmed the stories. Public indignation was rising. He rubbed his nose. Washington was furious. A Senator's wife had been raped and murdered. There was more pressure for federal intervention.

"SEVEN MURDERS, HOW LONG CAN THIS GO ON?" headlined an editorial in the *Times*. He turned the page quickly.

The advertisements for both *Times* and *Newsweek* had Orton's picture on the cover. CBS had announced an hour special on Orton's life.

Dempsey's stomach knotted. The pressure was building on Fairport. The pressure was building on the law-enforcement agencies. The pressure was building on him.

He stood up and flexed his shoulders. He'd find Orton, today. One way or another.

Little Louie, all 265 pounds of him, and Spider arrived in Fairport at about 9:00 A.M. in a rental white Oldsmobile convertible, with the top down. They had flown all night from Vegas on Trans World's Redeye Flight 60.

Louie's eyes were bloodshot. Spider had only slits for eyes. If they had any color, you couldn't tell. Spider always wore shades, even at night. The name was apt. He was big and gangly, hairy, fast and deadly. The boys had nicknamed him Tarantula because he looked like one. After a while, they shortened it to Spider.

At the Fairport interchange, the tollbooth operator reached out, took the quarter and shook her head in disbelief. A fat monster was driving that white convertible, with a big hairy spider sitting alongside.

Little Louie was sneaking into Fairport.

Grady, Briggs, Belli and Farrow were in a heated discussion around Dempsey's desk. The Chief seemed oblivious to it all. If he felt heavy pressure, his calm eyes didn't betray him.

Suddenly he broke into their babble. "Tom, anything yet on the paint?"

"Latex, washable. You can buy it at any hardware store. There was the one red stain where he painted her and quite a bit smeared on the statue when he lifted her up. This guy has to be strong. She was a full-bodied woman."

Dempsey nodded wearily. "I noticed."

Farrow continued, "That type of paint is easily removed. It can be washed off. It's not going to lead us anyplace."

"Find the car, you'll find Orton!" It was Mary Potter speaking, as she fixed another pot of coffee.

Grady realized how profound Mary's thought was. "By God, Mary, you're right. Orton has been driving all over town, leading us a merry chase. He's got wheels. What car is he using?"

"Piccollo took the plugs out of Orton's car. It's inoperative. He's not using that one," said Belli, pouring more coffee for each of them.

Dempsey took his cup back from Belli. "Thanks for the suggestion, Mary." He smiled at her as she left the room. "The car may be the key to locating Orton. If we knew what kind of a car he was driving, we'd have something to look for."

"Tom, you start with car-rental agencies. Check all of them within a fifty-mile radius. Spike, can you help with this?"

"I'm sure we can," answered Briggs. "Why don't we handle the stolen cars first? We can get a pretty accurate report through our computer network. After that, we'll go to work on the new- and used-car sales."

"Chief, we checked Orton's bank account and put a freeze on it," remarked Farrow. "He hasn't cashed a check since May 30th. Nothing out of the ordinary in the last two months. Certainly no car purchase."

Belli sighed. "Let's see now. We don't know what kind of a car he's using or whether it's rented, stolen, purchased or borrowed. As a master of disguise, he probably rented it disguised as a priest, a bearded hippie, or an old lady—"

Dempsey cut off Belli's monologue, looking right through him. "Let's think positively, Gus. We're looking for the unusual. Something that doesn't fit the normal pattern. If you find it, check the handwriting on the contract."

Mary interrupted the meeting. "Chief, the hospital is on the phone. Lefty Diangelo has been murdered. It's number eight. The six of spades was on his bed."

Lefty's room was cordoned off. The barrel of a .38 caliber pistol had been shoved into his mouth. The back of Lefty's head was gone.

Dempsey stood at the foot of the bed, the others behind him. "A silencer wasn't necessary. Could have muffled the sound of the shot with the extra pillow there."

Grady smiled slowly. "Well, at least today's victim won't upset many people. Diangelo was a cold-blooded killer. Good riddance!"

"Orton didn't kill Diangelo," Dempsey said flatly, as he looked over the room carefully.

"What?" echoed the others.

Dempsey repeated, "No, Orton didn't kill Lefty. Three simple reasons. First, he could have killed him the other night. He didn't, just maimed him. Second, this is a typical mob execution. It lacks Orton's creative flair. It's a simple rubout. Third, take a look at the six of spades. It's from a different deck. All the others were cards with a death's head on the back, made by U.S. Playing Card Company. This is a car with TWA on the back. The airline gives them out. I think Bicycle prints them."

"I'll be damned, you're right." Once again, Dempsey's deductive powers had impressed Grady. "Jim, you're the best."

"No matter what the papers say, eh, Sam?" Dempsey grimaced. "I think one of Lefty's heavy friends paid him a visit. He probably knew too much."

The floor nurse had arrived at the door, a big efficient woman in white. She was very upset. "I saw this big hairy thing sidling down the corridor. A big hairy ape. No, not an ape, it looked more like that big furry spider."

"A tarantula?" suggested Farrow, his brow creased.

"Exactly, that's it, a big hairy tarantula, with sunglasses."

Dempsey reacted instantly.

"That's another Vegas creep. Tom, get Piccollo on the radio, and tell him to stake out Rocco's. We've got out-of-town visitors. They may have come East just to kill Lefty, but they may be looking for something else. If so, it's probably hidden at Rocco's."

They were just leaving the hospital when they ran into Ned Nichols in the hallway. Dempsey introduced him to Sam Grady.

"I just came down from visiting Nellie Arbuckle. She's an important client of mine. I'm working on a sale of some three hundred acres she owns at Lake Candlewood."

"How's she doing?" inquired Briggs.

Nichols grimaced, gazed down the hall and spoke in a low

tone. "She's holding on by her fingernails. That old bat just won't give up."

On the way back to headquarters, Dempsey noticed the fog was lifting along the coast. A gentle breeze had come up. It was going to be another nice day, perfect for sailing.

Sam broke the silence. "That Ned Nichols is a cold one. I suspect that he'd kill his own father, if there was something in it for him—"

The police radio crackled for their attention. "Chief, another murder. There's a body hanging from the flagpole at the Fairport Yacht Club."

No one spoke. Dempsey floored the accelerator. Weaving through traffic, they were at the yacht club in less than twelve minutes. Two police cruisers were already on the scene. A crowd of police and spectators was milling about the foot of the mast.

It was a sad and terrible sight. Frouge's body swung gently in the light breeze. Two policemen, their uniforms covered with grease, were trying to climb the pole. They kept sliding down to the bottom.

"Chief, the body's hooked up there on that cleat. We can't get it down. How did it get up there?"

"Chop down the pole," suggested a young towheaded boy about twelve years old. "I'll run home and get an axe."

"You could shoot through the rope, and he'd fall down," suggested a young girl with long pigtails. "I saw them do that on television."

"They're going to shoot, they're going to shoot," several of the kids began chanting.

"Keep quiet and move back out of the way." Briggs was shooing the kids back.

Dempsey surveyed the scene. This murder had Orton's flair. It was obvious how it had been done. He'd explain it later. Simple, but fiendishly clever. Christ, Orton even had the morning fog going for him. Now, how to get the body down quickly?

The crowd was growing. Photographers would start arriving any minute. "Let's get this body down before the television crews get here," Dempsey ordered at the top of his voice.

He turned toward his assistants. "Do you have any climbing spikes handy? Better yet, get the fire department on the radio. Get a cherry picker or a hook-and-ladder truck down here."

It was almost ten minutes before the fire engine arrived. Dempsey noticed several movie cameras taking pictures. An ABC mobile television van had arrived. Briggs was busy talking to a group of reporters.

"Orton probably pulled up the body with a rope attached to that metal ring. He could have tied it with a hitch. We use them in the small boats all the time. Once he had the ring over the cleat, he pulled one end of his rope and it jerked free."

Under Dempsey's direction, the fire truck backed into position next to the flagpole, extending a long ladder up to the junction of the mast and the crosstree. A fireman scaled the ladder, took a long rope and ran it through the pulley, then attached it to the metal ring. Two other firemen on the ground held the other end of the rope. When he freed the ring from the cleat, they lowered the body to the ground.

"It's John Frouge," one heavyset woman shouted. Several others screamed. One fainted.

"Mary Frouge is in the clubhouse. I'll get her," shouted a blonde in a tennis dress. She was running toward the door before anyone could stop her.

Farrow spotted the six of spades in the hatband of the commodore hat almost instantly. The card had a death's head emblem on its reverse side. Frouge was dead; he'd been hanged. Orton again. What a way to go. Choking, he swallowed hard and gazed out at the Sound.

Doc Brody knelt down and examined the body briefly, rubbing his watery eyes and shaking his head sadly. He gave Dempsey the choke signal, then signaled to the ambulance attendants to remove the body.

There was a commotion on the deck of the clubhouse, and Mary Frouge emerged, frantic-eyed and shaking. She walked directly toward Dempsey. "Jim, they say something has happened to John. What? How? He was coming here to meet you."

"To meet me?" Dempsey's face registered his astonishment.

"Yes, you called last night and asked him to meet you here this morning. It was about racing in the Nationals."

"Mary, I never—"

"Yes, you did. I talked to you myself. I know it was you." Mary's voice had risen. She was now shouting hysterically. "You lured him here. Why did you do it?"

The spectators crowded forward. They heard nothing more.

Dempsey's mouth was open. He could feel his heart pounding. At that moment, Mary saw her husband's body being loaded into a police van. Her whole life was being carried away on that stretcher. She screamed, lunged toward the stretcher, tripped and fell to the ground and finally lay there, moaning.

Dempsey caught his breath. "Get her into the ambulance. She's in shock . . . needs secation and rest." Doc Brody and two attendants quickly surrounded her.

Then he turned to Sam and in a low voice asked, "What do you make of this twist?"

"Well, if Orton could impersonate Rocco's voice, fool everyone as DeMarco, imitate a television repairman as well as a state policeman, and make everyone believe he was Harold Green, I guess he can impersonate you."

"That's all I need right now," Dempsey muttered. "One of me is enough." He felt numb, wishing he could feel something inside him. Anything. Even fear. There was nothing.

Grady, with a genius for compassion, patted him on the back. "There's an old saying, 'Victory is sweetest when you've known defeat.' When we catch Orton, it will be pure honey. We'll savor it together."

As they walked to their cars, they overheard several of the kids talking. "Do you really think the Chief did it?"

"Nah, it was Orton. He's a master killer. The police can't catch him."

Driving away from the yacht club, Dempsey saw Ned

Nichols' face in the back of the crowd. He wondered aloud, "Now, what in the hell would Ned be doing out here watching us?"

In New York, Filbert Flagg was meeting with the president of NBC and John Churchman, recently returned from China. Flagg was trying to persuade them to conduct another live interview from Fairport with Dempsey, Briggs and Grady.

"But John, it will be twice as big as the last one. Think of the audience. We'll have at least forty million homes watching."

"No way. I'm not going to do it. Forty million, did you say?"

"It might be a way to lure Orton out into the open," Flagg continued, knowing he had tweaked Churchman's interest.

"You must be kidding. It's too dangerous. He's a crazy, with blood all over him." Churchman shuddered.

"We'll provide wall-to-wall security. You'll be in no danger."

"I don't worry about dying. I just don't want to be there when it happens," Churchman quipped.

"John, you ought to be willing to stick your ass on the line for the sake of the network," snapped Flagg.

"Not on my life! You stick your ass in your ear," Churchman stalked out of Flagg's office and slammed the door, leaving the two network executives staring at each other.

The private phone in the Man's office rang. He answered.

"Hi, sweetheart." It was Jeanne.

"Just a minute." He put the phone down, crossed his office and closed the door.

"Pussycat, I'm glad you called. I was just thinking of dropping over."

"That's why I called, lover. I'm in New York on a special assignment, fashion photographs at the U.N.—The Third World Look. It was my agent's idea. I'll be back late tonight, and tomorrow I'm going to get you out in my slow boat to nowhere."

"I'm disappointed. I was looking forward today to that box lunch you promised."

"Sweetheart, tomorrow's the day. Save up your delicious self for me. I'm at least a quart low." She blew him a big meow.

After they'd hung up, the Man drummed his fingers on the table. He'd call Gayla. Jeanne wasn't the only pussycat around.

He dialed Gayla's number. The phone rang for a good two minutes. Pussycat, pussycat, where have you gone? Damn. Gayla must have been called away on a flight. Stewardesses! You can't depend on them. They're too flyaway. They're never around when you need them, too busy moving their tails for the airlines.

Oh, well, there was always Barbara. Sexy, sensuous Barbie. Funny, the last few days, she'd acted so exhausted. He'd call her later and stop by.

For just a moment, he let his mind dwell on those tight-fitting blue shorts. What an unbelievable ass. He closed his eyes and leaned back in his chair.

Catherine Orton had finally been located. The California State Police learned that she and her mother had been traveling in the Far East on a four-week trip. They contacted them by radiophone in Kuala Lumpur.

"Impossible!" was her flat answer when told her husband was wanted for seven murders. "David wouldn't kill anyone. He hates violence."

She had no idea where he could be and had no inkling of what personal business could cause him to leave Fairport at a moment's notice. "David is meticulous. He would never leave without telling me, never leave his patients, and never leave without canceling the newspaper. Mother and I will fly right back."

But hearing the terrible news, Catherine Orton's mother had suffered a mild heart seizure and had been placed under sedation and hopsitalized for shock. Catherine couldn't leave her mother, at least for a few days. The California police had reported that she had sounded believable and sincere. The Malaysian authorities confirmed the heart attack.

She also told the Claremont police that her mother had purchased the tickets for the trip and had mailed them, accounting for the fact that none of the local travel agencies had any record of travel plans or ticket purchases by the Ortons.

In Alameda, California, David Orton's seventy-one-year-old mother asked for protection from FBI, reporting several phone calls threatening death unless she revealed where her son was hiding.

"I have no idea where he is," she said. "Haven't seen him in almost a year. My good David wouldn't kill anyone. I got down on my knees last night and prayed and prayed and prayed. God told me that my son hasn't killed anyone. I know he's innocent."

Piccollo, three other policemen, and four state troopers had Rocco's Cadillac agency under close surveillance. It was staked out with a man at each corner. The agency had been closed since Rocco's death.

At 10:35 A.M. a car pulled into the drive. Three men in business suits got out, walked toward the side door and began jimmying the lock.

Through his police bullhorn, Piccollo shouted, "Freeze."

The three men jumped as if shot. Their leader started to reach inside his suit coat, then saw the shotguns leveled at them. It was James Thatcher and his team of Treasury agents. "We're federal agents, we're here to help," shouted Thatcher.

"Welcome to Fairport," apologized Piccollo, as he looked over their credentials, briefing them on his team's mission. Thatcher agreed that his men would join the stakeout, at least until lunchtime.

At 11:30 A.M., a white Oldsmobile convertible pulled to the curb across the Post Road from Rocco's. Two big men sat in the car for at least five minutes, staring across the street. Finally they got out of the car. When Piccollo saw them, he wet his lips. These two had to be the ones they'd been waiting for.

Thatcher whispered, "Let them go into the building. If

they came here from Vegas looking for something, it's got to be important. Let's see if they can find it.''

Piccollo agreed wordlessly and signaled his men not to interfere.

Little Louie and Spider dodged through the heavy traffic, emerging in front of Rocco's unscathed. Louie waddled and the Spider sidled directly to the side door, Rocco's old entrance. The fat one took a key from his pocket and swung the door open. Spider removed his sunglasses and eased inside, gun in hand.

"Did you ever see a hairier guy in your life than that Tarantula creep?" whispered Piccollo. "Watch him. He's fast and he's deadly.''

"Watch out for the other one. Don't let him get close to your privates," whispered back one of Thatcher's men. "He's got a mean reputation.''

Twenty minutes later, Little Louie and Spider emerged back into the sunshine, both blinking at the sudden light. Louie was carrying a heavy package.

"Freeze," called out Piccollo. Spider instinctively snapped a shot at the sound. Louie reached for the Special under his armpit.

Seven shotguns went off together. First one barrel, then the other. Louie and Spider both melted to the ground, oozing away like snowmen in the hot sun. The thin man that's imprisoned in every fat man escaped slowly from Little Louie's body.

Thatcher was delighted to obtain the brand-new front and reverse plates for the fifty-dollar U.S. Treasury Federal Reserve note. "They're perfect, absolutely perfect," he exlaimed over and over.

Thatcher brushed off his Brooks Brothers suit and adjusted his monogrammed tie. In just one day on this assignment, he'd done the impossible, recovering printing plates the government didn't even know existed, saving millions of dollars. If his report was written right, Washington would give him a promotion, a substantial pay increase and maybe a special bonus. He'd done so much, and the local police and FBI couldn't even catch a murder suspect.

The federal agents walked away into the sunshine, looking for a good French restaurant. They were planning to celebrate their success before returning to Washington.

They left Piccollo and his team to clean up the mess.

Barbara awoke at 12:15 P.M., still drowsy. Like a sleepwalker, she shuffled to the bathroom and sat down. Her fuzzy mind tried to reason.

She was worn out physically. Emotionally, she knew her man loved her, turned her on, lit her fuse and opened the gates to paradise. But he was draining her dry, leaving her lifeless. Her tender insides still quivered. He'd gone on and on, long after she couldn't take any more.

It was a thrilling, throbbing sensation, feeling like a thousand little butterflies touching her, brushing her with their wings, one tiny flutter after another. She was still sensitive, on edge, totally switched on. All of her feelers were still out. It would take only the tiniest push to get her going again.

She dared not touch herself, even to pat herself dry, afraid the feeling would start again and wouldn't stop. Every time he'd touched her, it was a gossamer trip. Leaning over, she turned on the faucets in the tub. Maybe a hot bath would help. Then a cold shower.

He'd come by again today. She'd never be able to say no . . . to his loving hands . . . those incredible deep flutters . . . closer and closer together . . . then that continuous, shuddering orgasm . . . then a deep sleep again. Tomorrow, she'd be a little weaker. Where would it all end? After the shower, she'd eat a good breakfast and take a double dose of Geritol. Maybe Vivian could come over. Vivian was a new neighbor, a divorcée, who had acted very friendly. With a neighbor here, he wouldn't stop by, had to protect that damn wife of his from scandal. A day's rest. That would give her time to recover strength. Probably be all right tomorrow. Then she'd welcome him with open arms, and legs.

As soon as she finished breakfast, she'd call Vivian.

The news of the murder of Frouge, the eighth murder in the last eight days, pushed all other stories into the background.

Every half hour ABC television ran excerpts from the footage they had shot showing John Frouge's body hanging from the flagpole at the yacht club.

The excerpts made the police look totally inept, as they climbed ten feet up a greased pole and slid back to crash on the ground.

When the Man first saw it, he almost rolled on the floor in laughter. All they had to do was speed up the scene and run it over and over to ragtime piano music. It would be better than an old Keystone Kops routine.

Particularly damning was a close-up of Mary Frouge, shaking her finger at Chief Dempsey and shouting, "I know it was you. You lured him here. Why did you do it?"

The Man grinned happily. He'd undermined Fairport's confidence in Dempsey. Now he'd tear him apart.

As soon as he returned from Rocco's, Piccollo reported to the Chief. Dempsey was effusive in his praise of Piccollo's actions, concluding, "I'll put in a recommendation for a raise."

Piccollo knew he wouldn't get it. Fairport didn't have the money. But he was pleased by the Chief's thought.

Dempsey learned at 1:20 P.M. that Nellie Arbuckle had died. Right after Ned Nichols left the hospital, Nellie had complained of a sharp pain in her chest. Could Ned have given her a gelatin tablet? He made a note to check out a a few details about Ned's relations with Nellie. But finding Orton came first.

The private hot line in the Man's office rang at 1:30. It was Barbara.

"Thanks for stopping by last evening. That was pretty special. I was floating loose somewhere up in the clouds."

"I thought I might stop by later. My motor's still running," the Man responded.

"That's why I called you, hon. I've got a new neighbor coming over. Vivian. I don't think you know her. She called and was lonely," Barbara fibbed, "so I asked her over."

"Can't you get rid of her? I'm anxious to see you."

"Sweetheart, I'll see you tomorrow. I really need at least a day's rest. I've got battle fatigue.'' Barbara blew him a kiss and hung up, relieved.

The Man kicked his desk in frustration. Damn. He couldn't seem to throttle back. His whole system was racing, needing constant relief from the tension built up by murder.

Still no answer at Gayla's. Jeanne was in New York, and now Barbara had company. Vivian. Was that the new girl he'd noticed the other day? The one with the tight-fitting yellow sweater? What a pair! A real booby trap. Maybe he should stop at Barbara's and entertain them both. What the hell was he thinking?

He adjusted his left pants leg and kicked the desk again.

It was early afternoon when Dempsey, Grady and Briggs entered police headquarters. Mary Potter was waiting, a look of fear on her face. She handed Dempsey an envelope, saying, "Another one. The lab checked it over. It's clean. Rice said it was typed on Orton's machine."

The envelope was marked "Number 3 in a Series." It was addressed simply "El Chiefo Dumbo." It was postmarked June 7, 11:30 A.M.

Dempsey fumed. The letter had been mailed on Saturday morning. It was now Monday afternoon. The post office had been closed Saturday afternoon and all day Sunday. Another letter from Orton. He was becoming a regular poison-pen pal!

He slipped on a pair of thin latex gloves and slid the letter out of the envelope. Briggs and Grady watched closely.

Inside, there were two notes, one inside the other. The outside one was prophetic. It read:

> The Mail must go through—
>   but not on Sunday
> By the time you read this—
>   it will be Monday
> Too late
>   to help your friend
> The Frog
>   has met an untimely end—
> He croaked.

"Shit," exploded Dempsey. "This letter was mailed almost two days ago. We should have told the post office to deliver any letters addressed to me, even on Sunday. We could have saved Frouge."

Briggs spoke up. "Spilt milk. You're sawing sawdust, Jim. Who could have guessed? What's the other note say?"

Dempsey put it flat on the desk. Briggs leaned over and read it aloud.

"Your eyes are red
Your moods are blue
My ace is cold
And so are you.

"Just bait a hook
And wet a line
Then count dead fish
I'm up to nine."

No one spoke. Grady's cane tapping on the floor was the only sound in the room. They looked at one another. All three knew. Orton said he'd killed nine. They'd only found eight. King through six. He was telling them they'd missed the ace.

Briggs sat down heavily. "Our trail is as cold as a witch's tit. The bastard knows it."

Grady leaned heavily on his cane. "If the ace has been dead for eight days, he would be stone cold."

Dempsey stood stock still, eyes flaming. "Eight days. A corpse would smell up the town. He'd have to be buried, embalmed, or on ice."

" 'My ace is cold.' It's gotta be ice." Briggs jumped to his feet, shouting, "All the reference to fish, Jim. Baker's Ice House."

Dempsey's stomach churned. He knew Briggs was right. "The nerve of the s.o.b. Let's go!"

He rose from his chair, buzzed for Belli and Farrow and shouted instructions over the intercom.

On the way, Dempsey explained to Grady that four years

ago, Bob Baker had installed a large frozen-food locker in a shed behind his store. It was used to store large catches of fish and fresh game by sportsmen in the area. "Orton uses it all the time," he concluded.

They were halfway to Baker's when Grady spoke up, his voice puzzled. "How the hell? The lab said Orton typed the note on his machine. But how?"

From the back seat, Briggs blew a cloud of cigar smoke, then said, "Sam, that's a hell of a question. His typewriter's been locked up tight since last Thursday."

Grady looked thoughtful. "Orton's either sneaking into headquarters and typing lousy rhymes under our noses or—"

"I don't think so, Sam. I'll bet he typed his notes before last Thursday. He could have done it, if . . ." Dempsey hesitated. "If he's operating to a set plan. A definite schedule . . . with victims selected well in advance."

"Shit," exploded Briggs. "I'll bet he hasn't had to change a one. It's split-second planning."

Dempsey accelerated through a yellow light, then turned his head and asked, "Intriguing, isn't it?"

He pulled his cruiser into the parking lot behind Baker's. Belli, Farrow and two squad cars of policemen arrived moments later. Belli hadn't forgotten to bring workers.

Briggs opened the padlock to the shed with his own key. Grady nudged Dempsey in disbelief, and Jim explained that most of the sportsmen in town had keys, ending, "We'll get the list from Bob."

They entered the food locker. Grady had never been there before and was astonished at the size of the installation. His first impression was of a room full of white coffins. There were at least sixty large Styrofoam chests in the freezer area, all white and all of the same make, shape and dimension. At least half were stamped "Baker" in bold, black stencil. The rest were marked with individual owner's names. Another thirty or so empty, clean chests were in an adjoining room.

Dempsey turned to Belli. "Gus, have your men open every container. If it's too cold to work in here, bring them outside."

Grady interrupted, "Jim, before you start opening these containers, have your men go over them with a metal detector. That son of a bitch might have set a booby trap. That's all we'd need.''

Two policemen heard Grady's comment and turned pale. "We've got a Coin-Master in the wagon outside," one of them volunteered.

They went over each container carefully with the detector, with negative readings. Opening each one, they glanced in. Finding nothing unusual, they unwrapped and checked each piece of fish.

The twenty-fourth container caused Belli to let out a shout. "The ace of spades!"

Removing the top package, Belli had spotted the playing card. He held the package in his two hands.

"Chief, the packages in this container are all different sizes. They don't feel like fish. I think we've got a body, at least, we've got parts of . . ."

Belli turned pale green and dropped a round pumpkin-shaped package back into the container.

"What's the date on the newspaper?" Dempsey moved forward to see for himself.

"Sunday, June 1," read Belli.

Briggs peered over Dempsey's shoulder. "That checks. It's Orton's first victim, the one you claimed was missing, Jim, stored here all the time. I'll be damned."

The outside of the container was stamped "Nichols." The body had been stored in one of Ned Nichols' containers.

Dempsey knew the same thought was running through everyone's mind. He said aloud, "Nichols? That probably doesn't mean anything. The empty containers in the other room have all of our names on them. It would have been easy for Orton . . ."

An uncomfortable look crossed Dempsey's face, but he kept his voice expressionless "Gus, have one of your cruisers bring this back with us to headquarters. We'll have the lab and Doc Brody take a look at it. There's got to be some identification.

"Leave the other crew here and have them go through the rest. Make certain that there's only one body in cold storage."

On the ride back, Grady asked Dempsey whom he thought

Orton had been keeping on ice. He didn't answer immediately, just stared straight ahead.

Finally, he broke the strange silence. "I took a guess. Yesterday, I thought we'd find the ace of spades. I wrote it down, put it in an envelope. It's in my desk. When we get back, I'll give it to you. When we get an identification from the lab, open it. If I'm right, they'll identify him quickly."

"Why don't you want to say?" asked Briggs, chewing hard on the plastic end of his small cigar.

"Because . . . it's too diabolical. It'll blow a hole in everything. The media will eat us alive."

Grady looked at Dempsey. "You mean it's him?" His face paled.

Dempsey nodded his head.

Briggs and Grady exchanged glances. Suddenly, they all knew. They rode the rest of the way in silence.

The lab report came in at five minutes after five. Doc Brody reported this one in person, looking years older. The strain lines had deepened around his mouth and eyes. He shook his bald head sadly and then blurted out, "It's David Orton. The corpse is Dr. David Orton. The poor guy's been dead for eight days."

Orton had been killed and dissected late on June 1 and put on ice almost immediately. Brody didn't know what had killed him yet, but promised a full report later.

They sat in the conference room in stunned disbelief, totally deflated. Sam Grady slit open Dempsey's envelope. He passed the slip of paper around. It read, "The ace of spades will be David Orton. The Man has been blowing smoke up our noses."

They were back to the starting point, back to square one, hadn't even passed Go, back to the Man. He'd had them chasing a dead man, a nonexistent ghost. No wonder they couldn't find Orton. No wonder none of the leads checked out.

Now there were nine murders to solve. Dempsey rose slowly and walked to the blackgoard. He spoke softly. "The cocksucker fooled us totally. We've got to go back to basics. We've got to start at the beginning."

He wrote on the blackboard, the squeak of chalk against the slate the only noise in the room.

Date	Murder	Method	Marking (Spades)
June 1	David Orton	Unknown/Dissected	Ace
June 2	Selectman Donnelly	Dynamite	King
June 3	Hetty Starr	Snakebite	Queen
June 4	Judge Waller	Poison	Jack
June 5	Paul Fredericks	Stabbing	Ten
June 6	Warren Petty	Electrocution	Nine
June 7	Tony Rocco	Choked	Eight
June 8	Marie Benson	Carbon Monoxide	Seven
June 9	John Frouge	Hanging	Six

Farrow broke the silence "Chief, I'd better call off the search for Orton's car. I guess he wasn't using one after all."

Briggs checked his watch He leaped from his chair. "My God, I'm supposed to call the Governor."

Grady rose also. "Jim, I'd like to use the phone in your office. I've got to report to Washington."

Dempsey asked Belli to prepare a media release on the finding of Orton. "Lay it on the line. Don't try to sugar-coat it. Give them the facts. Honesty is always best. My mother drilled it into me. We're going to be torn apart. But we probably deserve what we get."

Jim Dempsey was alone in the room. He breathed deeply in an effort to control the emotion that rose inside him. He'd never felt more despondent, more helpless. He sat with his head in his hands, closing his eyes to think. "Goddammit!" he said, feeling a tear run down his cheek.

The Man moved fast, with the element of total surprise, since no one knew where he would strike next. The Man seemed to know every move the police made, seemed always to be close by. They'd have to go back and look for the motive behind each of these murders. There had to be one.

Walking to the window, rubbing his burning eyes, he

wondered if he was letting his emotion swallow his intelligence. He had to get his whole mind working. Somehow. He had to be a positive force, with a positive attitude. The town he loved was being torn apart and needed leadership. It was up to him to provide it. There was no one else. Besides, no one could outwit him. Breathing deeply, he felt better.

Grady and Briggs returned almost simultaneously. Both looked crestfallen. Briggs kept shaking his head.

"The Governor's on my ass. I made the mistake of joking about the Man's ace in the hole, and she chewed me out, but good, and gave me an ultimatum."

"You're not alone, Spike," Grady commented, out of the corner of his mouth. "We've all got our asses in a crack."

Briggs ignored the comment. "Well, I told her to call a spade a spade. Not only is this joker wild, but he's playing with a marked deck, shuffling, cutting and dealing the cards as well, drawing to inside straights, because he names the wild cards, after the hand is dealt. She didn't think my analogy was appropriate, and told me that if the Man turns over all thirteen spades, she'll trump me personally. Then the Governor hung up."

Dempsey looked up, a hint of a smile in his eyes. "Let's hope for everyone's sake the Man's playing nine-card baseball and not fifty-two pickup."

Briggs put his hand to his forehead and pressed his temples. "I've got this splitting headache again."

"So do I," Grady said, wincing. "The aspirin business must be flourishing. I don't think we're getting enough sleep. When we catch this prick, I think I'll retire, or at least take a long vacation."

Grady kept some new information to himself. Over the phone, Bob Dillinger had registered no surprise that Orton was dead, and wasn't the Man. He told him that, on a hunch, his agents were trailing six men. "My nose itched" was the only explanation Dillinger offered, confident that one of the six was the Man.

Grady respected Dillinger's desire to operate independently, and didn't ask him to identify his six suspects. Nor did he ask where he'd gotten the extra agents, knowing that, with his contacts in Washington, Dillinger could requisition an army if needed.

Grady asked Dempsey why he'd suspected Orton wasn't the murderer. The Chief went through the theory that the fingerprint evidence was the only really hard evidence against Orton. "And it was just too pat. Clear fingerprints, but only on small, portable items. The type that could be easily planted at the scene of a crime."

"How do you think he got them?" Briggs was now pacing nervously.

"Easy enough. The Man physically controlled Orton's body. Let's assume he overpowered or drugged him. It would be easy to put the fingerprints on a series of small items in small plastic Baggies for safekeeping, until he was ready to use them."

Grady's mouth opened. He nodded his head affirmatively. "Of course. Simple, really simple."

As the meeting broke up, Dempsey suggested that each of them think back over the nine murders. Review the details, murder by murder. "We need a clue. We desperately need a thread to lead us to the Man. Each of you should come up with what you think is the most likely path to explore."

Briggs suggested they check out the embalmer. He was clearly making more money than anyone.

One-quarter of Fairport's population commuted to work in New York every day. It was known as a bedroom community. Nestled snugly in exurbia, it was one of those privileged communities with exclusionary zoning laws. It represented the secure "good life." The commuters were used to returning every night from the urban jungle to their tranquil, affluent, safe suburb. John Frouge had been one of them. Suddenly, everything was backward, upside down. Their town had become the symbol for evil, a jungle with a bloodthirsty predator in its midst.

On the evening New Haven trains from New York, almost all of the commuters were reading the *Post*. Its entire front page was devoted to a picture of John Frouge hanging from the flagpole.

The headline read, "ORTON'S VICTIM NUMBER EIGHT. WHO'S NEXT?" The first six pages were devoted entirely to the Fairport murders. Each day the *Post* had expanded its coverage of the sensational murders. In just one week, the paper's circulation had doubled.

The discovery of Orton's body was not in the newspaper. But it was being bulletined every fifteen minutes on both radio and television and spread quickly by word of mouth through every commuter train. People huddled in groups, talking in low voices tinged with fear.

At the station, commuters were met by members of the newly formed "Protect the People Committee," passing out leaflets. They announced a meeting for 8:00 P.M. Tuesday evening at the high school for the purpose of forming neighborhood vigilante groups.

On Main Street, long lines of people waited outside Gunn's Gun Shop. Huge window banners proclaimed, "New Shipment. Just In. Remington 20-Gauge Shotguns—$199.95. No Permit Necessary."

Fred Gunn was selling shotguns right out of the shipping containers without unwrapping them. "It'll work, we'll guarantee it," he told Gus Rizzo. "If it doesn't, bring it back. We'll give you another. Next."

Pop was jubilantly thinking to himself, These murders are the best thing ever happened to Gunn's.

Tom Winchester bought four boxes of shotgun shells, saying, "If the police can't protect us, we'll do it ourselves."

Once again, the nation had been jolted by the news from Fairport. The evening television poured it on. The nation ate it up. Orton was dead. He wasn't the murderer. No, he'd been the Man's first victim, set up to look like the murderer by the Man, the sinister Man.

The news was unbelievable. People shook their heads in disbelief. "Did you hear?" It was the only topic of conversation. For five days, their media had told them over and over, thousands of times, that Orton was the murderer. It had become a fact. Like other accepted givens, Orton was the killer. Find him, and the murders would stop.

This belief had become as firmly planted in America's collective mind as certain advertising truisms. Avis tries harder; Maxwell House is good to the last drop; Ivory Soap is 99 $^{44}/_{100}$% pure—it floats; Clairol—does she or doesn't she? She does; Winston tastes good!

It had to be Orton. If it wasn't, who could one believe? Maybe Avis didn't try harder; maybe Maxwell House was bitter at the bottom of the cup; maybe Ivory sank; maybe the Clairol girl didn't; maybe Winston was blah!

If Orton wasn't the mass murderer, who was? It was back to the Man. Who the hell was the Man?

The nation demanded an answer.

In blue jeans and sports shirts, Belli and Farrow walked slowly into Luigi's Bar. A pale streak of light entered with them. It was swallowed by the darkness. They groped their way toward the rear booth. O'Cello saw them enter and lit a fat Cuban cigar. They moved toward the cloud of smoke.

They slid into a booth, and O'Cello grunted a greeting.

"I told ya." He showed his yellow teeth.

Belli nodded for both of them. "We shoulda listened. Policemen make mistakes. After all, they're human."

O'Cello grunted again and pushed two beers across the table. "I ordered for ya. Only got a few minutes." He glanced nervously around. The other tables were still empty.

Farrow noticed that O'Cello was perspiring freely. His light silk suit was damp. He had the sudden thought that the Sponge probably absorbed his own sweat.

Belli leaned forward and in a low voice asked, "What else can you tell us about—"

O'Cello's raised eyebrows stopped Belli in mid-question. He beckoned them closer and in a hoarse, nervous whisper spoke. "Drugs . . . it's shit . . . I lost three close friends, and then . . . my sister dead. Big Boy got them all." The Sponge shuddered violently. His eyes closed.

Belli and Farrow waited patiently.

"Some pals of mine . . . if they knew we'z talking . . . my tongue would be in a garbage disposal."

Farrow and Belli exchanged glances. O'Cello's dark sockets were watering profusely, and he dabbed at them with a hand-embroidered silk handkerchief.

Belli waited almost a minute and then he tried again.

"We found the funny money . . . the hard way. We have trouble understanding the other . . . We've never had any problem."

The Sponge nodded. HIs yellow teeth showed again.

"Fairport. If your whole town was on fire, I w'unt piss on it. Odd, ain't it? They're poppin' greenies in circles all around ya. Yer nest is clean. It's obvious. A vulture doesn't crap where he sleeps."

O'Cello leaned back, eyes scanning the room again. He rocked forward, then caught himself, and said nothing, his hand clutching at his cigar like a child's pacifier.

"Who? How?"

The Sponge licked his lips and shrugged. "I told ya before. A big drug operation. Fairport's dead center. That's all!"

He looked around again. "My life doesn't mean anything to ya. It's important to me . . . I've repaid ya. Give me five minutes. Ya stay glued." He reached out his fat hand for Belli's.

Farrow started to protest, then stopped himself.

O'Cello slid out of the booth and disappeared into the darkness.

The two detectives stared at each other helplessly. Farrow's hand tightened around his can of beer.

"Shit, we don't know any more now than we did before."

Belli's dark eyes flashed. "I'm not sure. Remember, he talks in riddles. Twice now he's told us it's drugs. The word is wrong. 'Drugs' is a layman's term. It doesn't fit O'Cello. He's telling us something."

Farrow looked at Belli, excitement rising in his face.

"Drug operation . . . dead center . . . a drug center. We've only got one."

Belli nodded.

"McAlpin's! Christ, old man McAlpin is square as a box."

"Maybe so, but this last week . . . it's enough to lose faith in both Santa Claus and the Easter Bunny. McAlpin's not in their league. Let's stake him out."

As they left the bar, Belli laughed. "Sometimes it's better to be lucky than smart."

Farrow grinned and put his hand on the other's shoulder. "You must be very happy, then."

Vivian had been happy to accept Barbara's invitation. She'd met only a few people in Fairport, and was lonely. She was becoming a kitchen drinker. Some new friends could help her win this quiet little battle.

She and Barbara got along famously. They chatted away all afternoon. At six, Barbara made them martinis and invited her for dinner, a simple but elegant steak and salad. They ate outside, on the patio, by candlelight. It was a warm, balmy evening, and a pleasant breeze blew across the terrace.

Vivian was a fragile, pale woman with deepset, dark eyes and an ethereal manner. Her haunting good looks were accentuated by a cool lemon jump suit with harem pants. Barbara liked her. She was sympathetic, considerate, understanding and compassionate.

At 6:30, the phone rang. Vivian could tell it was Barbara's man. Probably married, Vivian thought, or else why wouldn't he live with Barbara? She could tell that Barbara was holding him off. After the call, Vivian offered to leave, felt she was interfering, but was told please don't. Her car in the driveway would provide security. No one would stop by.

Barbara's whole story came pouring out, then, tears, and all.

Vivian comforted and consoled her and agreed to stay for the night. Later, after Barbara stepped out of the tub, Vivian rubbed the tension from neck and back muscles. She made her way very, very delicately, then touched her. In one moment, all of Barbara's butterflies fluttered their wings in unison, off on another gossamer trip. The butterflies grew larger and larger and fluttered faster and faster. Her excitement built. She was helpless.

It was a most glorious night for both of them, a unique emotional experience. Vivian was accomplished at what she was doing, very gentle, soft, sensitive, tender, loving, with everything at a slow, unhurried pace. Her lips and tongue were everyplace.

Very early, Barbara discovered something amazing and glorious. This lovemaking wasn't tiring her. In fact, slowly, but steadily, she was picking up energy and strength from it, obtaining an energy transfer, recharging her batteries.

She had also discovered Vivian's weakness, the moment she touched her breasts. They were supersensitive. Vivian couldn't resist that, and was even more helpless than Barbara had been. It was like a circle . . . endless. It went on all night.

Now, totally relaxed, Barbara's confidence returned. She knew that in the morning all of her normal vitality and energy would be restored, it was surging back into her body. She was in total control, felt wicked, her heart singing. Bring on her man. She could handle him now. If drained, she'd refill her reservoir from Vivian.

It was touch and glow time again. She reached out for Vivian's breasts. Her butterflies fluttered, then speeded up. Vivian, too, had found paradise.

Judy Rogers took off her reading glasses and leaned back from the desk in her hotel room and poured herself another cup of tea. It tasted flat. She'd crammed three days of research into one day, and her eyes knew it. She rubbed them, rose, walked into the bathroom and rinsed her face again with cold water.

After talking to Peter twice, she'd had a long conversation with her office. The finding of Orton's body had shocked everyone, but her instinct warned her that the death of Nellie Arbuckle might be even more significant. Nellie was very heavily insured, and already two companies had called Bond & Bond. The office had immediately dispatched a message to Fairport with copies of the policies. Her death was listed as an accident. Judy wondered. Arbuckle's death could hold the key to everything.

Peter was looking forward to their meeting on Wednesday evening, just two days away. Her pulse quickened. They'd never even had a date yet. She laughed. There was something exhilarating about their relationship that kept both her heart and mind open.

Orton hadn't sent her the daisies. Who had? She pushed the question into the back of her mind.

Judy slipped off her shoes, sat back at the desk and made another note on her pad. Stomach knotted with excitement, she sensed something. She was uncertain what, but still it sent a strange thrill through her. Nothing was solved, but there was a pattern developing.

It had started with one simple premise. In insurance fraud involving murder, people kill for money. Everything else is incidental. As far as she knew, of the ten deaths in Fairport, nine murders and an accident, Starr, Waller and now Arbuckle were the victims with important money.

Sometimes people killed innocent victims to draw suspicion away from their real purpose. But nine murders. That was far too many. Money was probably the key motive, but not the only one.

A number of prominent people had been murdered. Hetty Starr, Judge Waller, Warren Petty and Marie Benson. The death of any one of these individuals would have obtained important national publicity. She added Arbuckle to this list. The death of the minister, Paul Fredericks, would have been of local interest only. But a crucifixion . . . of almost anyone! It was a murder for maximum publicity. Why? She didn't know yet.

That left four victims. The least important on the list were Donnelly, Rocco, Frouge and Orton. Finding Orton was of national significance, but only because he'd been the object of a nationwide manhunt. Her mind was racing. The little pieces were starting to fall into place.

Judy's flesh crawled. All four were Rotarians, and all members of their executive committee. That was interesting. It was fascinating. There were eight other members of that committee, Baker, Briggs, Dillon, Dempsey, Hoyle, McAlpin, Nichols and Tilden. Of the eight, she'd isolated three for close scrutiny—Dillon, Tilden and Nichols.

Don Dillon had written insurance policies for Hetty Starr, Judge Waller and Nellie Arbuckle. Tilden was a suspect in bank fraud. She was positive he was guilty, but knew she couldn't prove it. The old fox was too sly. Tilden had also been a close financial adviser to Nellie. She planned to dig into that relationship. Ned Nichols stood to gain the most, perhaps millions, from the deaths of Starr and Waller. She wondered how close he'd been to Nellie.

Lighting a cigarette and drawing a deep breath, she let the smoke out slowly.

The remaining five members of the committee? The Man had already tried to kill Jim. The rest were likely victims, too . . . each staring death in in the eyes. Only the fit would survive. . . . Was that cynicism or realism? Oh, for the grace of 20/20 foresight. Tomorrow, she'd start talking to them.

Surely, all the law-enforcement agencies—all those men— had brains enough to realize the surviving members of the executive committee were in danger. That was simple enough for even a man to understand.

The Man had enjoyed a quiet dinner with his wife. But later, she'd reproached him angrily when he'd suggested sex.

"You're becoming impossible. That's all you think of. I'd like you to get back to normal. This everyday nonsense has got to stop. I'm not a machine. You don't push a button and turn me on. I've got to feel in the mood, and I can't feel like it every day. I do pretty well upholding my end. I clean and cook and do my chores. I do everything for you to make you happy. I'm not an everyday person and I'm certainly not a twice-a-day call girl!"

"Oh, shit, the lecture again," the Man muttered to himself. He went upstairs and took a long, cold shower.

Now, hours later, with his wife asleep, the Man was seated in his den, reviewing his day. He was ecstatic. The plan was perfect. News about Frouge and Orton had been devastating to Fairport and Jim Dempsey. The media were now referring to the Man as the greatest killer of all time. They'd seen nothing yet. He'd watched them take down Frouge's body. The elephants were so clumsy. Also, he'd thrown suspicion on the Chief; he even felt a twinge of sympathy for him. Jim was trying hard, but didn't seem to be thinking as clearly as he used to.

Now that Orton was no longer a cover, it was time for phase two. He rubbed his hands together expectantly. The elephants would charge off in three directions at once, stomping the ground, shaking the earth, trumpeting and getting nowhere.

This afternoon, he'd felt someone was shadowing him. It had to be either a federal agent or an out-of-town private eye, not one of the locals. Well, they couldn't have learned anything. Tomorrow, a trap was set for the tail. He'd nail the tail, right to the elephant's ass.

The stereo clicked off. Damn rock music, music by the inept for the untutored. Reviewing his plans for the next four murders, detail by detail, he knew each one should go smoothly. There was no reason to change anything.

He took his notebook and went down to his private arsenal and checked the equipment for the next day. It was all set. This impersonation was demanding, even for him, but it would be perfect. The latex nose, the fishskin that would go on the eyelids to change their shape, the rubber cap that would be glued to his forehead, the hairlace wig he'd wear, all was in order. Humming while he worked—"Little old lady passing by, catching everyone's eye"—he locked the wine rack back into place. When this was all over, those three specific bottles of wine would be the sweetest wine ever. He'd savor each drop!

He went back up to the desk in his den, two steps at a time. The black marking pencil crossed out John Frouge, the Commodore, the six of spades, victim number nine on his list. Some people were born to be murdered. The Frog was one.

As an afterthought, he put a checkmark next to David Orton's name. One of his four key murders. The Orton ruse, the ace of spades, had worked very well, just about the way he'd planned.

Just wait until June 14, and the ace of hearts. He clapped his hands together. That one was diabolical. He'd burn in hell. The notebook went back into its secret hiding place.

He poured himself a cold glass of beer. The foam ran over the top and down onto the table. Ignoring the puddle, he returned to his chair in the den. The wife was probably right, he'd have to cool it . . . too turned on. That might lead to his exposure. He laughed at the thought. His sex drive was phenomenal, at least triple or even quadruple what it normally was. It was getting away from him. In the old days, Gayla, Barbara, Jeanne and old "what's her name" were enough. Maybe he'd better branch out, spread it around a bit.

This Vivian was worth looking into. But in the midst of these murders, that was too dangerous. Better stick to the plan, adhere to his normal pattern. Maybe Vivian had gone home . . . he'd whip over to Barbara's for a quickie. No, that tail might be out there waiting. He'd have to ditch him first.

It would be better to discipline his thinking and actions. Plenty of time for sex later. He sighed. Time to take another cold shower.

10

Tuesday, June 10.
A Deadly Dose

SUSY NICHOLS slept fitfully. Those dreams. Nightmares that revealed a large man standing and opening his arms over her, his face always in the shadows, coming closer and closer. Now, this was the second dream. The man was holding a huge eyedropper in both hands. It had a familiar shape. It was just inches above her lips, dripping sugar, little drops of liquid sugar, sickeningly sweet. She swallowed some and then gagged.

She moved closer to Ned, and suddenly was awake. He wasn't there. The bedside clock blinked 6:00 A.M. What the hell was Ned doing up at 6:00 in the morning? There was music coming from the den, that Sinatra tape again. Ned was acting stranger every day. She was afraid he was going money-mad and feared that someday he'd reach too far and go over the edge of the dollar precipice.

Susy rolled over and tried to go back to sleep, vowing to make an appointment with Dr. Markum. Maybe he could explain the meaning of that dream.

Nichols knew he was operating at peak efficiency. The program of autogenic training had blocked out all distracting psychological factors. Aware that anxiety neutralizes a person's optimum performance, he had no anxiety. No fear.

In college, he had taken a course in hypnosis, and through the years had developed the ability of self-hypnosis, practicing it daily. It had greatly increased both mental and physical performance. Now he could use autogenics to psych himself up, to obtain the maximum effort from his powerful muscles. He was both physically and mentally fit.

Bright sunlight streamed through the windows. Ned, deep in a yogalike trance, was oblivious to the music from the stereo, meditating in a state of self-hypnosis. His subconscious was totally in control of his muscle memories, no doubt, no inhibitions. Like a great athlete, his actions would be totally coordinated, reflexes automatic, no tenseness, relaxed, no anxiety, no fear.

Today his performance would be exceptional. The body's feedback system would produce maximum strength. Anything tried today would be a super performance. If necessary, a call could go out to the body's super-maximum potentials. Up to now, it hadn't been necessary.

Briggs and Dempsey. A pair of Keystone Kops. What the hell had they ever done? Let them try to get along in the business world, where they had to produce results or else. He'd eat them alive and spit out the bones. Physically, they were strong, tested, tough. Especially Dempsey. But neither had his hidden resources. The motivation and strength derived from this daily mental training, his TM. But why think about them?

His mind dwelled on more attractive subjects. Ned's angels. The three of them were fantastic. Each with her own unique appeal. Then why did he always end his sensory thoughts with an image of those tight-fitting blue shorts? That incredible ass. It was just a matter of time. Sooner or later. He wet his lips.

Snapping out of the trance, he checked his watch, clicked off his stereo and headed to work, muttering, "This is a big day. I've got a lot to do."

Once again, the Man was on the move. Leaving the house at 7:15 A.M., he noticed a dark-blue Granada parked at the curb across the street. As he drove, he watched the Granada ease away from the curb, execute a sweeping U-turn, and settle back a half-block length behind.

Right, he was being followed. There was no reason to shake the tail. Not yet, anyhow. Better to pretend he hadn't noticed. Poor bastard, probably had sat out there all night. Tough shit!

He'd alter his plans slightly. It would be difficult getting to both Jeanne's and Barbara's today. Fuck the tail. There had to be a way. Damn Gayla. Where was that eye-popping blonde? As much as possible, he'd stick to the normal routine. Seeing the girls was no crime. They'd never prove murder that way. It might actually direct suspicion away from him. No one would believe that the world's greatest killer would have time for lovemaking, especially with more than one gorgeous chick.

The girls didn't know anything. They would be his alibi, if needed. Besides, most mass murderers in history were impotent, except for that bearded hippie Manson. Men kill because of sexual frustration. The police psychological profile would call for an impotent male. Clearly he didn't fit the pattern. He hit the steering wheel, then checked the rearview mirror again.

Who the hell was the shadow? Why? What had he done? If stopped, he'd say, "I ain't done nothing, officer." It had to be the FBI. The locals would never put a tail on him. They didn't have the manpower.

It couldn't be Grady's men; had to be another group of feds acting independently. If they were shadowing him, they'd have tails on at least five others. If they're tailing six suspects with three shifts each, that's eighteen tails. The elephants have got eighteen tails attached to eighteen fat asses. What a three-ring circus.

He'd nail the tail. Wipe him. No, that would make him a prime suspect. Better to find out for sure who else was being tailed, and waste one of their shadows. That was a damn good idea. Then he might wound his own tail, making it look as if one of the others had done it. Maybe killing all eighteen of them would be the best idea. He'd cut off their tails with a carving knife. A cartoon from childhood floated across his mind.

He had to shake the tail for at least an hour today, to kill the next victim. Shit, shaking all the tails was the only way, or they'd realize he was the only suspect loose at that time. The surveillance was going to make it tougher. No doubt

about it. It was pressure-cooker time. All right, play it one
murder at a time and play it carefully.

The Man pulled his car into the parking lot, parked, and
entered the building where he worked. He ignored the blue
Granada that pulled into the parking lot behind him, parking
at the opposite end of the lot.

Dempsey's entire staff sat quietly, waiting for the 7:45 A.M.
meeting to begin. He was on the phone with Briggs. The
conversation seemed ominous and one-sided.

He put down the phone and swung his chair toward them,
his face grim and tight-lipped. The strain showed. He looked
older, especially his eyes. They had no luster, seemed drained
of emotion. Farrow and Belli passed a worried glance between
them. In a low voice, he began.

"I want to talk about logistics. The Man has committed
nine murders in the last nine days. We've been able to cope
reasonably well up to now. The reason . . . we've had a
prime suspect, Orton. Everyone was looking for one individual. Attention was focused on a specific description of a specific person. Even so, we were inundated with calls and
barely managed to keep afloat."

Dempsey rose from his chair and stood behind his desk. His
voice was calm, but the tone of authority had increased
noticeably.

"Today, it's just the Man. We don't know who he is.
Pretty sure he's a white male, approximately six feet tall,
maybe taller, and weighs one-ninety to two hundred pounds.
Everything else is conjecture. I don't even have enough for a
solid sketch. We're now asking the public to come forward
with any information or suspicion—no matter how unfounded.
The public is anxious to help. They're concerned. They want
this bastard caught.

"Today we'll get hundreds, perhaps thousands, of telephone
calls. The department has set up a special number, 800-
259-9999. I'm detaching Sergeant Martin to organize this
effort. Briggs is loaning us Sergeants DiLeo, Marcus and six
troopers."

Dempsey turned and talked directly to Martin.

"Now, Bob, we've had offers of manpower from all surrounding towns. I want you to borrow as many policemen as you need. Special task-force headquarters are being set up in the high school. All calls with information about the Man will be switched to you. The telephone company is installing sixty phone lines in the gymnasium. They should have at least twenty ready by now. The rest will be operative by this afternoon. The Women's League has offered to work the phones. They'll take down the details of every call, no matter how unrelated they may seem."

Farrow noticed that the color was back in Dempsey's face. He was now speaking with his old take-charge voice, that spoke in well-defined capital letters. Tom gave Belli a thumbs-up signal.

"Your responsibility will be to check suspects against the physical description we now have. Your staff will handle the initial investigation, the preliminary screening. The minute you turn up a real suspect, you clue us in. We'll be there to play hero." A faint smile flickered on his lips.

"Since our description is so general, we're going to be deluged with calls. Girls who are angry at their boyfriends and every crackpot with a grudge against a neighbor. Wives with two-timing husbands. They'll all call. But there's no other way. We need a lead. Every phone call must be checked."

Dempsey pointed at Martin. "Every one. A streak of irrational behavior. It may be one little thing that trips him up. It generally is."

As soon as he could, Rice called Belli aside. The tall blond glanced around and spoke in a low voice.

"I got the report back from the forensic lab in Bethany. I was right. The teeth marks on the two sets of Tiparillo butts are identical."

Belli's mouth opened. "But Orton was already dead—"

Rice held up his hand. They entered the office and he shut the door behind them, his face glistening with excitement.

"You're right. There's only one explanation. Those butts had to be the Man's. He left two at Orton's, when he killed him, and two in the fringe of the woods, where he painted the

Senator's wife. We found some specks of paint on those. It matches."

"He'd have to be a chain smoker."

"Like some people we know." Rice grinned. "I've got an idea."

"There's a first time for everything," Belli said, returning the grin.

"Seriously, we've got a solid clue. All we need to do is find the matching teeth marks."

Belli stared at him silently. The idea was slowly taking shape in his mind. He nodded his agreement.

"If we don't find a match, at least it eliminates a few suspects."

Rice cautioned. "Label them carefully. Don't be obvious. We're dealing with a maniac. And say nothing. Absolutely nothing . . . to anyone."

There was a flush of excitement on Belli's swarthy face. He turned to leave, then turned back.

"Briggs . . . he's mine. That bastard is a Tiparillo volcano. And he mangles the tips to ribbons. By the way, what happens if someone notices?"

Rice grinned broadly. "Give him an evasive answer. Tell him to butt out!"

Grady, Briggs and their key men arrived at police headquarters at 9:00 A.M. It was a group of grim, unsmiling lawmen who gathered in the conference room. Rice had made sure there was a clean ashtray at each chair. He'd also set two packs of Tiparillos on the table.

"It's bait. I'm chumming," he whispered to Belli.

Dempsey was standing in front of the blackboard, on which was listed everything known about the Man. Most of it was conjecture, but one side of the board was almost filled, emphasizing the basics—white male, about six feet, athletic, 190-200 pounds, forty maybe, clever, pro at disguise and impersonation, strong, quick reactions, has arsenal of exotic weapons, with some working knowledge of explosives, electricity, rattlesnakes, knots, poison, surgery, typing . . . He paused, looked around and asked, "Anything else?"

Belli looked down at the floor, nervously. The Man also smoked Tiparillos. It could be the most valuable clue of all. Concealing information . . . oh, shit!

It was Grady who put into words what was in the back of everyone's head. "This is no ordinary mass killer. We're up against a brilliant mind, perhaps a genius. Few people possess all those talents." His cane pointed toward the board.

Dempsey didn't comment. He was mentally checking Ned Nichols' abilities against those shown on the blackboard. There was a surprisingly close match, and Ned had a motive.

Briggs reached for one of the Tiparillo packs, unwrapped the cellophane and slid out a small cigar, looking at Grady as he lit it.

"This must be an unusual town. I know a lot of guys . . . take Jim . . . I'm not sure about rattlesnakes or his acting abilities, but he's got the rest of those talents. The same is true for Nichols . . . Baker . . . Dillon . . . even Hoyle. All pretty active, all about the same build."

Dempsey stared hard at Briggs. "How about yourself?"

"I can't stand snakes." Briggs grinned. "Damn good thing we've been working together this week. We know where we've been."

Farrow made a mental note. It wasn't the Chief, but Briggs, Nichols, Baker, Dillon and Hoyle. Easy enough to check their whereabouts at the time of each murder. One alibi is all anyone needed. Otherwise . . .

Belli gestured and spoke. "Chief, until Orton's fake fingerprints threw us off, twenty-two bombing suspects had been eliminated. Solid alibis . . . couldn't have killed Donnelly. The other twenty-three . . . thrown out because their fingerprints didn't match Orton's. I'd like to finish . . . among those fitting the Man's physical description."

Dempsey nodded affirmatively and looked at the others.

Farrow acknowledged Dempsey's glance, rose from his seat, snubbing out his small cigar, and walked to the blackboard, turned around and jotted some notes before speaking. Belli slid the ashtray Farrow had used over next to him.

"A crazy . . . with no motive . . . just blind killings . . . there should be no pattern among the victims." Farrow paused, then stepped from in front of the blackboard, revealing what was written.

sex of victims	—seven men, two women
residence	—seven Fairport, two out-of-towners
profession	—all over the lot—from actress to psychiatrist— no pattern
wealth	—four millionaires—Rocco . . . three well-to-do, two average means
clubs	—one FYC, two Longwood and four Exec. Comm. Rotarians

"Two things stand out. The first, wealthy victims . . . a huge pot of money in some of these estates. That could be the Man's motive. The second, and I think most significant"—Farrow gestured toward Briggs and Dempsey—"four of your committee have been killed. That's a third . . . and, Chief, he tried to kill you, that would have made five. That's a definite pattern. For some reason, the Man is killing off your group. If we knew why, we'd have him."

Briggs blew out a lungful of smoke, then remarked coldly, "McAlpin, Tilden . . . they don't fit . . . too old. That leaves six. If this keeps up and only one of us is left, he's the Man, guilty as hell. Shoot the bastard on sight."

Dempsey interrupted. "The six of us have to be suspect. Tom, go over each one with a fine-tooth comb. Eliminate us as suspects. Any objection, Spike?" Dempsey watched Briggs' face closely.

"None," snapped Spike, glaring at Farrow. "But keep personal matters out of your investigation, sonny. Check the murders, but don't turn up any scandal. No gossip. This is a small town."

Dempsey noticed that Spike's face had colored noticeably. So he had something to hide. The rumors were true. Spike clearly didn't want Alice to know, and there was really no reason.

"Those are fair ground rules, Tom," said Dempsey. "Keep anything personal to yourself. Report it to me only if it's important to the murder investigations."

Spike looked somewhat relieved, but still seemed agitated.

"Why don't we put tails on the whole group?" suggested DeLuca, somewhat tentatively.

Shuster, DeLuca's partner, muttered aloud, "Behind every fool's face is a fool's mind. I should have known, the bastard's pulled a muscle in his head."

Dempsey cut him off. "That's not as wild as it sounds. Spike, if you'll loan us the men, we'll put tails on all six. God forbid, next murder, we'll know exactly where each one was."

Briggs hesitated. He ran his hand over his close-cropped head.

Grady agreed instantly. "If a suspect is not at a murder scene, he can't be guilty. Tails will give the innocent ironclad alibis. The Man just won't be able to keep it up. There won't be any suspects left, except for the Man himself."

"That's probably his plan," Dempsey commented ruefully. "The greater the risk, the greater the thrill. Every murder increases his danger of being caught. Every suspect eliminated increases his excitement."

Briggs stood up. "O.K. I'll see if I can turn up the men. I'll get on it." He left the meeting abruptly.

"Let's wind this up," suggested Grady. "You guys must have iron bladders. My eyeballs are floating."

Dempsey agreed, and the room cleared quickly.

As he walked down the hall, Dempsey thought, Spike's got about as much tact as he does patience. None. There's something behind the way he acted . . . check him out. First I've got to see Ned Nichols again. Everyone's forgotten, he was at the church . . . saw Fredericks on the cross. He didn't deny it.

Hell, I was questioning Ned when Sam called with a positive make on Orton. Nichols has a hell of a financial motive, stands to inherit millions from both Hetty and Judge Waller. He was at the club when we lowered Frouge down and at the hospital just before Arbuckle died. Ned has to be a prime suspect.

Grady was still in the men's room, looking around carefully, checking the empty booths to make sure they were alone before he spoke. "Jim, the Colonel's behavior surprised me. What's he hiding?"

"I'm not sure. He's got a short fuse."

"It's obvious. Under pressure, he turns nasty. Today he seemed almost as cold as your other buddy, Ned Nichols."

The Chief said warmly, "You old codger. I've been thinking the same thing. Let's you and I do a bit of number-one checking on the two of them. Let's start with Nichols. He fits almost every clue. I'd love to know his movements all last week."

In Rice's office, just off the lab, Belli and Rice were busy dropping Tiparillo butts into separate plastic Baggies. "I'll check them as soon as I can," Rice said. "We got four from Briggs. They're chewed to hell, look promising. We got one from Farrow. Just a few teeth marks on it. We got one of the Chief's. No marks at all. He doesn't chew, he sucks the tip."

Belli pondered. He wondered how the hell he would get butts from Nichols, Baker, Dillon and Hoyle. "I always knew I'd wind up picking up butts," he said, shaking his head.

"Boy, from now on, smokeless is the way to go. It's Happy Days. Just a pinch between your cheeks and gums." Rice mimicked a snuff dipper.

At 10 A.M., four prominent psychiatrists and five psychologists met in a private room at the Fairport Inn. They had been recruited at Dempsey's request by Sam Grady from hospitals, universities, medical schools, law-enforcement units and private practice throughout the Northeast. Their purpose was to sketch a psychological portrait of the Man.

Lou Piccollo, Doc Brody and Slade Custer were to be present throughout the meeting, providing background information and answering questions about the murders. By 11:30, it was apparent to Lou the day was going to be a long one. Even he could tell from the psychiatric jargon that the nine experts had nine different theories.

"The Man has nine lives," he whispered to Brody, "one for each murder."

"What crap! How'd you like to be paying sixty bucks a half hour to these shrinks for mumbo-jumbo?" asked Doc, leaning back in his chair and closing his eyes.

Piccollo turned and glanced at Brody. "They say insanity is hereditary."

The Doc grinned. "It must be. I got mine from my kids."

Barbara was up by ten. She was busy puttering about her kitchen, watering her plants and starting another load of wash, humming to the music coming from her stereo. Her heart was humming, too, happy, contented, fulfilled and full of vitality. Up went the ironing board. As soon as Vivian awoke, she'd serve her breakfast in bed. Glancing at the clock, she decided it would be brunch instead. There was a split of Piper Heidsieck in the refrigerator. Champagne, a perfect way to toast their newfound friendship.

Barbara had never slept with a woman before, but felt no guilt. She had always been curious, but never that interested. Vivian had been incredibly gentle, kind and caring. There had been no anxiety, no pressure. She'd been excited by her soft touch and caresses, a totally different sensation, a feeling of being desirable, wanted, needed. Theirs was an emotional closeness, almost a communion of souls. She had a warm inner glow. The ironing was almost finished. She'd clean the pool. No, she wanted to be here when Vivian awakened. She'd wash the floor next, but first she put the load of wash into the dryer.

The world was such a beautiful place . . . the cuddling and hugging, the warm, soft body sleeping next to her, it all felt so natural. Joy smiled at feelings deep inside her. When she touched Vivian's breasts, a fire went surging through her, the squirming and the moaning, the look of indescribable pleasure on her face. Then, when Vivian absolutely couldn't take any more, she relieved the tension. Her own heart had leaped each time. Every new layer of discovery had been better for both. Vivian's skin was soft and smooth, like pure silk. She was so vulnerable, like a puppy dog. Their lovemaking had been mutual, unhurried and pleasurable. Now the floor looked spotless. She'd wax it.

. . .

Farrow and Belli talked to Dempsey. Both had decided they'd feel better if Dempsey knew that McAlpin's was possibly the center of a major drug ring.

Dempsey listened, his face expressionless. His shoulders sagged at the news. McAlpin's. That was really unbelievable. Fairport was fast being revealed as a modern-day Sodom, or was it Gomorrah? One by one, his friends were being exposed as up to their ears in shitty business. Ten days ago he would have laughed at the rumor, but not now.

"How reliable?" he asked.

Belli and Farrow exchanged glances. The dark one said softly, "Very."

"Stake it out. Unmarked car at the front, one at the back. Three eight-hour shifts. Change cars and markers every shift. Gus, you set up the duty chart for this. What are we looking for?"

The redheaded detective spoke first. "A shipment of hard drugs, either in or out."

Dempsey's eyes flicked from one to the other. "Is that all?"

They nodded together.

Dempsey sighed. "You're forgetting one thing. Our Man thinks he's Robin Hood. If your source knows McAlpin's is a drug pipeline, the Man may know it, too. If so, he may try to kill McAlpin."

Dempsey's whole body seemed to come alive at the thought. He spoke now with enthusiasm. "This could be the big break. The drugs have to be of secondary importance. This may be our chance. Your men are to check anything unusual . . . anything at all. But, top-priority, we're looking for the Man."

As the two detectives were leaving the office, Dempsey called after them, "Oh yes, fellows, I hope you thanked the Sponge."

Dempsey saw their backs stiffen.

Back in Farrow's office, Belli said, "It's a damn good thing we told him about McAlpin's. He's got eyes everywhere. He knew we were lying."

Farrow put his hand on the other's shoulder. "Relax, we didn't tell him a lie. We were just a little creative with the truth."

In the police lab, Paul Rice listened once again to the tape of the Man's call the previous Saturday evening. He heard the amazement in his own voice on the tape. Even the gulps were audible.

He'd recorded each one of Rocco's statements onto another tape, and now had a fifty-five-second tape of just the one voice.

Damn, that had to be Tony Rocco talking. He knew it couldn't have been. At that moment, Rocco was a stuffed corpse parked in front of police headquarters. They'd all assumed it was Orton impersonating Rocco. But now they knew that the impersonator was the Man. They had the Man's voice on tape. Fifty-five seconds of the Man's voice on good-quality tape.

Rice was totally intent on what he was doing. Late yesterday, he'd ordered a sound spectrograph from Soundscope, Inc., in Stamford. The machine had been delivered and set up just twenty minutes earlier. Rice was nervous. There was no authorization to order the spectrograph. He had no idea how much it would cost. He didn't want to know. Fairport couldn't afford it. The police budget was already overspent. Fuck the budget. He'd ordered it on a ten-day trial basis. Soundscope had guaranteed they'd take it back if Rice didn't like it. He'd paid the twelve-dollar installation fee as a personal donation. He had ten days and no time to waste.

He played the tape of Rocco's voice again, this time into the sound spectrograph. This machine reduced the speech into electronic "pictures" called spectrograms, or voiceprints. In no time, the machine spit out the spectrogram. It was so advanced it was simple. He now had a voiceprint of the Man! A matching print would do it. He'd phone possible suspects on one pretense or another, record their voices and make voiceprints. He'd find the match, and they'd have the Man. The spectrogram went into a large manila envelope, labeled "The Voice of the Man," then into his desk drawer.

The literature claimed that voiceprints were as accurate as fingerprints. Rice wasn't sure. He knew that voiceprint evidence was not acceptable in Connecticut courts. That was a long way off. Before they tried him, they had to identify and catch the Man. The voiceprint could do it. At least it would indicate whom to go after.

The Chief would have to be told about the spectrograph, but . . . he'd have to screw up his courage. Rice looked about and put two large typewriter covers over the machine. Maybe, just maybe, no one would notice it.

It was late morning. The Man walked to his office window and looked down at the blue Granada. He could see the agent sitting in the driver's seat, one eye on the morning *News* and one eye on his car. The Man smiled and lit a Tiparillo.

The gall of the Feds. They'd put an amateur gumshoe on him, a car spotter, nothing more. The Fed was baby-sitting his wheels. Today it would be easy to ditch him . . . just borrow one of his associate's cars. One of them was out of town for a week. His car was parked on the other side of the building. Perfect.

The tail would never miss him. He could hear him now on the CB. "Yes, Inspector, he's in his office, car still parked in his slot. I've got my eye on him. Yes, sir, never get by me."

Damn amateurs, wasting the taxpayers' money. But just in case the tail got nosy, the instructions to his secretary would be to hold all phone calls. He was in an important conference and couldn't be disturbed, for anyone.

"Ahem." The voice was soft and tentative.

Dempsey looked up from his desk. Mary Potter stood there with a file of papers.

"If you have a minute, Chief, the girls and I have developed a 'What If?' plan."

A question flickered across Dempsey's face as he gestured to a chair.

Mary answered his unasked question as she sat down. "What if the Man is not one of your committee?"

Dempsey nodded, then said quietly, "Let's see it."

Mary leaned forward. "We started with a question. Is there any possible way to develop a comprehensive but manageable list of logical suspects from everyone in town?"

Dempsey's eyebrows raised.

"We made some assumptions. First, the Man lives in Fairport. Second, he's between the ages of thirty-five and forty-four. Third, he's six feet tall or over. And last, he's mobile. He drives a car."

Dempsey smiled slightly. "I'll buy your assumptions. Go ahead."

Mary handed him a typed chart.

Fairport—1970 Census Data	*No. of Men*
White Males	
35–39 years old	584
40–44 years old	957
Total 35-44	1,541
Assume 10% population growth (since 1970)	
Today—total white males 35–44	1,695
White males age 35–44, six feet tall or over (at 15%–from HEW study)	254
White males ages 35–44, over six feet tall, weight 190–200 (at 50%—our estimate)	127

Dempsey sat studying the chart. Mary rubbed her hands together nervously.

"They're only rough estimates, but it does show that it's possible to develop a manageable list."

"But how?" Dempsey looked across at her, his brow furrowed.

Mary smiled hopefully. "Drivers' licenses. The Motor Vehicle Department. They've got it all on computer, by town, sex, age and height."

Dempsey's face lit up. "By God, Mary, it would work. It's brilliant. Get them started on it." He rose and almost hugged her.

Mary stood up, her heart singing. "I called Wethersfield and used your name. They've already started. By tomorrow morning, we should have a list of approximately two hundred and fifty male drivers, between the ages of thirty-five and forty-four, six feet tall or over. We'll have to figure out how to narrow it down from there.''

Dempsey patted her on the back. "Mary, we might even have to set up a weigh station, getting down to about a hundred suspects. Let's check everyone thoroughly.''

As she walked toward the door, Dempsey said, "Mary, thank the girls for me.''

Mary nodded. They didn't know. She'd better tell the other girls about her "What If?" plan.

Judy Rogers emerged from the Fairport Savings Bank. She stood in the sunshine, blinking hard, checking her watch. It was 11:07 A.M. Damn, already late for her appointment. It was only three blocks to Ned Nichols' office. She'd make better time walking.

The morning had been spent going over accounts and ledgers. With Tilden out for the morning, she'd had free access to Nellie Arbuckle's files. Engrossed, she'd lost track of time. Her mind was a kaleidoscope, a blur of colored bits and pieces that fluttered at the far end into a pattern that was beginning to form.

She could see Sam Tilden's grinning face under a shock of white hair. With large incisors and long whiskers, he resembled a huge, white, money-grubbing rat. The few loose hairs she'd find this afternoon.

It was a warm day. As Judy walked, the perspiration sprang out in a flood all over her body. When she reached the bronze plaque that announced "Nichols and Dimes," she was soaked through. What a name for a law firm, she thought.

When the receptionist announced her, Ned Nichols came quickly out of his office, eyes twinkling, smiling. He greeted her warmly and ushered her into his inner office, his hand firmly on her arm, then closed the door behind them. As he did so, she reached into her purse for cigarettes, and at the same time switched on her mini-recorder.

"So you're Brenda's little sister. Quite a resemblance." Nichols ran his tongue along the inside edge of his lips. She was young, soft-scented, silky-skinned, attractive . . . and those blue slacks . . . she had the same perfect ass as her sister. It must run in the family.

"Sorry I was late," Judy said, sitting across the desk from Nichols.

"Don't apologize, Judy. Don't ever apologize. It's a sign of weakness."

Judy was startled by Nichols' directness and the forceful tone of his voice.

"So you're with Bond & Bond. Are you a hired gun?" The lawyer was grinning.

"Just our brains are for hire, Mr. Nichols." Judy smiled back.

"I like challenges," he said. Inwardly, he laughed. Bond & Bond was slipping. Imagine sending a girl to interview him.

They talked about Hetty Starr, Judge Waller and Nellie Arbuckle. Whenever Judy asked important questions about their estates or insurance policies, the lawyer became evasive.

"It's privileged information, Judy dear. I believe in saying nothing and repeating it often. If you want answers to questions like that . . . well, that's what courts are for." He grinned again, totally relaxed.

He would have won the battle of silence, so Judy switched tactics. She mentioned Dempsey, and Nichols' eyes flashed and his face clouded.

"He's a brilliant waste, nothing but a small-town cop. It's a job to keep small minds occupied. Hell, he's got brains, skill, energy, but what's he ever done? Chase robbers. His achievements don't measure up to his talents. The same is true, in spades, for Briggs."

Judy leaned back, listening carefully. Then she bent forward and asked, "How do you measure success?"

Judy was surprised when Nichols didn't hesitate.

"Money. It all comes down to the size of the bank account, doesn't it? A person without money . . . he's nothing. A nobody."

Judy sat there biting her lip. Nichols spoke calmly, methodically. "Life is a game, and the way you keep score is with money." He glanced at her. "You don't understand me, do you? Few people do. That's why I'm successful, and they're not.''

Judy nodded, thinking to herself how wrong he was. It was so easy to understand him. He was another greedy, money-grubbing rat.

Nichols reached into the mahogany humidor on his desk and took out a small cigar, extending it toward her.

''Will you join me?'' he asked with a smile. ''I've always wanted to offer one to a lady.''

Judy shook her head. ''No, thanks.'' She tapped a cigarette out of her pack. Coming around the side of the desk, he lit it. She sensed his real intention and drew away quickly.

Nichols sat back down. ''Dempsey and Briggs . . . have got real problems. I don't follow their activities. Business is my game.'' He put his head back and blew out a mouthful of smoke.

''It's obvious Dempsey's got himself caught on a hook. The more he wriggles . . . it's pathetic.'' Nichols patted his steel-gray hair with his hand. ''His rubber band is stretched tight. If he's not careful, it's going to snap.''

Judy had opened her mouth to object when the phone behind Nichols' desk rang. His eyes flicked to the closed door, then to Judy, hesitating. He swiveled around and answered it.

''Right. I'll be there. Probably close to one.'' He dropped the phone back on the cradle. Judy made a mental note . . . probably a private line. He had a separate, intricate phone-intercom system on the desk.

As he turned back, she said, ''To be fair, Jim's under tremendous pressure.''

''It comes from inside, Judy. Not from outside. You have to learn how to handle pressure. That's a real reflection of your inner strength.''

He waited for his words to sink in, waited for her to speak next. When she didn't, he added, ''Both Jim and Spike live in a circle of people who pat them on the back. They get to believe it. They're both aging fast, goin' round the bend.'' He chewed viciously on the cigar's plastic tip.

Judy's forehead creased. ''How about yourself?'' she asked.

Nichols' chest swelled. "Judy, since I found autogenics, the dial of my life has been turned back. I'm getting younger every day."

The clock on the shelf over the artificial fireplace struck 12:30. Nichols stood up.

"I'd love to invite you to lunch, but I'm tied up with a special . . . client. How about dinner?"

Judy was not prepared for the question, but recovered quickly. "That might be nice. I'd like to meet your wife."

Nichols' face colored slightly. "I meant just the two of us. We could talk about more pleasant subjects over a few drinks."

Judy looked at him, half with contempt and half with wonder. "I don't think so. Thanks anyway. I have some reports to fill out. Perhaps another time."

He put his hand on her arm and whispered gently, "If I can give you some advice?"

Judy stared at him, animosity in her eyes.

"This town is no place for a soft, innocent girl like you. It's a mortuary. It can bury you alive. Go home . . . change the things you can and leave the detective work to the men." The lawyer was grinning from ear to ear.

Judy almost spit at him. She had an uncontrollable urge to jab a finger in his eye, remembering just in time that she wasn't Wonder Woman.

Leaving his office, she said over her shoulder, "A man gets what he deserves."

Nichols was still grinning. Right. He'd buy that. That was his philosophy. His eyes watched her Underalls disappear out the door.

Judy's knees were trembling as she emerged back into the sunlight. She'd never met a more cold-blooded man. He wouldn't blink an eye before blowing off her head. The search was over. Nichols had to be the killer rat, and a vicious one.

How to warn Jim? Nichols saw him as a piece of overripe cheese, a tidbit to be snatched when ready. No, she'd set a trap for this rat herself. It would be totally unexpected. She knew the right kind of bait. His eyes had given it away when he'd looked her over.

• • •

The Man met Jeanne on the dock and lifted her lightly aboard the nineteen-foot Mako. He chuckled at the large number on the stern, *69*, and the small sign, "I may be slow, but I'm ahead of you." She had already stowed the picnic hamper with their lunch and a large ice bucket containing two chilled bottles of Chablis out of the sun under the control console.

He quickly started the Johnson outboards and cast off the lines from the boat to the dock, and they skimmed out into the Sound, heading toward Long Island, eighteen miles away. The water was calm, with only a light breeze blowing. The sun was hot, but the humidity was unusually low, with the temperature in the mid-eighties. There was not a cloud in the sky. It was a perfect summer day.

"How far would you like to go, kittykat?" the Man asked.

"As far as you'd like, lover," Jeanne answered, reaching over his shoulder and pulling the throttle back to idle. She pulled him gently down to the pillows she had spread out on the deck. "I promised you a box lunch in exchange for a quart of heavy cream," she purred. " 'The owl and the pussycat went to sea, in a beautiful pea-green boat.' Let's see, Mr. Owl, if you're the horny type!"

It was soon evident to the Man that his pussycat had been eating catnip. She was excited, revved up to a fever pitch by the idea of fulfilling her fantasy of making love in her open boat, out on the Sound, in public, in broad daylight. They must be nuts. He reached up and turned off the engine. The boat drifted lazily. It was then he saw the small bumper sticker on the inside of the gunwale—"Do a Mouse a Favor, Eat a Pussy."

Forty minutes later, they had finished their lunch and both bottles of wine, finished everything. The dessert had been pure bubbling sweet sugar from a flowing honey pot. As she slipped back into her filmy see-through bikini, he stared at her beauty.

She was gorgeous. Long flowing red hair framed her dazzling white smile. The erect nipples on her firm, well-formed breasts showed through her bikini top. An even tan covered her entire body and accentuated her small, silky patch of wet, curly red hair. His pussycat looked totally satisfied.

A contented, throaty "meow" came from Jeanne. "Darling, why don't you get a divorce and marry me?" The forthright question was totally unexpected. It hit hard in the pit of his stomach. He stared at her silently, wondering if it was the heady combination of wine, sun and lovemaking, or a change for the worse in her biorhythm pattern. He should have expected it. Redheads were temperamental, overexcitable and aggressive.

"I'm serious," Jeanne said earnestly. "I love you. You love me. We enjoy each other and could be so very happy together. I'm lonely, especially at night, tired of going to bed by myself and thinking of you. You should be there next to me. I want you for breakfast, lunch, dinner and midnight snacks."

Jeanne talked on, her deepest feelings now exposed. The forbidden word "marriage" had been mentioned. Retreat was impossible . . . would reveal a feminine weakness. No retreat . . . she had to have him, permanently, or not at all.

The answer formed slowly in the Man's mind. But once it had taken shape, it was right. He smiled, kissed her tenderly and said, "That's a great idea. I've been thinking about it for months. I've wanted to work it out first, but since you brought it up . . . we'll work out the plans together, kittykat."

He started the motor for the short trip back to the dock, and Jeanne was ecstatic. She kissed him with renewed intensity. It had taken months of screwing up her courage to mention the subject. The plan had worked. Making love in the open air, under the sun, in front of God and everybody, had turned them both on. It was some sensual experience, almost too much.

He'd marry her. She hadn't dared to believe. It would take time, but the waiting would be easy. Maybe something would happen to his wife with this wild killer loose in town. You could never tell. It was a magic moment. She still couldn't believe it. Tears came to her eyes.

Jeanne rubbed the back of his neck, thinking of her $200,000.

"Lover, I've got some money saved. If it would help you get free sooner." She could spare half of it.

"No, but thanks anyway. I'll handle the financial end." The Man kissed her lightly on the top of her head. Marriage? That redheaded broad has been two-timing me. I saw the scratches on the inside of the gunwale, right above the bumper sticker, the footprints, upside down. That wasn't the first time she's made love out there. Some turn-on—and now the bitch is playing multiple choice.

Gentle kittykat is turning into a man-eating tigress. I could push her overboard, hold her head under. A simple drowning. It would be easy. No, the police might connect us. That's too risky. I'll stick to my original plan. It's perfect. Besides, I need her. Now more than ever. He noticed his erection starting again. The thought of her murder had stimulated him.

Two close flashes of reflected sunlight from another boat caught his attention. Could those be binoculars? Had his tail been able to follow him? Impossible. Was someone watching? No, he'd checked earlier and hadn't noticed any boats close enough to observe anything. Had to be a couple of fishing boats in the distance.

It was too early for blues. Damn fools wouldn't catch anything. The choppers weren't running yet. Last year he'd pulled in an eighteen-pound beauty at the mouth of the Housy, using bunker chunks. But that had been in late August.

The flashes again. If it was a tail, what had he seen? Jeanne's bare ass. That's all. In doing her number, she'd been crouched on top the whole time, bottoms up, her favorite position. The tail would report a tale, about a piece of tail. The Man laughed.

He docked old 69 smoothly, secured it and lifted Jeanne onto the dock. She kissed him lovingly and whispered, "Thanks, hon. I've had a vision, and didn't dare hope it would come true. Now I've got a dream that we'll both make come true. I'll make you very happy, Tiger," touching the bulge in his trousers.

Tiger, oh Christ, now Jeanne was calling him Tiger, too.

●　　●　　●

It was early afternoon. Andrew McAlpin emerged from his private office at the rear of the Fairport Drug Center. He was nervous and doing his best to conceal it. Momentarily, he expected another shipment. Fifty additional bags of pure Mexican heroin, with a street value of well over two million dollars. His contacts were anxious, too, and were daily increasing the pressure on him to deliver more. "Damn Fagins," he muttered.

There were only two shoppers McAlpin could see in the prescription area. One was nervous Mrs. Rizzo. She existed on Valium, ate them like gumdrops. Like so many other housewives in Fairport, she was hooked on tranquilizers. The other shopper McAlpin didn't recognize. She was an old, stooped woman with an ivory-headed cane, a big woman who hobbled badly, probably as a result of an arthritic hip. Lately, strangers made him nervous, even old ladies. He'd be happy when she left the store.

"Madam," he inquired solicitously, "may I be of help to you?"

"I'm just looking, thank you." The old woman nodded sweetly to him and turned to leave.

McAlpin watched the old crone disappear into another section of the store. She was wearing a faded old cotton dress with a flowered pattern. From the rear, it looked more like a slipcover to an old easy chair than a dress. With one hand she clutched her black leather purse close to her chest. With the other she maneuvered her cane for balance and hobbled along. McAlpin had tried to look at her face, but a ridiculous large black hat with a broad brim shielded most of it from view. What he could see was ugly, real ugly, with scraggly gray hair hanging down almost to her shoulders. He guessed she was close to eighty years old. Certainly harmless enough.

Thoughts of his own mother crossed his mind. She would turn over in her grave about his heroin dealing. Damn, why did the old lady have to come into the store and make him think of his mother? Where was the delivery van? That loud stereo music annoyed him, but it would cover their conversation in the office. Telling the girl at the cash register he was not to be disturbed, McAlpin disappeared into his office and locked the door. Unlocking the safe, he noticed that only two glassine bags were left.

At 2:30 P.M., both cars on stakeout reported back to headquarters. Nothing unusual. The car in front reported two women shoppers in the store. The car stationed in the rear reported that McAlpin's had received earlier deliveries from Johnson & Johnson and Pfizer.

The two men on stakeout were advised again to maintain their cover and report immediately if they saw anything unusual, especially anyone fitting the general description of the Man.

At 2:32 P.M., McAlpin heard a knock on the inside door. Damn, the girl had been told he was not to be disturbed. The delivery would be here at any moment.

Angrily, he unbolted the door and swung it open. He was face to face with a hideous-looking old lady, with bulging, slate-gray eyes, the same lady who had been browsing in the store. He moved to slam the door, but she thrust her cane forcefully into the soft pit of his stomach. He expelled a gulp of air and reeled backward. The woman moved agilely into the room and clicked the door behind her.

Recovering from the shock of the woman's initial blow, McAlpin eased slowly toward his desk. "What do you want?" he asked, crouching, still holding his stomach, breathing raggedly, eyes almost reptilian.

"Don't reach for your gun." The old lady spoke in a very quiet but husky voice. McAlpin knew he had heard that voice before.

McAlpin, only two feet from his desk, lunged for the drawer. Thwack! The cane made a reverberating sound as it shattered McAlpin's wrist. Whack! It smashed his other one. A double scream lodged in McAlpin's throat, but got no further. The blunt end of her cane against his larynx kept it inside.

McAlpin made strange gurgling sounds and slumped down in his desk chair, irises dilated with fear, trying to collect his thoughts. He couldn't scream, and even if he could, he knew no one would hear over the store's stereo system. He thought he was going to pass out from the pain, hoped so. Didn't.

His search for sympathy in the old woman's face was wasted. Those bulging, slate-gray eyes. He'd seen them before on those television warnings. Those were the eyes of the Man. Good God! The old woman had moved like a man. The Man was a woman. No, the woman was the Man. He didn't know what to think. Pain addled his mind.

From McAlpin's safe, the Man removed the two glassine bags of heroin and set them on the desk. Then from a black leather purse he removed a long hypodermic needle. McAlpin's eyes stared blankly as he watched the Man load the hypodermic with pure heroin. Through his searing pain, he managed to squeal out, "What the hell are you doing?"

"I'm giving you a dose of your own medicine. A big bopper."

"Oh, no, no," McAlpin begged. "Please, you can have all the money."

The Man pushed back McAlpin's short-sleeve shirt and jabbed the needle full length into the vein in his right arm, unloading the entire contents of the hypodermic.

McAlpin emitted a horrible, guttural scream and writhed uncontrollably, until the powerful drug hit his blood system. It was a deadly blast. He slumped back in his chair, unconscious. The Man loaded the hypodermic again and plunged it into McAlpin's chest.

"Two freebies for the price of one, Andy old buddy," the old hag snarled, her face wrinkling into a hideous grimace. Then she pushed McAlpin's body into an upright position at his desk.

The Man put his hypodermic needle back into the black leather purse, pulled up a chair behind McAlpin to wait for the delivery van and unscrewed the end of his cane. He removed two small hypodermic darts from the black purse, filled them with the pure heroin and loaded them into the specially designed cane rifle.

Less than ten minutes later, he heard the van pull up outside. Then came the signal; two raps, pause, three raps. "It's unlocked. Open the door and come in," he commanded in a perfect imitation of Andrew McAlpin's baritone voice.

The clean-cut blond young man with the golden beard opened the door and peered into the dark office, pushed two large drug cartons into the room, turned and closed the door. He couldn't see clearly in the dim light and took a moment to readjust his vision from the bright sunlight outside. Finally, his eyes fell on McAlpin sitting behind the desk.

"Hi, dad. I brought you fifty bags of pure gold, just like I promised. Let's see the bread."

The young man did not see the old lady sitting quietly behind McAlpin, but with reactions honed to an animal sharpness by a life of constant fear, sensed another presence in the room. "Who's there?" he blurted, reaching for his shoulder holster. The old lady adjusted her cane slightly, and *plip*, the first dart struck the man's right shoulder, instantly numbing his chest and arm.

"Golden Beard, one won't kill you, but two will. Put your arm down." It was McAlpin's voice. "That's it! Sit down in that chair. That's right. You've got enough heroin in you to make you an instant addict. You'll learn what real craving is like. You're close to the edge. One little push, you'll go over. There's no return from hell."

The Man rose, walked over, and with his gloved hand removed Golden Beard's pistol, tossing it on the floor. Then he pushed a pad of paper and pencil in front of the other. "Now, unless you want the next dart in your heart, write down the names of your heroin contacts."

Golden Beard started to object. Then, taking another look at McAlpin's lifeless body, he swallowed and shrugged. What the shit, he thought. I got nothing to lose, plenty more horse where this came from. With his mind entering a state of euphoria, he messily scribbled down eight names and addresses with his left hand.

The Man moved quickly now. He bound the huge blond tightly to the chair. Rapidly unloading the cartons and piling the bags of heroin on the desk, he placed the list of heroin contacts under the top bag, then taped the playing card, the five of spades, to an engraved bronze plaque on McAlpin's desk. The inscription read, "To Andrew McAlpin: In recog-

nition of his service to the youth of America, with thanks—
Boy Scouts of America.''

The old crone took one last look at McAlpin. His face was
tissue-gray, eyes blank and sightless, staring off into eternity.
Shaking her head slowly and screwing on the tip of the cane,
she hobbled unhurriedly out of the office, through the store,
down the street to her "borrowed" car, and drove away.

After removing a quarter of a century of makeup, the Man
returned to his office. He rechecked the Granada. It was still
parked in the same spot. The agent had removed his coat and
loosened his tie. The Man checked the time. It was 2:55 P.M.

At 3:00 P.M., both cars on the stakeout at the Fairport Drug
Center made their half-hour report. Nothing unusual. There
was only one customer in the store. A white delivery van
from McKetchum Drugs was still parked at the rear entrance.
The driver had been inside since 2:44. "Dullsville," the
policeman reported.

It was 3:15 P.M. when the telephone call came in to police
headquarters. Andrew McAlpin had been murdered. Dempsey,
Grady, Belli and Farrow were at the murder scene by 3:25.
Two police cruisers had already arrived, joining two very
distraught plainclothesmen on stakeout duty.

The murder spoke for itself. Andrew McAlpin was seated
in back of fifty-two bags of heroin piled on the desk, his face
a grotesque mask of death. A note detailed eight heroin
contacts. A young man with a beard was tied to a chair,
raving out of his mind, soaring high on heroin in his own
multicolored Disney World. "It was an old lady. A hundred-
year-old witch . . .''

Dempsey's face was a mask. A mask so perfect it hid his
boiling emotions. He examined the office carefully.

Belli's swarthy complexion had darkened from frustration.
He looked almost black. "The bastard did it again. Right
under our noses. A stakeout front and back, slips through—in
and out. He's a fucking phantom!''

There was an anguished look on Farrow's face. "We should
have nailed him. The Sponge tipped us. We lost him. And the

beard here delivered a load of horseshit right past our pickets.'' He glared at the two plainclothesmen.

The two looked down at the floor. Finally, one spoke. "Lieutenant, I swear not one man entered the store in the last two hours . . . Oh, shit.'' He hesitated and looked around as if for sympathy. "It had to be that big old lady. The one with the cane.''

"That confirms the ravings of this yellow-bearded creep. Take him away before I shoot his balls off. When he comes down out of orbit, get a statement. He's an eyewitness. He saw the Man.''

Dempsey dismissed the two plainclothesmen, then turned to Farrow. "Tom, get Piccollo at the Inn, and whatever men you need. Pick up these eight heroin contacts before the news of this murder gets on the street. You've got no time to lose. We can't let these pushers slip through our fingers.''

Farrow moved fast. He knew the importance of these busts, knew that these pushers were street-wise. They had magic hands that whipped those glassine bags around. It was Tinkers to Evers to Chance and gone. With luck they could break up the area's major drug ring. McKetchum involved? Impossible. They were one of the area's most respected firms. But then who would have suspected McAlpin, either?

Doc Brody had arrived from the Fairport Inn and examined the body, then turned away as the bagmen removed the corpse. Eyes running, face streaked, his heavy body sagged into a round lump.

"He killed him with an overdose. Probably a stableful of thoroughbred, grade-A horseshit. Plunged right into the heart. Goddam. McAlpin was a close friend of mine. He should have known better than to be involved in this type of crap! I just can't believe it.''

Dempsey had never seen the Doc so upset. There were tears in his voice.

Dempsey and Grady met Briggs in the parking lot of the Inn at 4:30 P.M., and briefed him about McALpin. He told them he'd turned up a team of trackers, scheduled to be on duty tomorrow morning. The three of them went inside for a

meeting with the team of experts who had been developing a
psychological profile on the Man.

It had been agreed that Dr. Leonard Track, Director of the
Forensic Psychiatry Unit, FBI, would be spokesman for the
medical group and would give their report.

Dr. Track stood at the end of a long table. He was a
smallish man with a thin body and a perfectly shaped oval
head, dominated by unusually large eyeglasses. He spoke in a
clear, resonant voice that belied his frail appearance.

"First, we'd like to caution you that what we're trying to
do—sketch a profile of the Man's mind, his thinking and his
behavior pattern—is not an exact science. None of us have
ever met him. We don't know his biography, never interviewed him, never tested him. Our conclusions are based
solely on his notes to the police and the nine murders—we
hadn't heard about the tenth until just a moment ago." Track
looked apologetically at Dempsey, as if they should have
known.

"It's difficult to establish patterns in mass murders of this
kind because there fortunately aren't many of them, and they
differ so drastically from one to another. This murderer is
totally different from all others in three ways. First, his
murders are planned. Second, he's used a different method of
killing each time. And third, he's killing on an everyday
basis."

Grady glanced at Dempsey, as if to say, "Doesn't he think
we know this?" Spike sighed audibly. It was a low whistling
sound which only the three of them could hear. It was an oral
fart, Briggs' unique way of saying "Bullshit," without
speaking.

His introduction over, Dr. Track launched into the compos-
ite psychological profile.

"We believe your killer, your Man, is a paranoid schizophrenic. In simplest terms, that means he's suffering from a
progressive mental disorder. A mental derangement with conflicting impulses, emotions and ideas. His thinking has become
conflicting impulses, emotions and ideas. His thinking has
become unrealisitic, and illogical. He suffers from delusions

of either being persecuted or of being a great person, or both. He also has hallucinations and monomania, which is the obsessive pursuit of one idea. In this case, murder.''

Track leaned his thin, angular body against the table. ''Your Man is also a psychopath, which means he's mentally unstable. A psychopath breaks the normal pattern when you look for a motive. Death, itself, may be his motive. He's totally unpredictable.''

Track took a sip of water, then continued. ''His behavior and personality are now dominated by private fantasy. He may have progressed to the state where he lives in a world of his own, with imagined activities of fictitious people. It's hard for him to differentiate between what's real and what's fantasy. The murders are probably a game. A game in which he's competing against society and the police, in particular.''

Under his breath, Grady muttered, ''Yeah, so far, it's solitaire. He's turning over his cards, one by one.'' Grady patted his ivory-tipped cane.

Dempsey leaned forward, fascinated by what Track was saying. It's what he'd suspected right along.

Track looked directly at the lawmen. ''By hallucinations, we mean that the Man probably hears voices. He believes these voices to be real. At times, they may even be in command of his actions. Visual hallucinations may also be present, and may be bizarre. His schizophrenia probably developed early in his life. He's probably kept it bottled up for years. For such a person, one experience at killing makes subsequent killing easier.''

Track cleared his voice. ''If anything, he will become increasingly more violent. As for murder, he would feel no remorse at all, killing as casually as you would swat a fly, or step on an ant.''

The lawmen exchanged worried glances.

The FBI psychiatrist continued. ''Your Man may be exacting revenge—revenge against who knows what—by proving his power over the lives of his victims. This feeling of power is, in a sense, the motive for his actions.'' Track looked at the lawmen again. ''Not everyone who is paranoid is dangerous.

But just about everyone who becomes dangerous and homicidal is paranoid.

"The Man will go out of his way to seem perfectly normal. He'll do his best to maintain his daily routine, doing nothing unusual to attract attention to himself, no jewelry or flashy clothes. The secret of the Man is invisible, deep inside of him. It will not be noticeable to casual observers. You will have to dig deep to uncover it."

Track peered over his eyeglasses, then pushed them higher on his nose. "The Man probably had a disturbed relationship with one or both parents. He probably fantasized about killing one or both of them. In some way, he's isolated, withdrawn from the world, a loner. He probably has high intelligence, perhaps he's brilliant, but possibly holds a menial job. Most individuals of this type can carry on for years in a society, because they have isolated themselves. It's only when their hallucinations become so commanding that they set out to commit violent acts. Most people with similar symptoms won't hurt anyone. But every once in a while, there's an exception. He's your Man."

Track hesitated for a moment, looked at his notes, then plunged on. "Some paranoids seek life-styles that will protect them against their most feared impulses. For example, men who fear their sex drives occasionally become priests. They block the fear out of their lives, for good. A man who wrestles with a compulsion to kill, might just become—or want to become—a policeman."

Briggs, Grady and Dempsey all grimaced and looked at one another.

"This type of individual would normally be impotent, with low self-esteem and a raging need to establish masculinity. His sexual frustration might result in the murders. However, the rape of Marie Benson would indicate that the Man is not impotent. It is probable that he has crazed sexual fantasies. The sexual instinct is the source of biological energy driving all human nature. It is possible that the Man could be at the other end of the spectrum, very proud of himself, and highly oversexed. The ever-building tension inside him could provide him with a phenomenal sex drive. He may even be married.''

The word "married" jarred Briggs out of his own private fantasy. It was those tight-fitting blue shorts again. She'd been bending over. Was she wearing anything underneath? There were no panty lines. What an ass. Track was still talking. He'd have to pay closer attention.

"The world of paranoia is a raw-nerved one at best. At least part of the Man's mind feels persecuted. He may feel that the objects of his hatred are actually holding reign over him, in which case he's wrestling with demons in his own head. The Man's schizophrenic life must be tearing at him from all sides. In a word, gentlemen, he's completely mad, insane, crazy. Pick your own word. If you take him alive, he'll never stand trial.''

Track shook his bald head. Dempsey had a vision of an egg tottering on one end.

"Once you catch him, and we can talk to him, we'll tell you exactly the experiences and ideas that led to his bloody madness. But, in the meantime, this is the best we can do.''

Track looked around at the other doctors, who were nodding in agreement.

"I'd like to close on a bright note. Whoever the Man is, he probably wants to be caught. He desperately wants and needs recognition and credit for his actions. As a result, he may take unusual and unnecessary chances. He'll flirt with the danger of discovery, which will increase his risk of capture.''

The psychiatrist finished, scooped up his notes and bowed slightly. Dempsey stood up and thanked Track and the other doctors for their thorough report, then asked the doctor if he could brief the profile down to its essential elements for release to the media. Dempsey wanted a profile given to the media within the hour. It might soften the impact of the Man's tenth murder. Track agreed.

Walking outside, Sam put his hand on Jim's shoulder and spoke softly. "The mind is so complex. You think you can communicate with people through love and understanding. And then, in the back of someone's head, the shit hits the fan. . . .''

• • • •

Sam Grady drove directly to the Holiday Inn in Bridgeport. Bob Dillinger's agents had been following six anonymous suspects and he was anxious to get a firsthand report.

This morning, he'd put several facts together. Dillinger's itchy nose had given him six suspects. There were six surviving members of the committee who fit the Man's general physical description. Dillinger's itchy nose was a pure horseshit cover. He was a damn good detective.

If the agents had tailed the right suspects, McAlpin's murder should have revealed the identity of the Man. At the very least, it should have cleared the suspects. Riding to the Fairport Drug Center with Dempsey, he'd noticed the darkblue Ford Granada following them, and again, on the way to the Inn, it had been there.

He knew that Dillinger had rented six inconspicuous darkblue Granadas from Hertz, but hadn't mentioned the tail to Jim. Dempsey couldn't be the Man, but Dillinger had to find that out for himself. It was eerie being followed, surprising that Jim hadn't noticed the tail.

Good God, could he have a tail? He checked the rearview mirror. Four cars back was a dark-blue Granada. Oh, shit, thought Grady. What a waste of taxpayer's money. Parking in front of Suite 2A, he noticed that the Granada had gone by with the flow of traffic. Maybe it had been a coincidence. The return trip would be interesting. He knocked on Dillinger's door. A booming voice said, "Come in, shithead, it's unlocked."

It was a red-faced Dillinger who saw Grady enter the room. He apologized. "I'm sorry, Sam. Thought it was one of my surveillance team. I brought four hand-picked professionals with me. Then the fucking bureau sends me six amateur gumshoes. Bumblers. Today, I put them on my six suspects. They have nothing to do but sit tight on them. There's a murder in broad daylight and what do we get? Nothing! Not a friggin' thing."

He was raving, not trying to control his anger. This was a side of Dillinger that Grady had never seen before. Dillinger had a reputation as a perfectionist. It was probably deserved, thought Grady.

"What happened?" asked Sam.

"The six were supposed to be experienced shadows. They turn out to be shithead car watchers. Each thirty minutes they report in by radio. At one P.M. all six suspects were still in their offices. Lunchtime, I should have smelled a rat. At 1:30 P.M. all six are still there. Same at two, two-thirty, and three P.M. Sometime around two-forty, McAlpin was murdered. I checked my men. How do they know their suspect is still in his car? Believe it or not, all six answered, 'Because his car is still right here.' Six shitheads! I found out later at least three of the suspects had been out to lunch. How'd they get there? Two walked. One rode with a friend. My team reported them in their offices the entire time. I've got them coming here momentarily for an ass-chewing. We've had our murder for today. I'm sure the Man won't hit again until tomorrow. That clever bastard's not going to be caught by shitheads."

"Can you prove that any of the six were in their offices? Can you eliminate any as suspects?" Sam asked, thinking of Dempsey.

"Not a one. However, we've got six cars we can eliminate. None of those was at the murder." It was Dillinger's attempt at humor.

"Are you still sure you've got the right suspects?"

"Positive."

"How do you know?"

"My nose, Sam, it still itches."

Grady realized that he was not going to learn anything, particularly with Dillinger in such a foul mood. He was disappointed. The suspect list hadn't been narrowed. On his drive back to the Fairport Inn, he kept one eye on the rearview mirror. No one was following him. So Dillinger didn't suspect him after all. It was only when he pulled into his motel that he remembered that the six tails were meeting with Dillinger up in Bridgeport.

• • •

Vivian was walking on air. Barbara really cared. Her desperate days of loneliness were over. After the most wonderful night of her whole life, she had slept until 12:30 P.M. and been served breakfast in bed, complete with champagne. Barbara looked radiant, beaming and happy. Their eyes touched, nothing more. Even that was thrilling.

Vivian went home, changed into a filmy pink pantsuit and was back by three. It was a sparkly day, and she rode her bicycle the two blocks back to Barbara's. Giggly happy, the two of them finished a second split of champagne, telling each other their life stories. Vivian had been surprised when Barbara told her to stay and meet her special man, but didn't show it.

They both heard the Man's car in the driveway. Vivian watched Barbara rush to the door, and reacting to their intense kiss, had a moment's pang of jealousy, a pinch of envy.

"This is Vivian Smuckers." He smiled, a handsome smile, shook her hand warmly, and said, "Vivian, with a name like Smuckers, you've got to be good." All three laughed. In the exchange, she had missed his name, or maybe Barbara had never mentioned it. The Man recognized her instantly as the girl in the tight-fitting sweater. He felt light-headed, fuzzy.

She liked him instantly. He was all man. She was about to excuse herself to leave, when Barbara told her man to go into the other room. As soon as he'd left, Barbara whispered, "Vivian, I'd really like you to stay."

"No, three's a crowd," she said, but it was too late, for Barbara had unbuttoned her blouse and reached for her nipples. The light went on. Vivian's gasp was audible. She was instantly reactivated, turned on. She then undressed the quivering Vivian, slipped out of her own clothes, and led her into the bedroom. The Man was lying on the bed naked. Vivian's heart leaped when she saw his size. It was by far the largest she'd ever seen.

The Man wasn't sure what was going on, but he didn't intend to discourage them. Double your pleasure, double your fun, his favorite fantasy come true. The Man was faced with an abundance of candystore goodies. Two honey pots and four big red lollipops.

He touched Barbara first. The reaction, as always, was instantaneous. She touched Vivian's breasts. Her reaction was equally exciting to watch. Then they both attacked him together. Wow, two turned-on women on his hands, on his everything, all over him. He was plugged in, all circuits go. The teamwork was fabulous.

Their sex was truly three-dimensional. A troika of pleasure, a trifecta. It was the old triple play—from Vivian to the Man to Barbara and then back again. All were now roiling at a fever pitch, tuned to the same wavelength. He was stoking two live volcanoes, each erupting on a continuing basis. Their warm flow was pure melted honey.

The Man had extended his horizons, added that extra dimension. Then suddenly he realized that he'd overextended, was being raped by two super sexpots, was being eaten alive. Their appetite was insatiable, each wanted a seven-course dinner, and he had only enough left for an appetizer. They were feeding off his energy. He couldn't give any more.

Barbie Doll had never been so aggressive . . . wasn't tiring at all . . . spring still wound up tight. She looked as if she wanted to get even, wear him out, exhaust him. She was succeeding. Old Faithful had never failed him before, but it was petering out. The fizz had gone. His reservoir was empty.

Rolling out from under, he turned Vivian's attention to Barbara. While they were occupied, he quickly showered and dressed, threw them both a goodbye kiss from the doorway and left. They didn't even look up.

Barbara was ecstatic. Her little plan had worked perfectly. With Vivian at her side, she'd become an inexhaustible, well-oiled, efficient perpetual energy machine.

Both went skinny-dipping in the pool. The cool water doused the smoldering fires in the volcanoes. Later they dried each other off. Back in the house, Vivian touched Barbara. She retaliated by nipping her breasts. They were off again into their own special world.

Happiness is a warm summer evening, when the soft, gentle butterflies are out!

•　　•　　•

By 8:00 P.M., over six hundred townspeople had crowded into the sweltering auditorium of the Fairport High School to attend the meeting organized by the Protect the People Committee. The windows were open wide, but the room was hot and soggy.

Friends and neighbors greeted one another, but there was no light banter. They were grim-faced and serious. Any man sitting alongside could be the Man, sizing them up for the next kill.

The tone of the meeting was set by the main speaker, Tom Winchester.

"We all know why we're here tonight. In the last ten days, there have been ten brutal murders. I need not recount them. Every one of you is familiar with the details. However, some of you may not be aware of the latest one. This afternoon, Fairport's beloved druggist, Boy Scout executive, church leader and public servant, Andrew McAlpin, was brutally murdered in his own store."

Winchester raised his voice. "The police are trying to say that McAlpin was involved in drugs. It's a cover-up for the inadequacy of our police force. It was another cold-blooded murder by the Man.

"The police either can't or won't protect us. They're stonewalling us. Both the state and federal governments sit idly on their asses and watch our citizens get picked off one by one. Just last Saturday night, Marie Benson, one of our closest friends, was snatched from our table at Longwood, kidnapped, brutally raped and murdered. When I tried to help, an FBI official hit me in the shin with his cane and told me to mind my own business."

Winchester was pleased by the murmur that ran through the audience. He had their attention and, rapidly overcoming his nervousness, knew that his sincere, direct approach was gaining broad support among the audience. He continued confidently. "The murderer obviously plans to keep killing. Many think he intends to kill at least fifty-two of us. I say ten murders is enough. Do you agree?"

There was a thunderous "Yes" from the floor.

"If the police won't defend us, I say it's time we defend ourselves. Do you agree?"

An even louder "Yes" echoed throughout the audience.

"An eye for an eye," someone in the audience shouted.

Winchester rapped for attention. "We're going to pass a pad of paper down each aisle. We'd like one member of each family present—only one member, please—to write down your address, your military experience and the weapons you own. Our committee will assign you to a neighborhood vigilante group. Fairport will be divided into six zones, each one headed by a colonel, with six captains reporting to him. Each captain will head a vigilante team of ten men. That will give us a vigilante army, with command officers, of about four hundred men.

"We'd like women to volunteer also, for administrative duties. We'll get back to you by phone tomorrow night with your assigned area. Your captain will contact you to set up a personal meeting. Patrols start Thursday night."

Winchester's remarks were greeted by thunderous applause. Women stood up. Men shook their clenched fists. Before the evening was over, the committee obtained 520 family signatures, of whom 440 men had some military experience or training, and 460 families had at least one firearm.

Gus Belli was stunned. He'd been astonished to see the ease with which a fascist army could be organized right in the heart of Fairport. Tonight this was a well-controlled, although angry, crowd. Tomorrow it could easily turn into a wild mob dealing out its own form of quick justice. He left the meeting early.

The Man, disguised as a hard-hat construction worker, was one of those cheering Winchester's remarks. He signed up for vigilante duty, using the name A. Mann, and Winchester's home address, claiming to have been a colonel in the Marines and to have in his possession a machine gun, a bazooka, a flamethrower, two rifles, and six grenades.

Judy Rogers sat up in bed rereading a copy of the psychological profile from police headquarters.

As she reached for a cigarette and lit it, a doubt niggled in the back of her mind.

The profile called for a loner. A man isolated or withdrawn from the world. That didn't fit with her conclusions. It didn't fit Ned Nichols. That no-good shit was certainly no loner. He was an extrovert.

Either she was wrong, or the doctors' profile was wrong. There had to be an explanation.

She put down her notes and reached for her telephone to call Peter Bond. A plan to trap Tilden was forming in her mind, but she needed clearance from the home office.

The phone rang as she touched it. Her hand sprang back as if the phone were alive. It had to be Peter.

"Hello."

A snarling voice on the other end of the line said, "Miss Muppet, you've got less than twenty-four hours to get your pretty ass out of town. Or . . ."

"Or what?" Judy asked, surprised by the calmness of her own voice.

"I'll take a big bite out of it!" the voice said.

"Who is this?"

A click on the other end of the phone was the only answer Judy got.

Thoroughly shaken, Judy sat on the edge of her bed trying to control her emotions. It had to be the Man. She'd recognized the voice. She'd heard it just a few hours before. It was the voice of Ned Nichols. She'd stake her life on it.

She reached for the phone to call Jim Dempsey. No, she'd wait until she talked to Peter.

Dempsey rubbed his eyes. He was tight-lipped. They'd been burned again. The situation was normal. It was terrible!

It was time for total suspicion, time to suspect everyone. The Man knew everything they were doing, and almost everything they were thinking. It had to be someone close. Could it be someone inside their tight little circle?

The Man knew about McAlpin. The stakeout? He must have, otherwise why the disguise as an old woman? Who had known about it? The Sponge had told Belli and Farrow. They'd told him. He'd told Grady and Briggs. The men assigned to stakeout duty knew. That was it.

If Ned was the Man, how would he have known about McAlpin? Dempsey's mouth was dry. He got himself a beer from the refrigerator.

The Man had used an ivory-tipped cane. The description sounded like a duplicate of the one Grady used. What the hell was he thinking? It couldn't be Grady, or could it?

There were no illusions now. The psychological profile had confirmed his innermost feelings. They desperately needed a break. Otherwise it would be taps. And the Man would be blowing the bugle.

It was late night. The Man was exhausted, yet exhilarated. With his black marking pencil, he crossed out Andrew McAlpin, the five of spades, number ten on his death list. Next to McAlpin's name he drew a skull and crossbones. Underneath he printed "Coke—for Kids." Then he crossed it out with a big X.

What a day! He was whirling the elephants around faster and faster. It was carnival time again. The carousel kept picking up speed. The Keystone Kops were running faster and faster, becoming a blur. They kept reaching for the brass ring that wasn't there and kept coming up empty-handed. Christ, his head was spinning. He needed some sleep. Tomorrow was another big day . . . had to be alert. Today had been full. He'd eluded his tail and killed McAlpin. That shit deserved it. Oh, yes, he'd also promised Jeanne to marry her. He yawned. Good God, he was tired.

Winchester. That fascist fink. Maybe he should put him on the list. Yes, he'd work him in somehow, take Belli off and replace him with Winchester. Let's see, that was the seven of diamonds. He'd fry him crispy-crunchy.

Tomorrow it was time to go after the common folk. Some unsuspecting young lady was going to get a lot of unwanted publicity. He'd give her instant fame. His Queen for a Day.

Moving around was getting tougher. It was wall-to-wall

elephants. No, not elephants, bulls! He must not get careless
. . . had to think clearly. Still no one knew who he was. No
one. He rose from his desk and sat on the couch.

The Man's head dropped back and he fell sideways on the
couch. Sometime later, his wife came downstairs, tiptoed into
the den and put a pillow under his head. Her poor man was
working far too hard. For the last few days, he'd been on
autopilot. Operating on instincts alone. She kissed his forehead.

It was then she noticed a black notebook on the floor. It
must have dropped when he'd fallen asleep. She picked it up,
put it on his desk and went back upstairs. Sliding back into
bed, she thought, Maybe I should have looked inside. It
might be his little black book. No, if there are other women, I
really don't want to know.

11

Wednesday, June 11.
Queen for a Day

THE MAN finished shaving with a final bold stroke, splashed cold water on his face and toweled it dry. Reaching for his aftershave lotion, he felt light-headed, fuzzy. The king's crown on the label jogged his memory.

It was the final match in Leningrad. Boris Starsky stared at the chessboard, his lips dry, face taut, eyes pinched and strained, head cupped in both hands, staring, staring. He reached his hand forward with quivering fingers. Hesitating, slowly, ever so slowly, he pushed his queen in front to protect his king.

The Man grinned broadly. Instantly, he moved his rook and took Starsky's queen. "Checkmate!" He was champion. The greatest chess player in the world. It had been so easy. He'd won every match.

The memory was vivid. The white queen's head was lopped off. Blood poured down onto the board. Now, the black knight seized the sword with both hands and cut off the white king's head, as well.

"Kill," shouted the voice in his inner ear.

With gouts of blood dripping from the blade, the Man took the sword from the knight and plunged it into Boris Starsky's chest.

"Kill," shouted the voice again.

The Man nodded his head. He slapped the aftershave onto his face. With a wide grin, he winked into the mirror and said, "Thanks, I needed that!"

●　　●　　　●

298

"Wacko. The guy's totally nuts. Bananas. Out of his gourd. But he's leading us around by our dongs," Dempsey muttered out loud at the breakfast table.

"Jim. Watch your language!" Brenda said reproachfully. "Cindy might hear you."

"Hey, I'm sorry. I must have been thinking out loud. Where's my little Buttercup? Haven't seen her lately."

"She's still upstairs dressing. I'll go up in a minute and make sure she's got everything on right." Brenda sighed wistfully.

Dempsey looked up sympathetically from his eggs and bacon. "Hon, I'm sorry I haven't been able to help you this week. I know it's been tough on you."

Brenda leaned over and kissed his forehead. "Darling, you've got enough on your mind. Don't you worry about Cindy. I'll take care of her." Then she lowered her voice. "Nobody leads you around by your . . . 'thing,' except me." She blushed at not being able to say the word.

Jim rose from the table, laughing. "Hey, you watch your language." They hugged one another tightly. Then he said, "Pour me another cup of coffee, hon, while I go up and say good morning to Cindy. Our psycho friend can wait another five minutes for today's game to start."

Judy Rogers stretched and clicked on the television set. In place of *Good Morning, America*, ABC was telecasting an hour-long special on the murders, entitled *A Town Gone Mad*.

Judy listened with one ear as she brushed her teeth, then, running the bath water, adjusted the television set so that she could see it from the tub.

Most of the show was a rehash of things she already knew. Halfway through the program they introduced two prominent psychiatrists. One was from Yale New Haven Hospital, the other from Columbia University College of Physicians and Surgeons. They were discussing the psychological profile of the Man.

She sat forward in the tub, listening carefully. Of course—she could ask a psychiatrist to explain how an extrovert could be the mass killer, when the profile called for an introverted loner. She'd call one today.

The man from Yale was talking. "He desperately needs publicity and he's probably enjoying his cat-and-mouse game with the police. Oh, yes, to him, it's definitely a game. He visualizes himself as Moriarity killing Sherlock Holmes, proving to them that he's more of a man than they can ever be."

The other psychiatrist agreed. "There's no doubt that publicity inflames this type of paranoia. It makes the Man feel important. Suddenly, out from under a rock, he's center stage.

"The tension inside a paranoid personality builds up until it becomes unbearable. His only release is murder. The question we must ask ourselves is whether all of this publicity causes the killer to feel challenged. If so, it might speed up his tension and his urge to kill. The media may actually be promoting his criminal behavior."

Judy climbed out of the tub and started to towel herself dry, mentally tuning them out.

The two psychiatrists were arguing about the guilt of the media connected to the Man's murders. The argument was almost ludicrous. No matter what they said, the media would report any major news event, and nothing grabbed people's interest faster than news about a killer on the loose.

Several minutes later, the program recaptured her full attention. It was a question that the moderator asked. "Dr. Thomas, earlier you mentioned the Jekyll and Hyde syndrome. A man with two distinctly different personalities, one outgoing, one withdrawn. Would you explain that, please?"

Before the psychiatrist could answer, Judy was perched naked on the edge her bed directly in front of the television set, with a pad and pencil on her knee.

The doctor from Columbia answered, "I was thinking of the multiple or fragmented personality. There's a remote possibility that the Man's mind could be ruled by one or more personalities, manufactured by his psyche. One personality may be perfectly normal, composed and calm. This personality could live a normal life. The other personality could be propelled by compulsive urges to act out his anger by killing.

Perhaps frustrated because the other personality has been dominant over him. Waiting for his chance, he hates, every minute, hates. When this personality gets loose, he kills.''

The other psychiatrist nodded in agreement and added, "The two personalities could be completely separate. One may not know of the existence of the other. One personality may be amnesiac to everything the other one does. Remember *The Three Faces of Eve*, or Sybil. the girl with nine different personalities, all in one body. The personalities can be totally different in age, or even of different sexes.''

The moderator interrupted to say that their time was running short. Dr. Thomas held up a hand in caution and concluded, "I think we should hasten to add that this type of mental disorder is extremely rare. In all medical history, less than one hundred and fifty authenticated cases of multiple personality have ever been reported, and almost all were nonviolent.''

Judy reached over and clicked off the television. Her mind was spinning. It sounded so farfetched—a killer hidden within another man's body. A killer who would emerge at will, kill, then retreat and hide behind the other personality. He'd be almost impossible to find.

She sprayed her underarms with Arrid, then reached for her panties and bra. The theory was worth looking into. It could explain how Ned Nichols could be such an extroverted, money-grubbing shit on the outside, while inside lurked an isolated cold-blooded murderer. She didn't know which Nichols she liked the least.

Before leaving his house, the Man once again checked his arsenal. He selected a 10-gauge goosegun and hefted its eleven and a half pounds. It was bulky, but had the range he needed. With full choke set at the tightest constriction, it had a dense shot pattern. At forty yards, he could put seventy percent of the shot into a thirty-inch circle. That would take a big bite out of her pretty ass.

The shotgun was returned, reluctantly, to its place in the rack. He'd use a quieter, more subtle method. He picked up a leather attaché case that held a hypodermic syringe full of cyanide and checked the mechanism. A simple flick of his thumb and a needle would be projected through a small hole in the front of the case. Within five minutes she'd be dead, with all the symptoms of a heart attack. Imagine, a massive coronary at the ripe old age of twenty-six. He grinned. That was more like it.

Walking out to his cruiser parked in his driveway, Dempsey noticed the blue Granada parked across the street. A hundred yards down the street, there was a green Impala. He looked under his car and checked beneath the hood. One bomb was too many. Sliding into the driver's seat, he muttered to himself, "Two tails. The Feds and Briggs' man. This is getting ridiculous. I didn't mind the Granada yesterday, but now it's becoming a parade. If we all creep along and turn on our lights, it will look like a funeral procession."

Dempsey was slow to anger, but now was really pissed. Here he was busting his ass to solve the murders. What were the FBI and state police doing? Hassling him. If they were going to hassle, he'd hassle back. Who the hell did they think they were? Had they forgotten who was in charge of this investigation?

At the second stop sign, he braked and swerved to the curb. Quickly leaping from the car, he waved both the Granada and the Impala to the side of the road. For a brief moment, both tails were undecided. They didn't know what to do. The Chief of Police was waving them to the curb, hand on his holster. They had no alternative.

"Out of your cars. Hands on the roof. Feet apart." With considerable relish, Dempsey kicked their feet back. He didn't frisk them, knowing they were both armed. A small crowd of spectators had gathered at the scene.

"What did we do, officer?" asked the young crew-cut driver of the Granada.

"Haven't you heard? We've got a nut loose in this town, killing people. He tried to finish me last week with a grenade, and I've still got bruises to show for it. I don't like strangers sitting outside my house waiting to waylay me. My wife

doesn't like it, either; nor my daughter. Let's see your identification! You first, burr-head. Reach for your wallet slowly.''

Dempsey took his time. He copied down their names and
descriptions in detail. The FBI agent gave him his identification card. Now the Fed's cover was blown for good. Briggs'
man was better prepared, producing a fictitious driver's license.
But the trooper's surveillance of Dempsey was finished, and
he knew it.

Dempsey pulled them both upright, looking nose to nose at
each of them, and softly said, ''Gotcha! Both of you. If you
know what's good for you, there'd better not be a next time. I
won't bother to warn you. I'm getting itchy. I'll shoot off
your kneecaps.''

The Chief got back into his cruiser and drove off toward
police headquarters, knowing the tails would be gone. Now
he was annoyed at himself. Shit, it was he who'd suggested
the tails to Briggs. Damn, anger was a bad counselor. Where
was his cool?

Ned Nichols had noticed the two cars following him. A brace
of bulls. Obviously they had nothing else to do but chase
honest citizens. The government was already poking into his
income tax returns. Fucking Infernal Revenue agents. They'd
get nowhere. The returns were so complicated it would take a
firm of accountants years to unravel them. They were a tangle
of snakes. He didn't even understand them completely himself. Some of the loopholes had loopholes.

So they wanted to play games. He'd show them what a top
driver in a Ferrari could do.

He timed the next stoplight perfectly, accelerating through
the first blush of red, turned a sharp left in front of the
crossing traffic and whipped right at the next intersection,
then up the ramp onto the turnpike. Off at the first intersection
and back into local traffic. It was clean and green all the way.

That had been too easy. He'd relish a real chase at top
speeds, leaving them in the dust. Now they'd probably go to
his office and wait.

He had no intention of going to his office.

• • •

Spike Briggs only had one tail. He hadn't assigned himself a
trooper as a shadow. How the hell could I do that? he'd asked
himself. Now I want you to shadow me today and see who I
murder! It would sound psycho. Besides, it would be stupid.
Wasting taxpayers' money. I'm not guilty, haven't killed
anyone, at least not recently. But . . . that Uncle Sam tail
could sure screw up my private life. Got to get rid of him.

He pulled into the fenced-in state police barracks parking
area ten minutes before shift change and walked briskly into
his office. Seven minutes later, in a trooper hat and reflecting
sunglasses, he emerged in the midst of a crowd of state
troopers. Twelve patrol cars roared out of the parking area,
heading in twelve different directions.

The federal agent was bewildered. Peering through the
fence, he could see that Briggs' Jaguar was still there. But
Dillinger had stressed he couldn't rely on just watching the
suspect's car. He'd call the Colonel's office just to make sure
he was there.

Briggs was laughing, mind repeating an old Marine command, "To the winds, march." The FBI had a lot to learn.
Every once in a while it would do them good to get out in the
field, out where the rubber meets the road.

He headed across town.

Both Bob Baker and Don Dillon shook off their surveillance
without even trying. Sometimes it's better to be lucky than
good.

Jan Baker had an 8:30 A.M. tee-off at Longwood. She
played to a forty handicap, but enjoyed the companionship of
her women buddies. When told her handicap, Bob had
wisecracked, "Not even Ray Charles should have a forty."
Today was a modified scramble event called "Hit and Giggle."

At the breakfast table, Jan asked Bob for the use of his car.
Her clubs were in the trunk, and she didn't want to transfer
them. Bob readily agreed. At 8:10 A.M., Baker's Mercedes
pulled out of his garage, turned left at the street and accelerated toward Longwood, followed by a dark-blue Granada and
a green Impala.

At 8:15 A.M., Bob Baker pulled unhurriedly out of his driveway at the wheel of Jan's Ford station wagon. Out of habit, he checked the rearview mirror. There were no other cars on the street.

Across town, Don Dillon had slept on the couch in his den. He was annoyed by the latest of Deborah's spending binges, and exhausted by the effort required to keep their heads above the waves of bills that flooded in daily. He had washed, brushed his teeth, shaved, downed a bowl of cereal and left his house at 6:30 A.M. Deborah was still dreaming of purchases yet to be made.

The FBI agent took up his position outside Dillon's house at 6:45 A.M. Briggs' surveillance man arrived promptly at 7:00 A.M. They kept their beady eyes on one another for some time. Meanwhile, Dillon was off alone starting his busy day.

At the Bridgeport Holiday Inn, Dillinger was ranting wildly to his team of detectives. "It's only nine-thirty in the morning, and we've lost contact with five of our six suspects. Revolving doors. They go in one end and come out the other. Show them a shadow and they run for daylight. Five homing pigeons. They fly away and we get what they left on the rock.

"Hoyle's in his real estate office, but we don't know where anyone else is. Incredible. The Bureau sent me a team of Grade A shitheads. I lectured them last night until midnight. It didn't do one damn bit of good. I wanted fly paper, got toilet tissue instead. I told each one, 'Screw up again, it's your ass.' When those five diddling amateurs report in, tell them to pack up and get back to their desks. They can ride in the rear of the bus, all the way to Washington. They're finished as far as I'm concerned."

Dillinger suddenly calmed. The black clouds of doubt parted, and the sun radiated through, showing the clouds to have been puffy white ones all along. It was all so simple. Once you'd defined the problem properly, the solution was obvious.

One day with four or five pros would do it. They'd pick out the right pigeon and wring his scrawny neck. If necessary, he could use his own detective team for surveillance . . . they knew how to play them tight. Better yet, he'd get the

Bureau to fly up a professional team of trackers, and this time he'd specify the ones he wanted.

It always came down to people. The good ones did the job quickly and neatly, the rest invariably fucked it up. You learn the hard way that there are damned few good ones. When you find one, you do whatever's necessary to keep him. You can always judge a leader by the quality of his walking-around guys.

Rising from his chair, he rummaged through his briefcase and located his top-secret, coded list of personnel that were graded superior, or better. He skimmed it quickly, checked four names, and then went back adding a fifth, just in case. That should do it. He'd eliminated Dempsey as a suspect himself, agreeing with Grady that the poor bastard couldn't be everyplace.

He reached for the phone and dialed the Bureau. It was time to use his clout.

The Man was on the prowl, looking for victim number eleven. He had decided very early in his planning that June 11 was the perfect day to kill a housewife. The planets were right, Venus was in her house and Mars was on the loose. Not any special housewife, though. It was important that she not be special, but just an ordinary "run-around-the-house" housewife. He had not selected a specific target.

In his total plan of fifty-two murders, this was the only victim he'd not chosen in advance. That, to the Man, made her special. The ultimate decision was to be left to pure chance, a sudden omen, a whim. There was only one criterion: She had to be perfectly ordinary.

He drove slowly through the downtown area, then along the river toward the Sound. He braked sharply for a black-and-white terrier that scampered across the road. Damn dog. Should be more careful . . . could get killed. He pulled into the next shopping center, parked and waited, looking for a sign.

Coming out of the drugstore was a bent, frail, white-haired woman with a cane. He judged her to be at least seventy-five years old. His mind flashed back to McAlpin's murder. No, she wouldn't do, too old.

An attractive, lissome blonde parked her car. Sensual, but not too far from innocence. Too young, he decided.

Walking past Mil's Meat market was a heavyset, middle-aged lady in a black-and-white print dress. Black and white. Like the terrier. Could that be the sign he was looking for? No. She had the face of a porker, a fat black-and-white Arkansas razorback. This little piggy went to market. This little piggy stayed home. This little piggy ate everything. He laughed, a crazy, crackling laugh.

Two girls of high school age bounced past, braless in their thin T-shirts and blue jeans. It was the jiggle season. He watched with interest, and couldn't help but overhear their chatter. "I told Jerry I wouldn't do it. Not on our first date. What did he do? Dropped me off and picked me up ten minutes later. Told me it was our second date. He's really cool."

"Did you let him do it? Did you?" breathlessly asked the second girl, as they bounced out of earshot.

A young mother wearily pushing a twin baby carriage. A pregnant young black, at least seven months along. Two hippies with broad hips waddled past. More like hippos, he thought. A punk something with black lipstick, green hair and revealing holes appeared. From the holes, he could tell it was a girl, but certainly not an ordinary one. He'd have to wrap her in a plain brown paper bag to take her home.

The Man was sorting them out. Perhaps this wasn't the place. Maybe another location. Then he spotted her. Instantly, he knew she was the one. He smiled, a crooked, evil smile.

It was the tight-fitting blue shorts, that was the sign he'd been looking for. In recent days, tight blue shorts had become an obsession. Her shifting buttocks disappeared into the supermarket. She flaunted her ass like a policewoman disguised as a hooker. Through the window, he watched the blue shorts pick out a dozen eggs, a can of cat food and a carton of Merits. She passed quickly through the fast checkout lane, collected her gamepiece and emerged into the bright sunshine.

Now her face was clearly visible. His heart leaped. Very ordinary . . . five feet two inches tall . . . mousy brown hair . . . plain oval face . . . a pleasing, plumpish body. She walked by. It wiggled. It waggled. But, by God, it was even an ordinary ass. The Man's instant-playback mechanism flashed to the other blue shorts. That was a special ass, this was an ordinary one.

Thelma Pickell was upset, but then lately she was often upset. She was on a downer. Paul was away on business, and seemed to be going away more often and staying longer each time. She didn't really know what he did. He added numbers on a machine and wrote them in ledgers. Went around to different companies to check their addition. It was very important. Still after eight years they didn't pay him very much. She kept asking if it was so important, why didn't they pay him more? There never was a very good answer.

Opening the door to their faded blue Volkswagen, she noticed another long green scratch. Some bippy bitch just threw open her door and put another mark on their car. Why did other drivers hate Volkswagens? The car was covered with dents, looked like a washboard. Even so, Paul would notice the new dent. You bet . . . her fault. Another day, and she was still treading up the down escalator.

On the way home, she went back over the reasons she was upset. Married seven years and no children . . . twenty-eight . . . three miscarriages . . . and now pregnant again . . . five days overdue. This time they just had to make it. Without a baby to glue them together, she was afraid Paul was going to split from ordinary Thelma.

She had done her best to make Paul love her, didn't even cry anymore when he tied her and beat her with the leather belt. The welts usually disappeared after a few days, but this time he'd been rougher. Every day the fear . . . now a hope, a desperate hope that things would get better.

She unlocked the door to their drab, three-room walkup apartment. It had a nice balcony overlooking Korvette's parking lot. In the summer they usually got an evening breeze, plus the odors from McDonald's. The food was put away and she opened the cat food, putting half of it in Boozer's dish and the other half in the refrigerator. The Merits were left on the kitchen table.

She felt uneasy and nervous. There was no reason. Her hands were wet, and beads of perspiration formed on her arms. What was she afraid of? She swallowed several times to get rid of the lump in her throat. It rose again, she gulped it down.

A bath was the solution. That would take away the tension. She liked it hot. Shucking off her clothes, which were clammy and damp, she wriggled out of her shorts and panties and kicked everything into the corner of the bathroom. Standing on tiptoes in front of the full-length mirror, she turned to look at the purple bruises. They weren't all that bad. Oh, if only Paul were home now.

The Man watched through a crack in the bathroom door. Mirror, mirror on the wall, who's the most ordinary one of all? How about that, some son of a bitch has been whipping her. Shouldn't do that to my precious little girl.

Silently, he glided forward.

As she slid into the bathtub, the nerves returned. This was crazy. It was broad daylight. Fear was supposed to be much larger and more ominous in the dark. Had she locked the back door? The Man was still on the loose, killing important people. Thank God she was so ordinary.

She ducked her head under the water, wetting her hair. She tried to raise it, but couldn't. A powerful force was holding her head under the water, a man's hand, with incredible strength. Struggling to free herself, she tried to scream, could feel the water enter her throat, press up her nostrils. She swallowed. . . .

"That'll teach you to two-time me out on your boat, you redheaded bitch!"

The Man was snarling, a fierce, wild look on his face. He released his iron grip on Thelma's head, and her body sloshed lifeless back and forth in the tub. With the toe of his shoe, he lifted the frayed blue shorts and put them on the seat of the toilet, flipping the playing card, the four of spades, face down into the crotch of the shorts.

He turned to the tub and looked at her body. No red hair. It wasn't Jeanne. The victim was perfectly ordinary . . . perfect for his purposes . . . better off dead. He knelt down and kissed her forehead, then whispered lovingly, "I'll see you in heaven, baby. Wait for me."

Gus Belli entered Rice's office with a triumphant grin, handing him four small plastic bags.

Belli spoke in a low, confidential voice. "They're labeled. I got three from Nichols. He's a butt chewer, in more ways than one. Two from Dillon. He mangles his, too. Only one from Baker. Just a couple of teeth marks on it. That covers all of them, except Hoyle, and he smokes a pipe."

Rice's face showed his excitement. "How the hell did you do it?" he asked.

Belli grinned again. "I come from a long line of janitors. It's amazing what you can find in the office trash."

Rice opened a drawer and added the new samples to the ones they'd previously collected. "I'll get all of these up to Bethany this morning. With luck, we'll get a report back late this afternoon."

Belli turned to go, then turned, reached into his pocket and pulled out a Tiparillo package, offering one to Rice. Rice stared, then started to laugh. Belli laughed with him, dropping the package into the wastebasket.

"I'd been thinking of taking up smoking," Rice said. "I'm low on tar. But now I think I'll wait awhile."

Tom Winchester was at police headquarters waiting for Jim Dempsey when he arrived. They greeted one another coolly.

"Morning, Tom. Understand you're raising a private army."

"Only to protect our families, Chief. But that's not why I'm here," Winchester replied. "I want to show you something that might help find this killer. After the meeting last night, a small group of us stayed on and started to assign the volunteers to various neighborhood groups."

"Your vigilantes," said Dempsey.

"Yes. Fairport's vigilantes," answered Winchester. "Anyhow, one of the volunteers used a fake name, A. Mann." It stood out because he used my home address."

Dempsey reached for the pad that Winchester held out to him. He looked at it. Printed on the fourth line in bold strokes was:

A. Mann—16 Bunker Place—Colonel, USMC—machine gun, bazooka, 2 rifles, flamethrower, 6 grenades.

Dempsey buzzed for Rice.

Silently, he offered his hand to Winchester. They shook. Then Dempsey said, "Thanks for bringing this in, Tom. It could be a break. It's probably the Man . . . smells like him. He may show up at your next meeting."

Dempsey walked to the window. The sunlight made irregular patterns on the sill. After a few moments, he turned to face Winchester.

"Could you schedule one for tonight? It's asking a lot . . . a special organization meeting. We'll have the place infiltrated in case he shows."

Winchester thought for a moment, then responded, "It would be a bitch, but . . . yes . . . we can do it."

The eagerness in his voice grew, as he realized that his committee might be responsible for bringing the Man out into the open—even catching him. "We'll set it up for eight-thirty tonight at the high school."

"Good," Dempsey replied. "Did anyone get a good description of this fellow?"

"We think it was a big guy in a green T-shirt and a yellow construction hat, one of those hard plastic hats, over six feet tall. Big, your type of build. He kept applauding everything I said." Tom looked at the Chief questioningly.

"Sounds like him," Dempsey said, buzzing again for Rice and finally shouting out the door, "Paul, come in here. I think we've got something."

Rice apologized for being on the phone. Hearing Winchester's story, Rice's face came alive. They spent the next twenty minutes developing a preliminary plan setting a trap for the Man. The rest of the day would be spent perfecting their plan.

Rice took the pad with the Man's handwriting to his laboratory. First he planned to check the ink, then get as many police graphologists as possible to study the Man's handwriting.

Seated at his desk in his office, the Man was thinking about the police suspects. Probably down to about six. Low enough for a while. In due time, he'd knock off some more. Right now, the risk was too great. The survivors had to be the suspects.

Damn, that's what made it so exciting. He could feel the chill deep in his spine, down in the marrow. The police were so close, yet so far, it was tempting to give them a hint. They'd get his next note today. Maybe he should give them a deadline. Detectives didn't like deadlines, and killers, especially clever ones, wouldn't respect deadlines. They'd go crazy.

The bulls were stampeding. They were running after red. Men with red shirts, red slacks and red ties. Girls with red hair, red dresses, and red stockings. Red lights were flickering everywhere. The bulls had red faces. They were milling about in a sea of red. It was red blood. The blood would drown them. They could barely keep their heads above it.

Suddenly, he was a continent away. Seville, Spain. He was the world's greatest matador. Manuel, the Man. The one and only. The giant bull charged—

The ringing of his private phone interrupted the Man's thoughts. Now he was totally alert.

If the FBI and the police were shadowing him, they probably had bugged his phones, too. His hot line, also. The ringing was incessant. Ma Bell was demanding an answer. No, that was too risky.

Sliding open the desk drawer and removing his Swiss Army knife, he flicked open the razor-sharp blade and with one slash severed the cord at the baseboard. The ringing ceased. With a pencil, he pushed the stump of the cord back through the round hole into the wall, then inserted the long length of the extension into the same hole. It looked perfectly normal.

Maybe Gayla the vibrating flygirl was back. If so, he'd keep her on speed six indefinitely . . . one long, perpetual orgasm. No, it was probably Jeanne wanting to know whether he had his divorce yet. Ha! Or Barbara—she and Vivian had probably worked each other into a ringtailed frenzy. Now they wanted him for those hard-to-reach places. He felt long, lean and mean, but they were double trouble.

That would have to wait. He'd call them from a phone booth as soon as possible. From now on, it was "Don't call me, I'll call you." Damn bulls. They were ruining his sex life.

At 9:45 A.M., Lieutenant Rice called Sam Tilden at the Fairport Savings Bank.

"Mr. Tilden's office, Miss Schermerhorn speaking." Rice had met Miss Schermerhorn. Efficient and cold, like a Burroughs calculator, with teeth prominent as the keyboard.

"This is Lieutenant Rice of the Fairport police. May I speak to Mr. Tilden, please?"

"I'm sorry, but Mr. Tilden is in conference." It was brisk and predictable.

"It's very important that I speak to him. It may be a matter of life or death." Rice clicked on his recorder.

There was a hesitation, then a period of silence on the other end of the line, and finally Tilden came on, laughing his banker's laugh. "What's up, Paul? Need a loan?" The bank held Rice's mortgage and the financing on his car.

"No, Mr. Tilden. We wanted to warn you and other key Rotarians. This murderer seems to be specializing in your group."

"I heard about Andy. It's a shame. Verna will take it very hard." Tilden's voice trembled. Sounds sincere, thought Rice.

"What would you suggest, Lieutenant?" Tilden had put back on his banker's cloak of formality.

"Nothing particular. Just be careful. We'll assign you a guard, if you feel you need one, and if we can turn up an extra man here."

"Sounds like too many ifs, Paul. That won't be necessary. I can take care of myself. It seems like you and Jim need all the men you can get. Good luck, and thanks for the warning." He hung up the phone.

Tilden sat for a moment, jumbled thoughts spinning around his head. The Man had killed Rocco and uncovered his counterfeiting. Yesterday he had killed McAlpin and exposed him as a major drug pusher. Did the Man know he was an embezzler? It involved millions. How could he know? How could anyone know? His tracks had been covered with infinite care. Or had they? Somehow, money always leaves a trail.

Successful criminals have no records. Only those who are dumb enough to get caught have records. He'd never been caught, but then how would the Man know about Rocco, or McAlpin? The Man's exposure of their secret activities had been a brutal shock. An avenging angel? Or was it a divulging devil? Christ, his mother must have mated with a scorpion.

It would be a good time to get out of town and let things quiet down. Let the police kill this murderer. Hawaii. Trish had always wanted to see the volcanoes, and there was golf on spectacular, breathtaking seaside courses. Those tourist courses would be four or five strokes easier. Miss Schermerhorn could make the reservations today. With luck, they'd be on their way tomorrow. The trip might be the cure for Trish's "hotties." First there was the meeting with this young broad, Judy Rogers. What the hell did she want?

In the lab, Rice ran his recording of Tilden's voice back through the spectrograph. He had captured only a few sentences, but with luck it would be enough. The voiceprint of Tilden emerged. Rice nervously compared the two. Tilden's voiceprint against that of the Man's. They were distinctly different. Firm proof that Tilden was not the Man.

He slipped Tilden's voiceprint into a manila envelope, labeled it "Tilden's Voice" and put it in his desk drawer next to the envelope containing the Man's voiceprint.

He dialed both Bob Baker's and Don Dillon's offices. Neither was in. Rice left a message for both to call back, emphasizing the urgency.

• • •

It was after 11:00 when Mary received the computer printout from the Motor Vehicle Department in Wethersfield.

She scanned it quickly. There were 238 names and addresses on the list: drivers who were white, male, age thirty-five to forty-four and six foot or taller. She'd been right. It was a manageable list. She'd estimated 254.

Mary looked up and saw Dempsey standing next to her, looking over her shoulder. He was nodding appreciatively.

"Good estimate. You were pretty close. I just wanted to check its accuracy."

She slid her chair sideways, and Dempsey moved closer to her desk, running his finger quickly down the list.

"Baker, Briggs, Dillon, Dempsey, Hoyle, Nichols . . . we're all on it. Good! Let me know how you plan to narrow it down."

Touching her shoulder lightly in thanks, he turned and went back to his office.

Mary sat, thinking. Yesterday, partly in jest, Dempsey had mentioned a weigh-in. Why not? She'd have to think out the details. Anyone who didn't show up would be automatically suspect.

Absentmindedly, she chewed on her lip. If she could figure out the method to catch the Man—she felt the thrill up her spine—it would make her career. Absolutely!

Down the street at the Fairport Savings Bank, Judy Rogers sat on the edge of a soft white leather chair across from Sam Tilden. He spoke first.

"I apologize, but this must be a short meeting. I'm leaving with my wife on a vacation trip tomorrow. It was planned some time ago. What can I do for you?"

Judy looked at the confident, self-assured banker; then she spoke in a soft, measured tone. "Mr. Tilden, I'm here, as you probably know, to check on the recent shortage. Remember, it was your idea. I understand the shortage was caused by counterfeit withdrawal slips run on your new color copier."

The crusty old banker flashed Judy his smile usually reserved for important customers.

"Yes. Damn crooks. Can't trust employees any more. It's the new breed. Not enough discipline in the schools, too much television, everyone's looking for the quick kill."

"You think it was one of your employees?" Judy asked.

"Had to be, but it won't happen again. We've installed a two-key system on the copier . . . can't work without both of them." Tilden reached into his pocket and fished out his master key.

Judy listened politely, then continued. "We can't trace who did it. The trail's dead, but you already knew that. One of the insurance companies that I represent will make good on the loss."

Tilden smiled, a broad smile, rose from his chair, extended his hand and said, "Thank you for coming. . . ." He looked at Judy, still seated impassively.

Now Judy leaned forward and spoke softly. "Mr. Tilden, you're a sly old fox. I believe in coming straight to the point. You're a very clever crook."

"What!" sputtered Tilden. "Now listen here—"

"No, Mr. Tilden, you listen." Judy's manner was quiet, firm and unyielding. Tilden sat back in his chair, a tic developing over one bushy white eyebrow.

"It took me two days to figure out how you did it. I'm not talking about the two hundred thousand you stole with the Xerox caper. I'm more interested in the million bucks, give or take a few pennies, that you've embezzled from Nellie Arbuckle over the last two years."

Judy watched Tilden's face intently. She could read people as accurately as accountants read balance sheets.

Tilden sat in open-mouthed amazement. The girl's estimate was off by less than twenty thousand dollars.

Bingo, thought Judy. The stunned reaction on Tilden's face had confirmed her suspicions.

"Mr. Tilden. You were Mrs. Arbuckle's closest financial adviser, her trusted banker, and each week for the last two years, you withdrew ten thousand in cash from her account. You're clever enough to have a power of attorney signed by her, personally handling everything yourself, taking the money out of the safe and punching withdrawals into the computer. Every Tuesday morning, you visited Mrs. Arbuckle, regular as clockwork, and presumably you gave the money to her. Only you didn't. You stashed it someplace."

Tilden rose from his chair, the flush in his face showing bright crimson under his white hair.

"You can't prove that. Nellie's dead. It's your word against mine." He was thinking of the piles of cash, ten thousand per bundle, stacked in the secret wall safe behind the mirror over Trish's dressing table.

Judy waved aside the banker's denial. "It was just too regular, Mr. Tilden. Ten thousand in cash every week."

Tilden's eyes were flashing fire. "Nellie was the world's richest woman. Ten thousand a week was Nellie's walking-around money. She was eccentric, liked lots of loose cash nearby. I only did what she asked me to do."

Judy sat back, her cool voice even and crisp. "As I said, it was just too regular, Mr. Tilden. Every week, ten thousand dollars . . . except for the two weeks you were on vacation. You insisted that no one but you touch her account. Everyone understood . . . she was the bank's biggest customer . . . she trusted you. With her faulty eyesight, you knew she'd never check the statements. and as long as the books balanced, the examiners would never notice anything wrong."

"You're whistling in the dark! With Nellie dead, the estate isn't going to want to investigate this. Her estate is so huge, hundreds of millions. Inheritance taxes will take such a bite. You're talking about a drop in the bucket. Hell, Nichols will spill more than that. Just wait till he gets his hands on that estate." Tilden's eyes reflected his jealousy.

Judy leaned forward again and spoke in a soft, confidential tone. "Mr. Tilden, I thought we might discuss a compromise. The size of Nellie's estate is not important to my client. But the two-hundred-thousand-dollar bank loss from the color copier is fully insured, and that's important. Now, the IRS would probably be very interested in your withdrawals from Nellie's bank account. They'd be interested in how she was able to spend half a million dollars a year in pin money. They have ways and means of proving these things. The IRS is not my client. If the two hundred thousand could be found, wiping out the shortage on the bank's books, my client would be perfectly happy. Nellie's pin money would go with her to her grave. Think it over.'' Judy sat back in her chair.

Tilden knew that the young detective was running a bluff, a carefully calculated bluff. But it was clear also that she wasn't kidding, and meant business. Rogers was drawing to an inside straight and betting heavily, without even looking at the card she'd drawn. Tilden knew that the girl could never prove her accusations.

He had a letter signed by Nellie, instructing him to withdraw the money from her account each week. Shit, the IRS could probably prove that Nellie would sign anything that Tilden put in front of her. She'd been legally blind.

He couldn't afford to have the IRS poking around. They'd quickly discover that Nellie lived very frugally, held onto every nickel. A miser, who didn't give to anyone or anything . . . probably didn't spend a hundred dollars a week, let alone ten thousand. Apparently this young bitch knew it. That was the strength of her bluff. He'd go along with her.

Tilden's face sagged, then brightened. He'd give up two hundred thousand in exchange for a million any day. It was a hell of a business transaction.

He smiled, flashing a surprisingly good set of teeth. ''Miss Rogers, I like the way you think. I do believe that a thorough search of the bank will locate the two hundred thousand. It must have been misplaced. I hadn't thought of that.''

''Today?'' she asked.

''It's now eleven-thirty A.M. I think we should be able to find the money by, let's say, three-thirty this afternoon.''

''That will be fine,'' Judy said, rising from her chair. ''Oh, and Mr. Tilden, I would suggest that you consider resigning from the banking business. Let's say when you return from vacation?''

Tilden bowed his head and nodded, slowly.

Judy turned and left his office. She'd accomplished part of her mission, trapped one of the money-grubbing rats. Tilden thought he was going to get away with a cool million. She'd agreed not to tell the IRS and wouldn't. As soon as Tilden returned from Hawaii, the FBI would be waiting. Peter Bond had already set the wheels in motion.

Tilden reflected on what had just happened. It could have been worse, a lot worse. The girl was clever, and had a devious mind. The bitch had guessed at the way he'd swindled Nellie. Not quite right, but too close for comfort. If she prowled around the IBM 360, Rogers might discover how he really dipped into big money. There was a lot of money to be made by robbing the rich, and his computer withdrawals from inactive accounts had yielded him over four million, tax-free. The withdrawals had been totally undetected. He'd programmed the computer to destroy all the evidence.

Tilden relaxed. As always he'd plan for the worst and expect the best. He'd stay in Hawaii until the Man was caught.

It was 11:45 when Bob Baker returned Rice's telephone call. Rice went through the same conversation he'd held with Tilden. Baker thanked him profusely, but said he was well armed and capable of defending himself. "I'm the best shot in Fairport" was the way he'd put it.

Rice played the tape of Baker's phone conversation into the spectrograph. It spit out a voiceprint of Bob Baker, and he compared it with the Man's. He almost dropped both of them. They were identical. He looked again. There could be no question. Bob Baker was the Man. Rice let out a shout of exultation. "We've got the cocksucker!"

Both Belli and Farrow came running. Rice, grinning from ear to ear, held the evidence in front of him and announced triumphantly, "We've got him. I know who the Man is."

"Who is it?" they both asked simultaneously.

"Bob Baker. Baker is the Man."

Farrow's face fell. "He can't be," he said, simply but forcefully.

"Why not? I've got the proof here. His voiceprint pattern is the same as the Man's. It's like a fingerprint." He started to explain, seeing their dubious looks.

"No chance," the redheaded detective said emphatically. "We just finished checking him out. Baker and his wife were at the dance at Longwood Saturday night, sitting at a table with the Tildens and the McAlpins. Baker was there the entire evening. He couldn't have been involved in the kidnapping of Marie Benson or have killed Rocco. He couldn't have incapacitated Whitey, couldn't have maimed Diangelo. Shall I go on? I've got a whole list. He was in Detroit the night Hetty Starr was killed. No, Bob Baker can't be the Man, unless we have more than one killer loose."

Rice was flabbergasted. "But I've got a perfect match here." He was almost finished showing them how the spectrograph worked when the phone rang. It was Don Dillon, returning Rice's call. The tall blond clicked on the recorder.

Five minutes later, Rice, Farrow and Belli watched as the voiceprint of Dillon emerged from the machine. They compared it to the voiceprints of the Man and the one of Bob Baker. All three were identical.

"The Man has to be Dillon," exclaimed Rice.

"I doubt it. I think you've got a faulty machine. I'd have it checked out thoroughly before you record any more suspects," warned Farrow.

"There's a nut loose someplace," said Belli, as he scratched his head. "I think it's in your machine."

As soon as he could, the Man swung by Jeanne's. There was a note addressed to "Tiger Baby" pinned to her front door. He opened it and read:

Lover, I had to run into New York today. My editor needs a few extra pictures of the U.N. Building. *Harper's* is going to feature my article on the Third World. Everything is wonderful. I love you. See you tomorrow. I'll eat you alive.

XXX
Kitty kat

P.S. I tried to call you this morning. Your phone must be out of order. I was cut off.

As he pocketed her note, the Man felt the bulge of his Swiss Army knife. Jeanne was right, she really had been cut off.

It was 1:25 P.M. when the next letter arrived. They were waiting for it. The envelope was addressed simply "The Big Bull, Mansville, Conn." It had been mailed from Fairport the preceding day.

Rice took the envelope to the lab and checked it with a fluoroscope to make sure it wasn't a letter bomb. Then he opened the flap and removed and unfolded the letter with surgical tweezers. He sprayed it with ninhydrin and checked for fingerprints. There were none. Rice shook his head. Both the envelope and the letter seemed to have been typed on Orton's typewriter. He slid the letter into a large plastic envelope, so that it was visible, yet could be handled easily.

It was almost 2:00 P.M. when the letter returned from the lab. Rice handed the envelope to Dempsey, saying, "We can tell that he wears thin latex gloves, probably surgical gloves of some type. I'd guess he uses them during his murders. That would account for the lack of fingerprints at the murder scenes. These gloves are almost like human skin, unnoticeable to the casual observer."

Dempsey stared at the letter for a few moments, sighed wearily, inhaled deeply, and began reading the letter aloud.

> "Roses are red
> White, yellow and pink,
> To play in my league
> You've got to think.

> "Violets and piggies
> Both are blue,
> You hate me
> And I hate you.

> "Get off your asses
> Get on the stick
> To stop me now
> You must be quick

"Spades are black
Heads are red
By tomorrow night
One will be dead.

"I don't plan to die
I've too much to do,
In the next few weeks
I'll kill fifty-two.

"I like to win
When I choose,
But most of all
I hate to lose.

"Six feet tall
All of that
Strong and agile
Like a cat.

"Who am I?
I'm the Man.
Catch me, catch me
If you can."

An unreal stillness hung over the office when Dempsey had finished reading. The Man was taunting them, like a phantom picador, sticking lances into the bulls, under their skins, well into their muscles, deep into their sinews. The blood was showing, and the pain was intense.

Briggs broke the silence. "He's got us by the balls, and he's squeezing."

Dempsey suggested they all sit down. "We'll turn the letter over to the psychiatrists. They'll make a meal out of this one. It'll keep them busy for days. But first let's see what we can make of it."

Belli and Briggs both started to talk at once. Dempsey silenced them with a look. "We'll get noplace this way. There are eight four-line rhymes, if that's what you'd call them. Let's take them one at a time. I'll give you my top-of-the-head interpretation. Each of you add anything that you think might be useful.

"In the first rhyme, I think he's just saying that he's good. He's outsmarting us. 'To play in my league, you've got to think.' He's in the big leagues, playing hardball. We're strictly little-league, playing with ourselves. So far, he's right."

Dempsey looked around. All of the others nodded in pained agreement.

"In the next one . . . 'piggies' . . . that's us. His hate is showing here."

Grady spoke up. "He obviously has an intense hate against society, the status quo, the establishment. That fits his profile."

Dempsey nodded, and waited for other comments. There were none, so he continued. "Next, he's telling us that time is important, moves faster than we do, moving like a butterfly, and stinging like a bee."

"A fucking killer bee," muttered Briggs.

Farrow shifted uneasily in his seat. "Well, he's acting, and we're reacting. He's on the offense, and we're on the defense."

"Right," said Dempsey. "We're hunkered on our asses, just like he says. We're sitting on the can. We've got to get on the stick. Either we slow him down or move faster ourselves."

Dempsey tapped the plastic envelope with his forefinger. "The next rhyme is the key one. He's telling us that he's going to kill again tomorrow, going to kill a redhead."

" 'Spades are black, heads are red.' " Grady broke in. "He doesn't say which he's going to kill. 'One will be dead.' He may be planning to murder a black, even a black with red hair."

Dempsey stared at Grady, who was twisting the tip of his cane. "A black with red hair?" he said incredulously. "That ought to be easy. Not too many of those around here."

Dempsey poured a glass of water from the crystal pitcher on the table and swallowed slowly. He felt dehydrated, empty. He could hear the water gurgling as it went down.

"That's the rhyme we've got to figure out. In the next one, he says what we've all been afraid of. He's going for the whole deck." Dempsey shuddered involuntarily.

Briggs whistled. "Fifty-two murders!" He clamped his teeth hard on the tip of his cigar, his mouth working on the soft, malleable plastic.

"Jim, do you think we should tell the media that he plans to kill fifty-two people?" Grady asked.

Dempsey shook his head. "No, I don't. I think we should let them know that he's sent us another note, but not publicize any of the contents. It can't do any good, and it would scare the shit out of everyone left in town."

Dempsey looked around the room. No one disagreed. "Take the next rhyme. 'I like to win . . . I hate to lose.' "

Farrow said, "That sounds pretty normal. Most of the people I know like to win and hate to lose."

Dempsey looked at Farrow's boyish face, then sighed. "Yes, but they play by the rules. The Man plays to win. Period. There are no rules in his game."

Dempsey tapped his forefinger on the plastic envelope again. "The next rhyme gives us our first hard clue. He admits he's at least six feet tall, knows that we're sure of that. Also, knows that we know he's strong and agile."

Briggs stood up and walked to the window. He turned and half sat on the sill. "Giving clues increases the risk. It must make it more exciting for him. It's more fun. He's on a high. That's what the psychiatrists predicted."

Dempsey nodded again. "It's a meaningless clue, but . . . you know, we just might be able to produce a real clue, by playing on his ego, his underlying desire to be caught, his willingness to take risks. Set up a dialogue with the Man in the media. Issue a challenge to describe his appearance. Report that we can't catch him because he's too smart and we're too dumb. Ask the bastard to be more obvious."

"It's far out, Jim, but it just might work. God, it's certainly worth a try." Grady's voice registered excitement.

The others agreed, and Farrow was asked to rough out a release for the press before 4:00 that afternoon.

"The last rhyme . . . 'Whom am I?' . . . that's what we'd all like to know. . . ." Dempsey's voice trailed off.

"He's a nobody who's made himself a somebody by killing," said Farrow.

Briggs walked from the window to the table to snub out his cigar. He spoke softly. "I notice that he's the Man now. He's taken our name for him."

"It's the power of advertising," Bill said wryly, "but we've at least eliminated one thing."

"What's that?" asked Dempsey.

"We can be pretty sure he's not a poet." Belli attempted a weak smile.

A smile flickered momentarily on Briggs' face, and then it was gone.

The meeting broke up around 2:40 P.M. The Man was probably going to kill a redhead, but since they couldn't be sure, they'd warn blacks as well as redheads.

Grady lingered for a moment, after the others had left Dempsey's office.

"Jim, you're wound up tight as a spring. He's getting to you."

Dempsey bit his lip before replying. "You're right. He's becoming an obsession."

"You've got to hang loose and ignore the funerals. We'll get him."

"I keep looking behind me. That bastard is close by. He's breathing on us, hard."

"He's got to crack. Think of the burden he must be carrying. Heavier than anyone can bear." Sam put his hand on Dempsey's shoulder as they walked toward the door.

"It's unreal, Sam. I'm frustrated, angry, tired, yet I'm calm."

Grady nodded in understanding. "No one could ask you to do more. Living with all this death has made me appreciate life a little more. We both should be thankful."

"Thanks, Sam. I appreciate your words." The worry lines around Dempsey's eyes seemed to lift and his face was suddenly a little bit younger.

Judy Rogers looked at the name on the mailbox. N. Nichols. She pulled her Mercedes into the long circular driveway and parked, walked up to the front door, and pushed the doorbell.

An attractive, middle-aged blonde in black slacks and a white blouse opened the door. She extended a small but firm hand. "You must be Judy. Come in. I've been expecting you. I'm Suzy."

She led the way through a marble-tiled entryway into a very attractive sunken living room. Judy's eyes took in the white leather chairs and couches, the modern chrome-and-glass tables and the Impressionist paintings.

"Would you like something to drink? Coffee, coke, gin?" The blonde smiled.

Judy declined with a polite "No, thanks."

"I'd offer you a snack, but I'm on a diet. I'm trying to take two inches off my rear and put it on my chest." She laughed, sitting down across from Judy. "It's hopeless."

"As I told you on the phone, I'm an insurance investigator. I need some background information on some people and hoped you could help."

Suzy nodded, exhaling smoke through her nose. She'd expected the police before this. With Ned's recent strange behavior, the need to talk to someone was almost an obsession. This girl looked harmless enough.

They chatted about others. Judy listened as Suzy talked about the Dillons—"Their hate is fueled by mutual disgust." That was an interesting comment.

It seemed that Alice Briggs had raised badmouthing of Spike to an art form. What a whiner. But probably with very good reason. In view of the last comment, the thought crossed her mind that there might be something going on between Suzy and Spike. In this town almost anything was possible. It would serve Ned right.

"I don't like to talk about my friends," Suzy continued. "If you throw mud, you wind up with dirty hands." She hesitated. "If you don't . . . well, you can't say much about them." She laughed.

Judy liked Suzy. Another time, another place, they could have been good friends. She was personable, quite attractive, with skin that, although well-tanned, had a transparent fragility, and her directness was refreshing. How could this woman put up with that boor of a husband and his philandering?

Finally the conversation turned to Ned. Suzy hesitated, looked around, as if afraid he'd appear in the doorway.

"I guess every man's a mystery. Even after fifteen years of marriage . . . he's very successful, you know . . . started at the bottom . . . we've come a long way up, believe me."

Their eyes caught each other's. She went on, "He goes after what he wants. He's dramatic . . . explodes, charges the atmosphere. He's a bull. But these days, who cheers for the bull? You know, he's a Gemini . . . two people in one."

Judy clicked on her mini-recorder. "Tell me about it," she said softly.

"I love the guy," Suzy started, then proceeded to pick him apart. Her voice was low and troubled, coupled with a tone of panic. She finished, "I'm afraid he'll self-destruct." There were tears in her eyes.

"Are you afraid?" Judy asked.

Suzy shook her head. "No. I've learned to live one day at a time. You can't go back, you know . . . This last week, despite the sunshine, every day has been like night."

They walked to the door and shook hands warmly. "I guess everybody's got problems," Suzy said.

Judy nodded and smiled reassuringly. Driving away, she was convinced that Suzy Nichols knew that her husband was the Man.

It was early afternoon when Rosemary Schwartz returned home to her apartment. Water was pouring down into her bathroom from the floor above. It was already two inches deep, flowing over the bathroom sill and sloshing down the hallway, where it was being blotted up by her wall-to-wall shag rug. She glanced into the bathroom and saw that a large chunk of plaster had fallen from the ceiling.

"Oh, shit," she said aloud. "A pipe must have broken upstairs." It was a disaster. Warren had no insurance.

She ran upstairs and pounded on Thelma's door. There was no answer. Rosemary ran back to her apartment and called the apartment manager. There was no answer. "Oh shit," she said again, and called the fire department.

The call came into police headquarters at 2:45 P.M. from the fire department. The Man had murdered victim number eleven. He had drowned a plain, ordinary housewife.

"Dead?" asked Dempsey.

"Very," replied the patrolman on the other end of the phone.

"A housewife?" Dempsey and Grady asked it together. They knew that the murder of a housewife would create mass panic. For a few moments the two men sat in silence, heads bowed, each with his own thoughts. Then Dempsey said, "It had to happen, and it finally did. Let's go."

It was thirty minutes later. "This is the worst," Dempsey wearily commented for at least the fourth time. He and Grady were wading through the ankle-deep water in Thelma Pickell's apartment. Her bloated nude body was still in the now-empty tub.

"Poor little Raggedy Ann." The police photographer was talking to himself. Rice's men were dusting for fingerprints. They didn't find any. Other than the four of spades in the crotch of her blue shorts, they'd found no clues, and they'd located no witnesses. The Man, the phantom Man, had killed a plain, ordinary housewife, killed her in a plain, ordinary way, had drowned her in her own bathtub.

Judy returned to the Inn at 5:15 P.M., pulled her car into the parking lot and walked rapidly across the lobby. There was still time to go over some of her notes, take a leisurely bath, dress and meet Peter. He was due in about 7:00. The radio bulletin about the housewife's murder had shocked her.

Unlocking the door to her room, Judy had a sudden apprehension. She threw the door open and jumped back into the hall, gasping. The room was in complete disarray, her clothes and papers strewn all over the floor.

Taking a Baretta .32 ACP out of her purse, she eased cautiously into the room, checked the closet, the bathroom and the balcony, and then looked under the bed. Satisfied, she locked and bolted the door. Her biggest concern was the reel of tape in the dresser drawer, the recording she had made of her conversation with Ned Nichols. It was gone.

She couldn't stay in this room any longer. It was too dangerous. About to call Dempsey, she put the phone down. The poor man now had the murder of a housewife on his hands. Peter would decide what to do when he arrived. Slowly, an idea came to her. It might speed things up. Her heart beat faster.

She picked up her papers and put them in her briefcase, collected her clothes, folded them and packed them in her suitcase, keeping out her sleeveless blue dinner dress, showered and dressed. She locked her room and took the elevator down to the lobby, checking at the desk to make sure Peter's suite had been reserved.

The best place to wait for Peter was in the lobby, out in the open among people. She'd call her sister later and, if necessary, stay with Brenda and Jim for the remainder of her trip.

Her body was still full of adrenaline from the excitement and fright, thoughts a jumble. The Man was trying to scare her out of town. It had to be Ned Nichols. He had taken the tape she'd made of their conversation, knowing the damage it could do. How could he have known? The miniature recorder had been in her purse the entire time. He had to be psychic. She snubbed out her cigarette and lit another.

By nightfall, the townspeople had been stunned once again. A housewife had been brutally murdered by the Man, the eleventh murder in eleven days. This was his most diabolical murder, a plain, ordinary housewife. Now everybody knew that he might kill anyone. Not only prominent, important people, not only rich or well-to-do men and women, not only famous people. Anyone. No one felt safe.

Warnings were broadcast on local radio that the Man had threatened to kill either a black or a redhead by Thursday evening.

Dempsey was quoted as saying, "The chances of seizing the Man are minimal unless he wants to be caught, or just makes a big mistake. He must give us clearer clues, help us, be more specific about who he's planning to kill. He can call police headquarters at any time. We're most anxious to talk to him. He's been too smart for us."

Rice frowned. The report from the forensic lab in Bethany had come in by telephone. Dr. Simms, the odontologist, had called personally. All results were negative.

Rice went over his notes again, this time for Belli's benefit. "None of the teeth marks on the Tiparillo butts that we collected matched the two that were found near the Bicentennial statue or the two in Orton's house."

Belli's dark face grew darker. He shook his head sadly and asked, "Was he sure?"

Rice shrugged. "He gave me a rundown on each sample. Here, judge for yourself." He passed a notepad over his desk to Belli.

Sample	# Butts	
A	1	Teeth marks only—not close
B	4	Heavily chewed—similar, but not exactly the same
C	2	Mangled—different bite marks
D	1	No teeth marks
E	1	Light teeth marks—different
F	3	Heavily chewed—very similar to B
control	4	Heavily chewed—corners bitten off

Belli looked questioningly at Rice. "Who's who?"

Rice looked around before answering. "They're alphabetical. Baker, Briggs, Dillon, Dempsey, Farrow, Nichols, and, of course, the control is the Man. I don't want those names on paper, for obvious reasons."

Belli nodded and asked, "This lets them all off the hook?"

Rice shrugged again. "It's not an exact science. Simms felt that A, C and E were definitely eliminated. Their bite marks were distinctly different. There was nothing to compare on D, except that he apparently doesn't chew his plastic tips. That eliminates him. B and F were similar, but not exactly the same. He couldn't be positive about them."

Belli looked around. "Briggs and Nichols. Well, Doc Simms

narrowed it down to the right two. I guess maybe I'd better collect some new samples," he said softly.

Rice nodded. "I was hoping you'd offer. Everything checks out right. But there's something very wrong, if you know what I mean."

Belli shrugged his broad shoulders, turned and left the lab.

The man felt light-headed and fuzzy. The tension was building inside him, and the warm feeling was down inside his groin again. He needed relief, and they'd be ready now.

Barbara and Vivian slept together most of the day, very comfortable with each other's companionship. Both felt reborn, needed, bosom buddies. Since awakening, they had talked almost incessantly, and had spent the last hour deciding whether they should live together. They finally decided yes, at least until it was time for Pat to return from camp. Now Vivian had gone to her house to pick up a few personal items.

Barbara had been thinking about how she would explain her new relationship to her daughter. Fortunately there was plenty of time to work that out. She and Viv would just have to be very discreet. Maybe Pat could go away to a private girls' school, one with horses.

Her man drove into her driveway in the late afternoon. Last evening, Viv had recognized him, but promised not to say anything to anyone. Later they'd chatted about his bitchy wife. Viv was the one who'd said she couldn't understand why he stayed with his wife. Especially with Barbara available. This would be a good time to ask him that.

At the door they kissed. She was pleased to see him. He was truly something. Then he touched her. In a microsecond, all was ready. Transformed, she forgot about her question.

His batteries totally recharged, the Man was ready for almost anything. By the time Barbara heard Vivian return, she had been completely satisfied. The Man's sex urge was now almost uncontrollable. He couldn't seem to throttle back. Barbara was approaching exhaustion, felt totally drained, but was content, knowing that later she would restore her strength from Vivian. She fell back on her bed and murmured, "Please make Vivian happy, too. A joy that's shared is a joy made double.''

The Man had thought a lot about Vivian. She was a luscious peach, ripe and juicy. He'd like to bite into her, to pierce the skin and enjoy the sweet nectar.

Finished with Barbara, the Man walked into the living room and turned his attention to Vivian, who had been waiting. He kissed her gently, and reached under her blouse for the control buttons. Eyes lighting with pleasure, she shuddered with joy, high in her sexual heaven, spinning sugar, mesmerized. He tore off her clothes and pushed her back onto the couch.

It was a fantasy come true, his dreams of dreams. She was lying naked, squirming and writhing in pleasure. He just kept rubbing and kneading her sensitive nipples. They were the size of acorns, and hard. He didn't touch her anyplace else and wouldn't let her touch him. Her radiant face registered pure ecstasy, on the edge of an earthquake, running for her rainbow, finding it, time after time. She climbed a mountain, reached the top, and then another, and then another, higher and higher, above the clouds, into the heavens, surrounded by stardust.

He watched in fascination and excitement. Each time her toes curled in, then out, then in again, legs spread wide in open invitation, then closed tight together and crossed, knees bent, back arched, toes pointed toward the ceiling. Her entire body tensed, then convulsed four or five times. She relaxed for a few moments, eyes begging, hands and lips reaching . . . for him. Then the cycle would start again.

Vivian was floating somewhere in never-never land, body glowing, pulsating, totally satisfied. The Man carried her into bed and tucked her in next to Barbara. He kissed them both goodnight. It was only 7:30 P.M. Tonight, in the battle of the sexes, the Man had clearly won.

He sat up with a start. Tiparillo ashes had fallen on his bare arm. Shit, he'd burned himself. He glanced down. A sticky, wet spot oozed through his slacks. Good God. It was all in his mind. His brains were leaking. It was a damn good thing there was another pair of slacks in his closet.

•   •   •

It was 6:45 P.M. when Judy saw Peter Bond's taxi arrive at the Fairport Inn. Judy saw him the moment he stepped out of the taxi. He looked so distinguished and handsome. She fairly flew across the lobby into his open arms. His kiss was warm and sincere.

Now, almost two hours later, they had found a quiet corner in the dining room. Peter's face laughed as she told him about Tilden's locating the missing $200,000.

"He'd simply misplaced it." She flashed a mischievous smile.

Peter shook his head. "That old bastard's not as clever as he thinks. The FBI will pick him up at the airport. They're not very smart, but once somebody points them in the right direction, they're relentless." His hand reached across the table and covered hers. His eyes flashed silently. "Nice work."

On the back of a napkin, Judy sketched out the motive for murder. It was simple. It was big money. Totaling up the figures, from assorted wills and insurance, Ned Nichols stood to gain over six million dollars.

Bond whistled softly. She was spouting facts and figures like a computer. How could a computer look so enchanting and smell so gloriously feminine? Her simplicity was so bewitching. He moved his chair closer.

As Judy talked, the more convinced Bond became that she was on the right track. Nichols had to be the Man. Her theory that Nichols had two distinctly different personalities was brilliant. It explained everything. Tomorrow they'd see Dempsey. It was all circumstantial, but what a strong case.

Judy too was convinced: Peter Bond was the man for her. He was like an elegant wine, smooth, full-bodied, and with great depth. This evening she'd felt safe, secure and confident. It had to be love. She sighed, and her heart bumped. Her career was important, but the greatest thing in life was to be needed.

Peter found her mind stimulating. She was roses and thorns, and he liked that. Her personality was slightly on the acid side, about pH 5.4. Along with a sensuous body, a gorgeous smile, and soft eyes, her class showed. For the first time in his life, he could feel the hook in his mouth. He loosened his collar and tie. Suddenly the music blared, stopping all conversation.

"Let's get out of here," he suggested.

"Rémy Martin would be fine," she said, kicking off her shoes and settling back on the couch in his suite, talking on as he poured the drinks.

Suddenly something in her voice made him tense. He sat down, concern showing on his face. Judy told him about the daisies, the threatening phone call from Nichols, the ransacking of her room, and the missing tape.

"For Crissakes, Judy, why didn't you tell me. Your safety . . . nothing else matters. I'm not leaving you alone."

Judy's eyes sought his, relief showing on her face.

"We'll pack your things and move them in here. There are two bedrooms," he added hurriedly, seeing her questioning look.

"My room is just down the hall. I'm already packed . . . I was going to call my sister," she added quickly, when she saw his raised eyebrows.

It was later, after Judy had put on her robin's-egg-blue lounging pajamas and Peter had finally taken off his tie, that he said he loved her. It was the magic phrase. Seeking his lips, she found them. As they kissed, their bodies melded together. She could feel his rigidness as he could feel the heat of her body pressing against him. Their deepest emotions surfaced and ran together.

The moon shone translucently through the window onto her bed. Slowly, they moved together toward their own personal moonbeam. The clock ticked far into the next day without either of them knowing. They didn't care, being far too busy with one another.

By 8:30 P.M., the auditorium of the Fairport High School was packed to overflowing. Townspeople jammed the halls and spilled out into the hot, humid night. Winchester was pleased. His group had done a remarkable job of spreading the word about the special meeting. They had met every commuter train at the station and had phoned every person who had previously signed up for vigilante duty.

Everyone's mind was on Thelma Pickell's drowning. The crowd was subdued and serious. Tonight most of the vigilantes had brought their families with them. No one wanted to stay home alone. As Muriel Winchester told Tom when she first heard about the meeting, "Oh, no, you're not. You're not going anyplace without me. Not until this crazy is caught."

Tonight almost all of the vigilantes were armed. Holsters containing pistols of all descriptions were strapped to men's waists. Loaded rifles and shotguns were everywhere.

Known only to Winchester and a few close associates, sixteen lawmen were also in the audience—Dempsey, Grady, Briggs, Rice, Belli, Farrow, DeLuca, Custer, Piccello and seven state troopers were all there in civilian clothes. Unknown to the local and state police, Dillinger and his four key FBI detectives were strategically located outside in parked cars. With special nightscopes, they scrutinized every person entering and leaving the building, photographing them at the same time with special wide-angle infrared cameras.

One by one, the vigilantes obtained their unit and patrol-area assignments. Fifty-two new recruits signed up for duty. Winchester took the podium and announced that armed patrols would begin the following evening. A loudspeaker carried his words to those who couldn't get inside the auditorium. He ended his brief announcement with a chilling thought

"Today, the Man killed a Fairport housewife. Tomorrow, he might kill one of our children. We must kill him before he kills us."

Dempsey winced. Someone was bound to get hurt. The vigilantes might prove to be more dangerous than the Man. He knew most of them personally. In general, they were serious, hard-working citizens, intent only on protecting their loved ones, but some were no better than slaphappy, gun-carrying fools seeking to make a reputation by gunning down the Man. He knew that with guns some men became ten feet tall.

Belli had suggested earlier to the Chief that they stop the vigilantes from organizing, but they'd decided that under the circumstances, it was better to let the citizens patrol. Dempsey knew that the Governor had called Briggs earlier in the day to advise him that she was prepared to order five hundred National Guard troops into town whenever Briggs requested it.

The meeting ended at 9:45 P.M. No one had seen the Man. The lawmen were disappointed. Dempsey spoke with Winchester for a few minutes and thanked him for setting up the meeting. He walked dejectedly to his car.

The Man arrived home late. His wife had been nervously waiting for him, jumping at every sound. Like every other woman in Fairport, she had been terrified by the news of Thelma Pickell's murder, and was greatly relieved to hear her husband's car in the driveway. She put down the poker in her hand.

At the door she asked anxiously, "Darling, who's going to be next? This poor woman who was killed today. There's nothing on television but the Fairport murders. When will they stop? It's so frightening. When will the Man be caught?"

The Man held up his hands at the barrage of questions, trying to reassure her. "Hon, you're perfectly safe. I guarantee it."

"How can you guarantee my safety?" she asked sharply. "You're coming home later and later each night. I get so frightened here without you."

Shivering and crying, she pleaded, "Hold me close." He held out his arms to her and hugged her tightly. "Mother called tonight. She's worried about our safety, wants me to pack up and drive into the city tomorrow, stay with her until this madman is caught. I'd miss you so."

The Man bit his lip. His face tightened. Then, looking down at her, he said softly, "I'll miss you too, but it's a good idea. Your safety comes first. Why don't you run up and take your bath. Put on some of that good-smelling perfume. I'll be right up." He patted her bottom.

Starting to say, "But we did this morning," she caught herself in time. From the look in his eyes there would be no denying him tonight.

The Man couldn't help himself. His need was absolute. After her bath, he attacked her with a sexual vigor that was almost animal. At first she enjoyed it immensely. It was wild and primitive. They tried positions she'd never known were even possible. Even hit two separate high spots. Finally, exhausted and totally drained, she begged him to stop. Reluctantly, he ground to a halt, a look of deep hurt on his face.

Later, the Man returned his special attaché case to his arsenal. He hadn't had a chance to use it. He'd taken the mini-recorder tape from the drawer in the hotel room. It might have had his phone conversation on it. When he'd gone back tonight, she'd moved out of her room. The bitch was sleeping in Bond's room. The youth of today. They had no morals at all.

Back upstairs, the Man pulled the blinds tightly closed on all the windows. There were eyes watching him, nightscopes. It wouldn't do for them to see him sitting at his desk checking his notebook. With his black marking pencil, he crossed out "unknown housewife," the four of spades, number eleven on his death list. Again the book was carefully locked away.

He clapped his hands together. Tomorrow was a special day. A day destined to create a major international incident. He'd give the hardnosed patriots a reason for some old-fashioned flag-waving. He laughed to himself. It wasn't going to be easy.

The elephants, the bulls, the pigs, the troopers, the dicks, the feds, the private eyes, the secret agents, the bodyguards, the vigilantes, the fucking lawmen were everywhere, and more and more of them were pouring into town each day. It was becoming difficult to move about, to kill without being seen. That's what made his plan even more exciting. He ran his hand through his hair.

That group of vigilantes. They were a laugh. Bound to shoot someone for sure. Had to make damn sure it wasn't him. He'd been at their meeting and been so well hidden and so well disguised that no one knew he'd been there. No one. No matter how many infrared cameras they'd used.

The police were asking for additional clues. They said he was too smart for them and they couldn't catch him. He laughed. They were using it as a come-on. They thought it was pure horseshit. It wasn't. It was true. Maybe he would give them some extra help, making things even more exciting. Especially since he knew what they were trying to do.

The bulls were in disarray. Clearly, Dempsey was tired, losing his confidence. But he was still dangerous. Briggs wasn't as bright as he'd thought. He spent too much time dicking around with his lady friends. Grady was a lovable horse's ass. An old fart who toadied up to the Boy Scout Chief. Dillinger was still an unknown. As an unknown, he had to be respected.

That Vivian had been a good replacement for Gayla. Not as pretty, but a damn good piece of ass. A soft touch and no inhibitions. None. A sensitive, red-breasted sapsucker. Pound for pound, she really put out. Just watching her squirm about, his mind had almost had an orgasm.

It was midnight. Paul Rice sat bolt upright in his bed, shouting, "The Man. It was the Man. That son of a bitch outwitted us again."

Awakened by her husband's outburst, Rita rose up on one elbow and sleepily asked, "Paul, what's the matter? Are you dreaming? Are you all right?"

Rice was out of bed now, pacing the floor and thinking out loud. "Of course! I called Tilden at his office. It had to be Tilden. I got Tilden's voiceprint. But when I called Baker and Dillon, they were both out. They called me back. That's it. I thought they called me back. They didn't call me back, the Man did. He impersonated them. He's obviously very good at it. That's why Baker's and Dillon's voiceprints both matched the voiceprint of the Man. It was the Man on the other end of the phone. That clever bastard! He must have found out about the spectrograph and tried to undermine our confidence in the machine. He damn near succeeded."

"Come to bed, hon. It's after midnight. You'll wake the kids," pleaded Rita.

"I'm going to sit up for a while," Rice said, kissing her forehead gently. Tomorrow he'd get voiceprints from everyone involved in person. He'd use a hidden tape recorder strapped to his body. Tomorrow he'd catch the Man.

The Man had been concerned on learning that the police lab had obtained a spectrograph. Sooner or later, Rice would obtain his voiceprint and compare it with the recording of him imitating Rocco. That wouldn't do.

He didn't really know whether he could disguise his voice to fool the spectrograph. It was easy enough to impersonate a wide range of people and deceive the human ear. But he doubted whether his basic voiceprint would change, regardless of the impersonation. Could the machine be fooled? He was sorely tempted to try. It would be exciting to take the risk, but there was too much at stake. First he'd finish the Plan. After all, his Plan was perfect.

Under the circumstances . . . no . . . couldn't take the chance. Must avoid a direct comparison of his voiceprint with the one Rice had of the Man. How to nullify the spectrograph? The answer . . . throw doubt on its reliability. He'd accomplished that with two calls to Rice, first as Baker, then as Dillon. That had slowed Rice down, but Rice was clever. It wouldn't stop him. He'd have the machine checked out. The elephants had to be confused further.

Earlier this evening, again in the guise of Dempsey, he'd slipped into the police lab and had located the voiceprints in Rice's desk drawer. His first thought had been to destroy them, but in a last-minute inspiration, he'd simply switched them instead. Risky, but not foolhardy. His voiceprint was now in the manila envelope labeled "Tilden's Voice." The voiceprint of Tilden was in the envelope labeled "The Voice of the Man." Rice would now compare whatever voiceprints he obtained from suspects against the voiceprint of Tilden. Let the padded, pistol-packing pachyderms play poppycock with that one!

12

Thursday, June 12.
Red Sails in the Sunset

INTERMITTENT BEAMS of sunlight streamed through the open blinds, awakening Judy. It was morning. She lay there, enjoying being still, and then slowly turned her head to stare at Peter, still asleep. He was every bit as handsome as she remembered.

Peter was perfect, but not for marriage. She wasn't ready yet. Her work came first. Maybe Peter would join her on her trip back to Hawaii. Bond & Bond was paying for the four weeks. He might as well enjoy them, too.

Moving closer, she leaned over and with her lips parted kissed him softly. He awoke with a big smile, remembering his dreams of a honeymoon in Hawaii.

Spike Briggs helped Alice pack the suitcases. He carried them down to the car, kissed their daughter, hugged Alice and gave her a tender goodbye kiss. Alice was surprised by the intensity of it. Why wasn't it always like this? It took parting to make her realize what a real, total man she had. He suggested that they still had time to go back upstairs for a few minutes. "You idiot, we just did. It was a big one, too." Then she kissed him again. His arms cradled her soothingly.

The sun was peeking through a hazy mist. By mid-morning, it would be another bright, sunny day. Across the street, Mrs. Thompson and her children were packing their car. All over town, families were packing their automobiles, heading in different directions, anyplace that was safe. They were refugees for the duration of Fairport's war with the Man.

• • •

The Man was seated alone at his kitchen table, finishing a bowl of Super-K and reading the accounts of Thelma Pickell's drowning. Little Miss Ordinary. She looked just like the sister he'd never had. The two of them would meet up there soon and be close friends. He'd never had a close friend, but then he'd never really had a chance to make friends. It would be nice to have a close friend. You have to get close to someone if you're going to stab him.

Damn the *Daily News!* Article after article about the Man. Pure horseshit! Made up out of whole oats. This one claimed the Man was an incompetent, unimportant nothing. What the hell did this stupid columnist ever do that was important? How many people had he killed?

The *Times* claimed the Man was impotent, killing out of sexual frustration. Ha-ha-ha. Hey, maybe that was it. The Man was totally frustrated. He couldn't get enough. Now, that was the truth. He'd write the *Times* and set them straight.

The damn *Post* was slipping. He'd been on both the front and back pages for the last six days. But last evening, the *Post* had him only on the front page. The back page showed a picture of Ali announcing another comeback. They were out of line.

Didn't everyone know that he, the Man, was the greatest boxer the world had ever seen? Numero Uno.

He felt light-headed, fuzzy. It must be the heat. It was a warm summer evening. Yankee Stadium was packed. The crowd was standing thirty deep in the aisles. He was in the ring with the one and only Ali. . . .

He flicked a left to Ali's face, then another, and another. Ali was puzzled, dazed. Fear crept into the corner of his eyes, a stream of blood coursed from his battered nose. The Man danced lightly on his toes. Disdainfully, he put his hands down at his sides, daring Ali to hit him. Ali swung blow after blow. Not one touched him. It was his impenetrable radar defense.

Ali was panting, his mouth agape, mouthpiece gone. The Man thrust his face close to Ali's and calmly spit right into

Ali's mouth. Ali gagged on the foreign saliva, choked, hands flew up to his throat.

That's when the Man hit him, flush on the jaw with his brass knuckles. As Ali went down, he kneed him in the groin. The old man shouted, "Kill!" Before they could pull him away, he'd kicked the fallen Ali twice in the head with his steel-tipped boots.

The Man laughed at his own wild fantasy. Maybe his mind was slipping, gears not meshing. Everything was mixed up, swirling. Hell, everything was all right. It would take a golden bullet to kill him. He was the Champ, the Greatest.

The Man pushed back from the table and back from the table and bounced to his feet. He danced lightly on his toes, dodging a few imaginary punches, shadow-boxed to the top of the basement stairs, skipped rope, going down the stairs two at a time, and suddenly tripped on the third from the last step. He caught himself just in time with a half-fall, half-jump, crashing hard against the far wall.

The painful jolt alarmed the Man. What the hell was going on? Had his glitterbug gone haywire? In the midst of executing the Perfect Plan, he was acting like an idiot, a looney. Christ, if he wasn't careful, he'd kill himself before being born.

He could hear the old man laughing, now. Today he was going to start using his exotic weapons. The thoughts quickened his pulse. He'd stick a rocket up the elephant's ass and blow his brains out.

It was now the twelfth day of the Man's murderous crusade. Fairport was writhing in torment. Ravaged, paralyzed by fear, mistrust and suspicion. A bitter yearning for revenge was growing hourly. It had started as a trickle, but now it was beginning to flood the streets. Rising, it rolled aside the fog of fear. The feeling was expressed by Will Whipple, proprietor of the Fairport Smoke Shop. "If I catch this Man, I'll cut off both his legs. Then I'll say to the police, when you give me the reward, I'll bring in the rest of the body."

The Fairport Building & loan Association offered a reward of $1,000 cash for any information resulting in the capture of the Man. This was matched by an offer from the Fairport *Press*. The total amount offered for the Man's capture was up to $96,500, as of 10 A.M., June 12. Bounty hunters were swarming into town, replacing the regular citizens who were streaming out.

It was midmorning. Once again all the top law-enforcement officials were hunkered around Dempsey's table. They were narrowing down their list of suspects.

Farrow fished in his pocket and came out with a cigarette. He lit it before starting his report. "Yesterday we agreed to concentrate on six suspects, try to clear them, or turn up the Man. As of now, about four and a half are in the clear."

Briggs stared past him, as if dismissing the words out of hand.

"The first thing we did was to put together a time frame of the Man's known movements during the past eleven days. I've sketched them out here on this chart." The tall redhead stood up and put a large chart on the easel lip of the blackboard.

Date (June)	Location	Incident	Time Frame for Man's Action
1—Sun.	Unknown	Orton killed	Afternoon or evening
2—Mon.	Outside City Hall	Donnelly—blown up	2:50 P.M. precisely
3—Tues.	Shore Haven	Starr—murdered	12:30–1:30 A.M.
3—Tues.	Okonokee	Wallers—murder set up by TV repairman	8:30–9:30 P.M.
4—Wed.	(No specific time for any action of the Man)	Grenade attack on Dempsey	
5—Thurs.	Dempsey's house		7:45 A.M.
5—Thurs.	Congregational Church	Paul Fredericks murdered	10–11 A.M.
6—Fri.	Fairport Inn	DeMarco overpowered by Man disguised as state trooper	4:20 P.M. (approx.)
6—Fri.	Gold Room (Fairport Inn)	Wiring of Petty's microphone	4:30–5:00 P.M.
6—Fri.	Orton's House	Trooper left motorcycle there	5:30 P.M. (approx.)
7—Sat.	Rocco's Cadillac Agency	Whitey overpowered	6–7:45 P.M.
7—Sat.	Fairport Inn	Lefty maimed	6–8:12 P.M.
7—Sat.	Rocco's—Police Hdqrs.	Rocco killed	6–8:22 P.M.

7—Sat.	Unknown	Call to Rice	8:22 P.M. precisely
7—Sat.	Longwood C.C.	Marie Benson raped and kidnapped	10–10:30 P.M.
8—Sun.	Bicentennial Statue	Killed and painted Marie Benson	Probably early A.M.
8—Sun.	Unknown	Call to Frouge	8 P.M. (approx.)
9—Mon.	Fairport Yacht Club	Set up Frouge's murder	Early morning or possibly night before
9—Mon.	Fairport Yacht Club	Hung Frouge	Between 7:30–8:00 A.M.
10—Tues.	Fairport's Drugs	Killed McAlpin, incapacitated pusher	Between 2:30–3;30 P.M.
10—Tues.	Fairport High School	Attends "Protect the People" rally	Between 8:30–10:00 P.M.
11—Wed.	Pickell's Apartment	Drowned Thelma Pickell	Between 9:00–11:00 A.M.

Farrow shook his head. "The Man's been so active that he's provided almost unlimited opportunities for alibis—that is, for someone who isn't the Man." Farrow glanced at Briggs. There was no eye contact. Briggs was ignoring him.

"Bob Baker is no longer a suspect because he was at the dance at Longwood Saturday night. The Bakers sat with the Tildens and the McAlpins. They arrived a little before eight and were there after Marie Benson was kidnapped. We have at least a dozen witnesses who will swear that Baker was there all evening. Also, he was in Detroit on business the night Hetty Starr was killed. He couldn't be the Man.

"Harry Hoyle was at the dentist's on Thursday, from ten to twelve. He was having a root canal. It takes time and it's painful."

Grady winced; he remembered the extensive work on his own teeth.

Farrow paused for a moment, picked up a piece of paper, then continued, "Both Dr. Brill and his nurse will swear to the length of his visit. That's about the same time Paul Fredericks was killed. We did find out, however, that after his military service in Korea, Hoyle was admitted to Camarillo State Hospital in California, where he was treated for paranoia."

At the mention of the word "paranoia," both Grady and Dempsey leaned forward in their chairs. They were looking for a paranoid. Farrow recognized their unspoken comment. "I know . . . but Hoyle's paranoia was caused by ophidiophobia, a terror of snakes," Farrow added, when he saw their puzzled looks. "He was bitten by a viper in Korea, pronounced cured, but I doubt if he could get within fifty yards of a rattlesnake. He certainly couldn't handle one. No, he's not the Man.

"We eliminated Don Dillon because he and his wife were having such a row Tuesday night that their good friends the Stanleys went over to calm them down. They arrived at nine and stayed for almost an hour. They swear Dillon was home, when the Man was at the vigilante meeting."

"What was the fight about?" asked Rick innocently.

Farrow hesitated, then answered, "It seems they argue often about money. She's a spender. But this time it appears that Deborah strayed from the fireplace, for a little extracurricular activity."

Briggs jumped to his feet and cut Farrow short, saying, "I thought we were going to ignore gossip."

"I didn't mention your name," replied Farrow coolly.

"You didn't have to. The implication was in your voice," snapped Briggs. "Deborah and I are just good friends. Occasionally we meet for a drink, let it go at that." He sat back down. Dempsey noticed that Briggs' neck was purple.

Farrow nodded, upset by Briggs' show of temper. It was almost thirty seconds before he continued. "Dillon's secretary swears that he was with a client in his office at ten-thirty on Thursday, when Fredericks was killed, and playing golf with Ace Dawson, a visitor from Kentucky, on Tuesday. They teed off at one P.M. and were putting out on the ninth green when McAlpin was killed. Dillon can't be the Man. He's clean."

Dempsey shifted uncomfortably and whispered an aside to Briggs. "Hey, buddy, it's getting down to a small group. There's only three of us left. Want to draw straws?"

Briggs grunted his reply. "Yeah. The three of us have sailed a lot of miles together. Sailors have more fun. It's got to be someone else, some landlubber smart-ass throwing suspicion on us."

"We eliminated you, Chief." Farrow was smiling broadly and noticed everyone else was, too. That is, everyone but Briggs. "We've worked with you every day and seen how hard you've been trying to catch this bastard. The same is also true for Spike, but . . .

"You asked me to treat you both as suspects, so we did. Chief, you're out because the Man attacked you with a grenade. It's true you might have done it yourself. It would have been possible, but we know how much you loved your 'Bullet.' There's no way that you would have destroyed that car. Someone else did it. We're positive of that."

Dempsey spoke up. "Pretty weak evidence."

Farrow grinned. "You've been too busy for us to even ask for your alibis, so we talked to Brenda. She swears you were home in the same bed the night Hetty Starr was murdered. Also, on Saturday night after Rocco's body was found, Rice called you at home at eight-thirty P.M. You were there. He called again after Marie Benson was kidnapped at eleven-fifty. You were back home again. Possible for you to have done everything and still have gotten home, but highly improbable. Plus, the quick action in saving Grady's life when Petty was electrocuted proves you're not the Man. All three of you could have been fried. We all know you're not the Man, but wanted to clear you officially."

Dempsey nodded. He knew it, too, but was disturbed. Christ, he was having trouble remembering what happened yesterday, let alone the whole eleven days. It seemed like a lifetime. There were big lapses of time. He checked his watch. It was almost noon. Things were happening so fast, his mind was racing to keep up. He was tired. Exhausted would be a better word. Where was the light at the end of the tunnel? There had to be one.

They were eliminating him as a suspect because of Brenda's word. What kind of evidence was that? Most nights she took sleeping pills and conked out. He could be out catting around and she'd never know. Tom would have to learn what constituted solid evidence. But . . . he definitely wasn't the Man. If there was any question, he'd take a polygraph test.

Farrow looked directly at Briggs. "We're trying to eliminate Spike. We don't have any real reason to suspect him. It's just that he hasn't given us a solid alibi for any time on this chart." Farrow hesitated. "For example, he claims to have been at the Fairport Cinema on Saturday night. We have witnesses who saw him enter alone around nine P.M. We have other witnesses who saw him leave about ten minutes later.''

"Was he alone when he left?" Grady asked.

"No, he wasn't," Farrow answered nervously.

"Careful," admonished Briggs.

Dempsey was thinking to himself. Brenda had gone to the early show on Saturday night, to see *Jaws* again. Maybe she'd seen Spike there. He'd have to ask her.

"Hey, I've got personal reasons for not wanting to explain my outside activities," Briggs commented, his neck purpling again. "I'm not the Man. Shit, you know that. Set up a polygraph test this afternoon and I'll prove I'm not."

Farrow glanced at Rice, who nodded affirmatively They could do it.

Briggs was desperately trying to change the course of the discussion. He didn't want Jim to know that he'd run into Brenda at the movies and had left with her. He'd bought them a drink at Maxie's and had followed her home. A direct pass hadn't gotten anyplace. He couldn't explain it. She just turned him on. It had to be that perfect ass of hers. Obviously, Jim didn't know. Farrow probably knew that they'd left the movie together and about Maxie's. Probably suspected the worst. Too bad. So far, it was his only innocent affair, the one conquest that hadn't been made.

Grady sensed the building tension in the room and changed the subject. "Spike, you've been working on tracking the Man since Day One. Can't you recall one meeting in your office during the eleven days that coincides with a time on this chart?"

Briggs stood up, then sat on the arm of his chair. "Hell, Sam, I roam loose. Operating solo is my thing. I'm like a free safety, covering the whole field. I don't keep a diary, don't know where I've been hour by hour, day by day, but I never miss an important meeting. The rest of the time, I free-wheel, hustle, push on. I don't look back and second-guess myself." Briggs threw up his arms, as if to say, Take it or leave it!

Briggs knew exactly where he spent his time, but didn't want to expose his string of fillies. The one trouble with so many affairs was that it took so much fucking time. Better to let events run their course. He wasn't the Man. They'd find out. Alibis were like fingerprints—most of the time they were partials, anyway.

Then, suddenly, he thought of one he could use. "Hey, I do remember." He stood up grinning like a Boy Scout being awarded a merit badge. "I was at Hetty Starr's funeral service. That was at four P.M. on Friday, the same time as DeMarco was overpowered by the Man."

"Can you prove it?" asked Farrow, staring intently at Briggs.

"Of course. I was standing next to Jim's wife during the entire service," replied Briggs.

"Good. If that checks out, we'll eliminate you also," said Farrow.

Dempsey thought to himself, I'm obviously not the only one who has trouble remembering events. Thank God. Briggs is having the same problem. It's odd, though—Brenda didn't say anything about seeing Spike at Hetty's service. Probably just forgot.

Farrow smiled. "Gentlemen, we're down to one suspect. Ned Nichols. He has a big financial motive, and we have yet to turn up a single alibi for him. Not one. As you know, he was seen by the sexton running out of the church right after Fredericks was killed. Where there's so much smoke, there has to be fire. I'd suggest we put him under constant surveillance."

"If it's not Nichols, then we're back to the Man," muttered Dempsey aloud. "We've got to catch this monster soon. Right now, Ned seems to be our only hope."

"That's about it," answered Farrow. "We're pretty sure it's Nichols, but we have no firm proof. Everything is circumstantial. We don't have one shred of hard evidence."

Farrow sat down. Belli then gave a brief report on his team's investigation. "We've come to the same conclusion. It's got to be Nichols. We were down to Briggs and Nichols, also. Eliminate Briggs and we've got only Ned left."

Rice reported the acquisition of the spectrograph and the results of his tests. "This morning I was able to eliminate the

Chief, Briggs, Baker, Hoyle and Dillon. The only voiceprint I haven't been able to obtain is Nichols'. His office says he took the day off. Everything points to him."

Grady asked the obvious question. "Jim, don't you think we should pick up Nichols, at least for questioning?"

Dempsey shrugged, then spoke with authority. "It's a close one, Sam, but I don't think so. We've got no hard evidence, nothing that would stand up. Ned's a lawyer and a damn good one. He's smart and glib. He'd be out of here in thirty minutes. Connecticut requires a grand-jury indictment to hold a murder suspect. We've absolutely nothing on which to hold him. He has a reasonable explanation for his presence at the church. Should have reported finding the body, but we can't try him for that. We need one thing that will stick."

The meeting broke up, and Dempsey called Rice aside. "The spectrograph . . . I'm pleased you ordered it, but next time, go through channels. It's proved its worth. Keep it." Relief showed on Rice's face. Dempsey smiled. "Don't worry, we'll find a way to cover it in the budget."

Grady limped alongside Briggs, his free hand on the other's elbow. He spoke in a low, guarded voice. "Spike, where I come from, one doesn't screw around with his friends' wives. Sleeping around scatters energy. I'd suggest you remember the rule of holes. When you're in a hole, don't keep digging."

Bob Dillinger hung up the phone and turned to face his staff. He did have political grease. The triumph showed in his face, exultation was in his voice "Green lights, we've got nothing but green lights. Washington has authorized fifty additional field agents. They'll start arriving today. Hartford has been told to make arrangements for them. As of now, Grady's group reports to me, for the duration of this case. We have total authorization for anything needed." He held up both clenched fists in the air.

His men cheered, and Dillinger's eyes swept around the room to take in the wide grins that had spread from face to face.

"Gentlemen," continued Dillinger, "the President himself

is vitally interested in this case. He wants this Man caught, and wants the FBI to do it. This action could be important to the future size and function of the Bureau. Politicians feel the consequences when the public becomes aroused. They get thrown out on their asses. Congress is already getting heavy pressure from the folks back home, and are worried that more publicity about the Man will encourage other bedbugs to crawl out into the open. The President is feeling the heat from Congress. The Bureau is getting it from him. We have been told to catch this crazy cocksucker and to do it fast.''

Dillinger held up one hand. The meaning was clear: no interruptions. He continued, ''Men, this has got opportunity written all over it, the once-in-a-lifetime kind. Promotions across the board, our big chance. Let's not screw it up!''

For the next two hours they reviewed their list of suspects. Dillinger summed up their progress. ''It's got to be Nichols. All the little pieces are falling into place. We've got our two best surveillance pros on him now. If he tries that Nicki Lauda stuff today, they'll blast him out of his seat. We'll nail him for sure the next time he tries a hit.''

Bert Thompson, the FBI's foremost electronic wizard, observed, ''Bob, we've got him in a straitjacket. He won't be able to go to the john by himself. We've got him wired for stereo sound, his office, house, phones, car. He's infested with bugs. If he as much as breathes at night, we'll hear it.''

Dillinger smiled, putting his hands over his ears. ''I don't want to know. Planting is a no-no.''

''Are you positive it couldn't be Dempsey or Briggs?'' asked Gibbs, the team's devil's advocate.

''Positive!'' snapped Dillinger. ''Grady claimed he'd been with Dempsey all week, a Siamese twin. He's no fool, one of the best men in the Bureau. Smart and honest. Maybe too honest for his own good. Grady swears the Chief couldn't be the Man, says Dempsey is the most sincere, dedicated and brilliant lawman he's ever met.''

''If he's so fucking good, why is the Man still running loose, making an ass of him?'' asked Gibbs.

''Let's not underestimate the power of a Man,'' said Dillinger. ''Enough of Dempsey. Since Grady is so enamored of him, we'll let those two play bump and run. It'll keep Grady out of our hair while we catch the Man.''

"How about Briggs?'' asked Gibbs.

"He's a stud. Uses women like most of us use Kleenex when we have a bad summer cold,'' Dillinger added as an afterthought. "At least five different ones this week. But one of them provided his alibi. Dempsey's wife, if you can imagine. I guess Briggs has been jealous of the Chief for some time. He's been sucking hind tit to him at sailing and maybe even professionally. Probably tried to get even by seducing his wife. She's got some spectacular ass, I've heard. One thing is certain—you can't be screwing and murdering at the same time. That guy is an enigma. On duty, he's a hardworking cop. Off duty, he plays hard, wild and loose, a real swinger. He's elusive and hard to pin down. A will-o'-the-wisp, even uses four or five different patrol cars a day. He's no murderer, though—just protecting the unbelievable game he's playing on the side.

"Men, it's Nichols. It's got to be. If it's not, God help us. We'll all be back at desk jobs.'' Dillinger looked grim and subdued.

Don Dillon was sweating profusely, feeling nervous, sick to his stomach and on the edge of panic. Judy Rogers, a private detective, had been checking through Hetty Starr's insurance, looking for fraud. He'd heard about Rogers' reputation. She worked for Bond & Bond, the top insurance investigators available anywhere.

He gulped. Perspiration soaked his shirt, adhering it to his skin, even though the air conditioning was on full. Shuddering with a sudden chill, he knew his apprehension was well founded. The forgery of Hetty Starr's signature on a back-dated rider to one of her policies was the work of a bungling amateur. It had been done out of financial desperation, but he'd been reasonably sure no one would ever check.

The firm's well-deserved reputation had been built over two lifetimes, his father's and his. They had never done anything wrong, until now. Yesterday the key to the Mint was in his hands, $400,000 cash, the amount he needed to get Deborah and himself out of a deep financial hole and save their marriage.

Today he sat in dread, in queasy anticipation of being exposed for insurance fraud. Conviction meant at least ten years in prison. Besides ruining his personal reputation, it would destroy the business. And Deborah would be long gone with the first man who waved real play money at her. What a foundation for a marriage. If he ever got out of this hole, he'd stop her wild spending. If not, he'd throw her out on her bare ass.

Judy Rogers had phoned saying she wanted to discuss Hetty's insurance. Dillon had tried a stall, but Rogers would have none of it. Now he'd better check the file to see what excuse he could possibly hide behind. Clerical error, perhaps. In his current state he'd probably blurt out the truth. That might be the best policy. He'd always followed it up to now.

Dillon buzzed for his secretary and over the intercom said, "Miss Porter, bring me the Starr file." Then he remembered that old reliable Miss Porter was on vacation. This week's substitute was Paul Mutt's secretary, Goldie Powers. Dillon corrected himself. "Oh, Miss Powers, bring me the Hetty Starr file. That's S-T-A-R-R. You find it filed under S." He wiped his brow with a tissue.

Goldie was a blonde with sprayed, teased hair and rhinestone-studded harlequin glasses. She was classically beautiful but totally dumb. He had finally decided to fire her, over Mutt's strenuous protests. Objections so violent that Dillon realized what was going on between them. It's always the boss who's the last to know, he had thought.

Ten minutes later she handed him the file and eased, legs akimbo, into the chair across his circular glass table, waiting for instructions. Her thin Dacron skirt rose nearly to her hips. Dillon's eyes blinked. There was nothing underneath. It was all curly and blonde, and totally available. No wonder Mutt wanted to keep her on. She watched his eyes and smiled. It was a your place, my place, or anyplace smile.

He tore his gaze away and glanced at the file. On top was a bulky manila envelope addressed to Mutual Surety Co. It was stamped and ready to be mailed.

"My God," he shouted, leaping to his feet. "This hasn't been sent yet. I gave this to you Monday morning to be mailed."

"Oh, Mr. Dillon," the girl wailed. "Have I done something wrong again?" Tears welled in her eyes. Her skirt rose another two inches.

With trembling fingers he tore open the envelope. It was all there—the fictitious rider, Hetty's phony signature. Goldie hadn't mailed it, she'd filed it. Relief flooded Dillon's body. He'd been saved by her incredible stupidity. Rescued from prison by her total incompetence.

He swept around the desk and seized her forcefully by the waist, lifted her and whirled her around. She almost fainted, fearing he would strike her. Instead, he kissed her on the forehead, saying, "Miss Powers, you are an angel. A protective angel sent from heaven to keep me from evil. You are beautiful, and perfect. I'm giving you a ten-dollar-a-week raise immediately, and a permanent job, as long as this is my insurance company. And Goldie, it will be mine until my son takes over."

She was too dazed for words. He walked her to the door. "Goldie, you've learned the secret of success. When you make mistakes, make sure they work to your advantage." He bent to kiss her again. This time she turned her trembling sweet, sticky lips to him and glued herself tight. For Dillon, it was a kiss of eternal gratitude.

Goldie Powers had no idea what she'd done. It had to be the way she sat. It always worked. The sight of her intimacy had strange effects on men. Mr. Mutt's reaction was more direct—it was wham, bam, followed by gifts of money. Apparently Mr. Dillon gave the money first.

Rice had borrowed a Hagoth voice stress analyzer from the state police. Now he was explaining its operation to Belli.

"It listens to a person's voice and measures the amount of stress in it. When there's no stress, then these eight green lights here stay lit."

"That means?" Belli looked doubtful.

"When all the green lights are lit, you know the speaker is

telling the truth,'' Rice replied. ''On the other hand, when eight red lights are lit, you know the speaker is under a great deal of stress. Maybe he has a tarantula crawling up his leg. But most likely he's just lying.'' Rice smiled.

''Can we try it out?'' Belli asked.

Rice grinned and switched the machine on.

''What's your name?'' he asked.

''Gus Belli.''

The eight green lights glowed steadily.

''Have you concealed any evidence lately?''

Belli stammered out, ''No.''

The eight lights flashed a bright red.

Rice laughed.

Belli grinned good-naturedly. ''The fuckin' thing works. Let me ask you about that waitress.''

Three minutes later, Jim Dempsey walked into the lab, looking for Rice. The machine was behind him, out of his sight. It was still on.

Belli asked, ''You're the Chief, right?''

''I was this morning,'' Dempsey said, frowning.

''Are you the Man?'' Belli blurted out the question.

Dempsey glared at Belli. ''Hell, no! Have you flipped or something?''

The eight lights glowed a steady green.

Both Belli and Rice grinned broadly. Then Rice showed Dempsey their new electronic miracle.

Judy told Peter over lunch that Dillon was innocent. His firm was totally reliable. Hetty Starr's insurance was in good order. Funny, she'd suspected Dillon at first. He certainly had seemed nervous on the phone and sounded as if he had something to hide. But there was nothing irregular.

Dillon probably didn't know that he was going to inherit $500,000 from Hetty Starr's estate. Judy suggested that they stop by together this afternoon and give him the good news.

By noon, the newspapers, television and radio had disseminated warnings to millions of individuals that the Man had threatened to make victim number twelve either a black or a redhead. Anyone in the Fairport area fitting this general description was urged to leave immediately. Those not in the general area were warned to stay away.

On her way home, Jeanne listened to four warnings on her car radio. Her strawberry-blond hair was tied in a ponytail and tucked up under a bright-yellow beret. She was determined to drive home to see her man. He'd promised to marry her. His private number was still out of order, and he'd warned her never to call his regular business phone. She wouldn't. It was no time to cross him.

Driving, Jeanne wondered. Why had she zeroed in on him, a married man? What was so special? It all came down to the fact that he was one big hunk of solid man, kind, considerate and compassionate, and smart and successful. Other than that, she didn't know too much about him. They really hadn't spent all that much time together. It was eat-and-run sex. But that was something special. If hormones kept your skin young-looking, she'd found her fountain of youth. She laughed.

As she pulled into her drive, she thought she'd spend the afternoon sunbathing on her terrace, daydreaming about her man.

Ned Nichols turned his Ferrari into the dirt road leading to the future Day Camp. It was beautiful, lush green countryside. The blue spruce towered above the winding road, forming a shadowy haven for ferns and deciduous plants of all descriptions. It was a cool, delicate, restful world, with a distinct character of its own. Nichols pulled his car around to the lakeside of the fishing lodge, noticing that the sides needed another coat of preservative stain. He removed a cooler and several packages from the trunk of his car and placed them next to a canoe resting bottomside up on the beach near the dock.

He unlocked the small fishing shack adjacent to the dock and selected several fishing rods, a small tackle box containing assorted lures, and a paddle, righted the canoe and slid it into the water. He put his gear into the canoe and fifteen minutes later was gliding across the lake to a favorite fishing spot.

Eyes were on him. He'd sensed it all the way up Route 7. These tails smelled and acted like pros. The thought of ditching them had never entered his mind. Let them enjoy the day in the shade watching him fish. He'd needed to get away from the pressures of his office and time to think things out by himself, time to plan his next moves carefully. The eleven murders were a jolt. The pattern of the victims had been so beneficial, it was almost as if he'd selected them personally. Was someone trying to frame him, to point a finger? It certainly looked like it. But who?

The lure flipped into the water. The action was almost automatic, a reflex. Over and over, no need to think about it. The canoe drifted and his mind drifted with it. He'd enjoyed making love to Jeanne out on the Mako. Stunningly beautiful, with that gorgeous red hair and a real appetite for life, a genuine goodie gobbler. There was another man, probably Briggs, and she was serious about him. It was a hunch more than anything else. Someone had taught her that sword-swallowing trick. That would be Spike's style. Lucky bastard. Women were his real avocation. They kept him going.

It was too bad Suzy wasn't more adventuresome. Damn. She had come close on several occasions, but at the critical moment always moved away and used her hands, claimed she liked to watch Vesuvius erupt. If she'd just try it once, who knew, maybe she'd enjoy it. He'd hated to see her leave this morning, but once he'd gotten used to the idea, was pleased that she'd taken their daughter into New York. They'd be a lot safer there until this maniac was caught.

Christ, he'd forgotten, he had to be the prime suspect. People thought he was the Man. Why not? He fit the physical description, and everything had fallen into place, for his benefit. Millions . . . almost seven million dollars . . . greed and avarice . . . the two building blocks of his career. He licked his lips. Others would complain that he was lucky. He made his own luck, working harder than anyone else he knew. But enough was enough. His ass was in a sling. It was time to clear himself.

What was needed was an unbreakable alibi. Everyone was convinced that one man had committed all eleven murders.

All he had to do was prove that he wasn't at the scene of one of them. But which one? He'd been close by when Donnelly blew up, seen coming out of the church by the sexton, before anyone else knew that Fredericks had been killed. That was damning. It made him look guilty as sin. He'd admitted to Jim that he'd seen the minister on the cross.

Surprisingly, they hadn't put out an APB on him, were plainly waiting for him to make his next move. Shit, he didn't have a solid alibi for any of the murders. Not one that he could really pin down. Damn. He and and Suzy were going to go to the dance at Longwood on Saturday night. At the last minute they'd decided to stay home. Home in bed with his wife. That would never fly as an alibi. It was too unbelievable.

He must be impressing his shadows that he was some fisherman. Not one bite. Shifting his position, he opened a cold beer.

On shore, the two FBI agents had joined forces with Briggs' trooper, perfecting their strategy. Nichols couldn't escape in any direction. If he returned to his car, all three of them would track him back to Fairport. If he landed on shore someplace else with his canoe, they had two helicopters standing by, and tracking teams with bloodhounds. Their high-powered binoculars watched his every movement. They had searched Nichols' Ferrari for weapons. There were none.

All three were in constant radio contact with their home base. The agents to Dillinger. The trooper to state police headquarters. His messages were relayed to Piccollo at the combined task force headquarters. The messages were repetitive. "He's done nothing, still fishing." The return messages were just as repetitive. "Stick with him. Sit on him. Don't lose him. There has been no murder today. We don't think any will be attempted until Nichols returns. We'll catch him in the act."

Suddenly the agents were startled by a wild laugh from the canoe. "He's cracking wide open," remarked the trooper. "Like an overripe grape, his head has fermented," commented one of the brush-cuts. "His mind is foaming," said the other.

Nothing could have been further from the truth. Nichols had just perfected his alibi, knew now that he could prove he wasn't the Man. There was just one big if to his plan. He reeled in the line and paddled slowly back to the dock. Twenty minutes later he was driving back to Fairport on Route 7. Driving slowly, methodically. It wouldn't have mattered, he'd decided: his tails would have planted a tiny radio transmitter in his car. He could play Nicki Lauda all evening and they'd be glued to his ass. His mother had always told him, "If you're being run out of town, get in front of the crowd. Make it look like a parade." It was late afternoon when Nichols and his entourage arrived in Fairport.

It was almost four when Dempsey and Grady rationalized that maybe the Man didn't intend to kill either a black or a redhead. They had been reviewing a list of potential victims compiled by their staffs. Dempsey asked, "Sam, we assumed a redhead from the phrase 'heads are red.' Who else is red?"

"What do you mean?"

"Maybe I'm getting punchy, but I've got a gut feeling. The Man isn't as direct as we're assuming."

"I can't disagree, Jim. Remember 'Fred.' What are you thinking?"

"It's a wild thought. But Communists are reds. We have a permanent Russian Cultural Exchange here, three estates down from Hetty Starr's place. It's called Happy Acres."

"And the 'head' would be their leader?" asked Grady excitedly.

"Possibly. But this week they've got a top commie here from Russia. He's addressing the U.N. tomorrow. It could be him."

"Good God!" Grady said. "What would his murder do to détente?"

"What a nightmare, and there's no way we can protect him. The Russians have their own private army at Happy Acres. They probably outgun the National Guard. I've got to call and warn them to tighten their security."

It was 4:15 P.M. when Dempsey called Oleg Kamonov, first secretary of the Russian Cultural Exchange. The Russian thanked Dempsey for his warning and assured him that the Third Secretary of the Politburo was well protected. He, Kamonov, had personal responsibility for his safety. Nothing could happen to him.

Dempsey put down the phone and commented to Grady, "It was thanks, but no thanks. They've got their red head locked securely in a vault."

At the special command post at the high school, Sergeant Bob Martin's staff now numbered 170. He had eight officers and troopers from the State Police, forty-two officers and policemen on loan from surrounding communities, and 120 volunteers working eight-hour shifts manning the phones, recruited mostly from the League of Women Voters, the Junior League and the Young Republican Club.

"We're being overwhelmed," complained Martin to DiLeo. The fatigue had ground dark circles under his eyes and pulled the folds of his face downward. A constant glare of fluorescent lights narrowed his eyes to slits. The past two days and nights had blended imperceptibly. He coughed and spit into a Kleenex. The sting of too much coffee burned his gut, and the stench of stale cigarette smoke clogged his nose.

"What a grubby business." DiLeo sighed. "Thank God, we only work on days ending with a y." A smile. He had been with Martin continually since their command post had been set up. Sleeping on cots in a classroom, they kept at their phone vigil, wondering constantly where the elusive, taunting killer would strike next.

In the last two days, an average of four calls had come in every minute, 240 every hour. They'd weeded them down to eleven hundred possibles who had to be checked and investigated. And the calls were still pouring in.

Sergeant Marcus walked into headquarters, looking beat. He threw himself onto a cot, saying, "I've been down with the girls, catching. There are calls from Nebraska, Texas, Florida, even one from Bombay, India. Weirdos. They all want to talk about the Man. Most are coming from jilted women. It's fascinating how the pattern has changed. Before the housewife was killed, most of the calls were from women warning us about ex-boyfriends whom they hated. After Thelma Pickell's drowning, they're turning in their current boyfriends and their husbands. I never realized how many unhappy marriages there must be. Men beating their wives. Crazed sex fiends. It takes something like this to bring it out in the open.'' He closed his eyes.

"We've got so many false leads, but we don't dare ignore them," said DiLeo. "It's people getting even with other people. They're trying to settle a personal score with a neighbor, an estranged husband, an ex-lover, a hobo on the street. We get calls from office workers—'The guy at the next desk has got crazy slate-gray eyes, he keeps leering at me.' We probe and find out he's five feet one inch tall. So many of the calls are rambling, incoherent and vengeful. This case is a magnet for every nut in the country. The Man shook the tree and the almonds are falling out. The squirrels have a field day. Dozens of kooks have called, each one claiming that he's the Man and giving addresses. We rush out and no one is there.''

Sergeant Martin grinned. "It's like trying to shovel fourteen pounds of shit into a thimble. It just won't fit. Over two hundred callers want Dempsey replaced in command of this manhunt. There's so much backbiting. He must have teeth marks all over his ass.''

It was early evening. Mary Potter sat at her desk, on the telephone.

When she had learned about the new voice stress analyzer, she'd had an idea. She could connect it to her telephone, call the men on her list, and ask them their weight. It might save a lot of time.

The lights on the machine blinked red again.

She asked, "Are you sure?"

"One-sixty-four, exactly," the man on the phone replied.

The lights blinked red again.

"Thank you," Mary said, hanging up.

She shook her head sadly. The Hagoth had been blinking like a pinball machine for the past hour. It was obvious that women weren't the only ones who were vain about their weight.

There had to be a better way.

It was fast approaching dusk. All over town, people waited apprehensively for the Man to strike again, to claim victim number twelve. As the hours ticked away, the tension grew until it seemed that all Fairport might suddenly erupt in one giant explosion.

On the beach at Happy Acres, Oleg Kamonov was pacing nervously back and forth. He puffed repeatedly on one fat Havana after another. That idiot Third Secretary insisted on sailing every afternoon. He was out there now in his Laser, skimming over the Sound.

He was responsible for the Third Secretary's safety. The mass killer they called the Man was still on the loose. How he wished it were tomorrow evening. In the morning, his important guest would leave the compound for his speech at the U.N. Then he was going directly to Kennedy Airport for his flight to Moscow. His dog would be shipped later.

The Third Secretary had enjoyed his visit, had sailed every day and then had drunk himself into a stupor each evening. He had developed a craving for Tennessee sour mash. The blonde, Dawn, that he'd personally recruited for his guest's enjoyment had been a real find. That dirty buzzard was heavily into bondage, and she hadn't objected at all, would do anything for the cause.

He was also certain that back in Moscow the Third Secretary would give him a solid recommendation. On three different occasions the Secretary had toasted him with sour mash. It might mean a promotion, but if it meant going back to Moscow, Kamonov wasn't sure he wanted it.

It was 7:25 P.M. Just thirteen hours and five minutes more and his responsibility for the Third Secretary's safety would be over. If only the clock could be turned forward. He looked once more out to sea. The Laser with the distinctive red star on the sail was rounding the last buoy on the triangular course. The Secretary had five minutes more before he signaled him to come in.

Kamonov continued pacing. At 4:15 he'd received a call from the Chief of Police warning him that the Man might possibly try to kill the "head" of the Russian delegation. It had been a shock that Kamonov really didn't need. Fortunately, at 4:25 the Chief had called back and said it had been a false alarm. That was the trouble with Americans. They kept changing their minds. They wouldn't be half bad if they were disciplined. It was a country where everyone was doing his own thing, a disorganized mess.

On his second call, Dempsey had offered a police launch to help patrol the shoreline. When he'd declined, the Chief had insisted. Finally, Kamonov had reluctantly agreed. Kamonov was under strict instructions to cooperate with local officials.

The launch had arrived at 6:45 P.M. Kamonov had been surprised to see that it was nothing more than a small white speedboat, with the word "Police" stenciled on the side. As far as he could determine, it was manned by a single policeman. The policeman had waved, Kamonov had waved back. Then the launch began patrolling.

Kamonov wasn't counting on the launch for security. He looked again. Each leg of the triangular course was patrolled by a Bertram 31. Each Bertram was flying a small ensign with a red star, and each was under the command of a KGB colonel, with two KGB lieutenants as crew. The boats carried three submachine guns in duffel bags within easy reach of the crew. Kamonov allowed himself a nervous half-smile. His unauthorized navy was one of the largest Russian fleets in the Western Hemisphere.

Out on the Sound, the Third Secretary was thoroughly enjoying himself. The wind was a brisk twelve knots, blowing from the Northeast. He was heeled over, cutting a foamy wake through the gentle swells. Once again he was sailing for Russia in the Olympics, this time for the gold medal. Tacking smartly from starboard to port, he headed for the final buoy, to see how close he could cut it.

On the shore at Happy Acres, a shrill whistle blew. It was relayed by a blast on the horn of the Bertram closest to shore and picked up in turn by the other two boats. The man at the helm of the Laser heard the whistle as well as the horns, and ignored them. He tacked sharply around the buoy, missing it by a scant eighteen inches. Now, with elation, he headed for the last buoy, on a downhill sled. Once more around the course.

He outranked everyone at the mission by a wide margin. Let them wait. That Kamonov, what a boor. A teetotaling boor. He didn't drink and he didn't know how to sail. However, Kamonov had introduced him to Dawn. She was something . . . had taken everything so far . . . but tonight he had a real surprise in store. He was going to tie her ankles, spread-eagled over the chair. Then she'd meet Lover Boy, his Great Dane. That dog's talented tongue would lash her into a frenzy, and then . . .

The horns blew again. Damn bureaucrats, trying to impress him. He knew he was perfectly safe, could outsail anyone. Reluctantly, he jibed and headed toward the shore.

The Man waited patiently. He watched the Laser with interest. The Russian wasn't a bad sailor, but he didn't point high enough and his sail wasn't trimmed properly. In a small boat you have to become part of it, and every action has to flow with the boat. On each tack, you have to shift your weight precisely. It has to be second nature. The Russian was sitting like a duck. A sitting duck. A dead duck.

Disguised as Bob Baker, he had "borrowed" his Donzi. It had twin Mercury inboard 150 engines. It could outrun and outmaneuver anything on the Sound, and run rings around the Russians. The Bertram 31 was fast and was a superb fishing boat. What the Russians didn't realize was that they were about to pit three good Cossack ponies against a champion thoroughbred Kentucky racehorse.

He hoped that Baker wouldn't be too upset by his quick spray-paint job on his Donzi. The white paint was still sticky. But fuck Baker.

The "police cruiser" edged closer to the Laser, knowing the course the Russian would sail. He closed to one hundred yards. The closest Bertram tried to intercede between him and the Third Secretary. He turned lazily away, paralleling the Laser's course, and waved at the Bertram. He wanted to be closer to shore anyhow before making his move.

Now was the time, at the twilight's last gleaming. He pushed the throttles forward, and the Donzi spurted ahead as if shot from a catapult. The Man swung the wheel sharply, aimed the nose of his boat at the Laser and picked up his rocket launcher. It was a one-piece, self-contained unit only thirty-six inches long, but it fired an eight-inch anti-tank rocket. It had the same impact as the shell from a long-range gun on a battle cruiser. He placed the crosshairs on the bow of the Laser and pulled the trigger. The Laser disappeared in the ensuing explosion.

In the rocket's red glare, the Third Secretary of the Politburo had just become the Man's twelfth victim. Whizzing by the wreckage of the Laser, he flipped a buoy overboard to mark the spot. On the top of the buoy was a small American flag. Stapled to the buoy was a playing card, the three of spades.

Momentarily, the KGB colonels hesitated, shocked by the rocket attack and reluctant to shoot at any American police boat a few hundred yards from the Connecticut shoreline. The few moments were all the Man needed.

He swung the Donzi from side to side in evasive action, heading straight for Happy Acres. He knew the Russians wouldn't dare shoot automatic weapons lest they hit their own people on shore.

Thirty yards from the beach, he turned sharply to port and flipped two grenades straight up into the air. A full-throated maniacal laugh pierced the air. Then he shouted, against the roar of the engines, "Who ever heard of the rockets' red glare, without the bombs bursting in air?"

Opening the throttles, hurtling over the water at a speed of almost sixty knots, he rapidly outdistanced the pursuing Bertrams. Soon the Donzi was out of sight. The Russians hadn't fired a single shot.

All three television networks interrupted their evening programming for special news broadcasts concerning the murder of the Third Secretary. The commentators outdid themselves with apologies to the Russians. The Russians, in turn, demanded a special meeting of the U.N. General Assembly. Happy Acres was cordoned off behind a curtain of silence. Armed KGB troops rimmed the perimeter. The 54th Division of the Paratroops stationed at Fort Bragg were put on special alert to be ready to move to Fairport at a moment's notice.

In Washington, the President used his hotline to the Kremlin to extend his personal apologies, representing those of the entire nation, for the dastardly murder committed by the Man. The diplomatic channels were filled to overflowing with top-level exchanges. *Izvestia* headlined "America is Sick" and commented that horror of this type was to be expected in a country with such a high rate of mental illness.

Later, Belli and Rice surveyed the murder scene from the real police launch. Although it was a bright moonlit night, there was nothing to be seen. The wreckage of the Laser had been towed ashore by the Russians. They had also fished the Man's buoy from the water, reluctantly turning it over to the Fairport police. First they had broken off the small American flag and torn it to shreds.

Dempsey, Briggs and Grady were back at police headquarters. All calls to Kamonov had been met with a solid barrage of *nyet*. The bears were growling, and were showing their teeth. Dempsey knew they wouldn't bite. If they did, they'd lose their safe little den and all the privileges that went with it.

Ned Nichols was innocent, was not the Man. That had been even more of a shock than the murder of the Russian diplomat. Nichols had played it smart. He'd created an iron-clad alibi.

Nichols had suspected that the Man would strike again, on his everyday binge. So he had made certain to be observed every minute of the day. First by sitting for six hours in the middle of Candlewood Lake. Then, arriving back in Fairport and learning there had not yet been a murder, he'd driven straight to police headquarters, sauntering in, elaborately casual. Since 6:30 P.M. he'd been glued to the bench in front of the desk sergeant, reading *The Power of Positive Thinking*.

At the exact time the Man had blown away the Russian, two policemen had had their eyes riveted on Ned Nichols. Three of the best tails in the country had also been watching him from different vantage points. No, Ned Nichols wasn't the Man. There was no way!

"Oh, shit!" exclaimed Dempsey, Briggs and Grady in unison at police headquarters. "Oh, shit!" growled Dillinger at the Bridgeport Inn. "Oh, shit!" commented Judy Rogers to Peter Bond at the Fairport Motor Inn.

This had been a trying day for all of them. They were all back to the starting blocks. Back to square one. If it wasn't Nichols, it had to be an outsider. But who? And why? They were all back to the Man. Who was the Man? After twelve murders, they didn't have a single clue. Not one.

"Oh shit!" groaned the public.

The Man pulled his car into Carroll's and ordered a chcolate malt, smiling warmly at the carhop. She looked a little like Judy. What a perfect ass. He laughed. It took one to know one. Maybe he should go over to the Inn and . . . no, he'd have to get rid of Bond first. That shouldn't be too tough. He was another playboy.

The Man was positive the police couldn't catch him. They'd never sort him out. Couldn't find him. He was well hidden, concealed within another person. Totally shielded, protected by his other self. They'd have to search the far reaches of the mind to find him.

In the simultaneous sharing of the same body, it was not a question of inhabiting space, but one of a shared being. Since birth, he had been subservient, the other self dominant. He had sat back and waited, waited patiently, planning his break-out. Only once, in childhood, had he been able to wrest away control of the mind. It was the day he'd killed his stepfather.

His method of escape had been perfected through the years. Slowly, ever so slowly, he had gained control of the body's sex drive. Controlling this powerful center, he was able to maneuver and take over more and more of the thinking functions. Now he was able to use the entire mind whenever he wanted. His other self was being pushed back into the subconscious. There was no risk. None at all. The other self didn't know what was happening, didn't even know of his existence.

Day by day, the Man meticulously adhered to his Plan. Each day he took over just a little more of the thinking process on a permanent basis. It was the glorious fifty-second day of the Plan when he would take over the mind completely, totally and permanently. That was the day the other self would be eliminated. That was the most insidious murder of all. There would be no body, no evidence of a crime, but his other self would be dead. He'd award him the two of clubs, posthumously. The Man would then be free, having total use of both the brain and the body. What glorious plans he had for the future.

His secret could only be discovered in the past. Since birth, he had always known what his other self did. He had inhabited the subconscious, his other self the conscious. Although the conscious mind didn't know what the unconscious mind was doing, the unconscious absorbed everything that took place consciously. The Man had watched, waited and hated every minute of it. He had wanted control and now was getting it. Strangely, his other self didn't know about him . . . and never would. The Man winked at himself in the rearview mirror.

Maybe, at the right time, the Man would solve the murders. He was the only one who could catch the world's greatest killer. Then, and only then, would the world discover his true brilliance. That decision wasn't needed now. It was a long way in the future. He still had forty murders left to go.

He finished his malt and wiped his lips with the back of his hand, checked his watch and wondered what Barbara and Vivian were doing. He felt light-headed, fuzzy. He closed his eyes for a moment.

The more Barbara got to know Vivian, the more she liked her. Viv was a kindly, sympathetic person, a true friend. No longer would evenings be spent sitting around, waiting for her man to drop by on his whim, to satisfy his basic urges. She had total companionship with Vivian. They communicated. That man and his damn hussy wife . . . he was always protecting her.

Viv had mentioned that it was odd that her man never took Barbara anyplace. Obviously afraid they'd be seen and his wife would find out. She'd become nothing more than a bedroom whore, available for his pleasure, for free, anytime he liked.

She'd change all that, get her man to take her out to dinner, or a movie, or dancing. Someplace where they could be seen together. Either that or no more sex. She was his Barbie Doll. Just a plaything. A toy. With Viv at the movies she could talk to her man alone.

It was late evening when the Man arrived at Barbara's, surprised to see Vivian waiting in the shadows at the end of the driveway. She greeted him with a warm, clinging, honeybutter kiss, then jumped away so that he couldn't touch her. Speaking almost in a whisper, she said, "Barbara wants to talk to you by herself. If you're lonely later, lover, I'll be home waiting. It's the little yellow cottage on the next block." She ran across the back lawn and disappeared into the trees.

When the Man entered her house, Barbara stayed totally aloof and wouldn't let him get close. She wanted to talk about them, about their future. The Man listened impassively and finally said, "Barbie Doll, I'm tired. It's been a long day. We'll go out to dinner soon. Tonight I'd just like to make love with you."

At the mention of the nickname "Barbie Doll," she burst out crying and ran into the bedroom, slamming and locking the door. He knocked at the door for several minutes. Through her wracking sobs, he could hear the fractured words. "Go away. Go back to your wife, leave me alone. I'm not a damn doll to be played with."

"Oh, shit. Women. They're totally unpredictable," the Man muttered under his breath. It was either break down her door or try Vivian's. The choice was easy.

Vivian's cottage was not hard to find. The outside light

was on and the front door open. Meeting him at the screen door, in a sheer see-through nothing, she was shining with a soft, sensual radiance, smelling of honeysuckles. "Hi, Lover. You made the right choice."

With all the seduction of a female cobra, she cooed, "I was just going to bed. Care to join me for a nightcap first?" The glasses were set out, two cubes of ice already in both. In just a moment the drinks were mixed.

"Pretty sure of yourself," the Man commented and gave her his best male cobra smile.

"Everyone wants to be loved, including me," she whispered. "Sometimes I get so scared that no one will ever love me again."

The Man pulled her to him and kissed her warmly. "I get the feeling that when life gives you lemons, you make lemonade."

She laughed and replied demurely, "Your eyes are softening. They were hostile when you arrived."

"I thought you might be trying to cross Barbie Doll. After she cared enough to share the very best."

"No, I just wanted you to know you're welcome here at any time. No strings attached. I just don't like couches. I like the comfort of my own bed." She rose catlike, extended her hand and led him into her bedroom.

Vivian's bedroom featured a large double bed and mirrors. There were mirrors everywhere. She obviously enjoyed watching herself.

She answered his unspoken thought. "You know, when you live alone, you either shrivel into nothing, or you learn to cope. There's never anyone to date, except somebody else's husband, so you learn the art of self-enjoyment. I've adjusted pretty well. The one good thing about being alone is that you don't have to look your best. Sometimes the highs are intense, but the lows are awesome."

The Man grinned. Vivian was totally uninhibited.

She read his mind, and smiled. "In here I let it all hang out. I had an X-rated grandmother . . . my mother was double-X . . . don't need drugs to get high . . . tonight I feel wicked . . . thought you'd like to watch for a while. You seemed to enjoy watching me squirm on the couch. Don't miss the good parts.''

With that, Vivian slipped off her filmy nothing and lay down on the bed. It was soon apparent to the Man why Vivian was so hypersensitive. She clamped a small electrical stimulator to each nipple. This left both of her hands free, and she knew how to use them.

Totally switched on, her eyes dilated and then closed . . . riding the ocean, one wave after another, afloat in pleasure, on a self-indulgent high, tantalizing him.

The Man's excitement built until it was uncontrollable. It was time to join in. Her legs spread wide, and he moved between them. Her motion was soft and fluid. Plugged in the way she was, she was sensitive all over, a compact bundle of energy, thrills, and ecstasy, everywhere he touched. She was pulsating and glowing, like a flickering neon. Tonight Vivian had reached for the outer stars and had found them.

As soon as the Man left, Vivian returned to Barbara's. She was still upset and had been crying. Her man had walked out on her.

Vivian cuddled her close, touching her warm moistness. Barbara responded, and the rest of the night was spent consoling and loving her. She had brought one of her stimulators and used it on Barbara's sensitive areas. The intense tingling sensations were a completely new experience for her. She went wild.

Vivian was ecstatic too. Barbara no longer needed her man. From now on, Vivian would take care of both of them.

It was almost 11:00 P.M. when the Man awoke, still parked at Carroll's. He looked around sheepishly, started his car and drove home.

The Man was well satisfied with his day's work. The world had been shocked. He'd rocked its two superpowers with a simple rocket. With a little luck, he might start a global atomic war. He chuckled. That wasn't part of his Plan.

With the black marking pencil he crossed out the Russian

diplomat, the three of spades, victim number twelve. He reviewed the plan for his next murder.

That money-grubber. There is a tremendous advantage in being totally unknown. When no one knows who you are, or what you look like, it's so easy to kill.

Twelve murders in twelve days. Time was flying by. But time goes quickly when you're having fun. Particularly when you're having fun with friends. And he was having a ball, feeling happy, contented, pleased with himself, successful, dominant, all-powerful. There could be no question now. He was the greatest killer of all time, and still forty more to go. One last spade, and then the ace of hearts. That murder would whirl the fuzz around. He'd make a giant fuzzball and shove it down their throats. For days they'd run after another nonexistent suspect.

Dillinger wasn't on his list, but somehow that Fed would have to be nullified. Maybe he'd shoot some Crazy Glue into his eyes. That would cloud his vision. The top Fed would get some well-needed shuteye. Permanently! No, it was better to keep Dillinger healthy. He needed the mental stimulation. The tough, professional competition. It would keep him on his toes.

Dempsey wasn't functioning on all cylinders any longer. He acted like his mental sparkplugs had been tampered with. Over half of them were missing. He was sputtering, misfiring, slowly running down. The crucial fire had gone out of him. Poor Jim was going to crash and burn in the center of his tight little world.

He was going to complete his Plan of Death. Fifty-two murders. He was supremely confident. The Plan was perfect. The air had electricity, a certain static, and sparks of fire, lighting his fuse. He was a modern-day Cain, a pioneer, treading into areas of murder that had never been tried before, looking at murder in a totally new dimension. It was truly exciting.

CONCLUSION

Friday, June 13.
The Cain Mutiny

"SHIT! NOTHING's ever easy." Dempsey looked at himself in the bathroom mirror. He had nicked his chin, and now, four pieces of toilet paper later, it was still trickling blood. A slow, lazy, red ooze.

As if hypnotized, he watched and waited for it to stop. Fairport was bleeding, too. The town he loved was slowly oozing away, being drained of its lifeblood. Twelve murders. He had to stop this Man, before it was too late for everyone. Too late for him.

He'd never thought of death before, and still had no fear. Rocking him in her arms, his mother had taught him not to be afraid, to be strong. He missed his father and wished he'd known him; hadn't liked his stepfather very much, and in return had been barely tolerated. There had been no affection. Strange . . . he hadn't even been sad when he'd died. It had been an accident—the fat slob had been overcome by fumes from the kitchen stove. His mother had cried, but he hadn't.

It was the day he'd become a man. He dabbed again at the patch of blood.

The Man stared at his face in the mirror. The creases deepened in his forehead. Worried now for the first time since the conception of his Plan. Not by anything he'd done . . . or the police. No, the Plan was perfect. It was that crazy old man in his head. He kept shouting "Kill." It was driving him nuts.

That old fart wouldn't shut up. He'd like to shove him back

into the background. Back to oblivion. Just once, stick it in his ear, or better yet, up his jumper. He reached for the aspirin bottle . . . poppin' them faster than the teeny-boppers ate their mothers' birth-control pills.

Who was the old buzzard? The Man still wasn't sure. At first he'd thought it was the Devil himself, but yesterday he'd caught a glimpse of the old man's face. It was like looking at the man in the moon. He could see only one side of him. The face was bearded and timeless, the head covered with snow-white hair, as old as imagination. It had to be Cain, the father of all evil. Cain, who commanded him to kill.

Could the old man be trying to take over his mind? That would be incredible. His Plan involved taking over the mind of another. He was doing it step by step in an orderly way.

There was no doubt about it. He had it made. Now, suddenly, the old man was interfering with his Plan. Cain wasn't satisfied, he wanted more killing. If he did, it would be Cain's plan, not his. The old man was crazy. He shook his head sideways in defiance.

Why was Cain inflicting this torture on him? He was coming unraveled, as if someone were holding a microscope against his soul. Cain was dragging him back, away from his future.

"You're a has-been. I'm a never-was," he shouted back into the inner recesses of his brain.

"Kill, kill, kill," the voice responded, louder and harsher.

"Give me a chance, old man. Don't follow me. I'm lost." The Man looked about helplessly. "Thou shalt not kill! Come out, come out, wherever you are," he said in a singsong voice.

Slowly, the Man bowed his head. Tears rolled down his cheek and splashed into the sink, head pounding now, the old man's voice reverberating from one side to the other. The man knew he couldn't win. He was Cain's disciple. Cain had picked him to do his bidding, to play his cards. That was the way the hand had been dealt.

The Man raised his head and looked into the mirror. He'd follow the light and come out. What light? Cain's light, of course. His directions to kill came from a Higher Order. John had said, "He who has the Son of God has life." Was not Cain the first son of Adam? He nodded. A direct line.

"Ask and it shall be done," he said quietly.

Cain's voice had stopped. The silence was deafening. The Man breathed deeply. His own senses flooded back. Fatigue showed in dark circles under his eyes. Wiping the tears from his face with his fingers, he splashed water onto his face.

Shit. What difference did it make? He'd work the grave-yard shift for Cain. If the old man went amok, they'd sky out together, he'd go down in flames, and take Cain with him, all the way to the bowels of hell. Cain had been there before. The old man could show him around. He'd be a celebrity. The greatest killer of all time! Apostle of Cain. The thought quickened his pulse.

Then he'd take a trip into time, out beyond the solar system. He'd be reborn and come back as himself. But next time, he'd have a mind all his own. The Man winked at himself in the mirror.

Dempsey winked back. The bleeding had stopped. Shaking himself out of his lethargy, he splashed some cold water on his face and patted it dry, beginning to feel better. Today maybe he'd be lucky. Today was Friday the 13th, no time to be superstitious. It was a great day to catch the Man, that murdering bastard. He walked out of the bathroom with renewed confidence.

In their suite at the Inn, Judy was picking at her breakfast, Peter reading the morning *Times*. She poured herself another cup of coffee and added some to Peter's cup. Behind his paper, he nodded his thanks.

Suddenly she gave a start. Her hand trembled, splashing the coffee over the rim.

My God. One person held the key. There was one person who had seen the Man, and had never been questioned. Everyone had forgotten. One small, frightened girl, who'd seen someone throw a grenade at her father's car, and kill her doll. Cindy. What was it she'd said?

Judy jumped up from the table and moved quickly to the

desk. Thumbing through her notes, finally pulling out one piece of paper. She read it quickly, read it again, then as if in a daze, returned to the table and sat down.

Peter put down his newspaper. His hand reached out for hers. "You're onto something," he said simply.

She nodded, excitement growing in her eyes.

"Peter, when the Man blew up Dempsey's car, his daughter . . . my niece . . . Cindy . . . was outside . . . saw it happen."

Bond's mouth opened. "Of course."

"The only thing she said was, 'Daddy, Daddy, he killed my dolly.' "

Judy paused. Bond stared at her face. "We all thought Cindy was talking to her father. Just suppose she was talking to her mother."

"Oh, my God," Bond said, jumping to his feet.

They ran for the Mercedes and had reached the parking lot when Judy skidded to a halt, remembering Brenda had taken Cindy into New York yesterday morning to stay at her mother's.

Out in the middle of Long Island Sound, the Man sat alone in the police launch, quietly smoking a Tiparillo. He could hear the dinging sound of a buoy and the cry of the seabirds. He took a deep drag and flipped the butt over the side, and through his binoculars, checked the horizon. There was not another boat in sight.

Moving quickly, he slipped a line off a cleat and cast off Nichols' Atlantic. It would drift aimlessly until it was found.

The Man took a last look at the Altantic. Standing, bound to the mast, was Ned Nichols' lifeless body. The arms had been lashed behind him around the mast, and a thin Dacron tube had been inserted into the artery in each leg. A pool of blood completely covered the floorboards of the cockpit. The two of spades was nailed to the mast above Nichols' head. In his shirt pocket was another letter. It read:

"You've asked for some clues,
I'll give you a few.
No matter the risk,
I'll kill fifty-two.

"Thirteen are now gone,
Your Spades are all dead.
The Ace of Hearts
Will follow poor Ned.

Knave of the night,
A demon from hell,
You've never met me
Yet you know me well.

"For who else in town
Will you call a hearse?
A mechanic, a clerk,
A waiter, a nurse.

"A doctor, a rich man,
A beggerman, thief.
And as a finale,
Your idiot Chief!

"These hints won't help
You discover the Man
But catch me, catch me,
If you can . . ."

The Man's face contorted into an evil grin. On the way out from shore, he'd taken his time, so that Nichols could watch his life ooze out. That money-grubbing shit. His millions wouldn't do much for him now. Not down where he was going.

A brief telephone conversation with Brenda and then with Cindy confirmed Judy's worst thoughts. Like all children, Cindy had that wonderful quality of honesty. She had seen her father roll a ball under his car. Then everything had blown up and her dolly had burned. She couldn't understand why he had killed her dolly. That's what had upset her so.

Listening to Cindy, Brenda had been stunned. Jim couldn't be the Man.

Judy shuddered as she hung up the phone. It had been a devastating moment for her sister, but perhaps the easiest way to find out the truth was from the mouth of her own child.

Peter put his arm around Judy as she told him the details of her phone conversation.

The Man was hidden inside Dempsey. Who would have guessed?

They talked to Grady first, then to Belli, Farrow and Rice. There was utter shock and disbelief. Grady phoned Dillinger. Quickly the word spread among the lawmen.

When Dempsey's car was located at the police dock, they gathered there, in twos and threes, waiting for the police launch to come in. They waited for Dempsey. They waited for the Man.

Through clenched teeth, the Man snarled a last goodbye to Nichols, then opened the throttles on the launch. The boat leaped forward. His head was a throbbing dynamo. That fucking old man. He hadn't kept their bargain, wasn't satisfied, kept shouting "Kill," wouldn't stop. His command was insistent, over and over. The Man put both hands to his head, tears streamed down his cheeks. "Kill, kill, kill." There wasn't anyone for him to kill. What did the old man want? He was the only person in the boat.

He could kill Dempsey, but it was way too soon. He didn't want to do away with Dempsey yet. He needed him. Dempsey was supposed to be his last victim.

Cain's voice was booming in his head. It was a crescendo. The Man's eyes bulged from the pain. No . . . kill the old man first . . . kill Cain. He laughed wildly. His portion of the mind was locked in mortal combat with Cain's.

In the distance, there was a crowd of people at the dock. Peasants! They couldn't stop him now.

He reached for Dempsey's shoulder holster. Now he could see Cain's face plainly, an ancient, parchment mask, looking at him in horror. Cain was no longer shouting "Kill." He was shaking his shaggy white head, pleading, "No, no, no."

Cain had tormented him too long. The Man screamed in defiance. "Today is a good day to die, old man."

Through Dempsey's open mouth, he aimed the .357 Magnum at the old man, and heard the beginning of Cain's scream as he tightened his finger on the trigger.

The crowd on the shore heard the shot and looked at one another. Peter Bond put his arm around Judy. She buried her head on his shoulder, thought of Brenda and was filled with dread.

It was hours later. They'd all agreed. Dempsey had tracked down the Man and had killed him. It was the only way.

Bestselling Books
for Today's Reader —
From Jove!

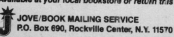

More Bestselling Books From Jove!